# PRAISE FOR K C ALEXANDER

"*Nanoshock* crushes everything in its path. Brutal, unapologetic, sexy cyberpunk, it is a steel-fisted punch in the mouth."

Scott Sigler, #1 NYT bestselling author of the Generations trilogy

"*Necrotech* is a speed freak rush down mean streets of the digital, the modified, and the just plain crazy. It's like razors for your brain."

Richard Kadrey, author of the Sandman Slim series

"*Necrotech* is a high-octane cyberpunk thrill ride that starts at full throttle and never slows down. Riko is an amazing, diverse, ass-kicking character that will leave readers wanting more."

Strange Horizons

"Scalding and brutal as a radiation shower, punishing as a street fight, and as sharp as a blade to the jugular, *Necrotech* and its badass heroine, Riko, will grab your heart in a diamond steel fist and squeeze it to a pulp."

Lila Bowen, RT Review Award-winning author of Wake of Vultures

"*Necrotech* bleeds with raw & unapologetic badassery. Riko is the cyberpunk heroine I've been waiting for, struggling with the truth that the tech we embrace to solve our problems just creates new ones, and no one has a chipset to fix hu... ... KC Alexander dials up the attit... ...renaline in this explosive de... ...d to Riko's next run."

Kevi... ...e Iron Druid Chro...

"*Necrotech* ... ...thrill ride in a fascinating cyberpunk ... ...ith one of the most interesting women pro...gonists I've read in a long time."

Stephen Blackmoore, author of the award-nominated Dead Things

"What I like so much about *Necrotech* is that Riko's arm isn't perfect. Much like my prosthetic or a wheelchair, it's an end to a means. Which is what I'm ALWAYS MISSING from transhumanism."
*Elsa Sjunneson-Henry, author of "Seeking Truth" in* Upside Down: Inverted Tropes in Storytelling

"Vulgar, vicious, and very very good! Alexander pulls no punches in this intense debut."
*Jason M Hough, NYT Bestselling author of* Zero World

"Sci-fi that's slick, sharp and snarky – KC Alexander doesn't 'write' so much as she fires words into your cerebral cortex with an electromagnetic railgun."
*Chuck Wendig, NYT bestselling author of* Star Wars: Aftermath *and* Invasive

"This book is a kick-ass thriller and Riko is a smart-mouthed, independent fighter who, despite her outward demeanor, loves human contact (sex) – male, female, it doesn't matter."
*Looking for a Good Book*

"Re-defining the scope and boundaries of cyberpunk science-fiction thrillers. KC's writing is like a solid right-and-left-hook combo that leaves you breathless. Pacy as hell, an engrossing mystery brewing beneath all that blood, gore and curses flying all around that kept me hooked to the end."
*Fantasy Smorgasbord*

"Mixing together high-tech imagination and conspiracy, this one is sure to satisfy the cyberpunk craving you didn't know you had."
*Kirkus Reviews*

"Pulse-poundingly action filled, with an approach to combat scenes which works brilliantly, putting one really into the fight the way the better class of video game does, making you feel not only the punches thrown but also the blows taken."
*Intellectus Speculativus*

"This is not my usual kind of book. It is so much fucking better than 'usual'. There's no lily to gild here. *Necrotech* is awesome. Go and buy it."
*Over the Effing Rainbow*

"Alexander does for sci-fi what James A Moore does for fantasy: create a world so brutal you keep expecting it to crush its own characters. Fortunately, the characters in *Necrotech* don't crush easily. A few pages in, and you'll find yourself rooting for a street warrior whose vocabulary is as brutal as her fighting skills."
*Cowering King*

"If you want a fuckingly good time, then *Necrotech*'s your book!"
*Matt's Cyberplace*

"Hard hitting and fun, it reads like a sci-fi action film."
*Pop Culture Beast*

"Riko's story will snag you harder than a grappling hook attached to a fighter jet... A colossal book that supersedes generic fiction labels."
*Sparring With Fiction*

"One of the fastest-paced books I've read, which packs punches both physical and emotional. You need this damn book."
*Write Code Do Science*

"A kick-ass cyberpunk novel and amazing female lead character."
*Glitter & Gorgons*

"*Necrotech* is fast, violent, profane, and utterly enjoyable."
*Lauren's Bookshelf*

# K C ALEXANDER

# NANOSHOCK

ANGRY
ROBOT

ANGRY ROBOT
An imprint of Watkins Media Ltd

20 Fletcher Gate,
Nottingham,
NG1 2FZ • UK

*angryrobotbooks.com*
*twitter.com/angryrobotbooks*
Fist of fun

An Angry Robot paperback original 2017

Cover art by Cody Tilson
Set in Meridien and Stomper by Epub Services

Distributed in the United States by Penguin Random House, Inc., New York.

US edition ISBN 978 0 85766 627 7
UK edition ISBN 978 0 85766 626 0
Ebook ISBN 978 0 85766 628 4

Printed in the United States of America

9 8 7 6 5 4 3 2 1

*Owning my shit.*
*Now own yours.*

**1**

You haven't lived until you've fisted a nun under the cheap light of a neon Jesus. With the material of her full-coverage habit shoved to her waist, back plastered to the gritty wall and vivid color streaking her sweaty, flushed face – goddamn, it's an experience. Her filthy lips wrapped around words I think are forbidden in the usual Catholic vernacular.

I have *serious* authority issues. I like a willing pussy, especially when some other bastard stakes it as sanctified ground. There's no way I'd pass it up when it's offered so sweetly as this one was. Wrist-deep in wet flesh, pressing the sister's shaking, writhing body against dank, humid-slick wall, I got off on making her beg as she rode my hand.

She came, too. But it wasn't to Jesus.

The torn remains of her underwear drifted to the muck at her feet. I grinned as the nun gasped for breath, pleased with the cooling slick of spunk on my hand. Wiping it on the back of my black fatigues, I imagined the stuff would leave a crusty smear when it dried.

Perfect. It'd leave crispy little cumflakes all over my employer's expensive desk when I sat on it. My little gift to him.

Grinning from ear to ear, I left the sister dazed in my wake. If she noticed that her shaking knees fell open – revealing the wet, reddened flesh I'd so thoroughly schooled – she didn't rectify it. A nice little send-off.

If I had a tie, I'd straighten it smugly before sauntering into the depths of Trinity Square.

My views on religion notwithstanding, she was *probably* a real nun. I mean, assuming the Judeo-Christ figure masqueraded as a pimp on the side. The testicular gangrene that run this zone call themselves the Good Shepherds, and they'd taken that whole bow-to-god religious thing to the wrong sorts of extremes.

My bar isn't exactly high, so if *I'm* calling it wrong, it's six kinds of revolting.

Their district is a putrid little pustule forgotten by everyone but the junkies gargling their own vomit and the scavengers that feed on that sort of thing. People too poor and desperate to live outside the Shepherds' care don't necessarily make it here as come crawling out of the filth they spawn in. The sickos aren't the worst.

Since most SINless worth an ounce of the junk we install in our bodies wouldn't be caught dead in places like this, much less claim it, the Good Shepherds get the run of the place. Not that it deserved anyone better. Places like this need a good old-fashioned fire. What it *had* was mutated syphilis in the shape of egotistical babyfuckers – and a whole lot of love for spreading the gift.

The earpiece attached to the curve of my ear crackled. A less than subtle cough. "You done, Riko?"

"I'm done," I replied cheerfully.

"That was disgusting."

I chuckled. I'd done worse to better. And better to worse. "Don't hate 'cause your porn subs don't play."

He choked. Not in the kind of laughter caught in a cough sound, but like he *choked*.

Poor delicate meatflower.

He deserved it. Thanks to his boss, I'd been tasked with strolling into Shepherd territory like it's no big deal, all in the name of meeting a source claiming to have information I'd bet a dead dog's dick didn't exist. Nobody down here could possibly have anything worth knowing. It was that kind of place.

I don't like wasting my time with useless errands. Too bad I didn't have a choice. Jobs had been hard to come by since I'd lost my hard-won reputation, which wasn't something I'd had to deal with for almost a decade. Ten years to build it, five months to break it. The past three weeks alone had been hell, and I needed to get my credits where I could.

Which explained why I was running a corp level errand with a corp level stick up my less-than-corp level ass. Or in this case, in my ear.

"Now that you're back on task," the operator said, clipped to the bone, "maybe we can, I don't know, *work*?"

Heh. "When's the contact supposed to show?"

"Twenty minutes ago." A little ice. A whole lot of effort to get back to level professionalism. "The contact point's not far from your location."

Back to wasting my time.

I strode to the open street, determined to see this through. If nothing else, I'd get to gloat about it later. And by that nun's holy vag, I would *so* gloat. I'd gloat my street-level ass off, rub that gloat all over my employer's desk.

Gloat and crusted nunjuice. I'm a benevolent motherfucker.

From cracked asphalt all the way up, hugging every

wall and frame and rotting façade, virtual signboards and vids filled every available space. There were so many advertisements infecting the bandwidth that my filters could barely keep up; didn't help most rolled on freqs a few years out of date. Meatspace lights lit up the rest in a haze, making it worse – the usual stuff in busted letters: flesh to wares, food to booze. A whole hell lot of religious iconery.

In short, a clusterfuck.

The fact I saw the bandwidth version of scabies torqued me on the regular. Normally, those of us without Security Identification Numbers invest in individualized tech – onboard apps to block the ads and bounce the bandwidth, optics with all sorts of special tricks; even our big-time tech gets scrubbed and reprogrammed to suit our personal needs. What blew my goat was that my chipset had gone cockrot sideways three weeks ago, and my mentor and personal streetdoc had tossed me out before I could get it overhauled. His cred, sky high compared to mine, would've dropped like a hungry twink on Ni-chrome's Stud of the Year if he hadn't. Cred wasn't a one-runner thing, unless you chose to run solo. Most of us need support.

I'd lost mine.

It sucked. It sucked in so, so many ways. When I needed repairs and checkups, all I had was a corporate doc on somebody else's payroll. That meant filters that *blow* when it comes to shitholes no suit would ever go.

The least of my problems, I'd admit, but an aggravating one.

My jaw shifted. I hooked my thumbs in the loops of my belt, rolling my shoulders like it'd help shed the baggage.

Despite all advisement, I'd come down without

anything heavier than a tactical jacket and a skinsuit to help regulate the cooler temperatures. One gun, a cheapie, was holstered in a stock rig under my jacket, and two serrated interceptors were sheathed at my hip and in my boot.

Just in case I had to get close and personal in somebody's guts.

I didn't expect to need anything more serious. My job on this glorious shitting day was to meet with a Trinity Square source about locally situated corp activity. And while I'd rather lick a hobo's crusty balls than come back to this shithole, any job with the MetaCorp brand in its crosshairs got my attention. They'd been fucking me since I got out – didn't even spot me dinner first. I didn't like that. Didn't know *why* they kept interfering in my business either, which pissed me off. Chasing them down, instead of the other way around, wasn't turning out as easy as I'd figured.

Chasing them down *here*? No way. Nothing of importance happened in Trinity. *Ever.* Worthwhile activity in this shitzone made less sense than tits on a fire extinguisher. This wasn't the kind of playground anybody worth dick played in, and especially not MetaCorp, whose capital chews up most corporations and craps them out again for funsies. There are only a handful of companies that could rival them, and not one of them would roll down here.

I grumbled under my breath.

The operator took that as a cue to preach. "Now remember, the key here is *tact*." He stressed the word. "We need the intel, and I've been warned about you."

I snorted a laugh. Tact? Not even on a good day. I had a linker for that.

Well, used to have. *Dammit.*

"MetaCorp will be deep underground, but that doesn't mean there aren't eyes everywhere. Be ready to coax the source with the credspikes we sent you with."

"Mm." If I didn't make off with them first. Punching the truth out of any source was my usual go to. Bribery is boring.

"We don't expect resistance. The source asked for you by name, so negotiation should be–"

"Whoa, time the fuck out." I stopped mid step. An ad ghosted in front of my eyes – *obedience to Our Lord's sacred appetite brings joy! eat at Jacob's Barbecue!* – and flickered out. I tucked one finger behind my ear, where the comm clipped in. "The contact did *what*?"

"Asked for you by name. It's a solid in."

I gritted my teeth. I would have facepalmed, but my instinct was to do it with my left hand. Since that entire arm had been blown off and replaced with a nanofactory diamond-steel tech arm, I'd learned to be more careful. I hit too damn hard these days.

"By name," I repeated. I almost shouted, but managed to zen it at the last second. I didn't need to announce my presence to the zone at large. I took a deep breath. "Oh-kay." I drew the word out. "They asked by name, and you didn't think *ambush*?"

When I got nothing back, I flicked the earpiece hard enough to send a feedback loop through the signal. It screeched. The operator tore off his own headset by the sound, his curses muffled.

My fists clenched. Unclenched. I took a deep breath, the mingled odors of rot and putrescence slicing through my nose. It only sort of helped.

I'd adopted a mantra. One I'd learned at my mentor's side. Lucky had pulled me off the street when I was barely out of the anglo res that didn't want me; a genetic throwback to the mixed blood that happens in a spunkpot like this city. I came out not white enough. Not prettily designed enough. Even though she'd gone through all the right channels, recessive genes can roll out anyway.

My mother was horrified. My father, whose ancestral genes I'd inherited, didn't care one way or the other. As in, at all. About anything.

I'd dicked out the moment I could. Got real, *real* lucky when a streetdoc named, ironically, Lucky scooped me up. Fucked if I know why, but he'd saved my life. Taught me how to run the street, how to be part of it – how to bend, maim and give better than I ever got instead of break.

Whenever I lost my shit, he'd stare at me with his sharp, no-bullshit stare. *Zen it*, he'd growl. If I didn't listen, I'd eat the floor. Took me a long time to realize that zenning it meant pulling my head out of the emotional part of my ass; focusing on the moment instead of rage and what-ifs.

Hard stuff. I needed anger management apps. Preferably ones where some digital voice told me how great I was doing while I punched the piss out of somebody else.

I whirled in place, searching the gloom. Hard to see much between all the meatspace and bandwidth chaos. Not that anything would help it look better. Everything sagged in the Square, even the cross lit by a spotlight somewhere to the east. Too much smog and filth to see fully in any direction, which made it a perfect setting for an ambush.

But by what? MetaCorp?

Too subtle. All *they* need to do is run a corp raid to get what they want. No law restricts corporate militia, and they hit the streets whenever they feel like it. There are thousands of obscure laws nobody's heard of, and guaranteed everyone is breaking at least five at any given moment. Makes it easy to claim any number of violations and ignore probable cause. Discretion isn't corporation credo.

It had to be something else. The last of my creds were very much on whoever my contact was supposed to be. A second player in this game?

A whistleblower from MetaCorp?

"Don't," the operator snapped when he'd settled, "do that again,"

"Eat a dick," I said tightly, squinting. "I need that kind of info *before* I go out. It changes *everything*."

"You weren't briefed?" A verbal shrug in his tone sent my heartrate skyrocketing into pissed. "Take it up with Mr Reed."

"Mr Reed," I snarled, "can go fuck himself."

Again, he said nothing.

Which meant I was aware of a whole lot of *nothing* around me. A lot of silence and dark and cold and ratruns where anybody and anything could hide. Now I didn't just feel like I was wasting my time – I felt like bait.

That motherfucker.

Malik Reed lorded over the Mantis Industries branch that funded the freelance runs I'd signed on for. He was a corporate shark and gaping asshole extraordinaire, determined to ride my shit all the way to the ground. Different than MetaCorp, at least – he had a buzz up his dick about them too, which was the one place we aligned.

Sort of aligned.

He didn't like hearing the word "no" as a rule. I relished saying it as often as possible – even though we both knew I needed the creds I wasn't getting from street-level jobs. And if any SINless runners learned I was freelancing for Mantis, I'd have more bullets jammed up my ass than I could handle. Only suicidal mercs sign up on corporate payroll.

I wasn't suicidal. Wasn't a traitor, either. I just needed to clear my cred before it cracked down to the bone. Playing gofer for a fuckmeister of the highest degree had to suffice for now.

Hearing that some source on the street had gone through Mantis Industries intel to ask for me by name? Not good. I'd made damn sure Mantis had no red tape to tag me with. My business was privileged fucking information, and doubly *fuck off* were Reed's irontight nondisclosures. Nobody had the guts to talk outside department lines. Far as I knew, not a *single* fixer had that info to sell. The only person I'd told was Indigo Koupra, and only because he'd been my linker – and closest thing I had to a friend – for six years.

Also, because I'd killed his sister.

Nanji's death weighed on him so much more than it did me, and I only kind of felt guilty for that. Mostly, I felt guilty for not feeling guilty, which meant I overcompensated by feeding Indigo corporate intel when I had it. It wouldn't make up for my part in it all, but I hoped it'd buy his silence long enough for me to fix whatever it was I'd broken.

I had an inkling. We both did. Rumor had it that I'd walked away with my girlfriend – Digo's precious little sister – and convinced her to tech up so fast she'd converted.

We call it going necro; pus-filled monstrosities that occur when you hit your tech threshold – the amount of machinery your body and brain can handle – and then scream past it. Something happens, hypes up the processing until the tech takes over the computer that is the brain, reprograms nanos, kills the meat it infects, and then tries to splatter everything around it for shits and giggles. Necrotech.

The second path to mobile meatsack is nanoshock; a lesser form of tech corruption. Not a deal breaker, if you catch it early. Nanoshock can be halted, your nanos recalibrated. Let it go too long, implant with more than your body can assimilate, or get rolled too hard for your nanos to deal, and that fever turns terminal. Full on conversion.

It's a smart merc's greatest fear. Even I watch my integrations. Every human has a different threshold, and there's no way to tell until you step over it.

Nanji hadn't just stepped over it. She'd been pushed. I'd watched her convert down in the lab we'd both been imprisoned in. When I went back, intent on burning the motherfucking place to the ground, Indigo and I found evidence that *I'd* sold Nanjali and other established runners to corporate interests.

Interests that had claimed me, too.

I didn't know. Couldn't remember. Somewhere along the way, something in my brain broke; those memories were wiped out.

When I'd finally come to, I'd escaped.

Nanji didn't. Her last words to me had been silent. *I'm sorry.*

Nothing else made it through before the overwhelming amount of tech installed in her spine finally shot her into braindead. Once the stuff had finished reprogramming her brain, Nanji was gone, leaving a corrupted system wearing her flesh like a dress.

My one regret was that I hadn't put the bullet in her

myself. I should have. Instead, I got nailed with the blame.

These were *my* problems. Nobody else gave a damn about anything else but the fact I'd turned my back on one of my own, and Indigo had every reason to doubt my innocence. He also had every reason to sell me out to the highest bidder.

The only thing that kept my shit in line right now was that I knew for a fact the Shepherds couldn't *possibly* be the highest bidder. Or even the best resource for revenge. I'd messed with them once before. They'd jumped me and the unit of Kill Squad I was running with while we'd been hunting down some of our strays. The Shepherds had the numbers, but that was about it.

Ten years is a *long* time to hold a grudge. I wasn't even part of the Squad anymore.

Besides, Mantis Industries and the Good Shepherds were as far apart on the social scale as an ocean and a drop of piss. Any crossover should have been impossible.

I fumed in silence, making my way to the designated meetup. The irritation that had filled my thoughts before now leaked into a puddle of nerves that pissed me off more.

Knowing what I'd just learned, I altered my approach to *buckled down and fucking angry*. When I made it to the right coords, no real light filtered past the crumbling edges of the bridge overhead. No sign of life, either. The place was wet, dark and freaking eerie. I rubbed my cold flesh hand against the back of my cold tech one. The damp in this pisshole was beginning to condense on the diamond steel, making it slick.

"What do you see?" asked the operator.

"Eat a dick."

"*Riko.*"

My jaw locked. "Nothing," I said through my teeth. "Fucking pause."

"Maybe they left when you didn't show."

"Maybe they left because your intel sucks," I snapped. Not that I believed that. This was too much a setup to miss because of a few minutes. My lips tightened. In the optics wired into my left eye, I watched numbers spike when I fisted my tech hand. The shadow remnant of my missing arm didn't hurt today, which meant the only feedback I got came through the implant that registered pressure, make up, and grip strength.

That was nice. It wouldn't ache when I punched somebody. And oh, would I punch the living *fuck* out of somebody today.

We both fell into an uneasy silence. One in which I leaned my back against the farthest support wall and pretended like I wasn't surveying my surroundings, feeling like a target with crosshairs locked on.

I didn't have to wait long.

# 2

My name floated from nowhere. "*Ri*-ko..." Emphasis on the first syllable. Rich with a tenderness I hadn't expected, creepy as necroballs hanging on a holiday tree.

I tagged it for modulation of the voice box, carefully tweaked for non-offensive and warm. Like... I don't know, something laced with a sedative. Wasn't any tech a scavenger invested in. It was the kind of intonation dirty old men pull on kids. Right before pulling out of 'em.

That meant a Shepherd. And I seriously *hate* Shepherds.

See, I'll fuck a willing nun till her judgment day, but I draw the line at rape and pedophilia. These ambulatory cankersores use religious affirmation as an excuse to do that and more. Their big kick is transubstantiation – as they tell it, the one who eats their holy sacrament becomes their Christ in all his glory.

That means any greasy little nutsucker can swallow a cracker, pop a boner, and let fly the holy seed. But only the men. The brothers and whatever. Their sisters, their chosen, whatever they wanted to fuck, had to bow down and take it.

What would Jesus do?

Whatever he wanted, apparently.

I knew an honest-to-god Christian who'd be *so angry* if he knew. I'd have to tell him one day. Mostly because watching my somewhat tarnished pocket detective go all wide-eyed and shocked had become a great source of fun.

*This* Shepherd, though. I recognized the voice under the modulator. Nothing fun about him. My anger fled, replaced by impatient exasperation. "Deacon fucking Carmichael. Can't forget me, huh?"

Not that I'd entirely forgotten him, either. Carmichael was one of those Shepherds who'd managed to haul ass out of the carnage before joining it. At the time, he'd carried the biggest stick like it'd pass for the biggest cock, and he'd promised to rape all three of us. Once in every hole and twice in the eye socket.

I'd left my mark – we all had – but I wish I'd been the one to shoot him. That gift had been delivered by another member of Kill Squad, right in the ass. On purpose, she'd said. I'd bet on shitty aim.

So that explained the named request. But not yet his link to Mantis. Or why he'd crawled out of his filthy nest to get me.

"Deacon?" His smirk translated without visuals. I couldn't place which direction it came from, either, which set me more on guard than I would've been had he shown himself. The whole area was like a freezing distortion filter. "No, no. I've risen to Our Father Christ's chosen."

"Whoop-de-dick-a-doo," was my congratulatory response.

"Is that how you greet an old friend?" A veiled threat in that voice thing, which made the fine hairs on my meat arm prickle. Warped *and* sweet. An ugly combo.

"Want another bullet up your ass?" I shot back.

"Hey," the operator interjected, "you want to simmer down, hotshot?"

No. And fuck him so very much.

"Neither a bullet nor another scar, thank you." A rich note of amusement, and not at all what I expected. "What you gave me was enough."

Not nearly.

He wasn't done. "You know, you were prettier when you were young."

Gross. *Ugh*. A thousand yottabytes of *fucking no*.

My flesh fingers itched. Soon as I found his scrawny little neck, I was wringing it. One-handed. Meat to meat, so I could feel the veins pop and vertebrae crack. My diamond steel arm would do more damage, easily process the amount of force it'd take to collapse his windpipe and register it in the optic feed I only half paid attention to, but it just wouldn't have the same rush.

Only first, I needed to know where he'd gotten his intel. On me, on Mantis and on MetaCorp. I wish I could have brought Indigo.

I wish he trusted me enough to do that.

I took a breath, grimacing. "Fork over your info before I skin your scarred ass for your desperate little brides to rub off on."

"Riko." The operator slapped a hand to his forehead. His voice had that sound to it. "Who taught you to negotiate?"

Nobody. Or rather, it never stuck. Digo had done all the talking; I'd done all the shooting, stabbing, glaring, breaking, maiming... Tactics and data are what linkers are for. Birdseye processing and boots on the ground direction, indispensable for any mission. He was my guy for all things – knew the best fixers, got the best jobs.

He'd once told me I needed to learn when to stroke my dick and when to stow it. Never figured it out. Stroking it felt so much better.

Carmichael's laugh rolled out like a warm, loving sigh. It took effort not to gag. "God, I love your fire." My scalp prickled. Wringing. His. Neck. "Why don't you stay a while?" he continued from the dark. "Let's catch up on old times. Tell me *all* about yourself."

My body tensed, hands clenching against the wall I leaned against. "How about you just give me what I'm here for? I won't," I added thinly, "ask again."

"Will you talk with me if I do?"

"Do I have to?"

"*Yes*," hissed over my comm. "I assume," came the too-melodic voice, "you want to ask me just how I knew about your little corporation fetish."

Ah, damn.

"The intel," the operator warned, as if he could hear my temper cracking. Given my heartbeat thudding bloody murder in my ears, he could. "MetaCorp is the end goal. Do your job."

Well actually, smashing this screwhead's face in had just become my end goal. "Fine." I spread my hands wide, showing my weaponless status to the dark at large. "We'll talk."

"Good girl." Light shimmered into view, a gleam to my left. He'd been hiding on the other side of the bridge. I straightened, pushed off the brick. Wasn't ready when that glow erupted into a pristine lance of bright white. Neon be fucked, the whole place lit up like daylight. Burned out the ads – and my retinas.

Sheets of red and orange popped in the back of my eyeballs. The data rolling through my optics stood out against the flash, cataloguing the worn brick my metal hand slammed against. Stone alloy, cement and ground up bits of whatever came before it.

Perfect for ramming a skull into.

He had performative dickery down to an art, I'd give him that. It took me a few precious seconds to see through the visual afterburn; he'd cracked my night vision with a ten-ton wrecking ball. Asshole.

By the time I could see again, Carmichael had fully formed like the miracle he wanted to be. The weird toga he wore already looked stupid, but the shitting thing was woven with filaments of lightwire. He was a sanctified beacon in the metaphorical – and literal – shadows. A religious wet dream.

His smile, behind a bushy auburn beard I was surprised his babyface had managed to grow, lacked half the teeth in the bottom left of his mouth.

*That* was my doing. Nanos don't regrow teeth. The rest were yellowed and brown at the edges, but most hadn't fallen out yet. I'd rectify that today, I swore to his sick fuck of a god.

He leered at me. "That's more like it. I assume you have what I asked for?"

I stared at him, blinking rapidly. "Dim it."

It took him a second or so to realize I'd meant the robe. He obeyed nicely enough. Odds were the thing screwed his vision, too. "For you," he said. Gracious, his scarred ass.

I let it slide. "You asked for me," I said, looping back to his question. "And creds. I'm here, aren't I?"

"So you are." His hands dropped. "My brothers tell me you enjoyed yourself on the way."

My lips twisted in a short smile. "You tailed me." I gave this one to him; I knew better and I'd gotten lazy. "Not bad. I hadn't noticed."

"Told you," the operator muttered.

Carmichael's back straightened, teeth a ragged curve. "We're stronger, Riko."

Uh huh.

I made a show of propping my foot up on the wall, leaning my head back to gaze somewhere over his head. The light had lowered, but my night vision refused to return. That irritated me too. In fact, this whole cunting thing irritated me.

Blah, blah, negotiate. Didn't need to hear it again. "So *that* must be how you found out about me, huh?" Wide-eyed bullshit delivered in sugar. I felt stupid. "All that strength and shit."

"You're awful at this." Resignation from the operator.

He could eat two dicks.

"I know people," the Shepherd purred, unaware of my eavesdropping babysitter. His heavy-lidded blue eyes settled on my face. Stared at me hard enough that my skin crawled right up my skull. "I know where you like to drink, Riko. Where you fuck in the corners and the business you want to hide." His remaining teeth looked rotting brown in the light of his robe. "And I know how *bad* you want MetaCorp."

Everybody knew where I liked to hang. The Mecca was nobody's secret. Everybody also knew where I liked to fuck. Also not a secret, and most comers – heh – welcome.

MetaCorp and my business? That part wouldn't fly. As much as I desperately wanted to see how far my nun-caked fist could go down his throat, I had to *talk* to get what I needed. Not my strong suit.

Fucking Malik.

I pulled out my best smile – one with less teeth than usual.

He flinched.

"Well, that sounds great," I replied, light as I could manage. "I got your creds." I tapped my jacket, where the outer breast pocket held the credsticks he'd demanded. Less than a usual payday but more than a Shepherd deserved. "And you got me here. So, fair trade, Carmichael. You know what I want."

That shiteating smile of his widened to the point the blackened rim of his empty gums framed it. "There it is," he said, that soft, welcoming voice all but vibrating in the air between us. "You're so much sweeter when you're a good girl, Riko."

Ugh. Like he had *ever* known me.

My fake cheer vanished. "*Oh*-kay." I dropped my foot.

His gaze sharpened, one hand out. "Don't move."

I would have ignored that, gone right for his fugly face with the bottom of my boot, but the operator's voice hardened on the line. "*Negotiate.*"

"Eat three dicks," I snapped. "It's a setup, you stupid cunt."

The Shepherd in front of me sighed elaborately, while the operator in my ear hissed.

Didn't matter. I got it now. Carmichael should have been frothing for this much cred in his bank. Instead, he was stalling like I was slow in the head. The pity he leveled on me only wrenched my temper higher. "Vulgar mouth," he chided. "You leave now and I can't guarantee your safety anymore. Our Lord told me that you need it."

His Lord could eat an extra dick on the side. So much dick to go around.

Enough was enough.

I closed the distance between us, knocked Carmichael's arm away and had a hold of his greasy beard before he could do more than manage a half step back in surprise. My flesh fingers twined into the coarse length so tight, his skin went bloodless where it pulled taut.

"Hey," I growled. "Father Fistula. We are *not* equals." He opened his mouth, hand pushing at the seam of metal at my shoulder. The plating claimed half my scapula, a harsh ridge between flesh and tech. It didn't move, and his nails found no traction.

I dragged the struggling Shepherd higher up by his beard, until he was on his toes and sputtering incoherently. His pocked and scabbed neck stretched, cords popped out in stark relief. The glow from his robes painted his upturned face in wild light and shadows, outlining every quivering pore.

I loved being tall. Having the kind of whipcord body that can bench assholes like him was just frosting. I smiled bloody menace into his panicked rictus, his eyelids twitching.

"Riko!"

"Shut up," I snapped into the comm, eyes on the father. To him, I said, "A few bullet points." I lifted one metal finger in front of his eyes. "I'm not going to freeze my ass off while you run your fuckhole like you have any standing." Another finger. "That sister what's her face? Just got her first and best orgasm in her entire shitting *life*, so you are welcome for showing her the light." His hands tried to go for my face. I batted them away. Metal knocked against bone, and he yelped. "And if you don't tell me everything you know right fucking now," I snarled, "I will nail your syphilitic nuts to your nostrils."

# 3

Watching his face transform from pain to fury fascinated me, in a weird kind of way. I mean, people didn't usually stare into my eyes and see a chance in hell.

He thought he did. His total lack of fear nagged at me in a big bad way. Stalling, obviously, but he thought he had an ace stashed somewhere.

One hand grabbed my wrist. "Swallow my sanctified cock, bitch." Saliva frothed on every word, spattering my hand and forearm. "I've got–"

I shoved a knee into his gut. Caught him as he bent over with a mangled grunt and jerked him back upright by his beard. Roots gave way.

His limbs flailed. Tears filled his reddening eyes. His breath wheezed, but he didn't stop. "I was going to let my brothers fuck you," he gasped. Pissy to the last. "But now I oughta send your corpse to Koupra." He spat in my face. "A favor."

I froze, fingers straining in his beard. His patter of spittle cooled on my cheek. I left it. Not the worst that ever hit my face. "Why." A demand, not a question.

Something snide and dumb had clearly popped into his head. He seized my wrist, trying to balance on shaking tiptoe as he sneered at me. "Turned on your

29

team. Caused your linker's sister to go necro."

My lips pulled back from my teeth.

"And it's no secret you've been panting for MetaCorp. Did you know," he added with a hysterical kind of glee, "they're looking for you, too? A few questions to the right people…" He laughed, high and tight. "You know you're fucked, don't you?"

Yep. But hey, good news: he wasn't wrong. It was no secret I'd been digging for info on MetaCorp. Or that MetaCorp might be trying to kill me. That shit happened on the regular among SINless. There were all kinds of jobs on the market – including ones quietly offered by corporate subsidiaries looking to score one up on other corp subsidiaries. Being off grid meant corporations used third parties to hire saints, and didn't have to worry about a trail leading back to 'em. Saints don't usually know who hires them – a good fixer keeps it that way.

Hypocrisy is an art.

The bad news was that he wasn't wrong about Indigo's sister, either. Nanjali Koupra haunted my recent past and foreseeable future in a nasty way. That the barest details of her conversion had leaked was old news – everybody knew I'd been reported dead, and that Indigo had a serious beef with me that years of runs couldn't bury. His sister *had* gone necro on my watch.

As for the rest of the chumheads out there gossiping like bored housewives, they didn't know I'd lost months of my memory up until that point. Only Indigo and Malik Reed did, and we kept it a closely guarded secret. Memory loss meant brain fuckery, and brain fuckery skirted too close to misbehaving tech for most. Misbehaving tech makes the jumpy ones think conversion, and threats of conversion earn a street funeral.

In short: a lot of blood and a barrel on fire.

Carmichael didn't seem to know that much, which was good. I smiled at the Shepherd trying to make like he wasn't all that hurt by his long and curlies in my fist. "Who is your contact?"

He leered. "You afraid?"

"Boy," I said, still smiling, "I will fist your skull like I fucked your precious sister if you don't–"

"MetaCorp," the operator yelled over me. "Get back on track!"

No. MetaCorp would be there tomorrow. Right now, the source that linked me and Mantis took precedence. *Then* I'd verify MetaCorp's presence – not that I expected any. Then I'd rip the Shepherd's throat out.

Then cumflakes on Malik's desk.

My fist tightened in Carmichael's beard. "Who." A jerk. "Is." Another, wrenching his head. "Your." Tears streamed from his gritty eyes. "*Contact.*"

He sealed his mouth so tight, sweat seamed between his thinned lips.

I ripped my hand away, fingers full of matted brown hanks. The audible sound of thin skin tearing filled me with gleeful satisfaction, seconded only by his high-pitched howl.

Carmichael staggered back and bent over, hands clutching at his chin. While he struggled, swearing violently, I turned my attention to the vermin runs on the other side of the bridge overhang.

Trinity is one of those deep places that doesn't see the sun. A double-edged knife. On the one hand, minimal risk of sun poisoning. No need to rely on shields to keep the radiation out, either, so the spotty shielding on the fringes of this side of the city doesn't matter.

On the other, freezing fucking cold, wet and dark as the inside of a dead man's asshole. Plenty of room to maneuver. Lots of places to stab a body in the dark.

Lots of places from which to snipe an unwitting runner like myself.

Carmichael's demeanor had all but screamed ambush. He'd mentioned knowing people. Two and two didn't have to add up to four, especially with Shepherd trash, but this was so obviously a setup that I wanted to rip Shepherd dick off and ram it up Malik's nose.

"You won't get out of here," Carmichael spat behind me. "This time, we're taking you down."

"You and what nuke?" I scoffed.

"You stupid whore. *This* one." Based on the shadows stretching long and thin into the street, he flung a hand into the air. "Shepherds!" A triumphant scream. "Put her down!"

The operator sighed. Probably at me.

A Shepherd call, huh? Better than a sniper, anyway. I reached to the small of my back where I'd stuck my cheapie – a Somers & Phelps pistol with 10mm rounds and about twelve chances to kill as many motherfuckers as I could. They called it the Gritster. Yeah, I know. Corporations are stupid. But street names can be even worse, so Gritster it is.

Bottom line, it fires bullets and can be trusted in any situation not worth real effort. It was the only firearm I'd bother to waste on these assholes.

Maybe.

*Any* moment now…

Right?

The poor bastard behind me held his dramatic pose for a full, painfully stretched thirty seconds. I rolled my eyes to the dirty cross spotlighted above us. The only brightness in that bag of meat came from his clothing.

"Shepherds," he said again, louder. "Get her!"

Another pause.

The operator held his breath – I heard the intake. No exhale. Then, "Is something supposed to happen?"

Oh, man. No intel, just a dumb bastard with a grudge. No source, just the same dumbass who could have asked for real backup from that source and didn't. Anybody *that* informed had connections; had there been a sniper, I'd've been shot by now.

This was the last straw.

I burst into laughter so intense, my balance went sideways. I caught myself against the wall, howling with it. In my peripheral vision, Carmichael's mouth opened. Closed. I laughed and laughed until tears streamed down my cheeks until I had to brace one hand on my knee to keep upright. "You…" I gasped a snort, barely managing to get the words out. "You wanna call 'em again? I'll wait."

His lips peeled back around uneven teeth, fear and fury. He stepped back. Slowly. Like maybe he wouldn't startle me if he moved just slow enough.

The risk of taking on someone like me meant failure blew bloody chunks. Literally. He'd come after me with no plan, no reliable backup. No fucking weapon. If you're going to go after somebody over your paygrade, you'd better do it fast and right.

He sucked at both. Worse, he had just enough info on my soured reputation to be dangerous, and a line into my business that pissed me right the hell off.

Carmichael took a few more steps back, shaking hands digging into his robe. He wore filthy treaders under the flirty white hem, stained with the muck of the streets he claimed to control.

I tapped my nanosteel index finger against the Gritster's barrel. It clinked.

The way his head twitched, I figured he'd come in wired up for comms and wasn't getting any updates. Blood ran from the mange I'd made of his face, and the sweat rolling down to mix with it confirmed what I already knew: nobody was coming.

His voice lost the rest of any modulation his tech gave him, guttural with rage. "This isn't over."

"Uh huh." I scratched at my temple with the barrel. "So, about that contact…"

"You're going down!" Again with the saliva. The dude had *issues*.

"One more time," I sighed. "Your contact."

"I'll be the *first* to *fuck your bleeding corpse*."

Fine. I'd asked four times, broke my own record.

I smiled. Teeth. Stone cold murderous intent. "Get in line, chum."

He panicked all over again. As I expected, that light woven into his robe went fullscale blinding, a geyser of interference. He spun on one foot and took off, fabric flapping around his skinny legs.

Too slow. Too late. I raised the Gritster shoulder-height, arm stretched, and pulled the trigger. I didn't have to look at his stupid lightwire to aim. The asshole didn't vary his angle.

The report of the medium pistol cracked through Trinity; a sharp shock that pinged wall to wall. The bullet caught him in the back – the spine, rather than his ass this time. Much as I'd enjoy leaving him with another keloid, I wasn't going to risk it. With any luck, the loss of one of the source's contacts would put a blinder on.

Father Carpetstain hit the wet street and didn't move.

I dropped my hand back to my side, shaking my head. With the other, I tapped the comm in my ear. Hard. That feedback whine sang like an altar boy fresh off a

Shepherd. "Update for Mr Reed," I chirped.

"Goddammit–"

"No info to be had," I said over him.

"I already heard!"

"Tell requisitions I expect reimbursement for the bullet."

Something clicked. Not the comm. His teeth, maybe. "A full report *will* be delivered to Mr Reed."

"Awesome. Make sure you note how I didn't assfuck a Shepherd with rusted rebar."

"That is gross."

"Don't kink shame." Rolling my aching shoulder, I left the worst ambush attempt in the whole fucking history of ambushes and paced towards the vermin lane I'd marked as my way out. "Tell Reed he'd better pay me for his lousy intel or I'll do to his ass what I didn't do to Carmichael's."

An immediate click signaled a dead line.

I win. My ego did, anyway.

So, now what? The Shepherds had obviously abandoned Carmichael, which suggested they hadn't been on board with the bastard's halfassed plan. The stuff he'd known about Digo and Nanji still stung, but he'd been fuzzy enough on details to keep me from shitting my pants. Nothing everyone else didn't already know.

He'd said nothing about Mantis specifically, either. Just MetaCorp. And yet he *had* contacted Mantis to get to me. How?

*I know people*, he'd said.

Shit on stilts, I'd have to find the intermediary. And I'd have to do it before they tried this shit again. Next time, I might not be so lucky.

I didn't put the Gritster back in my harness. At this point, the sound of a gunshot all but guaranteed company. Scavengers, if nothing else. Cannibalism wasn't all that rare around the starving. Me, I wasn't into the kind of munching that didn't involve ass and snatch.

For scavengers, I was boots and walking meat.

**4**

I'd barely made it out of Carmichael's glow radius when a shot cracked over my head. Then another in quick succession. One bullet pinged off my tech arm, another missed by a meter and sparked as it kissed the asphalt.

Not a pro. I wasn't even mad.

My policies are simple: if it shoots at me, kill it. If it jumps at me, kill it. If it owes me a favor and doesn't pay up, kill it. Basically, kill whoever fucks with me. Fuck whoever doesn't.

Scavengers aren't the shooting kind. Guns are rare as virgins down here.

The Shepherds had obviously given up on smart forever, and without smart, would-be assassins don't stand a chance. I looked up, found the grimy teenager sighting through a modified, balls-old sniper rifle at me, and scowled at him. He was too damn close for that weapon, much less the too-large scope he'd glued on it.

My return fire tore into the exposed side of his face. I didn't even need to move to hit him, just aim up and done. His body dropped from the ledge, landed at my feet in a tangle of arms and legs. Tenderized organs audibly squelched. One corpse, ready for the buffet.

I caught the rifle before it landed on him, gave it a

once over, and tossed it to the side. Worthless junk.

As I stepped over the dead kid, the cheap wire wrapped around his ear went wild. I paused, tilted my head. Echoed shouts bounced between dank walls, caught on each other and multiplied. So, hey, the Shepherds *had* been around in some quantity. Couldn't tell how many there were, but I figured outnumbered was a fair bet.

Awesome. I could use that anger management therapy.

I left the corpse where it was – didn't pat him down. I'd bet my ass he had nothing on him. Killing the poor bastard was a mercy; only one way out of the Square.

Or two, if you're me. Which is how I ended up hauling ass through Trinity Square with a bitchload of pissed off deacons on my tail, no bullets left, and a growing harsh on my zen. Killing four of them thinned them out, but I'd run out of ammo. Shoulda brought spares in my arm. I'd forgotten to refill it.

Not the worst problem on my plate. Just the most immediate.

I took a breather in the shadow of the searchlight aimed up at the crumbling cross at the top of a dilapidated church, crouching on the ledge between the light and the dropoff to the streets below. My exit was on the west side, where I'd grab my piece of junk ride and meet up with my Mantis extraction crew. They'd get me into the Corporate sector without any extra questions, then I'd smugly sit on Reed's desk while yellowed flakes of nunjuice drifted off my pants. A little gonorrheal gift for everyone.

Gunfire echoed somewhere in the bleak hell of Trinity Square, snatching my attention to the street below. A figure stepped into view. "Fuck!"

"Stop shooting at shadows," came a louder, closer yell.

"Go to hell!"

"Where'd she go?" Syllables bounced between slick walls. "Where is she?"

I grinned as more gathered around the first. What dreary light there was pooled like rotting halos in the smoggy layer of shit. Farther away, that spotlight of Carmichael's useless robe seared patterns in the pollution that settled in districts like this. A bleeding sun in a nuclear haze, just bright enough that one of the Shepherds' guns glinted faintly – a composite piece of trash called the Kago, but the rest of us call the Crappo. They're made from whatever'll fit, tend to 6mm rounds, with a sixty percent chance the fucking thing won't jam, overheat or explode on you.

Fixers on the low end of life grab 'em from corpses and keep selling them on.

They don't pack that much power, at least compared to what I'm used to. Didn't mean any one of these lowlifes couldn't get a lucky shot. My cred was already in the pisser; rumors of my demise at the hands of the Shepherds would just embarrass me.

"Shitting hell," seethed a deacon. His head, bald at the top, gleamed like a pale hole. "Where is she?"

"Lost her," said the first. His voice was high and tight, every word clipped to a splinter. "She got Carmichael, God take him."

"Good. One problem down." Another of the Shepherds tapped his own shoulder with the barrel of his Sauger Quad 54. A better piece than the composites, but top-heavy. Swinging one of those near your face is how an idiot blows his own head off. "We gonna pin it on her?"

Ugh. So that explained Carmichael's gambit. I'd just played the tool of some shitty gang's politics, and done them a favor while at it. That hurt my pride, those childfuckers.

Annoyed, I dragged my metal fingers over my scalp. My chin-length shock of bleached hair stuck to the sweat and ambient grime on my forehead and cheeks, causing my skin to itch in its wake.

I needed a serious sanitizing.

One of them growled; a darker, leaner shadow scouting the area in a slow circle. "We owe the bitch anyway. Sister Charmine's ruined."

"She still alive?"

"No body?" asked another, anticipating the response.

"Whore slipped us," he replied. "We'll find her."

"God damn her."

"Amen."

If that meant what I thought it meant, the nun hadn't just wised up to orgasms, but had gotten the fuck out of shit square while she was at it. Not sure how, but if she lived long enough to dodge the gang's deacons, she'd have a fighting chance outside this zone.

Samaritan service done for the day.

The crouching one stood. "Find this cyberbitch. She'll net us more dead than alive, so don't hold back."

"What about–"

"I don't fucking *care* what some heathen cunt wants," the apparent leader snapped. "Killing her boosts our Word, so gift this one the grace of a bullet. You hear me?"

Cunt, huh? Some heathen cunt, no less. Wasn't me, I'd obviously been designated the cyberbitch here.

One rubbed his head. "But the creds–"

My eyes narrowed as the boss grabbed the speaker by the front of his shirt and dragged him eye to eye. "To hell with a sinner's credits," he roared. "Bring Riko down and do it now!"

Credits. Sounded like a bounty, but not one anyone else knew about. Bounties tend to light the street network on fire, especially the *deliver alive* ones. That usually meant hell on earth for the poor sucker caught in the crossfire – fun gossip.

Less fun was my head in said crossfire. Who wanted me alive that badly? And secretly, too. I should have heard about my own cunting bounty.

Carmichael's source? Had to be whoever directed him to the Mantis contact.

Another Mantis department? Possible. The factions aren't known for playing nice with each other. Corporate espionage plays like basketball to most suits. Points are points, only in creds and tech and influence.

The role of the ball is played by everybody else in the way.

Fuck. In the end, all that mattered to me was that somebody out there knew two-thirds of my shit and had the opportunity to farm it out. Needed to find out who and needed to squeeze what else they knew out of 'em.

The guy playing prophet flung out a hand, gesturing the others to fan. "Eternal damnation to deacons who fail."

I rolled my eyes, pitched my voice low. "Hello, my flock," I intoned. "This is God."

They stared at each other. Looked around. "What the fuck–"

"Thou shit not," I continued, my voice deep and epic as I could make it. "Nor mess with bitches scarier than you." A beat. "Wait." I thought about it, bracing my hand against the lip of my perch. The cold cement cooled my overly warm palm. "Is it *than thou*? Shit thou?"

"Up there!"

I laughed as they finally looked up in unison. Too

slow. Goddamn, everything they did was too slow. My nagging sense of embarrassment was getting hard to shake. At this point, putting them out of their misery was the *nice* thing to do.

Two guns snapped up.

The leader of the group looked the most surprised – at least, I think he did. A black cross tattooed his skin forehead to neck, temple to temple. Made his eyes look very small, and his mouth very large and pink as it gaped.

Taking advantage of the moment, I stepped off the ledge.

Could have just left, I guess. Easy enough to lose them again. But screw that. I didn't want to play it safe. I was just angry enough to go in armed. As in, *armed*. With a piece of body tech that'd seen more shit than half these assholes.

Although it was machined to a functional shape, my arm would never pass for the real thing. Made of tough diamond steel, it didn't scratch easy and broke only when I pushed it – which I did, and did often. Nanofactoried tech like this meets in the middle of affordable and streetside functional, and I excelled at finding all-new ways to blow its capabilities to the max. Diamond steel gave it extra reinforcement, but didn't leave room for pretty. My dexterity would always be shot, my fine motor skills lacking.

Good thing I didn't aim for finesse. Instead, I aimed for that sickly pallid spot at the top of one deacon's head.

The Shepherds regrouped faster than I expected. Bullets pinged off the rusted ledge behind me. A few hit the spotlight, shattering its cover and snapping sparks overhead. The pocked and rusted cross above me went dark.

Score one for me.

Their faces lit up from the fiery shower, which only gave me a better view as I landed fist-first into the middle of the crowd. The skull beneath my hand crumpled. Then exploded out at the sides. Gray matter and bone shrapnel flew.

I got lucky. Splatter caught Crossface in the eyes. He screamed, wheeling back, flailing, mouth full of the raw stuff. I grabbed his Kago with my flesh hand, even as I wrenched my embedded fist from the depths of his buddy's chunked brainmeat.

"Jesus Christ," he swore. I think it was a swear; my pocket detective flinches like it is.

"Not today," I said brightly, swinging my borrowed gun around to knock it against the crouching deacon's eye socket.

A flash of pure panic under that uneven black ink. The pussy that passed for his mouth twisted, peeling back pink in the black leg of his tattooed iconery.

Then he found the balls he didn't know how to use. "Kill her!" he screamed. "Nownow*now*–"

No sense of self-preservation. Happens a lot.

I pulled the trigger just as another Shepherd surged at me from the left. The bullet tore through viscous eyeball and meat, skin singed from the heat of it. Crossface sailed backward, second set of brains turned to mush thanks to the bullet too weak to exit his hard head.

The second ganger cursed as I slammed my foot into his chest, a backwards kick that sent him sailing into a pile of rotting trash. Pulp and mildew puffed out around him, a cloud of noxious black.

I missed the growling goon that gifted me a bullet in the back. The report cracked like a pissant toy rocket, but a bullet was a bullet. "Fuck!" I grunted, jerking to the side. *Goddamn*, that hurt. No exit wounds, the Crappo just wasn't that powerful, but shit, it sucked. No exit wound meant dealing with it later. If I didn't, my nanos would build a pocket of collagen around it, creating a keloid seal. Nanos are good, but not *push out foreign objects* good.

Another reason I needed a functional streetdoc.

The Shepherd smeared with rot and practically foaming at the mouth jumped at me. I grabbed his arm, fingers slipping in the grime, and twisted harder than I should've had to. The move pulled at my new bullet hole and tore it that much wider. Pain ripped right up into my brain.

On the plus side, I rocked the guy into an armbar that ruined his day. Bone and gristle popped. He screamed, thrashed and punched and kicked whatever he could, like a kid throwing a tantrum.

When I didn't let up, the guy who'd tagged me rolled in hard and drove a fist against the back of my head. My skull snapped forward, head ringing. Sweat rolled down my back, cold and clammy. I was used to getting shot. Didn't make it physically easier.

I wrenched the howling, frothing deacon around, slammed him into his buddy. The Sauger Quad went flying.

I, uh, didn't expect one of them to have hold of my harness. Not sure which one, but at least nobody but those two were left to see me roll ass over snatch when they jerked me right off my feet.

I'd had enough.

Using the momentum, ignoring the sharp scrapes and bruises the broken asphalt ground into me, I rolled back up to a crouch. They struggled to detangle themselves. I stepped on the butt of the Quad by my feet, flipped it up, and caught it by the fore-end. Using its own weight, I pumped it once and had the barrel pointed business end first at the unfortunate deacons.

Both froze. One wobbled on unsteady knees, then fell back on his ass. "W- Wait..." His dark skin gleamed with sweat, eyes so wide the bloodshot whites practically glowed. "Our Lord said–"

"Oh, for..." I bent to bare my teeth at both. "Wake up, fuckos. He ain't helping!"

The other very, very slowly lifted hands twisted by scars. That was the one who'd dinged me with the Crappo. Point blank in the back.

Both knew what I knew – Sauger Quad 54s had a spray that hit everyone like bukkake made of rusted nails. I'd tag them both, and the floor, and the surrounding walls, in one shot.

I waved the shotgun. "You didn't even prime this thing," I said, disgusted.

They stared at me in silence. One's jaw set, fear a trembling line in it. His buddy was too stupid to look down the barrel of a shotgun and see anything but the inside of his own ass.

Ugh. Boring.

I tipped the barrel one way, then the next. "So, dickruns. Which of you d'you think your God wants to save?"

The stupid one glared mutinously at me. "Go ahead," he spat. "Martyr us."

I snorted so hard, laughter and saliva knotted into my sinuses and burned all the way down. Choking on the effort hurt like a bitch, but I'd be fucked right here if I let that one slide. "*Martyr* you," I repeated, croaking. I buried my nose into the crook of my elbow, eyes stinging.

Maybe he blushed. His jaw got harder and harder, his mouth thinner and thinner.

A figure moved in my peripheral. Keeping the Sauger trained on them, I lifted the Kago in my other hand and directed the trigger to the unlucky deacon. He hit the dirt, gurgling from the hole in his throat. Last bullet, too. I dropped the piece of shit. It bounced, skidded.

They stared at me.

"Martyr." I hocked up mucous in my throat and spat. The gob splatted by his feet. "Bitch, somebody's got to *care* about you first."

"Burn in hell!" the scared one managed.

Adorable.

Holding the weapon steady, I lifted my brain- and blood-spattered tech hand. Strings of meat seamed the middle finger I gave them. "You first."

I guess I hit the breaking point. Both turned and booked it; a Shepherd specialty.

Killing assholes was mine.

The Quad's blast scored the ground, the corner the quiet one tried to dive behind, and most of his exposed meat. Blood and flesh splattered. He hit the ground, twitching. The skinny one screamed as he planted face-first into the slimy street.

Nobody shoots me and lives.

I ignored the smeghead dying across the way, approached the little one and put a boot on his chest. The Shepherd whimpered, eyes rolling back in his head.

I wasn't even in the mood to savor it. This time, I shoved the barrel right into his gaping mouth. Teeth shattered on metal. He screamed around the barrel, and the acrid stench of ammonia drifted up to my nose.

"Yikes," I said, glancing at the stain spreading at his crotch.

So much for the martyr act. Tears ran from his eyes. His whole body shook, frozen to the ground. Whatever he said, I couldn't understand it around the shotgun. Blood and saliva dribbled down his cheeks.

*Sister Charmine's ruined*, they'd said. *Bitch slipped us.*

Such equality. Much love for the flock.

My lip curled. "Yeah, don't care. Tell me who your contact is. Who's the cunt you mentioned?"

His dark eyes widened, raw panic stretching every line of his face. He tried to speak, garbled nonsense.

I bent over. It tilted the barrel, which grated up into the broken shards of his upper teeth. "What?" I asked, cupping my filthy hand behind my ear. "I can't understand you."

He screamed, jagged gums grinding as he tried for words his shattered mouth couldn't frame. He openly cried. Wailing, gasping panic that hitched into hysteria. "I- I..." A shaking whine. "Ah 'o 'oh!"

My nose wrinkled. "What? Oh." I pulled the barrel from between his torn lips. "Oops, sorry."

"I don't know, please," he begged. "Please, believe me, I–"

My boot ground in. Something underneath it popped. He screamed. I let him, waiting him out. When he ran out of breath, I tapped his cheek with the Sauger. "Why are you after me?"

His hands twitched against my ankles, feebly grasping for something. Anything, I bet. Something to use.

All he had was me and the spread of his own piss. I smiled down at him.

His whole body flinched, tried desperately to go fetal. Wasn't all me. The spray he'd taken did a lot of the anti-mobility work. "Not me! Didn't want to do it!"

"Nope." Another pat, metal to cheekbone. Harder. "*They* wanted me alive. You wanted me dead. Why?"

I watched the realization bloom into full-on terror in

his face. The babylicker was genuinely crying. Like he
didn't spend his days ass-deep in it every day.

The worst.

He thrashed, hurt himself doing it, cringed, cried
harder. His face cracked into fragments of snot and filth,
blood and shards of teeth, and he sobbed, "Somebody
hired Carmichael. Creds for you, that's it. That's all I
know! I swear to God, I don't know anything else!"

Pretty sad for a would-be martyr.

"Why dead?"

"Cred," he managed.

The Word, I realized. Shepherd lingo for cred. Easy
enough to understand there. Killing me would be a
massive boost for the dregs of the city. Killing *any* merc
would do it for these shitsuckers. Had Carmichael's
efforts at revenge made me an easy and coincidental
target?

That felt like a stretch.

"Who knows details?" I demanded.

His eyes rolled to Crossface's sprawled corpse.

Just fucking awesome. Two dead sources of
information. This wasn't my day.

"Well," I said briskly, removing my foot from his chest.
"Give my love to the devil." I looked down at him over
the barrel of the shotgun, and smiled. "I hear," I added,
licking my lips, "he's got a *huge* cock."

Full-fledged panic turned his sobbing back into
screams, and that was all I'd get from him, so fuck it. He
was too close for spray. Instead, when I pulled the trigger,
thunder and meat exploded outward. Hit the street and
everything else around it in a radius of disgusting.

Martyr, huh? These crunchnuggets and Carmichael
both, hiding behind that useless cross.

At least I'd walked away with *slightly* more information

than I'd started with. There was some source who'd tipped the Shepherds off enough to hit a Mantis contact with my name, and wanted me delivered to them alive. That same source knew about my hard-on for MetaCorp, and their hard-on for me. They knew I associated with Mantis.

The way I figured, they'd know more about things than I did. Things I *would* get answers for.

Hunting that asshole down had to be my next job.

I threw the Quad into the mess and walked away, seething. Goddamn. Shooting wasn't enough. I should've dropped napalm on the whole crew when I had the chance. All the blood and sweat had washed that dried spunk off my pants and now I just didn't have any reason – or patience – to deal with Malik and his stupid desk.

His sources sucked. More, I figured I wouldn't find the source in his turf anyway. If a leak had dribbled out of his department, he'd never tell me. He'd just execute the culprit and walk out unspattered by the shit.

I hated his face.

When I didn't want to fuck it.

Let the operator make the report without me. Let *him* debrief his boss. I was done. My leads pointed streetwards, not to the corporate sector. If His Gaping Asshole had a problem with that, Reed could deal with it himself.

# 5

I couldn't get out of Shepherd turf fast enough. Given the necessary circumnavigation, it took me longer than I wanted, and every kilometer of ragged asphalt under my piece of shit Vega V3's wheels ticked my annoyance higher and higher.

I don't like questions. Hate digging to find the answers. My usual methods involve shooting elbows and kneecaps until somebody chokes out the info I want. I prefer to leave the digging to Indigo and show up for the bloody rest. Without my linker – without his team at my back, the way it used to be – I didn't know *how* to get answers. Digo had always been eyes in the air for me. He excelled at processing info fast enough to re-evaluate the plan on a moment's notice. Finding another one was out of the question. Most linkers make solid contacts when they did good, which I needed, but the best linkers are hard to cozy up to.

What the hell was I supposed to tell him, anyway?

I couldn't rely on memory, and Indigo knew it. Couldn't give him any more details right now than *somebody knows my shit*. Thin stuff. It may not even help prove that I'd been set up in his sister's death. While I wanted to claim a frame job, how could I know? I couldn't say it wasn't me.

I really, *really* needed to say it wasn't me.

Doing things my way required hands-on access, but so far there wasn't anything to get my hands *on*. I needed help tracing this new problem. Malik Reed wasn't it.

Leaving him stewing in his polished offices made me feel a *little* better about it.

Once I made it out of the dregs, the sun had already vanished. The shade cooled the muggy press of summer from *fuck I'm dying* to *damn it's hot*. So, not great. Better than heatstroke by the side of the street, though.

Not everybody is smart enough to keep hydrated on boosts, boxes or booze.

Sanitation is slow to come by places like this. Most times, it's a privatized effort to get rid of the bodies, human or vermin. When the sun hits peak, corpses abandoned long enough explode out – which smells, by the way. It smells so fucking bad.

The rest of the seasons aren't that much cooler. We'd ruined that way back, when the government – and the corporate interests that funded it – gave up all pretense of giving a damn. The regulations came off and the money rolled in. The midwest cracked up in a methane apocalypse and the ozone, already straining, took a massive hit as more and more factories spewed out the kinds of poison forward-thinking countries had once banned.

Didn't help that a mini ice age rolled in for a few decades, letting everybody preach about how global warming had been beaten. Emissions skyrocketed. Good old us, we'd led the way for everyone else to deregulate until the ice age boiled over, and by then it was too late. Global warming had become the least of our worries – the rat race had been too focused on the money on the ground to think about what was going on overhead.

But we're stubborn. Humanity cowered together like the vermin we are, merged the larger cities along coastlines into even larger megacities. The widespread development of shielding combined with the mass production of nanos did the rest.

Any children born within the city are squeezed out with the standard nano package. It's programmed in, parent to kid. First thing they do is carve a Security Identification Number into the fetal brain, upload that data to the system. Those born outside the city only carry if one of the parents does, but the programming is patchy. The radiation shearing through the fucked-up atmosphere takes care of those poor bastards real quick. Even if they'd had fully capable nanos, no amount of repair can keep up without shielding.

Those of us inside the shields trade freedom for security, kept nice and tame with chipsets loaded up on all kinds of entertainment. The bandwidth gets us free access to thousands of vid feeds on our devices and, if we want it, stringently approved tech integration. More are available for a price.

No fucking thanks.

I rode my Vega to a place near the rack, stopped in a one-stop-shop for a radiation burst and new clothes. The low-pulse shower seared the filth off my skin, while the printers worked on new clothes. Nothing fancy. This place replicated clothing that nobody would mistake for brand, not with the shitty printers available by the item. I paid for a new deep-vee tank and electric blue drop crotch harems. Tight around the hips, loose to the knees, lined on both sides with crackling white vinyl.

For shits and giggles, I printed out a slim black tie. Mostly because I knew looking at it would eventually piss Malik off.

I paid for it all with some of the creds I'd jacked from the failed mission. As I checked myself in the mirror, I pulled the tie into a loose knot – no idea how to loop a tie, I just one-knotted it at my neck. On my way out, I traded in my filthy boots for new bright green copies.

Now *this* was Mecca material. I'd chucked the Gritster when I'd emptied it, so no need to pack it. I threw my empty rig over the outfit. Kept my knives, though. One in each boot.

Next stop, Indigo, and then a little recreation. By way of getting as crunked as my meatbag could handle.

I was half out the door when the chipset installed at the base of my skull thrummed; a haptic tap, like a finger poking at the top of my spine. A projected call, right to my personal frequency.

Just what I didn't need.

Grimacing, I connected the call as I made my way out and around the corner.

Nice thing about projection space is its ease of use. One part of your brain takes the call while the rest of it sleeps, rests, or idles by in absent observation of the area around you. I wouldn't drive with it – that's what comms are for, and also I couldn't afford another bike if I wrecked it – but it meant I could loiter at the side of the shop and still be aware of both meatspace and virtual. Though one, by sheer brain capability, always claimed dominance.

The usual bare room with its standard bare table and metal chairs loaded up. No additions, no tailored locale. The vibe felt scattered; a sign of spotty connectivity. Low res virtual space.

Wasn't Malik calling to chew my shit, then? Another saint? I could have installed projection identifiers, but it didn't seem helpful. Most of us changed our freqs too often. *Especially* when we fuck around with projection calls as much as we do. Comms are shit for long distance.

Sainted signals on the bandwidth are pirated and locked down, but if we try to use anything fancier than the baseline hack, it sucks up more data packets than a non-signal can keep invisible. Relying on the dark parts of the band keeps us more or less under the radar.

If we want more, we gotta pay up bigtime for the properly forged keys, code and official seals that let the leaks look legit. Not to mention pay through the ass for a lockdown on a steadier signal.

When tens of billions of connections jam the bandwidth at any point in time, and with limited resources available, it's pay up or deal. I dealt. My linkup still hadn't shown up by the time I'd settled into my virtual skin, so we were both slow loading.

As I folded my arms and waited, my caller finally took shape in the black space set as the connection point. Formality. You can just pop in and drop the link anytime you want, but *walking in* is a legacy touch that's supposed to give the projection more realism or something.

Not that I needed more of that.

Sometimes, I wish I'd had the foresight to really amp up my projected image. I'd've gone naked into the space and watched Detective Gregory Keith's face melt in shock. Instead, he got my usual – clean skin, updated ink, shiny red tank, black pants. Full diamond steel arm.

As usual, his pretty green eyes landed on that first.

Purists. Mad enough about big tech to stand on picket lines, just hypocritical enough to enjoy the bennies nanos shell out. I hadn't known that when I'd banged him about a year ago. Then again, hadn't lost my arm yet, either.

"You seem–"

"Wait," I interrupted, eying the austere room. I hated starting conversations in the box before the ads loaded up. It pissed me off.

Between one second and the next, a whirlwind of color and words – flashing advertising and vid clips, the same as everywhere – erupted on every wall. Eateries, spas, educational facilities, weapons manufacturers, beauty tools. Capitalistic greed at its finest.

You can learn a lot about a person by their advertising blast. Mine slapped up hues of weapon adverts, technical enhancement; the kind of stuff the good detective wasn't supposed to see. Only reason he could was that he'd gone and paid a low-end streetdoc to tweak his filters.

Greg was trying his cute little best to fit into the street role he didn't have.

His ads, on the other hand, rolled out a whole different kind of struggle. The number of eateries and spas didn't surprise me. The detective was dealing with marriage issues, and his answer seemed to include a hell of a lot of marital bribery. To find it, he was looking for a cure way, *way* over his paygrade.

Which is where I came in.

He shook his head at me, mouth tucking into a boyish smile. The skin by his eyes crinkled with it, giving him that *aw, shucks* vibe that made me want to break him hard and throw him to the streets he wanted to be part of so bad.

"I was going to say that you seem tense," he said.

I stopped just in front of him, mirrored his stance by tucking my own hands in my pockets. It let me bend in, rock back on my heels, and give him the kind of hungry smile I knew disturbed him. "This a link and chill, Greg?"

If he'd been standing in meatspace, I'd've watched him

blush. He wouldn't here. As ruggedly attractive as the detective was in general, he'd gone and paid to sharpen up his image. A little tanner, jaw a touch squarer than in reality. Brown synthetic leather jacket with sleeves shoved up on nicely tanned forearms, despite the fact he'd roast alive in that thing outside.

His smile, irritating me, had been given a little extra special bling.

It wilted. "Don't tease me, Riko."

Meh. Been there. Done that. A one-night decision, whole lot of fun at the time. He'd been a sweet boy in blue fresh off his promotion to detective, a Judeo-Christ devotee who'd gotten off on my wild side – at least, wild for *his* view of the world.

Time had left its marks on us both. Now he worked on the side for me. While I didn't have the creds to spare, I made up for it by slaving him out to Indigo. Talk about bribery. Greg made for a shitty bouquet in general, but Digo seemed content to use him for all a cop was worth.

Which isn't much. Cops make shit, overworked and with half the cred they need to do what they're supposed to. Aside from excellent health coverage – nobody wants an injured cop with excess tech in their station; going necro in a copshop would suck big rotting ass for everyone – police get jack access from the corporations that own them.

Keeping the peace is an ideal, one overturned by corp forces and political gain, and that's especially hard on the civic drones like Greg; blue down to the bone, he didn't stay shiny long. His badge, contrary to his projected avatar, had already started to tarnish.

Fuckos like the Good Shepherds aren't limited to Trinity. Dealing with the worst of the street takes its toll.

I wasn't in the mood to hold his hand today. "What do

you want, Detective Choirboy?"

He no longer rolled his eyes at the monikers I saddled him with. Served him right for trying to blackmail me a while ago, especially when he'd wasted it to make that bank he wanted so badly. Total loss of a good hand. Not that I'd discouraged him.

"More what I was hoping to do for you," he replied. He took a couple steps back, out of my reach. "I've got something on the two other tech centers you asked me about."

I rolled my eyes. "Chopshops, Greg. If you're going to do it, do it right."

"Says you," he retorted. "One of the places you flagged is registered. As," he added with a smug crinkle to his smiling eyes, "a tech center."

"Eat shit and die." I was a poor loser. "Which one? Not the Vid Zone." That place had looked like a chopshop above ground, but a hospital lab setup beneath it. Too covert to be registered. Especially if they'd been fucking around with necrotech conversion, or even just risking it.

As walking techmeat, the things operated under an overwhelming amount of programming. Or that was the theory. The signal courses wire to wire, infecting every system clocked in via physical lock. Makes the virus easier to deal with, and when it surges – plugging into a system directly and hopping local network to network – the physical limitations make it easier to burn the fuck down.

Only problem was that the Vid Zone had turned into ground zero for what I suspected had been an alpha test gone really, *really* bad. Data from the Zone had suggested that the balls-stupid technicians in that lab had been trying to weaponize the code, and a four-block radius had turned into a blight. The number of people who'd gone necro blew away all records.

Turned out that necrotech had learned a new way to spread. With nanos still occupying the meatsuit, reprogrammed with everything else, they'd learned to infect a living body and spread that virus. Nanoshock hit harder. Conversion followed fast.

To make matters worse, Reed suspected that the necro processors had learned to access the bandwidth. The signal was shaky, connections frail enough that it wouldn't hold, but this was scary stuff. We'd be so fucked if they learned how to stabilize.

When a necro surge is registered, civic responders roll in and burn the whole area to ash and slag. Scorched earth is the only way anyone knows of to burn out a blight. People infected via nanos would be slagged right along with it. I shuddered to imagine what the city would do if the bandwidth became the new vector.

I could barely wrap my head around the size of that threat, so kept my eyes on my own problems.

The rest was way over my paygrade.

"The Vid Zone is still a dead end. Battery is the one," Greg replied. "It's up closer to the 7th Long, far enough from–"

"I know where it is," I cut in, turning away. I paced to the far wall, glowered at an ad for something called Ecstasy Vacations – *ugh, Greg* – and considered my options. The 7th Long hugged the fringes of the corporate sector, but far enough away that a hit may not invoke reinforcements in time to be much good.

I could get in with a good team. Ransack the place – murder a couple screwheads – and get out with more data, if it still existed. But then, how long could I wait to hunt down Carmichael's source?

Which should I go after first?

The detective watched me as I turned back around, his hands still tucked into the pockets of his jeans. "It comes with bad news," he added before I could ask. "Whatever corporation registered it, I can't trace it past the shells. I've gone about six deep and hit a wall."

"Shell companies, huh?" I leaned back against the shop wall in meatspace while sizing the detective up in the box. The heat in one nudged up against the cool nothing in virtual space, creating a minor sense of cognitive dissonance. Always felt weird.

"It gets better."

"God fuck it, Greg."

# 6

Greg's cheek twitched, a muscle just under his eye. Poor sinner. He used to full-on flinch when I took his oh so pious Lord's name in vain. "The Battery center's been cleaned out."

"Come again?"

"Up for lease," he added.

"Motherfucker."

"And demolished on the inside."

I threw my hands up. His gaze flicked to the matte gray one, then away just as fast. To my chest, of course. Then away from that and to the floor. In a show of nonchalance, he leaned back against the table, propping one hip on it like some sunny boy vid model.

"Why the hell not?" I drawled. "What else could go wrong?" Before he could justify my bitching with a smartass answer, I added, "Salvagers get in there?" When possible, they rolled in to an abandoned hole and stripped it down in nothing flat. Parts sold. Not usually that close to the Corporate Zone, though there were plenty of sinners in the area. The place straddled the line between residential and fading, leaving a hell of a lot of room for surprise.

Greg shrugged. "The work order was registered two

days ago, with a deadline of twenty-four hours. Signed by the same shell."

"Ah." That explained it. Since he couldn't trace how far back those shell companies went...

God stick a dick, I should have been faster. Malik Reed and his gluesniffing intelligence team should have been faster. Red tape was supposed to be his specialty.

My fists clenched. I was going to have to hit the Capital sector after all. And then hit Malik.

And hunt down his analysts and beat them to pulpy mush.

Greg read it on my face. "Now you look mad. Sorry," he said ruefully. The asshole, he even *sounded* like he meant it. I'd nail him on that later. *Sorry* didn't have a role in the street.

"What about Knacklock?" I asked. The third and final listing.

"Chopshop," he said immediately.

Smartass after all. I flipped him my favorite finger.

He grinned. Didn't even try to hide it, even though it faded just as fast. "I don't have much more to go on there. It's out of my jurisdiction."

"Like Cuntville Incorporated isn't?"

"That's just *barely* in it." Another smile, this one wan. "At least on paper. Knacklock's bottom tier ghettos belong to you people more than us." Ghettos, huh? *You people*. Like he wasn't on the brink of becoming one. By choice, no less.

The sweeter irony of it was that he thought Knacklock and its surrounding zones were *bottom tier*. How fucking quaint.

I waved that away. "Fine, I'll handle it."

"I could, if I had access to some extra contacts..." He let it trail off, looking at me with pleading eyes he figured would do the job.

Not happening. Greg only *thought* he wanted to run the streets. If he cared so much about the wife he cheated on and the daughter he mooned over, he'd leave it well enough alone.

Fuck me if I wasn't protecting him from himself.

"Nope." I waved at him, a perfunctory goodbye. At this point in my evening, all I wanted now was a goddamn drink.

Greg's eyes widened. He bent just a little and stared into my face. He was barely taller than I was; wasn't his fault I'm a goddamn skyscraper. "Why," he asked bluntly, "aren't you yelling at me about all this? Normally you'd be swearing six kinds of purple."

Because I'd had worse on my plate today and I appreciated his info. It wasn't his fault that his job cut him off at the balls. "Whatever," I said instead. "Why aren't *you* at home with the wife and kid?"

That one got him. Another wince. The muscles around his mouth and eyes tightened. "I'm at the station."

"The hell you are." I closed the distance between us again, careful not to touch him. Baseline protocols, no real integration possible. I could put my hands on my hips because I knew exactly what my hips feel like. Could lick my bottom lip because my mouth was part of me. My processors didn't need to crunch the data, it was already locked in. Might've felt a little off, the touchy version of shit resolution, but I still knew.

I didn't know what Greg's skin felt like in his own projection, what his jacket was supposed to be. Better integration could fix that, but it required both of us to enhance or else the protocols fried. Between our shit connections, we'd probably short both.

I did not want to add *another* reason to need a doc. I

was full up.

"Fine," the detective said, looking at my face instead of down my shirt or at my arm, so there was that little spot of willpower in him. "I'm not at the station, but I'm still working. For you," he clarified, "instead of the city."

Poor civic drone. So earnest. Something about yanking his chain always helped perk my day a little.

I didn't get to play with street virgins often.

My smile widened.

"Uh..." He moved farther back. Bumped into the table. The connection protocols had that much built in – sitting on the base furniture wouldn't do anything. They just integrated with the projections, plain old tables and chairs.

In this case, they helped to block his escape.

"Uh, Riko?" He pressed both hands against the table behind him. Like he'd climb over it if he had the option. "What in God's name are you doing?"

"Nothing." I hemmed him in simply by moving close enough so he couldn't swing his legs without hitting mine. "I'm going to have to pay you, you know."

"Yeah." A short laugh, uncomfortable as hell. "That's the bargain."

"Mmhm."

His whole body braced as I leaned closer, tensed from projected hair to toe. "Hey..."

I tucked my face by his and breathed in his ear. His filters didn't know what my breath felt like, what it smelled like, how hot it was. The edge of his avatar juddered, leaving part of his prettily designed face lagging. "Tell you what," I murmured. "If you can find me, Detective Gregory Keith, you can fuck me."

I'd make Indigo pay him for real later.

Both hands fisted on the table behind him. He

snapped away from me from the waist up, leaned far enough back that his elbows hit the surface. Not quite out of danger, but he could look me in the face.

His face twisted into a pained expression.

I don't know what he'd meant to say. His whole body projected regret, hesitation. The kind of thing people do when they're trying to be goddamn *nice.*

I didn't give him the chance. I recognized pity when I saw it.

He hadn't earned that. He didn't fucking have the right.

I jerked upright so fast, the edges of my avatar left trails. "You'll get paid," I said shortly, and the hell with walking out that cunting stupid door. I shut down the projection so fast, it lagged on the detective's still open mouth. Vividly colored ads winked out, leaving me leaning against the worn shop siding, blinking rapidly in the sun.

What little pleasure I'd gotten from toying with the detective, the sense of purpose his data had left me with, twisted to pure rage. I shook with it.

No. Goddamn. Right.

I stomped to my bike, threw a leg over the busted seat and yanked the machine up into place. The engine squealed when I over-gunned it. Fuck him. Gregory Keith, the good ol' boy in blue from *gee whiz* nowhere, had taken my invitation and turned it into something that deserved sympathy.

Bullshit.

From the shop, navigating the way I did, it was only a few minutes to the rack. Getting there gave me time to zen. The wind in my face, the shriek of wheels and horns in my wake, gave me enough space to take a breath. It helped.

So the detective was a jackwagon. Fine. I'd let Indigo deal with him from now on; see if I'd help his sorry ass make extra creds.

Meanwhile, I'd make sure he got paid for this one. I'm an asshole, I'd never argue that, but he *had* given me something worth paying him for. A registered chopshop – tech center, my ass; Christ on crank, the detective irritated me – in Battery, and the last of them up for grabs in Knacklock.

After this, the places listed in one of those files fingering me as part of the problem would be tapped out. Unless Knacklock provided any leads, I'd have no more – not unless Digo or Reed miraculously came up with something. Reed had been about as useful as a crank addict on the curb.

Decisions, decisions. Seemed like every time I picked a path, more intel floated my way.

For now, I'd let Indigo know the deets. I'd hit Reed up later about his slow ass, but all I wanted right this second was to go drown in something poisonous.

# 7

Caught somewhere between the gloss of the corporate sector and entertainment districts farther south, the rack lights up the night like a raver on colordust. Top to bottom, marquee signs scroll in real time, screens flash and vids play across every signal. The ads cross over each other in a pixelated crush, while billboards and neon climb the buildings in every direction.

The people in the rack range from street trash to slummers, saints and sinners smashed together – a hive of humanity wrapped in vinyl, synth, light, and scraps. Dirt to semen to ink.

Entertainment district, hooker's wet dream, black market front, saint's haven. Mad, sexy, noisy, vivid energy. Nighttime takes it all to the max, swapping out the usuals for the real weirdos.

This was my go-to, and I loved it.

The Mecca isn't the only club that offers what it does, but its regulars don't go anywhere else. Owned and operated by a scary bitch called Shiva, nobody yet had busted her balls and survived it. Deals, fucks to give and take in whatever way suited, drugs. Even murder, if you've paid her fees.

Everything for everyone, but for a price.

The rack is buried in a zone that doesn't see much police patrolling. Not that it matters – the sinners in blue can't do much without getting themselves brutalized in a terminal way. Most of the clubs here have bouncers instead of laws.

And, oh yeah, a fuck-ton of blooded mercs protective of their turf.

My kind of place.

A neon lotus marked its doors. The club had been here longer than Indigo had – longer than most of us – and we'd all come together under that sign. Digo, Tashi, Fido and Boone. Valentine and me. When you find a mercenary team that doesn't stab you in the back, you keep them. Stay with them long enough, and you become family.

We'd been that. *Done* that. Every one of us rocked a lotus tattoo, different colors and different places. I'd etched mine on my left bicep. I'd had it laced with bright pink and orange vid-ink, popped the colors into a sexy glow when I wanted to.

Maybe blowing off my arm had been a sign. Maybe the metal that hellhole had installed on Nanji, massive spinal tech where her shades of pink lotus used to be, had been the end of it.

I hated that I thought about this stuff when I approached the Mecca.

I squared my shoulders hard, gritted my teeth, and shook my head fiercely. It didn't jostle anything out of my skull, but at least I *looked* like I owned the place when I strutted right on past the line.

Chromers, slummers, or would-be runners without the cred to back up the swagger had to wait. The Mecca filled up fast – and the staff knew how to build anticipation. Saints like me, with enough local rep to bypass it entirely, didn't have to stand in line. Perk of the job. While I knew my cred had taken a hit, I'd had more than most. The Mecca knew me. I knew everyone who mattered in it. The day my cred went septic, I'd hear it here first.

Verbally, if I was lucky. Via bullets, if not.

A few crunked out kids who didn't know better catcalled me across the lightrope. Twenty-something and, as Lucky used to call me, built to break. One leaned out as I passed, her green and yellow wire dreads falling over her shoulder. "Hey, dude! Can you get me in?"

Bared teeth do not make a welcoming smile. The girl shrank back. Vanished behind someone else; some other vacant nobody too engaged in the vid projection in front of his face to notice. "Slummer," I muttered as I pushed open the heavy Mecca doors. Not much wrong with 'em on their own slab of the rack, but they're sinners from the sweet side of comfortable playing dress-up for kicks.

They never seem to understand how much shit they don't have when they play with the big kids. Or how much gets real bad, real fast. Fun to poke at, worthless in a serious crunch. Down here, they could brush against whatever shade of danger they liked and get off on the rush.

Assuming it didn't kill them first.

The foyer's interior lacked the same crashing lights as outside, forcing everyone who came through to adjust. It gave the entry bouncer more time to assess the clientele. Tonight's guard dog was Jad – an enormous expanse of shoulder and muscle wrapped in a tight yellow tee, beautiful black skin, face carved out of smooth asphalt. He was an avalanche in meat form and that was only half the sex appeal.

Jad's smile was summer hot and very, very bright, his

shirt stretching over his chest as he raised both hands like he'd scored a point. "Riko!" He had a voice like a bass beat, echoed by the rhythm rolling out from the door behind him. "You armed?"

I stopped, flexed my tech arm, bared to the shoulder in my white tank. Practically painted on, the way I liked to roll.

Jad's black eyes flicked to the bend of my metal elbow, and the seams that gave it a close enough approximation of muscle at the bicep. He laughed. "You know I like your shine, baby girl, but not what I'm after."

Widening my eyes, I pointed behind me with my flesh hand. Popped my hip to the side so he could see the shape of my ass in electric blue. "This?"

Laughter rolling, he beckoned me closer to the faint entry light placed overhead. Scarred skin stretched over his knuckles, and old keloids reamed his forearms. No exposed tech, but all-natural signs of violence aside, I'd seen him bench more than his heavily muscled body should have been able to. Torn a mouthy heavy's head clean off her neck with his bare hands, and that was after he'd tossed her friends out for breaking the rules.

Jad was delicious manmeat on the outside, and a juggernaut on the inside. No obvious tech didn't mean none. Just that I didn't have a genesniffer on me and wasn't inclined to pry.

When I got close enough for him to inspect, he twirled his finger.

I spun slowly, just for him.

This wasn't anything personal. Jad was a regular just like me. We'd had this routine for a long time. And like always, he projected disappointment to see I wasn't armed. More specifically, with the assault rifle he'd been dying to get his hands on for years.

"No Valiant?" he asked, going for crestfallen. "You break my heart."

I laughed, shaking my head. "I don't just carry it to stroke it for you, Jad."

"When you gonna bring it in so *I* can stroke it?"

"Depends. When are you gonna let me stroke *you*?"

He snorted, waving me past. Again, wasn't personal. He liked the ladies just fine. And I liked the play. If I ever got his *fuck I'm coming* face, I'd probably like him less.

"Indigo's in," he told me, "but keep your knives in your boots." I bumped his huge knuckles with my right one as I passed. Scars to scars. The comfortable vibe I got from the exchange did a whole lot to lift my spirits. As did the place I've called home for a long time.

The Mecca had a distinctly Eastern Indian vibe to it, though more of a wet dream than anything accurate. Everything's fetishized to the max. Nobody knows, nobody cares, what the hell a culture used to be. We're ass to mouth as a people, anyway – things like cultural borders get melted along the way. Or wiped out entirely. Plenty of those in our ages-old habit of jacking our collective spunk all over the globe.

The wild bass beat of the music saturated every pore of the place, worked its way through metal and meat. Frenetic energy crackled in the club. Even the long fall of embroidered fabric hanging from the pillars shuddered at the flow. The best of it, the hardest of it, filled the dance floor.

Thrashdancing isn't for the faint of heart, body, or balls. And given the feel of the place, they'd be carting a few of each out after last call.

I planned to be the last badass standing tonight.

Near the door, a linker I knew pinned a screaming chromegirl against a wall. The lights danced off his half-naked back, and the way she clawed at it said she didn't need my help. Her ankles locked at his waist. I detoured by them, grabbed her feet and opened her legs wide enough to tuck around mine.

I fit my crotch to Shar's ass, pushing hard enough to lock him balls-deep.

Her eyes flared, met mine over his shoulder. Her teeth clenched in her sweat-slick face, while the fist wrapped in her long, frizzy hair went taut. Shar looked back over his shoulder, too, grinned when he recognized me. I looped both arms over his shoulders. "Gimme," was my hello.

He tossed me a wink over near matte optics. "Dibs."

"Not her. Hey, chromie," I added to the wriggling delicacy. The sounds she made mixed arousal and frustration. Cute.

Shar took a laughing breath. "What do you want?"

"What do you have?"

"Front left," he said, without missing a beat. "Lady's choice. I've got more if you want it."

"Shar's Special Roulette is fine." The hand I thrust into his front pocket didn't soften like flesh. He jumped as my metal fingers dug into his muscled hip and thigh, which only made him dig deeper in the girl's dripping snatch, earning us both a heavy groan. Practically begging, at this point. One heel about carved a canyon in my hip.

I grabbed one of the four small containers tucked into the inner seams and switched it out for the last credstick I'd walked off with. Then leaned over and bit the part of his neck where it curved into shoulder. Hard. Another jump. A frustrated noise from each.

"You're welcome," I told them both, laughing at Shar's pained glare. I unhooked myself, wiggled my fingers in goodbye.

Halfway between the entrance and the bar, my smile faded.

It's one thing to exchange pleasantries and bodily fluids. Another to hire the same runner for a job. Shar probably liked me just fine. Didn't mean I'd be invited to one of his runs.

Also didn't mean he wouldn't kill me if everything imploded.

I was painfully aware of this as I made my way to the bar, shell in hand. A one-pop box, and by the heft of it, an injectable. Sweet. No wait times. I slid it into the waistband of my pants; a solid little reminder of what I had to look forward to soon. So much better than now.

The bar was busy, like it always was, with saints and more clustered around the gorgeous piece of nanofactoried wood. The surface of it was too smooth for a place that hosted my kind, stained a purple so dark it often looked black under the lights. They replaced it regularly – a telling sign of creds earned and tossed away. Shit's not cheap.

No sign of Shiva in the crush, but it was early yet.

One of the bartenders saw me coming. He snapped his fingers at a knot of barflies, jerked a thumb back to the club's main floor to make space for me. They left obediently enough. Barlickers often did this early in the night. Give 'em an hour, I figured. They'd get bounced or fucked.

The bartender shot a welcoming smile at me. Babyfine face, nice cheekbones. Open-collared Kongtown silk with rolled up sleeves. Eyes that looked black in the lights – nearly every dark color did here – and tinted skin. Tan or otherwise, hard to tell. Tans aren't hard to acquire, but neither are the mixed-up genetics most of us come from.

Frankly, he looked like a snot playing hooky away from mommy's eye. Easy to play with, easy to lose.

"What'll you have?" the kid asked.

"A White Feminist," I said loudly over the music.

"You try the anglo res?"

"Ha ha," I drawled. I had, not that I'd mentioned that to anybody but Lucky, and I ran away the moment I was old enough to try. "Fuck you," I added.

He grinned at me. "I never get tired of saying that."

"What would you say if I asked for a Black Snatch?"

His grin widened. "Order one next time and find out."

"Uh huh." I planted my elbows on the surface and leaned forward. "Who the fuck are you, and what the fuck is on your head?"

The bartender laughed, giving his shoulder-length black hair a toss as he reached for a glass. Wolf ears sticking out of his hair flicked in tandem. "They call me Lance."

"Can you get them to stop?"

"You wouldn't believe how hard it is."

"I'll just bet," I replied dryly.

Lance wiggled those ears at me without moving his head. Nerve sensors. Hooked up to adhesive on the scalp, they react to the same electrical impulses interior implants use. His grin sharpened in a way I didn't expect from a baby boy named Lance. "The boss has a theme tonight."

She usually did. Now that I bothered to look around, I spotted signs of it all over the place. Bouncers didn't blend. They weren't supposed to. But the serving staff all had something in common – either wolf ears or flowers. An analogy to the carrot or the stick. I wondered how many of them played bait and switch, too.

Shiva was a mastermind in drag. Or not drag.

As saints go, Shiva holds the medal for mysterious

bitch. Crossdresser, drag queen, transwoman or cisgirl laying it on thick, nobody had the guts to ask. Or if they had, nobody knew about it. Didn't matter to me, save that she ran the place and didn't let any Tom, Dick or Blow walk on her. I'd gotten my ass kicked once or twice by her people, and she'd had a few others carted out for jumping me and mine without permission.

Her fees are reasonable – if she likes you. If she doesn't, the fees get extortionate. She'd still take the creds if somebody's that hellbent for it, though. Just business.

I liked her. I also wasn't shitbrained enough to think I was an exception to her rules; another reason how I'd know if my cred hit terminal velocity. Soon as she lowered her fees on my ass, I'd be as good as dead.

Lance set the Feminist down in front of me, gave me a warm nod with that edge of teeth. "Let me know if you need anything else, sexy thing."

"Puppy," I replied, meeting his eyes and giving him more than the edge of mine, "you are sniffing the wrong snatch."

Lance laughed, raising both hands in surrender as I took my drink. Leaving him in my wake, I made my way around the club, avoiding the dance floor until I was ready to rock it. Wearing my booze would be way less fun than drinking it, and I didn't want to start my night sticky and sober.

As I figured, Indigo had claimed the usual room – a back area with blue glass inset in an ornate mosaic over the arch. There were other rooms, some less spacious and others more so, but he had a favorite and stuck to his thing when he could. Our team had spent years staking this turf.

He'd kept the vinyl curtain open. His elbows rested on the surface of the table, which meant he was poring over his comp unit or a low-key projection. As usual.

An elbow clipped my nanosteel shoulder as I headed his way. "Ow, fuck, what the fuck!" A woman in red synth leather whirled on me, one hand cradling her arm. "Watch where you're walking, fucktoy."

I met her eyes, stared hard. She stared back. Her shoulders straightened like she desperately hoped I'd square up.

Not worth it. Didn't sense much intent on her; just another jackoff in a sea of 'em. Saying nothing, I turned back around and walked away.

Two of her girlfriends grabbed her as she surged after me. "Come on, it's not worth trying!"

"We just got here," added the other, her voice lower in tone and deeper.

Guess it worked. She didn't jump me, and I kept a wary eye on the crowd as I cut through it. Something must have gotten them all steamed up. I said as much when I ducked under the draped curtain, raising my glass in greeting. "Feels like a hunt tonight."

Indigo straightened, flattened a hand over the projection he'd been studying. It cleared the data, put his internal chip into sleep mode. Cool gadget, a backup data projector built into the palm of his hand. Couldn't even tell at a glance.

His dark blue eyes, a clearer color in the less chaotic private lights, looked tired even from my distance. "Shiva's gone for hunter and prey," he replied, shrugging. "Subconsciously has tails wagging."

"It'll make for good thrashing." I skipped the three stairs leading to the rise the booth occupied, set my drink down on the table. Made like I didn't see him snatch his work away from me. Made like I *expected* him to play his cards close.

It stung. I admit it. Aside from Lucky, I'd never been closer to anyone. Digo was a damn good linker. The best I'd ever run with. But no matter how long we'd run together, the rumors about me didn't cut me any slack with my ex-team.

I refused to admit I missed them too. Even Valentine, with his pay-to-play sculpted physique and his desert god façade, and we'd never really meshed in the first place.

The circumstances were just jacked enough – and our partnership just deep enough – that Digo had enough faith to give me a fair shake when evidence showed up incriminating my ass. Angry faith, but I'd take what I could get.

In a roundabout way, Indigo Koupra had saved me. Still did, in a lot of ways.

I sat, kicked my four-inch boots up on the booth beside him. "How's it going, blue man?" Light greeting. No bigs.

"Aside from the usual shitshow?" His smile didn't touch his eyes. Not the way I was used to. "Not much. You?"

I hated the way we tiptoed around each other.

Lifting my glass again, contents murky white with a gelatinous glob of black ghosting around in it, I threw back half. The stuff hit like sugar acid, with a kick that rivaled a gut punch from a heavy. The globule bounced around; a built-in chaser of awesome, and the real power behind the concoction.

Indigo's expression turned wry. "I feel you."

Probably did. Not that long ago, he'd been the type to roll with the punches, slide around obstacles. A logic and data man, tempered by Nanji's sharp instincts.

After everything imploded, he'd gone a little harder

around the edges. A whole lot meaner. These days, Indigo Koupra's features had thinned out, his body made of lean, ropy muscle. Swarthy skin and dark hair put him closer to his East Indian ancestry than many, but like the rest of us, didn't mean much.

He did shack up in Deli, though – the preferred haven for his type of people. No idea where. He had his safehouse on lockdown, like most of us. I used to squat wherever looked good. Moved often, baggage light.

We both had a little more baggage these days.

Today, Digo had left his long hair down. Straight as I wasn't; a deep, true black, with streaks of dark blue from root to tip. His thick black eyelashes looked extra dark today. Smudged, too. Eyeliner.

The vain bastard.

His sharp elbows returned to the table, a clear yellow glass of something by one. I think it was a Mecca special, I'd never seen it anywhere else. The hair I enjoyed admiring swept down to coil on the surface. "You here to play?" he asked.

"It's like you know me."

"Once," he said, and then sealed his mouth into a taut line. His gaze flicked away, darted back – guilt, then challenge. As if he hadn't meant it, then decided he'd own it.

I swallowed the hurt. And the anger it lit in its wake.

I missed so much about my previous life. My easy friendship with Digo and my team. The mentor who'd raised me fresh off the SINburn. Lucky had taught me the rules of the street, a hard man with hard rules, and I owed him in ways I'd never be able to shake.

They'd both taught me about cred. How it *really* worked and where it mattered. Without Lucky's zen and Digo's skill, I'd be so much chum in a back alley.

I missed Lucky, too. In ways I'd never thought possible.

That made this big fuck-off amnesia thing twice as bad and six times as fucked.

And it meant I couldn't jack Digo's shit about how he treated me now. Half a stranger, half a memory he couldn't shake.

I tipped my drink towards him instead. Wanted to down it fast and snag more. Once I shot up with the injector, all gloves would come off. I was going to ride and ride high, because goddammit, I was tired.

Indigo must have seen it on me. Or maybe I just imagined the subtle slump to his shoulders, like a clenched breath let go. "You look prepped to jank up."

"If I have my way."

"Heh." He tipped his head back towards the curtain. "Try not to black out in this mess. There's blood on Shiva's agenda." The music thudded like a reminder, lights strobing in every color. Winding up all those toy meatpuppets in prep for the go.

I glanced over my shoulder, studying the entry. The side rooms weren't kept as dark, but also contained less strobe. A compromise for those of us who used them to dip out of the chaos. It made the club beyond look violent, flashing and raging.

Exactly what I wanted.

I turned back, grinning. "Thanks for caring."

"I just don't want to pay Shiva's cleaning fees."

I snorted, but I couldn't laugh. A deep part of me ached.

No matter how easy it came, this banter wasn't the same as it used to be. Surface-thin, warm only in the sense that we were both lying our asses off; making like everything was okay. I don't know why he tried, don't know why I let him. I was *so* uncomfortable.

I shifted in the seat like it'd help.

"Suck it," I replied, in the same friendly tone. "Before I tell you what I found out, you learn anything new?"

His sharp nose wrinkled over a grimace. "A few things, but the one you need to know is about the Knacklock shop."

"Is it still open?"

"Not just open," he replied, "but active. Four major deliveries have come in and out of the area since the Vid Zone."

"Finally," I breathed, tapping my drink lightly. "A solid. What deliveries?"

"Unknown." Not surprising. Not a lot of chopshop sources brand their shit with their names or logos. That was just asking for a hit.

"Who runs it?" I asked.

"Doc by name of Hevin Kern."

"Do what now?"

He shrugged. "Hevin. With an *i*. No *a*."

"How literate."

Another shrug. "Not much on him, either," he added. "My usual contacts wouldn't go near it. I'm waiting for a few to get back."

"He that big a deal?"

Another shrug. "Like I said, there's not much on him. We don't usually wander around Knacklock."

Another point, and one I chewed on. Greg assumed all of us knew each other, because everybody on the wrong side of the SIN does, right? Ignorant chumhead. Truth was that Knacklock was so far out of my usual trails, I'd have to hire a guide to find anything.

It wasn't the worst of the wards, but it held no awards for the best, either. Maybe I'd be able to find a fixer willing to nose around. "Let me know if they get back?"

He nodded.

"What about the zone itself? Any sign of necrotech activity around the place?" I dropped my voice for this one. The room was quasi-private, but I refused to take chances.

"Not that I can tell," Indigo answered, lines gathering between his black eyebrows. "I can't just 'ject up my usuals and drop necro line like it's cred."

Valid. Very, *very* valid. Necro conversion isn't something mercs and techheads worry about until they start implanting the big stuff. For most of the smart ones, it's a bogeyman; keeps us in line. Wasn't the same with the actual code locked down in Malik's closed-circuit lab.

If Indigo hit up his people with news of necro in a box, he'd be committing suicide by saint.

I grimaced. "Got it." I lifted my metal shoulder at him. "Don't know about Reed's progress, but I'll let you know if I hear anything about that, too."

"Yeah." Not exactly ringing enthusiasm. "Have you been by Kongtown lately?"

I shook my head. "Not since I pulped Fuck It Jim." Speaking of fixers who'd tried to screw me. The scummy weasel had been part of whatever it was I'd done in my fugue. Sadly, I'd crushed his head before I got any answers.

Indigo tapped the table with his drink. "Don't for a while."

"Why?"

He smiled thinly. "You're not exactly subtle, Ree. Between the rumors and the saints you pissed on, there's a handful of warning signs. The rounin gangs in northeast Kongtown are looking to score."

Which meant they wanted a flag to plant in their camp.

The rounin gangs – also known in the area as ghosts, the friendless, or simply *bag of shit* depending on what area you ride through – all have something in common: no turf of their own or kicked out of the Kongtown families. Or both. Usually both.

"Oh-kay," I said, a long exhale. "You think they'll want my ass for a boost?"

"I don't know." He tipped a mouthful of sparkling yellow into his mouth, took his time swallowing as he studied the glass. Then, "Nobody's saying your name directly. Not to me," he clarified. "But you know how it is."

I did. The thing about cred is that nobody *has* to say anything. There are always those that do, which helps boost the word, but so much of it is based on social cues. Who's working with whom. Who got kicked out of what club, who killed what and where.

Fixers get off on this kind of social engineering, and mercs get off on using it.

Obviously, some had decided to get off on me. Couldn't be many, or else I'd be fighting off every screwhead looking for a break, but the fact Indigo said something meant my cred was sliding lower than I'd hoped. From cool shoulder to knives out. I sighed. "Last thing and then I'm out of your silky sweet hair."

That smile again. Like he couldn't quite nut up to it. "What now?"

"I got set up by a Shepherd."

# 8

*That* got his attention. Indigo straightened, gaze sharpening. "What? Trinity scum?"

"Yeah." My smile twisted, bottom rim of the glass rolling on the table as I spun it between my flesh fingers. "Far as I can tell, an old deacon with an old grudge worked it. The others let him die, but came after me saying something about a source wanting me alive." When he only stared at me, waiting, I gave him the answer he waited for. "Yes, I splattered them. No, I didn't let any of them run off to tell big daddy in the sky or whatever passes for their leadership. But…"

"But," he picked up when I trailed off, "you want to know what the fuck."

For all our issues, we connected on some fundamental levels. And stumbled over others. "That's the one." I leaned forward, metal arm braced in front of me. "You didn't set me up again, did you?"

Digo shot me a sharp frown and an emphatic, "No. Once was enough."

I chose to believe that. In his defense, he'd heard on the network that I'd all but murdered his sister at the time. I felt like I'd been dealing with some tit for snatch here, only I wasn't sure I'd ever get the chance to even the balance.

"Besides," he added, smiling wryly, "I already *have* you alive."

That slipped out of his mouth so easy, both of us froze. *Had* me alive. Now I was just... alive. Without him.

My jaw shifted. "Fine. I need to find out who hooked a babyfucking Shepherd up with a Mantis contact, using my name, and offering creds to capture me alive."

Indigo's nose wrinkled. After a moment, he gave me another headshake, like that slip had never happened. "That's not good." The fingers of his right hand tapped on the table. "You sure it wasn't Reed?"

"Reed has me alive, too," I pointed out, dry as bleached bone. "And as far as I know, you and Malik Reed are the only ones who know my connection there."

His eyes narrowed. "Right," he replied begrudgingly. "You have a good point."

"Yeah."

"But it wasn't me. Too elaborate. If somebody's got your number, that's a major problem."

"Yep."

He leaned forward, searching my eyes. "If there is somebody out there, a few Kongtown scrubs are going to be the least of your problems."

I smiled faintly. "Nothing I can't work out of, right?"

His silence was answer enough.

I didn't need an answer anyway. This was it. The sign I'd been braced for. Going from top of the world to Shepherd shitlist made no sense, not without the intermediary runs, but now I knew I could file Carmichael as just that.

The real issue started here. More than rumor, I was the target of an active move from some credsucker on my case.

We both fell silent. Me staring at my clenched fists,

him studying the bottom of his glass like he'd find answers there. Finally, when it stretched to the snapping point, he broke the quiet. "Up until this conversation, all I've heard are mutterings." Indigo finally set his glass down, pushed it away with his forearm. "But if there is somebody haunting your signal, that could change any second. I'll see what I can find."

"Thanks." A pause, then less terse, "Thanks, Digo."

His smile, cautious as it was, helped. "There has to be someone out there with something. Nobody operates in a vacuum."

"What about Jax?"

That smile vanished. "You want to owe him another favor?"

"I don't know." I rubbed both hands down my face. "I have to find the source that linked my business, put a bullet in them. Find the source of the Vid Zone laboratory and put a bullet in *them*, and then spend some time laying waste to make it clear I tolerate no shit. A projector could help."

Not that I had many to choose from. Far as I knew, there were only two 'jectors in the city. I had connections to one, but needing Taylor Jax was like ordering a full back tattoo from a dude who loved his needles and carved bone deep. Precise, sure, but it'd cost a shit-ton of time and cred and you'd owe more than you thought by the time he was done.

Also, you'd be walking around with his mark on your ass until you scraped it off.

The fact we'd been linked cock to cunt a few years back didn't help. We'd split messily. Now he clocked me as a rival; a compliment *and* a pain in my ass. Jax would screw with his rivals all he wanted, whenever he wanted, but he'd wreck anybody else who tried to muscle in. He was that kind of saint.

"Jax could probably find out," Digo said slowly, but the space between his nose and eyebrows wrinkled deeply. "Not worth the risk."

"Says you. It's not your cred."

"That's not what I mean."

It took me a moment. Then I swore hard. He was right. Again.

The thing about projectors is that they're rare as virgins for a reason, branded as kill on sight for every civic-minded Tom, Dick and Blow looking to score some points with big corporate. Of all the ways to uplink and connect, projectors are the only saints who still rely on barbaric jacks, implanting connectors direct into their neural processors and wiring through to the signal.

It was a brief fad a long, long time ago, but an important one. According to Jax, tech advanced so fast from that single point that jackplants quickly depreciated. We like our shit wireless, please and thank you.

In going to broadband, Jax once told me, we'd lost something pure in the process.

Didn't change the facts. The direct wires made them way more susceptible to conversion than any other saint teching up on the streets.

Add necro activity to the mix?

"Dammit," I finally said, scrubbing at my forehead. "No Jax." I laughed, sharp as the knives I still packed. "Nobody even knows how to contact him, the shithead."

Indigo shrugged, tense shoulders easing.

I pushed my drink to the edge of the table in prep to slide out of the booth. "By the way." Not subtle. I wasn't great at segues anyway. "I need work, and soon. My creds are tapped. Any offers?"

Indigo's gaze flicked to the door. Then to my glass.

Then at my face. My nose, to be precise. "Not with us."

Anger seared so fast, my fingers cramped around the table lip I'd grabbed to brace. The numbers spiked in my optic, threatening structural failure under my tech hand if I didn't let up. With effort, I eased the joints. "I know." A thin veneer over a snarl. "Thanks for reminding me. Where else?"

And yet another shake of his head.

"Come on!" I sat back heavily. My shoulder blades hit the vinyl padding hard enough to shake the booth. "You have to help me out. At least before this mystery asshole drops more shit on my cred."

The black line of his eyelashes narrowed in clear warning. "No," he said deliberately. "No, I don't. Careful, Ree. You're going to push yourself right out of what you have left."

Oh, snap. Snap and *fuck you very much*. He'd gone there. A warning, a line.

The shattered glass hollow in my chest squeezed so tight, I had to swallow hard to get it back down. He was right. Shit on piss, he was so right and I hated it. I'd just told him that my life was on the brink of exposure. He'd just told me to watch myself.

Indigo's hands were tied. He'd never hook me up long as this shit continued. He couldn't risk it.

Couldn't risk trusting me.

I downed the rest of the Fem in the glass, swallowed the globule whole. It'd punch me in the guts soon enough. I deserved that much. The thick-bottomed glass thumped on the table. "Let me know what comes up." Too mild. My throat ached so badly, all the words I wanted to say jammed up in there and stuck.

A nod this time. How fucking refreshing. "I'll be in touch."

Tense lines hiding too many unspoken things. We knew each other, Digo and I. Too well.

He affected calm as he leaned back in his seat and waved his yellow glass at me. "Watch the floor," he said, his version of goodbye. "There's going to be some serious thrashing tonight, and Tashi's already there."

Oh, good. Maybe I'd get a chance to smash the creepy pixie.

I left the room wishing there was a door to slam closed. Or punch. Or break over his head. I leaned against the mosaic wall outside it, trying to inhale oxygen through my too-tight chest. Both hands clenched into fists. I pressed them hard into my sternum, where everything gelled. It didn't help.

I'd lost him before. Lost my whole team when they thought I'd killed Nanji. I'd come back from the dead, but not her. I'd walked out of the void and left her to die. They'd abandoned me just like I'd abandoned her, because I couldn't explain what the hell I'd been doing for the months I don't remember.

But Indigo had given me the last shred of his faith – despite all odds, he'd run with me on a suicidal plunge into necro infested territory to see with his own eyes the place his sister had died. The ups and downs of my relationship with him shouldn't have cut through my thick skin. And yet...

This was so far down, I didn't know what to do with it. Good cred comes with freedoms lowstreet chummers only wish they had. Good cred gone bad becomes a cage.

Frustrated, shaking, I grabbed the plastic I'd picked up from Shar and flipped it open with a thumb. Hollowpoint needle and syringe to inject it with, one-button autohit and done. The stuff in it screamed danger orange, reflecting the light.

New designer drugs. Tweaked to the latest version of whatever the nanos couldn't bleed off.

That's the only problem with nanos. Designed to tackle just about everything, disease to regeneration, poisons are no exception. They adapt fast. Make junkies push harder for the next high, meltdown faster. Those of us with the right friends have direct links to new sources. Each time the system adapts, designers make different stuff to lock 'em up again. Good gig, if you can get it.

Tipping my head back against the wall, I tucked the needle under my tongue until it hurt, ensuring a seal. Depressing the injection switch, that little hurt turned into a quick jab and pain that lit the nerves in my mouth up like pepper spray and strych.

The stuff warmed the space under my tongue, seeped through my jaw. The first whisper of calm eased into my aching throat. I pushed away from the site of my own eviction, tossed the needle into a bin.

Now I'd go play. Because fuck this doubt and fuck this nagging sense of guilt and fuck Indigo, too. I didn't need him.

I snagged a purple and gold drink off a waiter's tray and forged toward the dancefloor. "Hey, wait–"

"Let her go," a woman said quickly.

I glanced back. The waiter wore flowers on his head. Nice shoulders, solid abs. No ink on all that ochre skin, and more flowers draped around his neck. Marked as definite prey – I could see why. Everybody had to be tough to live this life, but some just never shake the *eat me alive* vibe.

The waitress beside him, a busty dark-skinned femme with a mouth made to suck the chrome off a slummer's bridgepiece, gave me a wide, red-lipped smile. Wolf ears in her close-cropped buzz, enough junk in the trunk to lose your face in…

Oh, yeah. I recognized her, even if I didn't know her name. Maybe I'd try to find out later. A lot of us get to know the staff. Those who come down here know the game, or at least the basics of it. Sex can be a commodity or it can be fun; and if it's the former, Shiva gets a cut. If it's the latter, she doesn't give a damn as long as it doesn't affect her business. Staff that voluntarily vanish with the clientele while on shift don't have jobs to come back to.

Clientele that vanish with involuntary staff show up later in the chumhole out back. What's left of them.

But before pleasures of the flesh, I wanted the pain; something way more visceral.

I drank the Cellular Sunset, dropped the glass on the nearest flat surface. Bass pounded, met an answering kick in my chest. Didn't know if that was because of me or the shit I'd consumed. Didn't care. *Predator* was in my genes these days.

The smell of sweat and heat amped up the crazy.

Which didn't mesh with the knock at the base of my skull. Another haptic tap, merging with the music and the junk I'd put in my body to make me wince. Not cool.

Scowling, I loaded up the call.

# 9

The moment my consciousness embedded into my personal avatar, shelves of old-fashioned books greeted me. They lined one wall, floor to ceiling because why the fuck not, while a huge window streamed bright daylight to my right – pure and clean, well away from any hint of smog or pollution.

Sunlight smacked me in the face, forcing my protocols to adjust down the halo. As it configured, an enormous custom desk focused into view. Figured Malik Reed wouldn't make do with the basics. Anyone can alter their projection box. The more it changes, the more it costs, but that had never been a corporate problem.

Malik Reed, on the other hand, was *my* corporate problem.

I glowered at him before I'd even finished loading. "What the fuck do you want?" I said by way of greeting.

From behind the desk, he spared me the briefest of glances. Raised a disappointed eyebrow. "You're late," he replied, dropping his attention back to the projection slides in front of him.

The asshole was *always* at his desk. It didn't surprise me he'd tailored the dominating piece of furniture into his virtual space. He lived behind that desk. He probably fucked hookers on that desk, jamming a thumb up his own ass while swiping through stock reports with his other.

I liked to imagine bending him over that desk and pegging him six ways to raw. I'd shove that stupid hand-tailored vest he wore so far into his mouth that his smoky brown skin would turn purple at the edges of his strikingly sculpted face, make his tech work to keep oxygen flowing. I'd take his dumb tie and wrap it around his wrists so tight, those nanos would have to build bridges over the imprint the fibers would leave behind.

I have a libido. Sue me. Also, I really, *really* wanted to ruin his day. And if fucking him stupid didn't do it, maybe that wedding ring he sported on his left hand would seal the deal. Whoever had married him, she'd probably dance for joy if he gave her a reason to leave his sorry ass.

The screens covering his desk looked like gibberish to me, charts and shit, each different in data and format. Such a goddamn workaholic, he studied projections while *in* a projection. The sun caught in his close-cropped hair, picked out the brown sheen buried under black. It made the array of freckles that covered his cheeks and nose stand out.

Those freckles, cute on anybody else, did nothing of the sort for him. Cute and harmless weren't words that even existed in Reed's vicinity. Why he hadn't zapped them out of existence mystified me.

Why I liked them so much mystified me, too. I liked his face – top and lower lip full enough to put me in mind of a girl's, a wide nose and sharply angular jaw. He wasn't a soft-looking man. Given the sharp bone structure under his dusky skin, I suspected a genetic blend of anglo, black, and a handful of other landmarks from Native to mexi.

Striking as hell. Dangerous as masturbating with the barrel of a Sauger 877, safety off.

The hunger riding my high made *that* sound like a great idea.

Instead of waiting, I crossed the large callbox, slammed both hands on the other side of his desk. Right through two of his projections. The visuals flowed seamlessly around my forearms.

The contact tingled. Underneath my palms, it felt more like plain, featureless metal. I didn't have the kind of filters that could connect wholly with Reed's. Whatever he could feel, whatever he'd programmed in, I couldn't tell.

"What," I repeated, slowly and loudly like he was too stupid to put it together, "the fuck do you want?"

A gaze dark as motor oil and sharp as knives lifted, settled on my face. He didn't smile. "You," he repeated in deliberate mimicry, "are late." I hated when he did that.

"Gosh, I'm sorry." My eyes widened, fake concern. "I was just stopping to get a sweet little tie for our meeting." Partial truth. I did, in fact, have a tie on.

He wasn't the type to rise to my bait. But he sure did like to dish it. "It's casual Friday."

I snorted, eying his suit. "Guess you missed your own memo."

"You clearly did not read mine. Where is your report?"

"You got one."

"But not yours." One eyebrow lifted in an obscene amount of self-control.

In contrast, I smiled like I'd just fucked a nun and got away with it.

Oh, wait. I did.

"Does that report say whose ass I didn't ream?" I

leaned forward enough that he got an up-close view of my smile. And down my shirt. Not that he looked, the frigid bastard. "Does it include the fact your intel sucks in a big way?"

"It says," he said flatly, "you failed to negotiate with the source."

I rolled my eyes. "Your operator sucks, too. The source failed to negotiate with *me*." Now I raised both eyebrows. "And speaking of. Want to explain to me how a Good Shepherd knew to approach *you* with *my* name?"

"No." He swiped a hand over the projections. They winked out, leaving the surface of the custom desk gleaming. "It's not relevant."

When my smile faded, it faded fast. Settled into a thin line. "Try again."

"Why?"

"Because part of our deal," I snapped, "is no leaks. None of your shit up in mine. Less than three weeks after that agreement, someone hit up *your* shit for *mine*. Follow now?"

He tilted his head. Appraised my expression. I'd have loved to punch him, but I didn't dare do it in projected space. Damn filters. Filthy rich nutless wonder.

Malik shrugged. "He didn't know he was talking to my people." When he flicked his fingers at me, I read it as get the fuck off his pretty fake desk. I did not. Now Malik's lovely mouth hardened. Good. "His bad luck that his supplier of choice set him up with one of my scouts. Your bad luck he knew your name."

Oh, *fuck him*. Scouts were corporate versions of splatter specialists, but whose specialties revolved around stealth and murder. They're often used to infiltrate SINless territories, especially in the rack. Naturally, their heads subsequently show up in corporation turf, usually without attached appendages. As a matter of principle.

"A scout," I repeated. I finally pushed up from the desk, folded my arms across my chest and glared at him. "In an area where somebody knew to ask about me. You want to do the math, or should I?"

He did not math. He only watched me steadily. Patient as a serial killer stalking his prey.

Malik Reed was the kind of man who used silence as a weapon. Wait long enough, and people back down or fill the silence with more than they want to say.

Bitch, please. That tactic had never worked on me. And I was reaching a high that took my anger and rolled it right into hunger. Blood, sex, laughter and unfuckingtouchable. If I got any more zen, I'd pass the shit out.

*Bring it.*

I barely kept a straight face when he mirrored my stance. The material of his tailored vest crinkled as he folded his arms over it, drawing attention to the athletic expanse of his chest under all that prim button-down and dark gray tie. Not too wide of a build, a defined triangle from shoulders to hips, with long legs and pristine clothing to cover it all.

He wasn't even close to the size of the heavies I'd worked with, but nothing to scoff at. Unless you counted the fact he'd probably gotten it from a personal trainer.

I'd scoff at that all day long.

Malik was aggressively handsome in a way that screamed authority and power, not parties and charm. And he didn't, I noted, do anything to alter his avatar. My snatch did a little dance of *fuck he'd be a good lay*.

The jackwagon hit all the buttons I had – the good and the bloody.

"My scouts," he finally informed me, "have nothing

to do with our agreement."

Meaning hands off his business, huh? Yeah, right. "You're correct," I replied, setting my jaw. "They don't. Which means they're fair fucking game, so get your screwheads out of my turf or I'll take matters into my own hands." I uncrossed my arms to point a metal finger at him. "And if you ever, *ever* withhold job information from me again, I will take my contract and jam it so far up your ass, you'll be shitting fine print for a week."

A ghost of amusement flitted through his eyes. "It's a verbal contract."

"One that says I get job details."

"Unless it's need to know."

"Push it," I shot back, "and then tell me how *need to know* feels in your anal canal. You want boots on the ground, you won't fuck me over next time." I put the finger away before I forgot I was in virtual space. The urge to take his face in my hands all but overwhelmed me.

Whether to stroke it or crush it, I still wasn't sure.

Maybe both.

"Oh?"

I snapped out of my imagination. Glared at him, even as my lips twitched. *Crush.* Ooze. So delicious. I cleared my throat. "I meant what I said. Get your jackwagons out or I'll hand-deliver them."

"And if it costs you your position in my department?"

I opened my mouth, but hesitated just long enough that he inclined his head. That damned humor was back, like I amused him in some absent way.

Goddammit.

"Give me a reason not to tell," I demanded.

"Give me a reason to remove them," he replied. Didn't even miss a beat.

"Their lives aren't enough?"

"No."

"Because you think I won't find them?" I demanded. The tilt to one corner of his mouth said it all. I sighed, dropped my arms. "Malik, you're an asshole."

"I have one."

I wanted to laugh so badly. I half-turned away, scrubbing at my face with my meat hand. The chill between my physical body and the projected one prickled. "Did you just project me to flaunt that asshole at me?"

"No." The fact I heard his footfalls on the virtual carpet only strengthened my initial impressions. He'd paid big creds for this thing. I glanced over my shoulder to find him so much closer. Within reach closer.

Right. So my cunt straight up drenched in meatspace. That's how fucking good my high was – and how infuriatingly sexy I found him.

"I called you," he said in his smooth, aggressive baritone, "because your pet police officer failed to achieve his mission."

"How did…" I caught myself, curled a lip at him as I turned around to face him again. My hands tucked at my hips. "Never mind. You spying motherfucker."

"I have not ever fucked my mother," he returned. Deadpan. So serious.

I snorted a laugh, slapped my flesh hand over my mouth and tried to glower instead.

Malik checked the understated, too-expensive watch at his wrist. "I've located the parent company of Battery's tech center."

*Agh*, cunting sinners.

"Chopshop," I growled through my fingers. "Who is it?"

He ignored that with way more aplomb than the detective had. "Rest," he ordered. "Recover from your injuries, and sleep it off." He folded his hands behind his back. "Tomorrow, you will come to my office and we will discuss it."

There. The first spike of fury cracking through my high.

I took a step closer, fists clenching at my sides. "What did I just say, Malik? Don't you fucking hold info from me."

"I'm not." His thick black eyebrows lifted. "I am setting up an appointment."

Ooh, I hated him. I turned back around. "Go suck a necro cock," I shot back. "I'm going to find out who leaked my business. And," I added, voice thinning to ice and deadly promise, "if I find out it's one of yours..." I left the threat unspoken.

He extrapolated the threat, and took it farther. "What if," Malik replied slowly, deliberately, "the two are connected?"

I paused. Frowned. "What do you know?"

He stared at me. Silent. Judging, the ass.

I was not playing this. "Guess it's not important, then," I sneered. "I'll find out on my own."

He didn't so much as move a muscle. Just two words, delivered in that same aggressively blunt authority. "With what?"

In the reality of the Mecca, somebody ran into my chest. Rebounded, howling with laughter. My own nails bit into my palm, echo of the rage roiling under my skin.

I was so boned. I was backed into a corner and Reed knew it. I'd seeded what I could. Only had Indigo and Reed to sic on the trail of the leak, and here Reed was stringing me along. Lucky was gone. His vast network of contacts may have helped, nose to the ground sort of thing, but I had no idea where he was now.

With what, he asked? With nothing.

I saw red. And the fact it came with a core of hurt pissed me the tits right off.

I whirled, arm lifted before the rest of me caught up with the stupidity. High on the shit Shar'd given me, pissed at the shit Malik was giving me, and already hurting like hell. His words hit worse than a bullet and they shouldn't have.

I was made of tougher stuff than that.

My protocols, though. They weren't.

Malik Reed goddamn *smiled* as my flesh fist collided with his sternum. A part of me wanted so bad to break it. The rest of me knew I'd get nowhere in this box.

Sure enough, with little more than a mild ripple of sensation at my knuckles, the box froze. Both of our avatars flickered, his leaving lag trails behind as he turned away like I was nothing. Something popped in the back of my head, the haptic signal gone haywire, and I swear to shit, I heard something that sounded like a hollow, digitized laugh.

Snapped into bone-deep embarrassment, jacked up into a white-hot burst of anger, I tried to disconnect. Couldn't get a grasp on the signal. With a head to toe prickle, pins and needles shooting outward from the base of my skull, the room shattered, taking our connections with it. I came back to reality with a full-body jerk, careened wildly into a small group. Sweat on my skin and a fierce pain in the back of my head.

My chipset knocked back on me so hard, a surge of bile rose in my chest.

Arms caught at me. "Whoa," laughed a guy, his short hair glittering under the lights. He grinned at me, a mouth full of rainbow teeth in neon. "I'll have what you're having!"

A thin arm around my waist effortlessly put me back on my feet. Belonged to a lanky type whose androgynous features parted on a good-natured grin. "See ya."

The third with them was broadshouldered and heavily muscled. Taller than me by about four inches, even with my heels on. I knew her. Kilo. Never worked with her, but rumor on the street marked her a reliable heavy.

She stared at me. The thick ridge of metal carved into her ebony jaw lit with its own red light, shifted like she was going to say something. She didn't. Her eyes gave nothing away. Not warmth. Recognition. Nothing.

I grinned right back at her, straightened my poorly knotted tie with more sass than she probably liked. Rubbing the spot over my chipset, I turned and gave up on the fucking world for a while. Appointment, my ass. Discussion, my *ass*.

And a high burned out because Malik Reed wouldn't take me seriously. Now my frequency was shot, no ability to make or receive projections until I got it fixed. How I'd get it fixed was something else entirely. I had one doc, and she belonged to Mantis anyway, so no.

I missed Lucky. I missed him bad enough to think it often. My personal streetdoc, my mentor, my zen. He'd know what to tell me.

He'd kick my ass until I figured it out.

I clutched at my chest where it felt like I battled a constant hollow hurt.

The only cure I knew was a higher high, a jacked up night, and a thrashdance to get me through.

All three could be acquired. Right. Bleeding. Here.

There's an art to entering a thrashdance floor. A mix of instinct and reflexes that gets you over the border.

You learn by failing. A metric fuckload of times. I nailed it. Ducking a fist and sidestepping a knee, I threaded my way into the center of the pit and breathed in the music. The body odor of too many people in too little room, blood and elation. You lose yourself. You become part of the problem.

You bleed and you crack and you lay down hurt because laying down hurt feels *good*.

Colors of the people around me, the glossy shine of chrome and glitter and tech refracted from every angle. Painted lips and streaming hair shining in strobe. What the drinks I'd inhaled didn't manage, the drugs did. Tabs tucked between my lips, sucked off fingers belonging to strangers. Another injection I scored and jacked into the side of my neck. It hit like a heat wave and freezer burn at the same time, took the wild tangle of limbs and made them shine.

The crazy that happens to your brain when the nanos are riding higher than you is all kinds of fucked up. Losing it is only one of many, many effects. But I can say this: there's no cunting room for guilt.

# 10

Something scaly had died in my mouth. It was the only explanation for the taste of it as consciousness blurred slowly into existence. I couldn't manage enough saliva to swallow it down, either.

I was all too familiar with this feeling.

Pounding head. Limbs aching like a son of a bitch. My ass was raw and my junk throbbed. I knew what that meant, too.

One hell of a night.

My lips twisted up into a grin as I rubbed the crust from my eyes. There wasn't much light, only a fluorescent line built into a seam under the domed ceiling. Wasn't much room, either, just enough to get on your knees. Any more and you'd crack your head. Which someone had done, judging by the smear of hair and blood above me.

A hand tucked against my chest. My naked chest. I looked down. Shit. Somewhere along the way, the bar in my nipple had been torn out. Probably thrashed out. My nanos had healed it, but it'd scarred. Not a good sign for the state of my shit last night, and probably the same issue with the bullet I hadn't gotten removed. I'd have to get it redone.

A warm body curved back to back against mine, too awkwardly placed to belong to the hand I stared blearily at. With effort, I put together the pieces.

One arm. Inked in black. Attached to a lithe body with small breasts also inked. White skin too perfectly pale to be anything other than enhanced, and scars she'd left untouched. Mark of the badass. Her short green hair spiked out in all directions as she slept the sleep of the damned. Didn't know her name. Really liked the plating covering her right ribs, though. Bone reinforcement merged with extra armor. That was debilitating injury recovery stuff. Definite saint.

I vaguely remembered licking the seam between tech and flesh. She'd really liked that.

I turned my head with effort, wincing when my brains sloshed around inside.

Black hair. Lean muscle under swarthy skin. My nervous system clenched so hard, I almost swallowed my tongue. Until I realized the lighting painted his skin darker than it was, and I had not – thank the cunting gods of whatever the hell – fucked Indigo. That was a conversation I did not ever want to have.

Instead, as I propped up on my flesh elbow and saw the remains of one wolf ear still attached by a wire, I swallowed a snort.

Lance, huh? A curious glance down his body clarified why exactly they called him that. Too coincidental for a birthname, unless he'd been deliberately enhanced in the womb. Or enhanced himself later. Either of which were not the weirdest thing I'd ever heard of.

Amused and aching, I slowly scooted out of the tangle of flesh and sheets, braced one hand on the ceiling and reached for my discarded clothes. Wasn't expecting the arm I reached with to roll back on me in nerve-shattering rebuke.

"*Fuck*," I hissed, snatching the metal back to my chest. Cradling it didn't help. The nerves at my shoulder had long since seared to barbecue, which had immediately burned out any feeling when my arm had blown off. Far as I knew, not every amputee out there experienced this. Then again, we didn't talk about it, either.

Cauterized nerves didn't stop my stupid brain from filling the metal with some sort of ghostly echo – a desperate search for missing meat. When the thing lashed back at me, it screamed.

White-knuckled against the ceiling, I forced the glorified paperweight to move. Forced it to snag my clothes so I could get out of this capsule. The two slept soundly. Or had died. I didn't know, and I wasn't going to stick around to find out.

The entry point was all of four scoots away. I wasn't kidding when I called it a capsule – coffin hotels, built exactly what they sound like, and rented by the hour or night. They used to market to the business types who didn't have time to go home between shifts and eventually caught on to the dregs. Now you find them everywhere, often host to people like me doing things like this.

I pushed the door open with one bare foot and leveraged myself out of the tube. A few capsules up, primo suite. Somebody had splurged for the headroom and enough space for most of what we'd done. Better not have been me.

The floor was cold on my soles as I landed in a clumsy flail. The air was just as cold, full blast fans meant to blow the stink out of the place. Didn't work. It smelled like dust and mold. *And* the thick cloud of sex I brought with me.

Something clattered beside me, bounced and landed against my foot.

I looked down. A purple strap-on, size *ohshitwhat*. Like I needed a ribbed fuckstick, crusted over and well used, to explain what I'd been doing.

I snapped back a laugh before it escaped from my mouth, only to cringe when my head tried to pull itself apart. Rubbing at my eyes with flesh thumb and forefinger helped nothing but the sticky grit still attached to my eyelashes.

When I opened my eyes, blinking, my peripheral keyed in on a shadow. A boot.

*Behind me.*

My chest clamped down, heart leaping into my throat. My brain went red hot and I jumped, already whirling, one foot up and momentum solid. I leveraged a kick hard enough to crack bone at whoever was stupid enough to jump me this fucking early in a hangover.

My target was lower than I expected. My foot connected solidly with a face that didn't offer any resistance, slammed his skull against the bottom tier coffins so hard that it rang two like a bell. Three of the transparent doors went dark as blood splatted outward in a messy circle. Quick, hard and easy.

I dropped my foot again, panting as adrenaline collided with tired. This hangover needed a boost, a recharge or both. And the bullet still lodged in my back was beginning to pinch. I'd have to get that removed when I fixed my protocols.

I remembered that much, anyway.

The man whose day I'd ruined lay folded over in a heap, neck bent near in half, the rest of whatever smarts still in his head leaking out. I'd smashed in his face; looked like I'd broken a shoulder. Not that it mattered.

It wasn't me who'd killed him. Slack face and ashen skin said he'd been dead a couple hours, long enough to go cold. Merc, maybe.

And I thought *I* was having a rough wakeup. His hangover made mine look like a splinter.

I struggled to get my hungover ass into my wrinkled pants. My throat felt scratchy. My eyeballs burned, dried out. Shit, even my bones hurt. Worth it? Maybe. It'd depend on how long the hangover lasted.

I looked up at the open capsule door. A long line of something wrinkled and black swung gently from the lip. I reached up with my right arm, still trying to tug my pants up while shaking out my stinging foot. The tie I'd knotted around my neck last night tumbled free in my fingers. Spots of white decorated the wider end, and the threads had started to unravel at the edges.

Laughing while hungover is the worst possible thing. My head thudded in violent protest, sharper than before. I flinched, jammed the crumpled tie into my pocket. Dressed first. Hanging out with my nipples hardened in this cold draft wouldn't do me any favors.

I'd cut glass with these things.

Bracing myself, I bent for my dropped tank. The thing had landed half on the bloodstain. I'd be worried, but the stuff had dried to a brown smear long before I'd woken up.

Whoever this guy was, he'd pissed somebody off in a big way. The ink stretched out on the dead guy's neck gleamed vid-ink red, still sparkling. It would until the chipset drained down – he hadn't rigged it to blow, which was a bad call for a saint. It meant anybody could extract data from it, if they knew how. Most enforcement types did.

I didn't recognize the insignia, if it *was* one and not some dumbass idea on a dumbass day. I think it was supposed to be a scripted bunch of letters and numbers. For all I knew, it spelled *momma's boy* and he'd just gone all out.

I pulled my shirt over my head, grimaced when my shoulder howled at me. Goddammit. It was too early to drink my brain into letting it go, and I had no access to painkillers right now.

Grabbing my boots by the sloping tops, I padded barefoot down the long line of capsules. The bottom three tiers were tiny, coffin-sized. Not even enough room to flip over in. Cheaper than anything else, but stifling. Bigger mercs had to fork over for primo suites, but hey, life isn't fair.

I rubbed my sweat-grimed arm over my tired eyes as I rounded the corner back to the lobby.

Didn't see the fist coming. Sure as shit felt it connect.

My head snapped back on my neck, rattled my soggy brains ear to ear. My nose caught the brunt, cartilage popping as it sheared right back into my face. I screamed, surprise and rage. Dropped my boots as I threw my metal arm up to block the second fist. Her turn to yell, cursing as her knuckles met unforgiving diamond steel.

I jumped back. Blood streamed from my nose and throat. I spat out a mouthful, just as the red- and yellow-clad woman – curves, tall, a flash of red streaming behind her – spun in midair, slammed a blaringly yellow boot at my head. I barely ducked in time. Not that it helped.

She grabbed a fistful of my greasy hair, dragged me in a dizzying semicircle and locked me in place; bent over backwards with my arm twisted out in front of me, wrist forced at an agonizing angle. Shockwaves exploded up my spine. I only saw the faintest details of her face – yellow-brown skin, a glittering wink of red somewhere around the shape of a bared-teeth smile.

"Oh, *fuck this*," I snarled. I kicked up with one leg so

hard my knee popped. Ligament. Joy. That hurt almost as bad as the two vertebrae her forced dip ground together. Using the momentum of that swing, I rolled back over her.

"Ai!" Surprise and dismay.

Distance achieved. Not enough to breathe.

Taking advantage of the corridor I'd just left, I faded back as a flurry of fists and feet came at me. Elbows and knees. Black half-gloves, yellow shoes, copper skin. Full scale fury in the form of mostly meat, and one cunting *hell* of a right roundhouse.

I tried to give back as good as I got, but I was sluggish, wrung out already and in desperate need of a recharge. I drove my flesh fist into my assailant's gut, earned a grunt for my efforts. Her belt buckle cracked my knuckles; I swore long and hard as I grabbed the back of her neck and drove both knees into the same spot, one at a time.

Strangled pain from the both of us.

I didn't expect her to duck low and drive right into my grip, ramming her shoulder into my stomach.

We both staggered. Flailed in a tangle of arms and legs and lost balance. Bile and acid roiled up into my throat, mixed with blood and worse. She rolled away, taking any semblance of support with her.

I dropped to my hands and knees and threw up a bucketful of something that defied recognition. It splattered, splashing the slumped shell of the corpse I'd kicked into a second level of hell. It took a few more seconds of wrenching heaves before my intestines sagged back into place.

Yellow boots rimmed by studded floral designs planted right by the spreading pool, too fucking bright in my streaming eyes.

"Well, *somebody* had a night."

# 11

Ragged voice. Panting, but I recognized it anyway. It graveled when she laughed, legacy of a shattered voice box pieced back together by surgery when her nanos couldn't handle it. Was there when it happened.

"Shit," I rasped, then spit out another gobbet of sour mucus. Tasted a hell of a lot like Kongtown stir fry. Or what was left of it. "Fuck me."

"No bueno, babe. Thanks, though."

I couldn't take a breath without smelling puke. Which would only make me vomit whatever was left. Grimacing, I pushed myself back up to my screaming knees, shoved my grimy hair out of my eyes and wiped that same arm over my mouth. "Muerte," I spat when I could.

She grinned, unrepentant as she sank to her heels near me and laced her hands under her chin. "You look like shit."

"Suck my dick," I growled, sitting back heavily on my ass. I struggled for deep breaths. Everything just hurt more. "What are you doing here?"

"Saving your mexican't ass."

"The hell you are."

"It's true."

Yeah, and I was the one on my knees. "Funny way of

showing it." I glowered at her smug expression. "What the hell are you trying to prove?"

She shrugged, her shoulders wide under the yellow flak epaulets she sported over tattooed arms. Fringed. Because why the fuck not?

Typical Muerte. I used to run with her, back in the day when we were both Kill Squad specialists. She'd been the one to put a round in Carmichael's ass. I'd never seen her laugh so hard as then.

I hadn't heard from her for a few years, though her name cropped up on the network occasionally. Muerte was a fixer – saints who get what you need. Drugs, hookers, data, names, jobs, whatever. You need a guy? They *are* the guys. The best ones have fingers in a few holes.

Muerte had a lot of fingers, and a lot of holes.

She hadn't changed much. Her dark brown hair was longer than I remembered, ends fuckoff red and pulled up into a severe ponytail at the top of her head. Long straight-edged bangs just barely hit her eyelashes, fringing brown eyes ringed with neon green filaments. The optics fed her more information than my tech arm integration did, and she kept up with superhuman analysis. A lot of street roles overlapped on the fringes; she'd give Indigo a run for his creds if she had to.

Muerte was tall and curvy, with more vid-ink than I had in more places, square jaw and round cheeks. Insanely deep dimples, and she'd put sparkling red studs in both. Smile or not, they made her look irreverent as fuck.

The curved nanosteel bar under her right eye was new. Tempered glass divots following its bend no doubt recorded whatever she wanted, uploaded it to her personal datafield.

I scowled at her. "If you recorded this, I'll shit on your face."

Muerte threw back her head and laughed. That hadn't changed. She'd always laughed like she didn't have a single fuck to worry about, loud and rough. "Yeah, yeah. Did you know your freqs are burnt out?"

"Thanks. Go die," I added for clarity. I struggled to my feet, ignored her helping hand. "Did you have to knock me around?"

"Just testing you. Making sure your shit's in shape."

"When's it not?"

She snorted so hard, it echoed. "Like now?"

"Fuck you, I'm hungover." I did my best to ignore my body's killer payback. And the rapidly congealing pool of last night's fun. At least this time, I knew why I couldn't remember. Self-imposed amnesia wasn't the same as losing months to fuckery by some necro farming laboratory.

I used the opportunity to drag myself to my feet, avoiding the puke swamp. "What drags you into my hell?"

Her amusement upped by about six notches. She pointed at the open door to my primo suite. "You weren't exactly hard to trace," she said wryly. "A club full of looselipped hombres heard your plans. *Saw*," she amended, laughing again, "your plans."

Ah, balls. "So you followed me?"

Another shrug, and that wink of red in her smile. Which faded fast. "Short version, nena."

"Speak slow," I grunted, bending to stomp into my boots. It hurt so much. "And I'm not your girlfriend."

"You could be," she said on one breath, and then added with the next, "People are looking for you." From laughing to serious in seconds.

My chest tightened. Anger and exhaustion. Adrenaline swirling around with nowhere to go. It left me shaking. I snapped upright, had to slam a hand against a capsule to brace myself. "Say again?"

Muerte rose to her feet as well, dusting off her hands. "Some decent up-and-comers, looking to score a quick cred shot." A nod at the corpse. "He knew. Found him searching capsules."

"So?"

"Knife in hand."

"Looking for me?" I asked, raising a skeptical eyebrow. "Come on."

"Don't laugh." She turned, slammed one foot into the corpse so hard that it folded around her shin. Third level of hell, if not at least four more. Muerte's right foot had been replaced from the knee joint down, enhanced more than mine and machined beautifully into shape. She'd spent far more, I'd guess. Don't know. She'd had it as long as I'd known her, and why wasn't my business.

It explained her nightmare roundhouse.

The clatter as he tumbled into the capsules for a second time rocked a sharp echo in my head. I winced. "It's not safe to stay here," she said, totally casual for all she'd just snapped a body in half. "For the awkward fuck-fling wakeup, if nothing else."

I snorted. She was right, anyway. Mornings after? Not my thing.

Assuming it was morning.

"I got somewhere to be," I told her as I nudged the abandoned strap-on into the corpse's splayed elbow. The ridged dick on that thing looked good pointing to his flattened face. "So do me a favor and make this quick."

"Hot date?"

"Definitely be heat," I muttered. I bent, adjusted the

cuff of one boot. "What time is it?"

"Why don't you have that programmed in to your setup?"

"Because fuck you, that's why." I was beginning to repeat myself, but I didn't have it in me to try for more. "What time is it?"

She shrugged. "Almost ten."

"I hate you," I muttered. I hadn't gotten sleep. "You didn't crawl out of the Squad's territory to do me a favor."

"Actually?" She laced her hands together behind her back. "I'm hoping you'll do *me* a favor. In exchange for saving your ass."

"You mean kicking it?"

"In your defense," she said, chuckling, "you look like shit. Come with me," she added, humor fading. "It gets better."

Fuck. I rolled my throbbing shoulder, staggered my way back down the corridor. Muerte wasn't exactly an old friend, but we'd had good times patrolling together. I'd been young when Lucky forked me over to the Kill Squad. Too young to understand what was happening, too fresh. Dancer and her casual brutality had scared me to death.

I'd run. She'd come to collect me from Lucky's place; he let her take me. You don't run from a gang like Dancer's. She'd dropped me off again, unconscious and broken on his doorstep.

Soon as I'd healed, I went back. Probably my first real lesson. Never let them see you flinch. Muerte became something of a wingman, Dancer my example, and I'd learned what Lucky wanted me to.

Street rule number one: survive. At all costs.

Right now, I'd have to use Muerte to do it.

"Hey," she called after me. "You gonna take that home?"

I braced my hand against the corner she'd jumped me from. Summoned what dignity I had left and glanced back over my shoulder without biffing it. I followed the line of her finger to the plastic dick, shrugged the shoulder that didn't hurt. "Nah. I'll leave it for them."

She raised her eyebrows, obvious only because a corner of her mouth quirked when she did it. Her long bangs hid the rest. "Token of your affection?"

"Souvenir." I tipped my chin at the capsule still open over her head. "He'll wake up feeling it."

Her laughter followed me into the lobby.

I refrained from babying my aches and pains as I left, aware of Muerte's searching gaze on me. Spine, head, jaw, knee. The ache lower in my back came from something else entirely – I'd worked those muscles hard.

Wolf, my satisfied ass. Guaranteed I'd used that thing on him till he screamed.

Lance seemed to have returned the favor. Probably while I was plastic balls deep in the other one, which would also explain the fire in my arm. Maybe I'd worn it out. I flexed my fingers and rubbed at the seam at my shoulder like it'd help. Didn't. It wouldn't no matter how many times I tried.

Muerte passed me, hands tucking into the pockets of her bright red shorts. Her bobbing ponytail caught fire in the sun, first warning before light hooked steels through my eyeballs.

"Urgh." A groan.

Muerte's rough chuckle drew me farther out.

Morning or not, the sun had no mercy for my pain. It slammed into me the moment I left the unreliable sanctuary of the hotel, hit with a wave of heat so intense I was sweating by the time I made it to the sidewalk. A little cosmetic enhancement to my nanos could have taken care of the filth I'd accumulated, but I didn't want it. In my line of work, I try not to push my threshold with non-essentials. You never know when you'll need the room.

Like the loss of my arm.

Muerte obviously didn't feel the same way. Whatever other technical improvements she packed, I could only guess. The lack of bruising said skinweave of some kind, and her light as goddamn air step suggested enhanced recovery. Maybe pain dampeners. Both gave a little extra durability in a fist fight. On the plus side, her tech threshold hadn't been crossed yet. Would hate to see the business end of her focus if her dead flesh came at me.

I shielded my eyes best I could and scanned the street. Heat rolled off the asphalt in shimmering waves, baking the rack and everything in it. The nightlife had transitioned out to day walkers somewhere around dawn. Not much difference, save the weirder ones were sleeping it off. Now, only the usuals threaded through each other, on the way to whatever miserable achievements they had for the day.

Included in the standard civilian package are apps meant to turn life into a never-ending stream of acquired achievements, rewards for the slog the sinners call living – go to work; *ding!* finish your shopping list; *ding!* your fiftieth day in a row at the pachinko palace; *ding!*

The main interests of your everyday joes are breeding, consuming, fucking and feeding. Raise your kids or not, nobody gives a shit. But you get certain achievements for choosing, and no do-overs. Unless you pay for that, too.

The apps are the first thing a saint sheds after burning the SIN out.

Vermin in all shapes and colors plodded through the

heat, all of it comprised of tech and chrome and skin and piss and the overpowering scent of deodorant. Pamphlets and posters, discarded propaganda, littered the streets and sidewalks. Bandwidth to reality, ads and graffiti mapped the place.

Too many people. Most slogging through adspace I blocked, the sinners among them chasing the thrill of achievements clocked. Hookers solicited any random joes going by, hands on slick hips, scraps of clothing built to entice. A few had stopped, scoping out the wares – some with jaundiced skepticism, others with naked greed. One dude in the sweltering black vinyl of a goth kid had his nose shoved into the gleefully exposed armpit of a large, hairy crossdresser.

Every pleasure for the right amount of creds.

A three-man booth across the way flashed as morning-afters irradiated the stink of burned off booze, sex and junk too gross to wear in the sun. The air over the booths warped as radiation escaped from the vents.

Muerte snagged my arm to get me moving. My left arm. I sucked in a hissed breath, jerked it out of her grasp. She snatched her hand back at the same time, eying the bared metal. "What the fuck is wrong with you?"

"Nothing," I snapped.

She raised an eyebrow. "New arm giving you trouble?"

"It's not new." She didn't ask more. A relief. "Where are we going?"

She shrugged. "Somewhere not here."

"Why so secretive?" I demanded, rubbing the back of my sweaty neck.

"Because if anybody overhears this, you're boned."

"Again?"

"Not," she said with emphasis, unfolding a pair of narrow shades and sliding them on her face, "the way you hope to be." Counter to her duochrome approach to today's look, her shades reflected the city back in mirrored black. They also hid the telltale rings around her irises, letting her take in the surroundings at her leisure.

Muerte was an information junkie. She always had been, just now her implants were better.

Fuck. I matched her pace across the street, weaving through end-to-end cars and motorcycles, bikes and scooters shittier than mine. Horns honked. One at me. Or maybe the teeming crowd jaywalking with me. I gave them a flesh finger. Sneered through the mask of drying blood my nanos had sealed. My bloody teeth apparently made the bitch behind the wheel slam on their brakes. The woman in the passenger seat flicked her finger back at me.

Muerte didn't stop grinning. I'd always had this urge to punch her, catch her out of nowhere and do to her nose what she'd done to mine. Just to see if it'd kill her smile.

It wouldn't. But she'd sure as shit try to kill *me*.

I'd have to warm up for round two.

# 12

Dives litter the lower streets. They burrow in to every district worth being in, and they usually have the best food. Most come and go, swap out from this cuisine or that. The great ones linger.

Like scars.

Muerte knew a place I didn't. We set up on the back side, where we both had a clear view of the patrons and an easy way over the table. Just in case. Not everyone looked the part of badass looking for a fight; precaution beat a bullet in the back.

Story of my life.

She sprang for food and drinks. Greasy pancakes and oily shit they called coffee but didn't come close. I'd know. Lucky used to brew his own. No idea how, real beans are even rarer than virgins.

I added a recharge to the order, and asked for something sharp in my coffee. It came with a hot pink plastic knife hanging off the edge, its curved end already melting in the heat.

Ha ha. I plucked it out, flicked it at the wall behind us where it stuck, one of many accessories left by many patrons.

The place was fast. And greasy as a bad lubejob.

"Talk," I demanded the instant both platters hit our table. The ads playing across the grimy vidscreen built into it scrolled in a nonstop blast of news and junk. Filters wouldn't touch it; digital screens can only be hacked. "What's got you going for a personal hello?" Aside from my busted freqs, anyway.

"How are you not inhaling everything right this second?" she replied, already loading up her fork. "Madre, I'm starving."

I was too. A recharge would have gotten me by, but it'd been a while since I'd had pancakes. Or, for that matter, real food. Last time was with my corporate doc; a bet I'd lost.

This linecook mess would mop up at least half the hangover, settle the nanos I'd pushed hard last night. And this morning, no thanks to her. I folded one pancake in half, then fourths, and stabbed it in the center with my fork. "Three seconds to swallow," I said, "and then spit it out."

"That's what he said."

"Maybe to you."

This time, her laugh didn't make it through the pancake. She choked, had to slam back her coffee mix before she wore them both. Or I wore them both, given Muerte's sense of timing.

Took five seconds. I was counting.

When I kicked her in her tech leg, my toes cramped. Even through my boots. It jarred all the way to my cunting arm. Hissing in a breath earned me an eyebrow. "How'd that work for you?"

"Face next," I warned, jamming my fork so hard into the next pancake that the twisted tines sparked across the platter. "Round fucking two, only I know you're there."

Still snickering, she waved a hand at me. "Yeah, yeah. But look, don't punch the messenger. Again."

I nodded. Ate my pancake so I wouldn't tell her to bite my clit and get to the point. I was, I thought grimly, in a foul fucking mood.

She set her fork down, half her plate cleared. "You," she said seriously, "are sitting slightly left of some nasty crosshairs. Word is your cred's taking a dive, and that's catching attention."

"You're just now catching up to the gossip?" I asked around the fork in my mouth. "C'mon."

Her gaze drilled mine. "I knew the rumors. The notice is new. Chummers've been sniffing around Squad looking for information about you."

The pancake turned to rust in my mouth. I swallowed before it glued itself to my tonsils. "Yeah?" Affecting nonchalance, I propped my elbow on the table and pointed my fork at her. "When am I not on somebody's shitlist?"

"Not like this," she replied. None of that amusement filled her eyes now. "Saints've been hitting up our turf, and I hear your name raising a few digital eyebrows lately. Subtle stuff, at first."

"At first?"

"There's a player just good enough to dodge me and just rough enough to get my attention doing it," she said. "In his wake, I'm seeing patterns. Carefully dropped bits of gossip, skilled diversions."

"How skilled?"

Her jaw shifted, stung pride. "I run into more false stops than I do intel," she confessed. "Riqa, who the necrofuck did you piss off?"

I stared back at her. I knew this was coming. I thought I'd been prepped for it. Should have been prepped for it the moment Carmichael had called me out. Hearing it, seeing it carved all over Muerte's face, drove it all the way home.

First my team. Then Lucky.

Indigo had laid the final board and Muerte nailed it in place.

It wasn't *just* a leak. Wasn't just a stalker out to ruffle my cred. Somebody was fucking with me. With very, very real consequences.

I didn't realize I was gritting my teeth until Muerte reached over and tapped my jaw. I jerked, swatted her hand away with my throbbing left as I took in a deep, freakishly painful breath.

I thought I'd lost the life I knew the day I'd woken up in that lab. I'd only been fooling myself.

I set my fork down beside my plate and leaned back in my seat. Draping my left arm on the back of it at least took the weight off my shoulder, even if I hadn't stopped sweating since we sat down. Now I fought to keep my hands from clenching.

Somebody.

Was going.

To die.

"Can you find him?" I asked.

"I'm working on it. But in the meantime, you should know a few uppity pendejos are gunning for the cred boost."

"Specifics?"

She pointed her fork back the way we'd come. She had excellent direction sense. "That one back there? 401Nasty."

"Who?"

"Newly on the radar. Challenging the FriqaChiquitas for southside Caprese."

"Isn't your sister rolling with them?"

"Yeah. She's good for the news."

"No shit." That made the 401s a bigger deal than the usual scum. The Chiquitas were known terrors, hadn't lost a turf war yet. Brutal approach, no prisoners. In Caprese, that was the only way to scrape out a rep. "How'd they hear about this?" A pause. "And why haven't the upper tier runners weighed in?"

Muerte tucked her fork between her lips, idly let it rest there as she shrugged around it. "The digirat's signal isn't spreading that far. I *think* he's deliberately targeting the kiddies in the kiddie pool. Riling them up."

That made no sense.

I let Muerte go, sat back hard and dropped my head back against the seat. The blackened ceiling glistened, stained by countless hours of oil, smoke and grease. In it, I read layers and layers of spunkfucking frustration.

Sense or not, this was it. My cred had dripped far enough through the networks that some asshole had up and taken me on, using low rate runners and scumslurping dregs to do it.

Soon as it reached upper echelons, I'd lose everything I had left. So why the long crawl up? Why couldn't he go right to the top and smear me all the way down?

What the fuck was I, a psychic?

"I do not," I said grimly, "have time for this."

Muerte laughed, a short, sharp crack. "Who the shit does?" When she dropped her elbow on the table, chin in hand, I glanced back at her. "P'much everyone," she said around the bending tines, "knows you tangoed Koupra's bebe into necroland."

"Old news."

"Yeah," Muerte said, bending into the table to lower her voice. The permanent dimples in her cheeks winked, though she wasn't smiling. Her neon-rimmed eyes drilled into mine, and she took the fork from her mouth to point at me with it. "Except now they're saying you took creds for making her overclock her threshold." Then, even quieter, "There's a vid up for sale."

My eyes snapped wide.

"Something going for a price most, if you're lucky, won't be able to hit for a while," she continued. "I don't know if it's related to the rumors or not, but there's mucho speculation."

*No.*

"And a lot of fixers," she finished, stone serious, "will be sniffing it out."

There weren't enough curse words in the goddamn universe to fill this one. I lost the fight to look calm, fist clenched on the table, white-knuckled to the point of pain. Between my teeth, I hissed out a low, "Unfuckingbelievable." It hitched on the rising tide of panic climbing up my spine. "Have you seen it?"

Her dark eyes studied me. "No, Riqa, I haven't. No one has yet. To be blunt," she added in her graveled sense of serious, "I'd rather hear it from you."

My jaw popped. I forced my teeth to unclench. I jammed both elbows on the table and rubbed my face. My guts churned. Hangover. Bile.

*Fear.*

Goddammit. Fuckdammit. Shitfuckdammit!

This was bad. Worse than stalker level bad. That fucking vid *showed me* making a deal over Nanji's unconscious body. Showed me signing my thumbprint on a tablet and then *shaking the smeghead's hand*. Aside from the necro code sealed up in Malik's lab, it was the only evidence Indigo and I had walked away with.

Fake or not, framed or not, this would destroy me in

ways I couldn't even comprehend.

Was Digo the source? Only he'd seen that vid.

No, wait. *Reed*. Reed knew. He'd seen the footage. Tested me on it. He'd placed scouts at my hangouts – corplickers made to look like the saints they infiltrated. I didn't trust him as far as I could knife him. But what the fuck did he have to gain by ruining my cred? What would Indigo gain? Revenge would only work if Digo stopped associating with me altogether.

Why was everything so godshitting *confusing*?

I raised my head, pushing my tangled hair away from my face. Fear and fury screwed all the way down to the bone. "Anything else?"

She sighed, picked up her fork again to push the sticky remnant of pancake around. You have to eat the stuff fast, or it turns to mush. "Aside from the vid nobody's picked up on, there's one last thing raising eyebrows and stiffies." One finger tapped on the table. Nail clicking. "Did Lucky drop your ass like a corporate drone?"

"Oh, what the tits." I shoved my plate away so hard, it rattled all the way to the edge of the ads. Patrons looked up. I shot them a filthy glare. "Yes," I snarled, lowering my voice and turning that glare to her. "So fucking what?"

*Click, click.* Another fingertap. "You know his cred overlapped yours, right?"

I snarled again. Longer. Meaner. Jumping the table to grab her by the throat wouldn't net me anything, but my instincts didn't care. I had to grab the edge to keep myself from leaning any farther in, halting almost nose to nose. "If you're saying Lucky's cred took a hit–"

She raised her other hand between us, cutting me off. "No, Riqa. I'm saying that everybody knows you aren't under his umbrella anymore."

Oh. That was it? I scoffed, relief easing me back to my seat. "I've been on my own for years."

Muerte's hand lowered. "You still don't get it," she said, shaking her head. Her gaze, usually lined with the same shade of arrogant I painted mine with, had gone softer. "I'm saying that up until now, you've been enjoying his coverage. You didn't," she stressed as I opened my mouth, "have to be under his roof to reap the bennies. Lucky made sure of that."

What?

No.

I blinked at her stupidly for a few breaths.

Covered?

By Lucky?

I shook my head. As much to clear it as try and knock myself back into the moment. "I developed my own cred. I mean, sure, he taught me everything, but I've handled my own shit." *Until now.* "I took a hit, I lost enough rep that he no longer services my tech, but..." I paused. "How do *you* know he was keeping me under watch?"

As soon as I asked it, the answer came to me.

I was one of the few who hadn't known.

Muerte saw it click; I read it in her eyes. The pity shaping her mouth.

My teeth snapped together. Ground until something crunched.

She nudged her cold coffee across the table, closer to my hand. Her version of helping. "Lo siento," she said quietly. "But I wanted to make sure you knew."

What, that my cred might not have been as good as I'd thought? That I'd only played at saint while my benevolent father figure watched over me?

It felt disgusting. A protective layer like the Christ, all

guiding shepherd and shit.

And as my pride and rage and sense of cunting *loss* churned in my gut, Muerte watched me in apologetic silence.

Like I needed it.

I snatched the coffee cup in hand, drained it of as much as I could, and shattered the mug on the table between us. The screen underneath fractured, white streak turning brown as the leaking remains of coffee seeped into it. The sound cracked through the dive, piercing the clamor like a gunshot. Even Muerte jumped.

"Save your pity." I used the remains of the ruined mug to push myself out of the chair. "I'll deal with this without Lucky. And if you don't think I can," I added flatly, "then stay out of my way."

Muerte leaned back. Slow, but unfazed.

I spun, scowled at the sea of faces and eyes, and gave them a middle finger from both hands. "You hear me?" I snarled. "Stay the fuck out of my way!"

Not my finest moment. With the crunk of last night's bender all over me, coffee and blood dripping from my flesh hand, and confusion roiling under my skin, I yelled at a dive full of strangers and left Muerte to pay for the mess.

I'd make it up to her later. I had to, given the info she'd dealt me. Nobody gets shit for free from a fixer. She'd eventually tell me what she wanted, anyway.

For now, I needed to get out. Go somewhere else, *do* something else while my brain tried to sort through the mess. I wasn't built to think. But without Indigo or Reed in my corner, and both a suspect for trying to fence that vid, I had no one else to trust.

# 13

Of my two immediate problems, only one seemed in reach right now.

I stopped in a booth for a quick radiation blast, used by most of the city in lieu of water. Unless you're rich and well-connected, water is a deadly combination of toxins and lead. It takes a shit-ton of purification, and costs a fuck-ton of creds to install.

Malik Reed had showers in his building.

Lucky had installed an extra large sink in his shop that tapped into some pirated source.

Everyone else not taking cumshots on credlines got radiation.

The stuff approved for human use is weak enough that nanos can eat any cancerous side effects, but strong enough to melt everything else off. The booths, made to process as many people as possible, didn't fuck around. Hard and fast, in and out. Way better than disinfectant, which smells for days.

Once out, I didn't bother changing my clothes. Didn't feel like paying for more.

The recharge I'd consumed and a hit of hardcore nanocandy dulled the pain. My head did not rattle right off my neck as I guided the Vega onto the interzone and rode it all the way to C-Town. Hell, even the spinning panic in my skull mellowed slightly, space carved out of that meditative mix of wind and speed.

One thing at a time, right? That was Lucky's zen.

Lucky.

I just didn't know how to deal with that one. Not right now.

Maybe when I'd pulled cred up. My own cred. My own way.

The ugly little knot in my gut felt too much like rage to link to Lucky.

I was seventeen blocks into the corporate center when I rolled up on a towering glass penis-replacement. Runners called the place C-town. They called it the Capital, but we replaced the C with whatever we wanted: corp, cunts, cocks. Name it, it sticks.

Every corporation has kilometers and kilometers of turf in the sector. Shell companies, branches, side operations – locating the center of any of them is like searching for a virgin in a whoremine.

Whatever Malik Reed's offices were, they weren't Mantis central. I didn't know what Mantis central looked like. I imagined it was full of corporation fuckheads standing in line to wipe the boss's taint with reports.

By the time I made it into the underground parking garage, I felt much cooler. Much, much steadier. I'd nail this one down and go from there. The job in front of me.

Whatever else Lucky had done, his lessons remained solid.

The elevator rose fast enough that my ears popped, leaving me wiggling my jaw as the elegant doors slid open. I stepped out, straightening my threadbare tie like I was a businessman here to hit on the secretary.

This floor, comprised of this lobby and Malik's offices,

was too fucking big. The walls were decorated with paintings of long-dead artists, the extremely airy interior boasting real plants and tasteful lighting fixtures. Behind the nondescript desk occupying the central space, massive windows gave rise to an incredible view.

C-town is cleaner than just about anywhere else, with stronger shields to block out the sun's punishing radiation and a filtration system that keeps smog to a minimum. It leaves the area bright and clean, with a panoramic view of a portion of the city. Green spaces stood out from all the glass and glitter like welcome mats, similar gardens growing on building rooftops.

And all of it, of course, visible from the entry of Malik Reed's place of business.

My favorite?

The personal assistant watching me enter.

Hope Ramsay, like the desk, was nondescript – perfectly tamed dark blonde hair, features easy to look at but hardly anything to plaster on a vidscreen. I suspected genetic modification. Nobody could be born with just the precise amount of unassuming. Plain enough to be unthreatening, pretty enough to compliment the surroundings. Womanly figure without stepping a kilogram out of line, like every good assistant should be.

Another part of corporate credo. You make 'em extra hot or extra plain, but never ugly.

Hope looked at me over a pair of frameless glasses, her smile fading to a flinch. "You look like death."

"Aw, Hope, you worried about me?" I grinned at her, pulling back my hair from my face so she could see my eyebrows raise and lower suggestively. "I could stand some loving care, if you're offering."

Hope surveyed my outfit, stained tie and all. I took the time to rest my elbows on the tall desk, batting my eyelashes at her. "Riko," she said slowly, "how do I put this? You... need new clothes."

I laughed. "Talk sweet to me some more, Hope."

"Maybe from a reasonable distance away?"

"You break my heart."

"Sorry." Her eyes danced behind her lenses, not nearly so severe as her role on Malik's payroll demanded. But that didn't mean she left it entirely. Her gaze focused between the obvious, catching all the little signs most didn't. "You look tired."

I had no answer for that. I *was* tired. Sick and tired of this ghost on my tail and the questions I had no answers for. Sick of the pain dulled in my arm, and the subconscious awareness it'd just roll back up to agony again. Even as I stood here and chatted up the secretary, most of me braced in preparation. For hurt. For confrontation.

If Malik knew anything about the vid for sale, Hope would have to call in a cleanup crew.

I waved her concern away with my good hand. "Where's Mr Corporate Creed?"

"Preparing," she replied, gesturing back to the elevator. "Mr Reed will be in the munitions center."

I stared at her, hand flat on the desk.

She blinked up at me. "What?"

"You're letting me wander into the armory?"

Her pretty mouth turned up at the corners, one hand resting on her defined hip. "Yes?"

"By myself?"

"You are an adult," she pointed out, laughter in her eyes. "And under contract."

"Uh huh." I dropped my chin on the counter top, rolled my eyes at her. "Reed ordered you to let me in there, didn't he?"

"Of course he did." She reached across the desk,

gesturing me to stand up straight. I did. She had to stand on tiptoe to reach my shoulders – she was shorter than me, with that rounded physique I enjoyed so much wrapped in bland professional suits I enjoyed much less. "Hold still."

I waited, surprised, while Malik Reed's personal secretary unkinked the knot in my tie, straightened it out, and then tied it properly in the space of seconds. With a final flourish, she pushed the neat, perfectly folded knot into place.

"There," she said briskly. "Don't you look smart?"

Making a face, I hooked the knot with a finger and tugged it looser, earning myself an exasperated huff. "You may want to wash your hands," I told her.

Hope, unfazed by my attitude any day of the week, chuckled. "Sanitization is a lifestyle choice. Go down three floors," she added. "Follow the signs."

"Should I bring a ballgag or a paddle?"

"What?"

"Never mind." Laughing to myself, I headed for the elevator I'd just left, waved at Hope without turning around. "If you see Orchard, tell her hi for me."

"Tell her yourself," Hope called back as the doors closed. Her wave warmed me in places that had nothing to do with sex. Well, mostly. I'd tap her, given the chance, but she stubbornly preferred cocks and wouldn't budge on my suggestions to acquire one.

Not like fucksticks were hard to get.

Oh, well. Just because I hated corporate bullshit, and most of the execs who chew on it, didn't mean I had to hate every person in it. Hope Ramsay was good people. Loyal to Reed, so I didn't trust her if it came down to it, but I liked talking with her.

The elevator hummed a welcoming note as it slowed.

The munitions lab, huh? Mantis Industries specialized

in armor and bodygear, not weapons. The only real break they'd forged in the munitions industry had collapsed with their corporate partners some decades ago: the Valiant 14, with 12mm caseless rounds and an orgasmic rate of fire. The assault rifle was perfection in nanosteel, and had been a joint experiment between it and rival company TaberTek. The Valiant savaged everything in its category, poised to launch Mantis into arms as well as the armor they specialized in.

They'd only manufactured fifty final prototypes. Before the Valiant could hit mass production, the eternal meatgrinder of the corporate world got to grinding, and TaberTek went down. Cannibalized in boardrooms across the city.

I owned a Valiant; the second of two. The first had been stolen from me by my Vid Zone abductors, and fuck them so much for its loss. The second came with my freelance pay; signed, sealed and delivered by Malik himself.

I should have brought it with me. Riddling Malik Reed with his own company's failure smelled like sweet, sweet irony to me.

I followed the signs and arrows down thinly carpeted corridors and by more of those paintings Reed liked so much. Eventually, I reached wide double doors at the end of a hall and paused. The art and carpet clearly stopped at this point. Beyond, framed in narrow glass slats in each door, I saw white. Always white.

My stomach twitched. A tiny little movement that rippled up my spine, wiggled into a spot behind my solar plexus.

I did not like laboratories. Or hospitals. I didn't like anything that had to be kept cold and clean, that smelled of antiseptic and misery. Every time I paced through a pristine white environment, barren walls and overhead lights, part of my head started to scream.

Leftover reaction from that lab that'd murdered Nanji. I'd been fighting memories I didn't recognize as mine ever since – something about bashing my own head against white tile and people shouting all around me.

Orchard, the Mantis doctor, called it post-traumatic stress.

I called it bullshit.

I don't know why I'd expected the munitions lab to be anything different.

When I approached the double doors, my breath hurt in my lungs. The cool air scraped like razorblades across my skin, tucked sharp fingers into my flesh and hooked in. Here it was. The usual start.

Security cameras everywhere made me damn sure I didn't display any signs of this weakness, even as I sucked in air and forced myself not to shake. The images had gotten less sharp with time. Didn't stop my traitor brain from filling in the gaps.

Blood on the floor. Excruciating pain in my head.

A black hole opened up behind my sternum. A void that made me want to hunch over it, like I needed to nurse a wound.

The hell I would.

I shoved open the doors with more force than they needed.

Malik Reed was a creature of routine, right down to his clothes. Gray, sometimes a pop of color in his shirt or his tie. Always a suit. Always an attitude, like he owned the city and everything in it. Today's single-color blessing upon the peasants came in the form of a pale yellow button-down, pressed and tailored perfectly to Reed's physique. Tucked into crisp, light gray trousers and a

matching vest, he looked like an exec fisting the public
at a corporate picnic.

Five people in shades of gray camo cargoes and black
T-shirts stood around a plain metal lab table; five sets of
eyes snapped around to me. One pair did not. "You're
late," Reed said to the large projection dominating the
center of the table. It spun slowly. Blueprints, looked
like. A lot of missing information in it.

The rest of the munitions lab spread out in every
direction. Larger than I could map, with protective panes
set up around various projects and different departments,
the whole floor had been devoted to arms development.
Racks lined walls and shelves, various firearms and
prototypes of things I didn't recognize had been left
haphazardly on tables with parts strewn around them.

There were a lot of projections. A few tablets.
Technicians everywhere beyond the initial meeting
room we gathered in – many wearing protective gear
and all of them sporting badge IDs. A busy floor for a
company that doesn't do munitions.

Busy enough, I realized as the ache in my chest faded
to a dull throb, that my tremors had vanished. Why? Was
it the different environment? Less sterile. Less quiet?

Or was it Reed I refused to show weakness to?

Either way, I'd take it and run. I jerked my eyes back
to the group, curling a lip. "You didn't tell me it'd be a
party."

"You didn't ask." Reed pointed to a chair.

*Eat me* danced at the tip of my tongue. Didn't bother.
The group was already eying me like the short kid
in a game of basketball. I got close enough to see the
projection, stayed far enough away from them to draw a
line. "What'd I miss?"

"The whole thing," said a broadshouldered man.

Military posture, ID clipped to his collar. Channing. Cody Channing, obviously an enforcer. "Sucks to be you."

I shot him a bland smile. Bland only in the sense that it was mostly teeth and *fuck off*.

He glowered at me.

"Wait, is this why you wanted me here?" I lifted both hands, palms up. "You couldn't just tell me on the line?"

Reed finally looked at me. Gaze on mine. "Did you rest?"

"Absolutely," I lied. Didn't even miss a beat.

Skepticism all but radiated at me.

"Your version of rest needs reprogramming," piped up a woman with short white hair. She smiled back at me. *Also* all teeth. Ooh. I liked her already. "We have a job to do, and you'd better haul your weight or we're leaving you for the cleanup."

"Where's the job?"

"Should have been here for the briefing," said another man. Leaner, cocky. Thought he topped me on the scale. I smiled at him, too.

"Located in Battery," Feliz cut in. She shot the younger man a hard look, severe as an anglo axe to the face. "Shut up, Lindsay."

Awesome. Just *awesome*. The only thing worth locating in Battery was the second of my chopshops, which saved me the need to strongarm Malik into it.

He worked fast. And it was the first good news I'd had all day.

I grabbed the stained, wrinkled tie I'd donned just for the occasion and made a show of tightening it up to my neck. "Well, then." Nice and brisk. "Thanks for letting me join the club."

Every eye dropped to the filthy faux silk. Even Reed's.

Despite the pretty knot Hope made of my tie, not one

of the enforcers cracked a smile.

Killjoys.

When Malik finally raised his gaze to mine, I re-evaluated my impact. Framed by that perfectly shaped goatee, the slight lift of one corner of his mouth looked a hell of a lot more wicked than it should have. "Rendezvous with Dr Gearailteach," he said, looking at me but obviously talking to the others. "Wheels up in two hours. Dismissed." They nodded, turned away. "Riko," he added, tenor dropping an octave, "a word."

The team filed out, a stream of gray and black. "Ooooh," murmured Lindsay as he passed me. "Somebody's gettin' *reamed*."

I jerked my elbow back. The sharp edge connected with the hollow beneath his shoulder blade, bone catching on bone on the way to gouging muscle. He stumbled into Feliz, who braced with a curse that balanced the wisecracker's yelp.

He turned on me. "You friggin' *cunt*–"

"*Dismissed*," Reed repeated, deep voice so wildly authoritative that even *I* felt the impact of it in my gut. Which only made me angry. Really, really angry.

"But she–"

Only then did Malik's eyes leave mine, cool as the ice I needed to jam down my pants on the regular. The way the cords in his neck moved when he turned his head fascinated me. I wanted to trace every one of them. Maybe lick them.

Then see if they'd plink like an old guitar when I snapped them out.

The weight of his silence pressed down like a slow hammer to the face. They felt it. I felt it. Could I get any more pissed?

I damn well was going to try.

# 14

I took the opportunity to sling myself into a chair, leaned back and kicked my boots up on the surface of the shiny table. The technicians beyond those seals continued to work without much attention to us. Soundproof, maybe? Bulletproof for sure. Maybe fireproof, too. A killbox if something went wrong.

I wondered how many times something had.

Unable to stand up to the boss – probably unwilling, executive power and all – the enforcers turned and left, backs stiff. All pissed-off pride among their own.

Reed watched them, one hand slipped into his pocket. When the doors closed, a hiss of air in their wake, he turned back to me. "Would it kill you to let jibes pass you by?"

"Would it kill you to give me some prep?" I retorted. "You could have told me about this on the comms."

"You needed rest."

"Don't tell me what I need, motherfucker."

A flash of teeth. Not a smile. His eyes narrowed. "I assure you again that I've never fucked my mother," he replied flatly.

I waved that away. "Like you never thought about it."

Somehow, my rejoinder cut through his annoyance.

He paused, *actually* paused, to think about it. After a long, unnerving moment, he tipped his head. Acknowledgment.

I snorted.

"Since you are here," he continued, "would you like to know who legally owns the Battery location?"

"Oh, do I get to know?" Acid sweet. "Gee, thanks."

No reaction. "Trace the shells back far enough and it leads to MetaCorp, Incorporated." Evenly. As if he'd just told me his favorite color – which I knew. Gray. Because *gray*.

I scowled. "You knew this last night, didn't you?"

He shrugged, no fucks to give minus several more.

I threw my hands up. Which only made the seam at my shoulder stretch, then crunch. That cut through the pain-dampening effects real fast. "Fuck *damn*," I gritted out between clenched teeth, and forced myself to train my gaze on him instead of my arm. No weakness. "Throw me a bone here, jackmaggot. Given MetaCunt ran our asses ragged at the Vid Zone blight, your shitbrains manage to source any whispers that we'll see them in Battery?"

"Unknown."

"Figures."

We'd fought necros *and* enforcers that day in the Vid Zone, which nobody had seen coming. Initial evidence suggested the smegheads wanted the same thing we wanted – the necros had torn them up just as bad as they had us, and we'd walked away with the data.

Short victory.

Was it possible they'd been trying to retrieve their own data from their own fuck up?

I dropped my head to the back of the chair. One foot fidgeted on the table, leaving a black rubber streak on the surface. "You know it's been stripped, right? Do you have *anything* to go on?" Not that I needed much bait here. It'd still be nice to know.

"Sixteen hours ago you were frothing at the mouth for this." Dark eyes appraised me. "What changed?"

Everything. My mouth hardened into an aggressive line. Slowly, I laced my fingers across my stomach and asked, "Want to know what I learned today?"

"Basic math."

"You wanna try again, wiseass?"

He approached the table, bent with his hands on it. A power lean. Common suit tactic, especially the execs. And one that put him too close for comfort. "No. Get your feet off my table."

"Suck it up," I replied blandly. "Go on, guess."

His eyes narrowed. "For a woman with few allies and a great deal of problems, you are dangerously close to losing what little help you have. Why do you insist on pushing?"

It mirrored Indigo's caution too closely, and too soon. That stung. And I refused to take it from a corp tool.

"Fine." I sat up, feet firmly where he didn't want them. "How much are you getting paid for that vid, Malik?"

His eyebrow rose. "You're speaking nonsense. Get," he repeated slowly, "your feet off my table."

I searched his face. Or the mask he wore over his face, anyway. Nobody could be that stone cool, not all the time. Unless he was and maybe his wife liked that?

No accounting for taste.

"You heard me," I began, and swore when one large hand wrapped around my left foot. Swung hard enough that both legs sailed off the surface. I jerked upright before the chair tilted, surged to my feet. His strength always surprised me. The way that hungry part of my libido responded did not.

"Hands off the merchandise," I snapped.

"That's right," he replied thinly, and seized my dangling tie in one large fist. He jerked me close enough that the edge of the table slammed into my hips, catching on bone. This was new.

And hot.

And pushing my every fucking button. The violent ones.

"You," he said slowly, every word stretched to the max, "*are* merchandise. Contracted and paid by *me*. I expect–"

Yeah, right. Two of my fingers locked into a point in his wrist, and he let me go so fast it was like I'd grated his knuckles off. His expression blackened, white teeth revealed in a soundless lip curl. I watched him flex his tingling hand, the moment of whatever the hell was eating him turning into cool appraisal. Beyond him, a few technicians broke whatever willpower kept them looking elsewhere. Outright shock, furrowed surprise.

Yeah, I'd just assaulted their boss. Come at me.

"Screw your expectations," I said flatly. "You betrayed me, didn't you?"

He stared at me. Like I'd just grown an extra finger to flip him off with.

My turn to power lean, taking advantage of the space he'd dragged me into. "How much are you getting for that vid?"

"Riko." Flat calm, eerily cold compared to that heated display of aggression. "I don't know what you're getting around to and I do not have time to humor you. You have a job, you have a team. Anything festering in your childish brain can wait until after."

"You hear me out first," I shot back, low. Furious. Menace cut like knives – and to my shame, my voice shook.

He heard it. Damn it. Reed paused, arms folded across his chest. Jaw tight, he took a breath and let it out on a curt, "You have my attention."

My fingers bit into the metal surface. Only one side scratched. "You remember that vid I grabbed?"

He nodded, a single inclination so regal I wanted to punch his teeth out. No callbox protocols to interfere this time.

"I got notice today that somebody's pushing it to market." My flesh hand fisted, already sealed like I hadn't cut it on ceramic. "If it goes live, I'm as good as dead. You realize that, right?"

"What," he said evenly, "does this have to do with me?"

"Basic," I snapped back. "Cunting. Math."

"You have a mouth."

"I will tear your girly lips off," I snarled. "Only two of you know that thing exists." I leaned forward even more, shoving my own hips into the table so hard that the legs screeched against the pristine floor. My tech hand matched the sound, nails on rust and twice as loud. The abrasions left behind earned me a disapproving frown. "From scouts to ambush to my cred up for auction. Why do you fucking think I'm asking you?"

His sigh made me want to climb over the table and rip his lungs out. Shoving them up his ass, wet and pulpy, sounded like my idea of heaven.

Except I needed the job he'd put together. Battery wouldn't wait long.

"What makes you think Mr Koupra isn't behind this?"

Because I refused. I'd cling to that thread for as long as it held me. What the hell else did I have to lose? "I will," I promised quietly, counter to the flash of red in my vision, "come over this table. Watch your mouth or

I'll stuff your dick in it."

He held up his hands. Not placating. Not afraid. A reminder, a warning, to zen it. "If that seems impossible for you–" A touch of mockery, like he thought me naïve. "–perhaps you should consider the fact MetaCorp attained that information from the same place you did."

"Digo erased it all."

"If they owned the Vid Zone's center the way they own Battery's, they'd have other options."

That made more sense than I wanted. Slowly, I straightened. Pulled my body and my temper away from Malik Reed's reach, the throb in my shoulder sharpening to a trickle of imaginary nerves on fire. "You make a point."

"I appreciate your acknowledgment." Gone was the sympathy. Back was the quirk at the corner of his mouth, and unreadable dark eyes. "You're going to be late for your physical." A beat. "Again."

"Eat shit and die." I straightened that stupid tie again. "If I find out otherwise, Malik…"

I let the threat linger. No slouch, he picked it right up. "If you find out otherwise," he continued mildly, "you may do as you like with me."

Well.

I didn't expect *that*.

I shoved both hands into the pockets of my drop-crotch pants. "That doesn't clear you."

A nod.

"You realize I'm only working with you to get intel, right?"

"Of course."

"I'm going to do everything I can to beat your mooks to it."

"Do not kill them," he replied, "and you may do

whatever you want."

I stared at him. "You *really* don't care about people, do you?"

An eyebrow. "Incorrect. My tools are finely honed and specialized. Your efforts," he said pointedly, "will not affect mine."

Heh. I turned for the door. "Fine. I'll go play with your jackwagons."

"I expect," he said to my back, that authority he wielded like a knife sliding deep into my spine, "you will share your intel with me upon return."

My meat shoulder lifted, "I'll think about it."

"You're so kind."

"I know." I flicked a hand back in a dismissive wave. "It's a redeeming feature."

"Not as much as that ass, I believe."

I almost tripped on the floor. *Fuuuuuck.* A direct reference to the pink arrow I'd forgotten was bare at the back of my tank. I swear to Indigo's asshole, it annoyed me so much that Reed had an absurd talent at deadpan humor. I had *no* idea if he meant to, or if he was the world's ultimate straight man. I gritted my teeth and shot him a glare over my shoulder.

He'd crossed his arms over his chest again. Watched me go with appraisal in his eyes. More challenge than I wanted.

Didn't like that, either.

"Go fuck yourself," I said.

"I'm considering tech for that."

I hate him so very, very much. The doors closed on my laugh.

It didn't last long. The frayed remnants of humor vanished.

Somehow, I felt better about Malik's role in the vid's

leak. No way would he offer his skin up like that.

Not unless he had every expectation I'd fail. A nasty gamble on his part.

Childish brain, huh? That one stuck as I stomped down the corridor. Fuck him. Shows what he knew about SINless ways of life, and the thin glue that holds it together. His people would not love to have me among them. Not my fault. *They* were the ones who tried to nut up at me. What these suitfuckers don't realize is that nutting up means an easy boot to the testicles, and how was I supposed to resist it when the idiots are so quick to sack up in my face?

Whatever. Let them whine and cry when I didn't play nice. My goal was to beat them to any data in there, and I'd have to do it without Indigo to work his linker magic. I'd screw Malik's wife before I let that data fall into some asshole enforcer's hands. I was already feeling like my ass was hanging in the open.

The way I operated, I was going to bruise a lot of egos.

Sounded like Reed's problem.

Probably should have known better.

# 15

Another lab. This one very much a problem. A pristine white floor, pristine white walls. Med tech and metal exam tables, technicians in white lab coats. I sat on an aluminum stool, waiting my turn for scans, and tried to breathe through my cramping lungs.

Even with my head tipped down, the light in the med lab burned bright as Carmichael's gown, unflinchingly pure in color. White-blue, sharp enough to cut into closed eyelids.

"Hey, Channing, bet you I can beat your time." A woman's voice. One of the enforcers.

"The fuck you can," Channing shot back.

I flinched. It was so similar to a conversation between Indigo and me that I could barely hold my shit together. My eyes snapped open, the floor beyond my knees blurred.

Somewhere between the relaxed back and forth of my coerced team and the smell of disinfectant, I forgot to blink. Forgot entirely to breathe until the cramp in my lungs screamed. Then I tried to inhale slowly and quietly.

To keep my shit mine.

Kind of worked. Like a hard crash after an adrenaline

run. Focusing on the here and now, taking in the cold hygienic air and the plain white ceiling, wasn't helping. For every second I tried, I lost that much more detail. Until I couldn't remember what I was staring at. Couldn't remember what the fuck shone harsh and unflinching down on me, only that it cut through my nerves like a sawblade through a baby.

Blood on white tile.

Voices shouting.

Pain shrieking through my head. A sharp crescendo. Once, twice.

*Sedative, now!*

It translated to a quiet, insistent buzz. A low-grade hum that knocked somewhere around my chipset, centered at the base of my skull. Hated this sound. It cropped up now and again, and it made me feel... *haunted.* Claustrophobic. Like tearing off my skin was a good idea.

I was stuck. Stuck with the growing tendril of panic unfurling from the black hole swirling in my chest, stuck with the panic and anxiety and fight, flight, freeze instinct that swamped me.

I didn't fly. Or freeze. Wasn't the type.

*Can't fight.*

My fingers grasped at the edges of the table on either side of me.

*Cold. Hard. An autopsy slab.*

Blood on white tile–

*Zen it.*

Couldn't.

A blur settled in front of my staring eyes, a mix of white and screaming orange-red. "Hey." A quiet greeting. A soothing voice. "Riko." It cut through the noise, managed to isolate the only part of my brain keyed in to the here and now.

I blinked. My eyelids scraped over my dried-out eyeballs. My grimace showed a lot of teeth, but I straightened. Made like nothing had gone down. A quick glance at one of the large digital clocks scattered around the lab told me I'd been buried for twenty minutes.

Shit.

Unlike most people in her profession, Dr Orchard of the unpronounceable last name wasn't afraid of me. My attitude had never fazed her, which I found curious. She crouched in front of me, long limbs folded up, sharp elbows on her thighs for balance. Her wavy orange hair stood out in the whitescape of this hell like fire in a padded room.

I liked it. It was fun to look at, see all the little strands of yellow and red and brown in the pumpkin mass. Given a face full of freckles that did for her what they didn't do for Reed and her guileless blue eyes, I assumed she'd been born with all of it.

Those freckles winked and shifted as her wide mouth bent into a smile. A real one. "Welcome back."

I pretended like she'd missed me. "It's only been a couple weeks." I managed light.

Orchard knew better. She'd had my number since the day I'd tossed her over my shoulder in a fit of what she called traumatic flashbacks. It was, I knew, the reason she blocked the view between the others and me. Protecting my rep.

I just didn't know what to do with that.

"You able to stand?"

My back stiffened. Across the lab, my soon-to-be-teammates laughed and joked, snapped at each other in that familiar way longtime teams could. "Why the tits wouldn't I?"

Overt aggression.

A tinge of hurt crept over Orchard's features, creating an equal tinge of mirrored guilt. Which the black hole in my chest quickly latched onto.

Why the fuck was I so awful to her?

Because I was a goddamned cunt, that's why.

I set my jaw. "Thanks."

"I'm here for you," she said, hurt fading. Unlike everybody else, I accepted her sympathy. It was the kind of compassion you get from people who want to patch up your bullet holes and stich your stab wounds. She unfolded from her crouch, long-fingered hands beckoning me. And when I say *unfold,* I mean it. She was fine-boned and tall, like one of the genetically recreated birds they put in zoos. She sat in chairs like a kid, with one or both legs folded up, and on stools like she didn't realize she'd fall off with just a sneeze. "Let's get you prepped."

Another lab tech, a large man with blond hair, looked up from the projections he studied. Gunther Leto. Nice enough guy, but protective of Orchard and the lab. I hadn't broken anything so far, so he waved at me. "Heading out with this group?" he called.

"Seems like." Look at that, I managed to sound normal.

The enforcer next to him grimaced at me – probably the one teasing Channing. Her brown hair was pulled tightly back into a knot, the Kongtown cast to her features easily recognizable. Almost as tall as me, with muscled limbs hanging from her white medical gown and brown eyes spitting *not by choice.*

I was so on that wavelength.

Leto flashed me a thumbs up.

"Scans only?" I asked Orchard.

"Scans, physical health." She looked back over her shoulder as I followed her through the maze of equipment. "Do you still refuse to let me in?"

"Depends on where you're trying to go."

Orchard only smiled, a rueful shake of her head causing her curly ponytail to sway. "I wish you'd let me work on your tech."

Ugh. It was like I flirted with a brick wall, she was so clueless.

Fact is, the only time Orchard had been in my setup, I'd been delivered by an extraction crew with rebar in my chest and necro nanos flooding my system. I couldn't stop her then, and I had no doubt she'd recorded everything. I wouldn't willingly do it again.

We passed the white-haired enforcer, who shot me that feral smile of hers. "That's Banh." She nodded to the woman who was not Feliz. "You met Lindsay. My name's Damrosch," she told me. The wires hooked up to the adhesive on her chest vibrated with the waggle of her fingers. So not cute. "Make sure you remember it."

I shot her back my own kind of smile. "Thanks. I'll scream it next time I fuck your mom."

Surprising me, Damrosch threw back her head and laughed. It echoed through the lab, got everybody else's attention.

"Christ, Tera." Lindsay, obviously sulking. I couldn't see him in the mash of technical equipment, but he'd be hooked up somewhere too. Scans first.

"It's good to make friends," Orchard said mildly to us both. "Stop moving, please," she added.

Damrosch's grin remained. "Oops."

Orchard beckoned me to a curtained room – the same one I'd stepped into when I'd first visited. Same one in which I'd thrown her over my shoulder when

I first buckled. I'd gotten better about controlling it. At least in that I didn't jump her shit when she touched me. "Clothes off, gown on."

I was already reaching for the tie at my neck when Orchard paused. When she bent to look at it up close, her hair bounced over her shoulder.

She smelled like something sweet. Not candy. Flowers? The fragrance filled my nostrils. Somehow, it helped ease some of my tension. The scent was just so *Orchard.*

"Is that a *tie*?"

"Heh." My only response. I stared at the fall of her orange hair like it'd bite me in the face if I didn't pay attention. When she straightened again, I took a deep breath. Antiseptic washed away the lingering lightness of her hair, from sweet to acid. Why I did it, I wasn't sure. I just felt like maybe I wasn't supposed to smell something, be close to something, that *nice.*

"Has Mr Reed seen it?" she asked, laughing.

"Oh, yeah." He'd used it as a weapon, too, which I'd return in kind another time. I shot my hand up into the air and gave the room a general middle finger as I dropped the stained tie to the floor.

"I keep telling you. There are no cameras in here."

"I keep telling you bullshit," I replied, and stepped inside the curtained room. I left the thing open behind me as I peeled the dirty tank top up my sticky body.

Orchard tugged the thin barrier closed.

Giving up on any sense of good behavior, I kicked my boots off. Sent them smack into the sheet, which swung and flared out, revealing Orchard's electric blue sneakers under the hem of her white scrubs. Wordlessly, she bent to pick my boots up. And the tie.

Good freaking riddance.

Shimmying out of my pants took longer. Loose as

the harem pants were, they'd dried stiff. So had my meatsack. I was tired, hitting strained reserves.

Once I managed to peel the fabric away from my legs, the rest followed easily, leaving me bare to the cold lab air. I hesitated, dug my fingertips into my chest where my heart pounded hard enough to throb in my temples.

*Keep it together.*

Taking a deep breath put my metaphorical feet on the motherfucking ground.

I grabbed the curtain and threw it wide. Nakedness didn't bother me. I had less modesty than a pornstar on an up close and personal vag feed. Orchard, however, didn't share my interests. A white gown hit me with almost preternatural speed, immediately covering my body from breast to crotch. Catching it caused it to drape, revealing my shoulders, ribs, and most of my thighs. And all my ass, which I did *not* turn around and shake at her.

I hope she appreciated my restraint.

The ink on my right shoulder stood out in this obscenely stark environment like a colorful murder scene. I could also light the vid-ink up – made for some stunning visuals in the right place. Here, I didn't have to. The Dia de los Muertos skull on my shoulder, the visual mix of art and designs that crawled from shoulder to wrist, and the ornate Kongtown dragon sinuously etched down my ribs, hip and thigh were more than enough for these C-town types to handle.

I got no love for my peepshow. Not from Orchard.

The enforcer behind me, Channing, wasn't as obtuse. He tossed me a wolf-whistle for my trouble. I ignored him.

She led the way to a plain white wall, seams carved into its smooth paneling. A touch of a scanner opened one slot, and a medical table slid out. Nice and cold.

Minimal padding. "OK, you know the drill. Scan first. Then physical. Shower," she added, wrinkling her nose over her shoulder at me, "last."

"Are you telling me I stink?" I asked, all wide eyes and impossible attempt at innocence.

Her nose wrinkled harder – so hard that her eyes all but vanished and her freckles collapsed in on themselves. "Even your hair is dried stiff, Riko."

"I'll show you stiff," I muttered.

Orchard pointed to the table. "Put the gown on. And get up."

"I could get u… *mmph!*"

She snatched the gown from my loose hold and threw it over my head.

The crisp fabric settled on my shoulders, felt like spikes and rust and dried cement. It grated against my skin like it'd peel the damn stuff off, but I didn't flinch. Didn't run, either. A small fucking win. At least I was breathing again.

So far, so good.

Forcing myself to relax, I suffered through the same scans and exams the others did. Only I wasn't invited to the conversation. Not until three of us ended up clocking our physiology together, assigned treadmills to map our vitals.

Lucky me, I'd been put between Damrosch and the dude with an eye for ass.

For a good five minutes, none of us spoke. We just hit the treadmill and started running, sensors occasionally beeping to indicate another measurement taken. Damrosch's track moved faster than mine, and mine was faster than his.

Didn't take long for the shit to fly. "You gonna make it, Chanchan?"

I kept my eyes forward as he snapped, "Go kiss a dog's ass, Tera."

Heh.

"You volunteering?" she shot back, and laughed when he grunted. Then her attention turned to me. "You look like you're going to pass out."

I wasn't.

When I didn't say anything, she clicked her tongue. "What, too good to mingle with the rest of us?"

That got me. I sneered. "You're the ones trying to nut up."

"Pretty sure you started it," Channing volunteered. No sass. Just a statement. I shot him a similar look. He met it with a chuckle. None of us had been running long enough to work up a sweat. "Seriously, what's your problem?"

"She doesn't like corporate tools," Damrosch cut in. Her turn to sneer.

I rolled my eyes. "Don't put words in my mouth."

"Oh yeah?" She eyed me sidelong. "Then what is it?"

Steadily holding my pace, I turned my answer in Channing's direction. "I don't like corporate tools."

His chuckle transitioned to a laugh.

"Bitch," Damrosch crowed. "I knew it."

Shrugging, I bumped up my speed. Sweat gathered along my spine, under my breasts. I'd be soaking this white sports bra soon. The tiny shorts given me and Tera weren't my favorite – I preferred the boardshort style given Channing. These rode up. Fucking institutionalized bullshit.

We both spent too much time digging the lycra from our ass cracks.

Didn't stop her from bumping her speed, though. Challenge on, huh?

Gritting my teeth, I held this stride while the rest of

me adjusted. The machines beeped per half a kilometer, splitting our growing breaths and occasional pants into uneven moments of silence.

Channing left his machine alone. "If you hate it so much," he said after a while, "why sign up?"

Because I had to jack whatever I could out from under prying eyes, and I'd run with corporate cunts if that's what it took. I blew out a breath. "None of your business."

"Pay?"

"None," I repeated tightly, lungs squeezing, "of your business." The speed was taking its toll.

"Do you owe Mr Reed a favor?"

I snapped him a hard look. Caught the bottom of my shoe on the rough treadmill surface and barely managed not to eat shit.

Damrosch's snicker snapped my brain into gear. "Fuck you," I said between gasps. "You aren't going to distract me."

They both laughed.

Tera bumped her speed up.

Setting my jaw, eyes ahead, I did the same.

Ten minutes in and we were both gasping. Even Channing had started to shine, though he'd maintained his pace. Sweat rolled off my face, dripped to the treadmill. My arms scattered droplets around me. Both enforcers obviously felt the same.

Of the three of us, Damrosch and I would hit the distance marker first. Channing would come in third, which I'd take. The question was who'd take first.

She pushed her speed higher.

Groaning silently, I did the same. We couldn't see each other's numbers, but fucked if I'd lose to a corporate puppet.

Sixty seconds of this and I couldn't think of anything else but the effort. Three minutes more and I refused to die on this treadmill. I could long-distance jog for hours, but this? This was almost sprinting speed, and I wasn't sure I'd manage it much longer. My lungs screamed, a cramp in my side stretching from hip to shoulder. Hell, even my tech arm was beginning to weigh down on the shoulder girdle that kept it in place.

Tera gasped for breath, strained and struggling.

The doors opened behind us. Leto's voice. "Tera, Riko. You're up."

"Oh shit," Tera yelped, and I knew why. Legs shrieking, muscles seized, we both tried to stop and we both ate treadmill. My knees gave out, feet glued to the rapid track, and my face smashed into the front controls. Then the treadmill.

It took a chunk of skin with it. All the sensors pulled free, taking more skin with them, and snapped back to the controls. That clattered, too.

By the time I'd rolled onto the floor, panting for breath and groaning, Channing was laughing too hard to keep his own pace and had to step lightly to the sides to keep from joining me. To my left, Tera lay sprawled on her back, mirroring my efforts to breathe.

Leto, three steps in the room and frozen in place, studied the tableau. Lips trying so hard not to curve, he said sternly, "No playing on the machines."

Channing's laughter went up an octave.

"Who hit first?" Damrosch wheezed.

"Riko hit the floor first." I shot him an exhausted middle finger.

"The finish," she managed, struggling to get up on one elbow.

Leto sighed, features struggling for patient. "Riko did."

Tera returned the finger back at me. "Die in a fire."

"You first," I said, dropping my head back to the floor.

# 16

I'd earned some ground. Or at least some wary inclusion. Banh, Damrosch, Lindsay, Channing and Feliz. I committed their names to memory, as much to stay in communication during the run as give them shit over the comms.

I was putting that to good use now. "Channing, quit pissing around and get that door!"

Rapid fire forced me behind the abandoned car I'd stalled at. Banh, at my back, braced her Sauger over the rusted hood and laid down cover fire that didn't do squat. Not a single break in the barrage of bullets coming back at us.

She ducked down as they pocked the metal. The car rocked.

"Eight!" It came through the headset sharp and short. Kongtown slang. Bitch had just called *me* a bitch. "Do you know how to shoot that thing?"

"Woman, please," I snorted, squeezing off another burst. "They don't understand the concept of cover, suicidal bastards." What's worse, we couldn't see jack and shit, just the occasional flash between cyclical reloads.

"Why the fuck is this area abandoned?" Lindsay demanded. "I thought Battery was residential mixed."

"Mostly." Feliz's voice came clipped. "But yeah, there should be more activity here."

"Sealed," Damrosch volunteered, almost lost beneath another round of firepower aimed our way. Once it eased up, she added, "Probably zoned off for a raid."

"You mean ours?" I said dryly.

"Channing," warned Feliz, tucked somewhere behind a crushed dumpster three meters away. "You close?"

"I am working on it," came his growl, low and tight on the feed. "It's not exactly a stroll down Fenroll Park."

His job was to crack the main door, by fist or by fire. He was Mantis's equivalent of a heavy, which operated best in close combat – serious amounts of strength and various ways to avoid a KO. Boone, Digo's usual heavy, used tech for that. He'd replaced his legs with wide foundation feet, earning him rock steady balance and a kick like a goddamn railgun. Not to mention I'd seen him work the stuff like a battering ram, fuel a hydraulic jump and stomp stuff into mush. People, mostly, and the occasional wall. Or door.

Or car.

Riot shields.

Boone was a heavy of many, many strengths.

What Channing brought to bear remained to be seen.

Flanking Feliz – only an idiot leaves the coordinator unprotected – Damrosch scanned the streets. Heat pushed down on us like a sweltering blanket, making everything hard to see through the constant barrage of heatwave. My boots sank four centimeters into melted asphalt, tar oozing up around the soles. Made every step fun.

Through my heads-up display, a series of numbers, figures and indicators flashed. Over a hundred degrees outside, a calm seventy inside the regulating armor.

Thirty rounds left in my Sauger, which did not bode well for our initial assault. I had more clips, of course, but at this rate, we'd blow our loads on cover fire the assholes didn't care about. Sui-fucking-cidal.

I ignored everything else fed into the HUD but the thin green line around the team. It helped identify them in the dark, through smoke, or in the chaos of a fight. Reed's people had upgraded since my last experience in a Mantis combat suit, allowing a blend of sensors and network to place each person. Meant we could see each other through barriers, to an extent.

Wasn't perfect. They occasionally glitched in one direction, or lagged half a step behind. Yay for beta testing in the field.

To make it worse, red lines *should* have marked our enemies. Problem here was that I didn't see any. Could have been another glitch, could have been the limits of the network. Could be these assholes had better tech than we did. It was supposed to be empty. Guess whose intel sucked again? Well, Greg's too. Emptied out, my ass.

"They're either locked behind serious stealth gear," I said, slinging my assault rifle back into the crook of my arm and dropping to the street. "Or the heads-up is shitting the bed."

"No stealth suit is that good."

"Lindsay," I said between clenched teeth and repeater fire, "I will take your ass in that bet."

Trick offer. I knew from firsthand experience just how good stealth gear could be. I'd come face to face with MetaCorp thugs with integrated tech that made them all but invisible to the sensors in standard helmets. Had to use your goddamn eyes to see them coming, and who the hell went bareheaded in a gunfight?

Given this place had MetaCorp ties, it wasn't that much of a leap.

"Focus," Feliz snapped. "Channing?"

"Six seconds!"

"Shit," hissed Damrosch, a tight sound of pain.

"Tera?"

"I'm fine," she said, too loud and too fast. "Only clipped. These aren't standard twelves."

"I clock 'em at armor-piercing and fuck you," I muttered. "One of these will blow a lung out."

"Maybe *yours*, snowflake."

I smirked as I peered down what limited sight the Saugers had.

I held my fire, half under the back of the sagging car, finger resting on the trigger guard corporation engineers insisted on. The asphalt, only barely cooler under here, stuck to my gear.

Nothing about this place looked like a certified tech center. But aside from the quality, the Vid Zone chopshop had been the same. Shitty façade, internal badass engineering. I mean, except for the part where it caught on fire and filled up with slavering killbots.

On the very, very slim plus side, there was no sign of necro activity. Regardless of Malik's reassurance, I wasn't letting my guard down until we'd cleared the place. All I knew was that this hadn't turned into a blight. No necros crawling around, no burn team on standby. Relief beat the sheer terror of a once-human sack of meat coming at you any day of the week.

Just in case, I'd padded my requisitions with one of my own heavy handguns – a M422A Tactical Revolver, .525 caliber and designated by runners as the Adjudicator. It blew holes through people you could put your fist in.

Which would all be moot if we got stuck here because

our heavy was using his brain instead of his metaphorical dick.

So backwards, motherfucker.

"Screw this," I muttered, and rolled out from under the car. A bit awkward, given the asphalt didn't want to let my knees and elbows go. The sound I made slicked through the comm. *Squelch.* Super classy.

"Riko, don't–"

"Too late," Banh snarled.

Word. I was already darting across the street, closer to the entry than any of these fuckers had gotten – save Channing. I slammed my back against a heavily armored electrical unit, crouched low enough that my head wouldn't make for easy target practice.

"Blowing in three," Channing said over the crackling report of gunfire that just would not quit.

"Finally!" Lindsay shouted.

"Who you blowing?" I added, bending around the protective cover and squeezing the trigger. Three times, three round bursts. A bullet screamed so close to my head that its wake scored a groove at the bottom right side of my helmet.

I jerked back so fast that I left black streaks on the metal. My heart pounded, no doubt recording those vitals to the Mantis analysts. Yaaaaay.

Channing ignored me. He really liked doing that. Instead, he took off running, gesturing with his hand repeatedly as bullets pinged and sparked and tore up the ground around him. Blue light ignited at the farthest corner of the wide doors, getting brighter with every second.

He'd meant explosives, not a controlled entry. Motherhumping son of a bitch!

*Boom.*

Precision is supposed to be the hallmark of specialized teams. At least when it comes to company policy. I'd expected something quieter, neater. Something that'd laser its way around those doors and blow them off their hinges.

Those hinges did not blow.

Everyfuckingthing else did.

My faceplate lit up like a Deli celebration, flashing, sparking, *red red red*. Too slow to do anything but throw my goddamn hands up in resigned laughter, I caught the blastback full in the face and chest. My heart slammed into my spine, my ribs collided with each other. Lungs kicked back, guts flattened, metal arm thrown wide. I had to brace my feet and legs so tight, I sank further into the blistered street. Grunted as the protective cover on a nearby electrical unit tore off its bolts and rocked into my chest, then rolled off my shoulder and sailed to the street.

Even my comm link audibly shattered, throwing a feedback fuzz so loud that it sliced right through the blast's subharmonic pressure. I clawed at my helmet in defense, yelling.

And then it was over. The static in my ear eased off, giving way to voices I couldn't quite track.

I'd like to say everything went silent. It sort of did – I could tell that nothing moved, save the debris still dropping off the façade. Not even weapons fire to break it. I shook my head rapidly, ears pulsing like I'd just taken one of Muerte's kicks to both. The helmet hadn't shattered, but my whole face felt squished anyway.

And in between my ears, rattling around in my skull, an aggravating buzz. Shit. I hadn't felt that – heard that? – in weeks. Not since my chipset had rattled something loose in the Vid Zone and left me half-deaf with the noise.

It'd been fixed once. Maybe I needed a full chipset replacement. The tech wasn't supposed to rattle so easily.

I turned slowly. Blinked at the group as they rose from their impromptu cover positions. I couldn't see their expressions, but hey, it didn't matter. I'd take this one.

I threw my hands up into the air. "Victory!" I yelled, too loud through the angry thrum in my brain. Two helmets jerked. "Still motherfucking standing."

Audible groans, noises of impatience. Slowly, they clarified into actual words.

"That was reckless," Feliz snapped.

"Stupid, you mean." Lindsay strode forward, clearly with every intent to knock my shoulder with his. He closed the gap fast.

"You're going to get us killed," Damrosch added curtly.

Ladykiller with the temper didn't count on the straight arm palm I checked that shoulder with. Harder than the aluminum car dented by the blast behind Banh. I didn't push. Gave him the chance to swing that shoulder back and out of reach.

"Watch out," I said, smiling.

Silence seethed on the line. Until Feliz gestured over our heads, two fingers in a single sweep down. "Move it, we have work to do."

That we did. Not a single shot had been fired since Channing blew the door. Compared to the barrage pinning us down before, that felt off.

"Think I killed them all?" Channing asked, his tenor surprisingly melodic when I paid attention. He paced past us, careful through the debris. No squelch of tar, though.

I looked down. "Whoa."

He looked down too. A large fan of asphalt had hardened, lighter gray than the sun-beaten tar around it. Didn't try to suck the grit off my boots as I stepped onto it.

Much to my pleasure, it was his turn to strike a victory pose. Although he was much more subtle about it – a thumbs up in my direction. "I do good work."

"When you get around to it," I said, laughing. It turned into a wince as one ear buzzed so loudly, I lost my sense of balance. I locked my knees, fought through the eerie sense of vertigo. Goddamn nerve tech.

"*Wah*." Banh elbowed her way between me and Channing, forcing a gap. "Are you guys seeing this?"

Whoops. We were not. Too focused on the immediate – which naturally included pushing corp-licker buttons while admiring the size of Channing's exposed metaphorical dick – we'd missed the *real* shocker of the day.

The doors still stood. Scratched and covered in soot, hinges secured in the frame and utterly unfazed by our attempts at breaking and entering.

The rest of the wall around had literally exploded into countless pieces of carnage. Plaster and splinters, crumbled stone and cement, twisted beams and unrecognizable steel thrown in every direction.

"Well," I said after a moment. "He *didn't* get the doors open."

I swear I heard Channing's laugh, a lot more relaxed than it was at first. I'd wear him down.

"Coordinates lock the facility about twelve meters away," Feliz said, ignoring us all in favor of the data streaming over the monovisor inset into her faceplate. "Since that's impossible, looks like we're going vertical." She tipped her head to me. "Bitches first."

"We drawing straws?" I asked blandly. "Or just giving Lindsay the win?"

A hiss rattled the link. He tensed up beside me.

"Just go," Feliz snapped.

I strode past them, assault rifle tucked under my arm, barrel down. It saved the stress I'd put on my arm later, though adrenaline always made the aches and pains go away. Best drug there ever was.

If only it swatted the wasps in my head, too.

The team followed me, coordinator in the middle. Silence on the line.

I tilted my head. "Why don't we have an operator?"

"I double," Feliz answered, finally shooting for professional voice. "Last job, you lost contact underground. We assumed the same would happen here."

"Fair enough." And underground was where we headed.

Much as Greg suggested, very little was left of the interior. Then again, Channing hadn't helped that. We crunched into debris, boots cracking on rock we couldn't see and heads-up displays working overtime to catalog surroundings in the billowing dust. It was the perfect time for an ambush, but none came.

The tension in the air should have been way worse.

Instinct told me we'd find nothing here. "This floor's empty," I said, deviating from the fan we'd spread into. "Find the way down and we'll find heavier resistance."

"Heavier than that?" Damrosch asked skeptically.

"Dunno. I can't find traces of whatever nailed us down."

Channing chuckled, the green outline of his broad shoulders lifting. "I am *not* sorry."

"What makes you think we won't find anything?" Lindsay demanded. He kicked through a pile of rubble, like he needed to prove me wrong. His boot met twisted, blackened metal. "There was some serious firepower coming out of here."

My turn to shrug. "Waste time if you want. I'm gonna look for a way down."

"Feliz." Barely short of a whine.

"Let her look."

I'd take that. Frankly, I needed to get to whatever was down here first, and the more they ignored me, the better. I left the enforcers picking through whatever was left. Maybe looking for bodies, maybe looking for their asses.

I wish I'd had Indigo's eyes. I'd settle for half his brain. Instead, I was stuck with me – my gut, my fractured memories, and the limits of my own brain. Which preferred blowing up walls instead of looking for doors, and fighting assholes instead of working through jolted chipset feedback.

Turns out Channing's crack had done more than just blow the front wall.

The back wall of the joint had warped under the pressure, leaving canyons of exposed steel. I tapped on one swath of dusty metal. Large flakes of plaster dropped like turds to the mess at my feet.

I hooked my Sauger back in its place on my harness, studied the surface.

"This is weird," Channing said. I glanced over my shoulder. They still sifted through debris. Still looking for remains in the blackened hunks of twisted steel buried in it all. "It's like nobody was here."

"Automated, maybe." A thoughtful appraisal from the coordinator. "These look like turrets."

Which would explain the fearless shooting.

I didn't honestly care. Turning my attention back to the wall, I shook out my left arm lightly, took three steps to the side. Right… about…

*Here.*

Pulling back my arm, I aimed for the spot where the plaster and brick had fractured in a near-perfect vertical line. The enforcers didn't notice. They sure as shit did when I drove my diamond steel fist so hard into the wall that it shrieked like rusted brakes on a spiked rail. The remnant of the clinging façade exploded outward in a new shower of debris, and every one of the mooks behind me shouted, cursed, shrieked – heh, Damrosch.

"What the fuck are you–"

I cut Lindsay off. "There's your door."

"The fuck that–"

"Shut up, Lindsay." Feliz walked forward with more purpose than I credited her, passed me without a word, and tore down a hanging hunk of filthy plaster.

"No shit," Channing murmured.

I grinned fiercely. Goddamn, punching that had felt good.

I'd regret it later, once the adrenaline wore off. The drugs already had.

Feliz touched the door with a gloved hand. A circle of projected light spread out from her fingers, rotating as she did her coordinator thing. Fancier than Indigo's, but that didn't mean as good. Unless it was, and I had new anti-sec measures to tell him about.

He'd have to do the research. The anti-sec protocols in my netware weren't made for anything harder than your average cyberlock.

After a silent moment, Feliz drew her hand back. "It's not locked," she said slowly. "No security at all."

"In the whole thing?"

She shrugged at me. "Anything below has a closed system I can't access from anywhere else. We'll find out."

"Sweet," I replied, pulling my borrowed Sauger back out. "Time to–"

"–get in goddamn line," Feliz cut in. "Channing, you're up with me. Banh and Lindsay at the tail end."

Which left me with shortmunch. And our coordinator in the lead. Fanfuckingtastic.

"Fine," I said, so very, very sweet. "But if Lindsay puts a bullet in my back, I'm going to give his corpse to the 'philias at Sodomy Morgue."

"Gross."

"Don't kinkshame," I said blithely. It wasn't the morgue's official name, but that didn't mean the moniker wasn't earned. Most of us avoided the place. Tried extra hard not to die in range, too. It was that bad.

I propped my left hand against the door. With effort, I braced my weight and shoved it slowly open. It did not creak. A good sign. "We still rolling out bitches first?"

I didn't have to see Feliz's face to get her annoyance loud and clear. "Shut up."

"Yeah." I knocked the butt of the Sauger against my shoulder. "I'll get *right* on that."

## 17

Another elevator, another moment of tense silence. We'd gone through three already, each leading to landings with zero activity. Just enough room for a new elevator door to fit. Not a single camera to watch the space.

"This is stupid," Lindsay sighed, jerking his head to the plain surroundings. "Why so many stops?"

I had theories. Like, if there was any emergency involving, say, necrotech conversion, it'd be harder for them to crawl to the light of day.

I didn't say that. Wasn't even sure it was true, except it made sense to me. Was it possible that Malik's analysts failed to clock necro activity because it was so far buried? Even if we were looking at another, much smaller surge, it seemed unlikely that they'd find a way back to the surface. Whatever smarts the necros had before conversion, it didn't translate over. Pushing an elevator button? Maybe by accident.

To their credit, the team snapped to readiness the moment the platform stopped moving. Six barrels came up at the same time, covering the wide corridor the doors opened on.

A nanosecond of silence before I ruined it. "Gosh," I said in breathy wonder. "That synch was just beautiful, guys."

"Go get dead," Banh snarled. "And give it a *rest*."

I didn't get the chance to retort as she brushed past me hard enough to knock my Sauger aside, boots stomping on the bare floor. I grinned at her back instead. "Well, fuck me, *someone* hasn't had her rice today."

She stopped. Didn't turn. "You're the SINless here."

"Guys," Feliz said firmly.

We ignored her. "So?" I scoffed.

"So there's nothing to stop me from carving the number four in your heart."

"Double death to make a bitch," I shot back. "Guess who'd win."

Banh came from ghost-side Kongtown; her slang marked her Cantonese heritage. Four sounded a lot like canto for death, eight for bitch.

Feliz snapped. "Enough!" She threw a hand between us. "Next asshole to open their mouths gets served."

With what, I didn't ask. Probably a write-up to Mr Reed. *Pfft.*

Lindsay, made braver by her temper, clipped my right arm as he pushed past.

I *could* have punched the back of his helmet, but that would probably net me a time out. I needed to get into this place. Fucking with my team wasn't doing me any favors.

Instead, I took a deep breath and fell silent, sliding my ass into line with the rest of the good little mooks. Beside me, Damrosch gave me a double-fingered salute. Fierce kitty. I tucked my gloved index finger between hers, rubbed her silent insult suggestively.

She snatched her hand away, faceplate jerking right back around to face front. With monumental effort, I refrained from laughing.

We proceeded in formation – only one direction to go.

Once the edge of Feliz's threat wore off, Channing broke the silence. "I hate how eerie it is," he grumbled. "There should be alarms or something."

"At least resistance."

"At least," Banh added tersely, "some kind of branding somewhere. Looks corporate to me."

MetaCorp, to be clear. Malik hadn't told them that. Need to know, huh? I shook my head.

I watched Feliz's helmet dip as she checked her links frequently. "Readings are hard enough to get down here."

"Think it's an ambush?"

Of corp-sec thugs? Eh. I'd seen worse. I'd *felt* worse. This didn't have the same intensity as the Vid Zone's festering mausoleum. Empty, yes. Hollow, absolutely. Channing had used a good word. *Eerie*. But somehow… harmless.

Biting my tongue, I followed Channing and Feliz to the end of the hall, stepped to one side to cover them as the coordinator studied the new entry. I wrinkled my nose as she prepped her anti-sec scan. "Don't bother," I said. "It's unlocked."

"You couldn't possibly–"

Channing slapped the keypad. The doors unsealed. "It's unlocked," he repeated, surprised. More empty hall, a short one that led to a wider space.

"Like magic," I muttered.

Feliz peered at me over her shoulder. "How did you know?"

I shrugged. "Seems the pattern."

Lindsay nudged me in the back of the knee with his boot. "Or," he said with more intensity than the moment required, "you've been here before."

My snort was all I'd give him. Frankly, I didn't know

how I'd known that. But the fact remained that the place, aside from protective turrets, had been abandoned. Why lock an empty lab?

My head hurt. I caught myself tapping at the side of my helmet more than I wanted to admit. It didn't help.

"Let's go," Feliz said, and once more picked up the pace. This time, we moved quickly, each covering our respective quadrants. "It could be a trap, so eyes open."

Lindsay muttered to himself. Not so quietly that we couldn't all hear it. "What I'm saying."

"Not exactly the brains of the op, is he?" I asked.

Nobody said a word. Which made me wonder if they'd taken him seriously.

For fuck's sake.

Feliz held up a fist – universal sign for stop. We paused, surveying what little we could see of the area. Wall on the left leading some eight meters in. Straight shot into the unknown. "Nothing on the HUD," Banh said.

"Not that they're working right," I replied.

Feliz's helmet shook back and forth. "The walls are a complex steel alloy. It seems to be causing interference on the bandwidth. We're only getting partial data."

I sneered. "I thought Mantis was supposed to be *good* at bodygear?"

Her faceplate turned. Couldn't see her expression, but read it anyway. *Shut up.* Yeah, yeah, I got it.

"Channing, point," she said, turning back. "Riko, cover him."

The man tapped his left shoulder, suggesting I flank his left side. I sighed. He rounded the corner first, Sauger at the ready.

I'd barely put a foot on the floor when the damn place erupted into chaos. Channing got the first round of bullets to the upper chest and shoulder – his right.

Thunder shattered, sparks flying every which way. His rifle's muzzle flashed, sprayed wide as he staggered. "Back!" Feliz shouted, hooking his arm and jerking him off his feet. I leapt back, joining the rest of them as they plastered themselves against the wall. "Shit," she hissed.

Channing slammed into the space beside me, pounded chest armor shredded and blood gleaming at the edges. "Shit," he repeated, gasping.

"No shit," I said, breathing hard. Nothing like a surprise fucking by bullets to amp up the adrenaline. The pissy wasps in my skull retreated.

"You OK?" Banh demanded.

"Missed his vitals," Feliz answered for him. "What did you see?"

He shook his head, shoulders rounded. "Nothing," he gasped. "No one."

"Came from the right," I added, "about eighteen meters deep."

"A trap?"

"We go slow–"

"Slow is what got us trapped outside," I interrupted.

"We go *slow*," the coordinator repeated.

Goddammit. My patience thinned out to nearly nothing. "Fucking dickless wonders," I snarled. I pushed past them all, dodged Feliz's arm and rolled out into the open space. On cue, bright flashes popped from three angles – a hail of bullets slammed into the floor around me, burned past my helmet.

Feliz whistled sharply through her teeth. "Riko, for godsake, get back here!"

Nope. Too slow. Not listening. Sprinting to the opposite end, autofire tracking my every move, I barely kept ahead of the deadly storm. Bending my knees sent my heartbeat into overdrive – the slimmest second where I slowed enough to risk my ass. Channing's larger build was an easier target than I was. I was prepared, and faster.

As I leapt up, hardcore tread on my boots planting solidly on the wall, Feliz shouted over the comms. "Take advantage of her distraction. Go, go, go!"

Fair enough.

Only thing I could grab onto was a seam carved high in the left wall. I jammed my gloved diamond steel fingers into it, barely managing to hook the tips of them into the groove. It gave me a vantage point they didn't have, moments of surveillance that gave me more info at a glance.

No fucking trace of people.

Four goddamn turrets chewed through ammo at an obscene rate, same kind as the ones outside – chunky things with heavy barrels and thick plates protecting the control. The rate they spat out armor-piercing ammo peppered the air with nonstop chaos.

The enforcers finally jumped into action, dropping to the floor to sight around the corner. Except Channing. A shower of sparks erupted over their heads. The walls dented beneath the force of each bullet, ate some and shot others back. "Watch the ricochet," Lindsay yelled.

Impossible to keep track of it. What didn't stick in the alloyed walls bounced in every direction, forcing the others to play safe.

I'd work with that.

One turret caught on to my position, turned slowly to lock on. Green lights lit up around its barrel, one by one.

"Riko, get back – Banh, seven degrees!"

Nooope.

I pushed off from the wall, rolled in midair and landed square in front of two bullet streams crossed in an X. The insanely fast rate left an open vee to stand on, but the draft caused by each registered in my HUD.

Oh, *fuck*, yes.

The turrets on each end struggled to pick targets, while the second from the left rotated slowly. Scanning. Were they remotely manned?

I ducked low, flung the Sauger out to my side and pulled the trigger. Smaller ammo than what they rocked pinged off the armor plating. Shit. No time to work it. A ring of green lights in my peripheral was all I got – barely enough time to hit the ground and roll.

Sparks exploded up from where I'd stood, metal shrieking as shrapnel flew in every direction. It scraped against my right side as I pushed up to my feet. For once, the armor soaked it. About cunting time.

*"Riko!"*

"Eat my ladycock," I yelled, sprinting once more for the wall. Trick worked once. If it worked again, either the damn things were remotely operated by dogdick stupid corpscum or they were automated.

My levels of pissed jacked up with every second.

I ran up the wall, pressure hard on my soles, squatted in to make myself as minimal a target as possible. Caught the same lip. I bent forward and thrust my momentum forward, running hard along the wall.

My legs screamed. Thigh muscles burned. The turrets didn't see me – and if dogdick stupid operators weren't the reason, I'd shoot someone on principle.

"Where the fuck is she going?" Damrosch demanded, shrill on the comms.

"To get herself killed," Lindsay snarled.

Feliz's voice crackled with impatience. "Riko, stay with the team."

*Nooooope.*

My glove sheared down to a thin layer as I sprinted across meters of siding. Vanished entirely in a wisp of smoke as the groove hit my tech fingers. An additional layer of metal grinding against metal made the cacophony worse, grated nerves and ear canals and my body right down to the bone.

Finally, a turret saw me coming.

It raised its sights, started shooting reams and reams of ammo before it locked on. Two seconds and I'd be too close to target.

Only got one.

Bullets slammed into my right hand, hit the assault rifle I carried outstretched for balance. The impact numbed my arm to my elbow, but not so much that I didn't feel my fingers snap when the momentum tore the Sauger from my grasp. I screamed bloody fucking murder as it sailed into the chaos, stumbled with it. Agony, fiery splinters shoved into every nerve of my hand and all the way up into my brain, howled.

So much for the ugly hum I fought. Between bullets and pain, I ran out of processing power for anything else.

I didn't stop. Wouldn't.

I'd seen the double doors behind the turrets. And where turrets had been set up, something juicy lay beyond.

Every thudding footstep, every flex of muscle to keep me upright and moving hurt so bad, but it didn't matter now. What was done was done; street rule number two: broken bones and bullet holes mend. Just don't get killed on the way to the win.

Wrenching my sliding fingers out of the seam, I launched off my vertical runway and sailed over the turrets.

Landing, I admit, wasn't nearly as cool as I'd hoped. I

collided with the doors, absorbed the impact on my tech arm, hip and leg. My knees knocked together so hard that I felt it through the armor, head slamming against the inside of my helmet. My damaged hand crunched, raw torture rolling tears and sweat down my face. Don't care who says otherwise, without pain dampeners – which were a stupid risk among the reckless – the flesh does what it does. Tears of pain are as regular as blood and piss.

I fell gracelessly to the floor and sucked in gasps of air through gritted teeth, body locked in a clenched spasm until I could get ahold of it.

"Holy shit," Damrosch said on the comms. "She did it."

"Get those turrets offline," Feliz ordered.

Oh, so *now* I was the hero?

Extra nope. With that bag of dicks Malik wouldn't touch, just for flavor. I'd warned him I'd do what I could to get ahead of his people. I'd played nice all the way here. Now I had the perfect excuse to keep them off my back.

I wasn't *just* being a bitch. If I let them tail me, Feliz would demand access to every bit of data and I'd have to shoot her if she found anything I needed to hide. Like any more evidence incriminating me in a series of mercenary flesh trades. Or maybe that I was somehow involved with the necro jacking of the bandwidth back in the Vid Zone.

The others wouldn't like it if I shot their coordinator.

So I'd have to shoot them too.

Which Reed wouldn't like.

Fuck it all. Saving their stupid lives was the easier option. They could thank me later.

I struggled to my feet, gave the machines a cursory

glance. The extra thick guard protecting the processors didn't cover the back end. Could circle round and rip out the targeting, but fuck it. I wasn't wasting four bullets of my six-shot Adjudicator on tech, nor did I want to risk electrocution.

Leaving the turrets to their rapid fire spray, I turned my back on the group and kicked the doors.

They slid open.

"Riko!" shouted Feliz.

"Fuck you, traitorous bitch," Lindsay yelled at the same time. I wondered if his face was red. "I'm going to jam this gun up your ass so hard, you'll wish you were never born!"

"I'll let you know what I find," I said as the doors closed behind me. "Stay in that hall and you'll be fine."

A slew of voices, curses, orders crackled through the comm. Too late for me to make sense of them. I pulled my helmet off, dropped it behind me as I studied the new hall.

Always with the halls.

Always with the metal on metal on boring.

Sighing, I lifted the Adjudicator from my harness and paced silently onward. Fortunately for me and my fuckingly bad luck of late, I could only reliably use the heavy gun in my left hand. I'd fired it once in my right, and the kickback had nearly shattered my forearm. Lesson learned. Not that I could right now.

My flesh hand burned. A trail of blood spatter left behind me meant enough blood loss that I'd need a recharge, some protein boosts, and enough alcohol to put everything else to sleep. Either that or Orchard would look at me with those sympathetic eyes again.

Just what I didn't need.

Too late to worry about it now. Between the bone

rattling landing I'd only barely achieved and the ache in the back of my head, I wasn't walking out of this one unscathed anyway. May as well add some blood to the bruises. Made for a better story. *No shit, there I was in a necro factory...*

The first door on my right was closed. No windows on either side, no signs of anything around it. I paused, metal hand tightening on my weapon. Last time I'd been in a place like this, it'd been crawling with ambulatory meatsacks torn to shreds by godknowswhat. Each other, maybe. More than one door like this had spewed murderous necros.

Sometimes, I still heard the screams as they shredded our last teammate alive. A corp kid. A rookie.

He hadn't gone pretty.

My breath shook, and I was glad I'd tossed the comm. I could feel my blood humming in my ears; stress made the throb in my head worse. So bad that my eardrums vibrated with the interference, overwhelming pain.

I closed my eyes. Took another deep breath. Let it out slow.

Adjudicator raised, I reached out and nudged the keypad with the heel of my flesh hand. That hurt, too. Everything smegging hurt. I'd deal.

The door slid open.

I braced, flinching. Which pissed me off more. I was better than this.

Especially since nothing came at me. Nothing moved in the room. Nothing even decorated it. No furniture, no lab desks, no chairs. Bare floor and bare walls, not white. Thank fuck, not white. Metal walls, unpainted, lit to a faint sheen by fluorescent lights built into the ceiling.

Something, I realized as I looked up at them, I hadn't considered.

If this place was so empty, why were the lights on? They'd all said it was empty. Greg had even logged it as up for sale. The whole area had been buried under that façade Channing had blown, and its entry hidden.

So why the lights? Default generator?

Maybe I was overthinking it. Hooking into the power grid wasn't that hard.

I proceeded down the corridor, passed doors that opened under a simple tap of the locking screens. Scoped them from the outside before continuing. Door after door, hall after hall. All empty. All lit.

My nanos eventually sealed the shredded meat ammo had made of my hand, knitted the bones I hadn't set. I'd have to re-break them to get them straight again, but I didn't have time now.

Another door slid open, this time without my triggering it. I immediately leapt to the side, gun up, shoulder blades colliding with the opposite wall. Another sharp jolt to my head had me wincing, but not nearly as bad as the guts that had sloshed up into my throat. I breathed so hard, I hurt.

At least the Adjudicator didn't shake in the unyielding grip of diamond steel. Even if the rest of me sure as shit did.

"Zen it," I whispered. "There's nothing here."

Nothing but a bank of monitors lined up along the far wall. The first ray of cancerous sunshine today. "Hello, babies." I dropped my arm, barrel pointed at the floor. No cameras mounted anywhere in sight. No turrets; lucky me. Nothing but empty floor and metal walls.

With twisted fingers, I poked at the various dashboards built into a counter beneath the digital ribbon. It didn't take me long to figure it out. I was no linker, much less one of Indigo's caliber, but I knew my way around standard stuff. The netware installed in my metal arm allowed me to bypass minor security measures, which provided my first clue that it was *my* turn to be sniffing the wrong ass.

Or in this case, assholes.

*No data found. Please try a different command.*

My lips tightened as I ran input after input. Line after line of data scrolled down the screen, most involving systemware and mechanics. No matter what I tried, large text blinked on every monitor at the end of every scroll.

*No data found. Please try a different command.*

Son of a necro *whore*.

# 18

A helmet hit the ground at my feet as I strolled back into the blistering heat. It only kind of bounced, leaving a dent in the softened asphalt. I nudged it off my boot. "Hey," I said brightly, "you made it."

Lindsay, Bahn and Feliz faced me in a semicircle, helmets off and murder in every stare. Lindsay's fists clenched and unclenched, his blue eyes spitting raw hatred. "You are the *worst*–"

I frowned at him. "If you start frothing, Lindsay, I'm putting you down."

"That is fucking *it!*" He launched himself at me with his whole body, tense as the iron rod shoved down his throat. Skill be damned. I caught him chest to chest, staggering under his weight, and took the opportunity to slam my head into his. He howled as the bridge of his nose cracked, jerked back and stumbled with his hands covering his streaming nose.

I swore upside down and sideways, holding my forehead with my crooked right hand. Don't care how badass I am, my forehead had no reinforcement. It *hurt*.

Feliz stepped in, seizing me by the collar of my armor and hauling me close enough to feel the fury burning in her eyes. "You left your team," she gritted out. I tracked

Banh circling in my peripheral, heading me off at the back. "You left us to fight through the mess instead of finishing the mission and getting Channing out."

I grabbed one of her wrists. "Is he still alive?" I demanded.

A curt nod.

"Then he did his job."

"You bitch–"

My only working set of fingers bit down on her wrist so hard that her skin paled. The pressure I cinched in wasn't enough to shatter bone, or so my optic reading assured me. Instead, as she let me go with a jerk, I stuck a leg out and yanked her arm past me like a dance gone very wrong.

She tripped on my foot, and with my help, whirled right into Banh as *she* came at me. Shouldn't have discounted Lindsay. As the women tangled together, struggling to right themselves, a hand twined into my hair. Pulled hard enough that my back bent before I could rotate into it.

That was mothercunting *twice*.

Fire crackled across my scalp as roots pulled; I spared a moment of empathy for Father Assmichael and his scruffy beard. Shortlived. I pulled an arm up, too late to brace. "Fucking bitch," Lindsay panted, and drove his fist into my face.

It hit my blocking arm, but without strength behind it, the curve of my elbow slammed into my own face. The edges of my armor gouged in to my skin. My lip split open.

"Cunting traitorous street trash!" he yelled, going for another shot.

Enough was goddamn enough.

I always carry interceptors. Knives, steels – hell, even

swords come in handy, though the short ones are easier to conceal. Only thing that made me think they weren't out to kill me was the lack of sharp things in their hands.

I wasn't as nice. They got their chance.

I snatched the serrated blade from my harness, flipped it edge out. Lindsay went for another punch, fists honed to hurt, and I slashed out and up – caught his hand and my own hair in the edge and *yanked*.

My hair pulled. Roots tore. Lindsay howled as hunks of my hair fell to the ground. Blood soaked a good portion.

I snapped upright, grabbed Lindsay's arms – his hand bled like a bitch – and used his effort to leap back. The momentum fueled the boot I rocked into Banh's chest. She staggered back, barely avoiding Feliz.

Who'd pulled out an asp.

Fanfuckingtastic.

I rotated so hard against my grip on his arms that Lindsay shouted. Elbows hyperextended. One shoulder popped out, obvious even beneath his armor. That hit a high note of raw pain muffled when my forehead slammed *again* into his face. Blood spattered mine. Bone dug into the ridge of my eyebrow.

More blood, this time dripping into my eye.

Rage fueled every nerve, lit my senses with napalm and gasoline. The pressure in my ears whined under the thundering roar of my aggression, but I didn't care. Didn't stop to think about it, to analyze. What mattered was that somebody, everybody, died.

The word popped out of nowhere: *eradicate*.

With fucking *pleasure*.

Lindsay landed back on his ass, hands plastered over his face, blood welling between his fingers. Verbally losing his shit into his palms wouldn't save him. Only a miracle could.

I ducked as a leg sailed over my head, dropped to a knee and jammed my metal elbow back into Banh's thigh. Femurs are hard to break. I managed it, felt every splintered snap of it radiate into my shoulder. She shrieked, swearing upside down and too fast in canto I couldn't follow.

It left me exposed to Feliz's silent assault.

The baton whipped into the side of my neck, a halo of red and white pain exploding in my sight. Cold sweat erupted from stinging scalp to booted toes. For a strained moment, I couldn't breathe. Couldn't hear anything but the shattered pulse of a hammered artery struggling to keep up; fury carved in stinging wasps.

Sheer muscle memory kicked in. I dropped, rolled, kipped up to my feet and blocked the next attack with nanosteel. The asp was already up and swinging again. She was fast. Hell, she was *fuckingly* fast. Steel in her expression, she sidestepped me and drove the weighted baton into my side. My knee. This stuff I wore wasn't geared for this.

Torture radiated from each spot. Rippled out and met somewhere in the middle. Gasping for breath, I set my jaw. "You are," I said between gritted teeth, "overfuckingreacting!"

"*That*," Feliz panted, still managing cold as ice despite the quick pace of her assault, "is why you will *never* amount to anything but guttertrash."

Fine. Bracing myself, I sidestepped and threw myself at her. She hadn't expected me to risk the barrage of pain she'd already leveled. Clearly, she hadn't watched me with those turrets.

A baton to the side of the head is nobody's idea of a good time. Only thing that kept me from screaming was

the fact I'd surprised her. She tagged me with the middle
of the length, lashed out again and hit my left shoulder.
At least that part didn't feel anything. Mostly.

Soon as I stopped swearing, I'd feel the shit out of this.

For now, I surfed adrenaline like the drug it was
and launched myself to her left side. I hooked an arm
around the back of her neck, rocked my knees forward
and carried her full force to the ground. By the time she
caught herself, I'd already clambered around her back,
wrapped my legs around her waist, locked my ankles, and
squeezed hard enough to drive the air out of her lungs.

My diamond steel fist drove into the back of her head.
Her head snapped forward, hit the ground. Flesh grated,
blood ran. My right fist wasn't in the best shape, and I
screamed with her as I followed up with another punch
from it. Didn't stop me. Adjusting my knees on her
biceps, I pinned her in place and delivered heavy punch
after agonizing punch after metal punch. Until her face
was a bloody, sticky mess against the tarred street and
bone shone yellow and red through her flesh and she'd
stopped screaming.

I didn't notice when the extraction team arrived.
Burly arms thrust under my armpits, locked behind my
neck and dragged me spitting and swearing off Feliz.
Banh was already being carried out, her leg held out and
knee sidewise.

Lindsay's face was a shockvid in progress, disinfectant
wash turning his mask of blood into a horror show.

Didn't see Channing or Damrosch. Didn't fucking care.

Malik Reed owed me big. Shitty team, shitty intel.
Shitty fucking contract.

I was so far over fed up, I longed for the days I wanted
to tear out his throat. So, so much nicer than what I
wanted to do now.

# 19

A holding cell. They'd put me in a shitsucking padded cell, white on white on white – which made no sense because by the time I was done, I'd punched the door bloody. I barely had room to measure the fucking thing in three strides. Punched *that* wall, too.

They hadn't counted on metal shredding whatever cunting *fluff* covered the scratchproof walls underneath. Or on my anger overwhelming any sense of pain or ugly I should have been wading through.

Hell if I even knew where I was. All I knew was that I'd savaged the white until I was no longer screaming curses and threats at the cameras. Until I could breathe through panic cut with a hunger for blood so intense that I swore to every lens watching that I'd rip the intestines out of whoever came through that door. And eat them. For funsies.

I ran out of epithets long before I ran out of steam, and by the time I'd thoroughly wrecked the insultingly spartan prison, I ran out of that, too. I stood quietly in the center of the room, bloody hands hanging at my sides, face tilted up to the ceiling. Closing my eyes gave me only shadows.

Capturing any kind of zen felt impossible.

They hadn't even let me change. I'd shed the armor pieces all over the floor. My skinsuit, shiny black and formfitting, kept me from soaking in the icy air. Like they blew it in on purpose to either cool me down or make me uncomfortable.

All it did was piss me right the shit off.

What was the problem? I'd been sent in with a team that did its job – got me a path inside. I'd scoped it out. Came back with the data.

Or to be precise, zero data. Just a whole fucking bunch of automated systems programmed to lay down hell at anything that moved. No data in the banks. No nothing. Just machines and a fucking hum in my head that told me I should've found something else. *Anything* else.

Instead, I'd snapped. Even as I stood in the cold room and breathed in real slow, I recognized I'd lost my shit.

Wasn't the first time. I'd have to start considering that I was far more fucked up than I let on. And worse, that everybody else knew that. Reed had once warned that brains were untrustworthy – that like any computer, they could be hacked.

It wasn't that I doubted that kind of skill, it's that shit like that is beyond the realms of norm. It'd take some serious, *serious* power and credits and time and *skill* to pull it off.

So I couldn't remember four months of my time. Three months of which, according to Digo, I'd been wandering around sounding and looking normal. That left a month missing in that lab.

Not even close to enough time. Hell, biotech took longer – you don't just regrow a limb over the course of a few months. Brainmeats? That took far longer.

So here I was. Back at cunting square one with nothing to show for it. No intel, no leads on whatever spunkdumpster had decided to expose my shit. No idea if Indigo or Reed had betrayed me; no idea what I'd do if they had.

How was I supposed to press on *now?*

A muffled thump at the door had me opening my eyes. I tilted my head to glare as it slid open; the kind that pulled out and to the side.

Malik braved his intestines first, cool as ice and unruffled in his gray suit. Or so he'd like everyone to think. I saw different. Honed in on it. The corners of his mouth pinched, eyelids tight. If his cheekbones got any sharper, he'd cut himself in the mirror. A glance at the mess I'd made only squared his jaw into barely contained fury. Hell, I could practically feel the heat in his eyes burn the cold away.

Well, at least I had that going for me.

He threw my clothes at my feet. "You," he said flatly, "are out of your mind."

"Sort of the problem, isn't it?" I replied, neither facing him nor picking up my clothes. I just kept him in my sidelong periphery, head tilted back. "I mean, it's not like your worthless bank of shitsuckers are helping in any way."

He waited me out, black lashes a thick, narrowed ream around glittering eyes. When I fell silent, he clasped his hands behind his back – all patient businessman, but for the lie it was – and looked pointedly at my hands. "Look at yourself," he said, just this side of a sneer. "You've got the blood of *allies* on your hands, Riko. Blood on your face. That wasn't MetaCorp or Mantis or OGEnterprises you tore apart, those were allies."

My gaze returned to the ceiling. "And?"

A sharply razored silence. Then, shiny black shoes tapping gently, he circled around to look me in the face. I gave him that one. If only to meet his eyes with the utter apathy I felt for him seeping out of every single pore.

Not that he seemed to care. "You're not thinking," he said flatly. "And the more you don't think, the less you get."

"Not," I returned in flat mimicry of his tone, "that I'm getting anything anyway."

"What did you find?"

"Your munches didn't tell you?"

A tic at his jaw. A single beat at his temple. "You did not tell them."

"Oh." *Eat me*. "Silly me."

He stared at me.

I stared back.

When it stretched near to snapping, I gave him what he wanted. Deliberately, so he knew I'd made the choice myself. "The place was fully automated, with turrets set up for maximum carnage. Only bank of computers left had nothing but defense protocols. In short, *Malik*, your people netted me a whole lot of nothing. *Again*."

An eyebrow rose. "You didn't wait for Feliz to get in there?"

"Why?" I scoffed. "So she could look at nothing, too?"

He took a slow, deep breath. Wide nostrils flaring. Let it out just as slow. I could smell the smoke on his breath. I hadn't noticed it before. Something spicier than nicotine and tar.

I blinked. "Hold on," I said, throwing up a bloody hand between us. "Hold on a fucking second." I stared at him. Hard enough to make that second eyebrow join the first. "Do you smoke *cloves*? Is that even a thing anymore? Does your wife know you spend a fortune on greenhouse habits?"

Possibly I couldn't push him further. I'd never seen

him look so laser-focused fury. For the first time, I braced. Not for his usual authoritative attitude, not for his random bouts of amusement, but for something uglier. Something that crawled under that freckled mask and promised shades of murder I didn't think he had in him.

Executive assholes don't get to where they are by playing pretty.

And if he laid one finger on me, I'd break every bone in his body and rub my asshole raw on the rest of him.

Did he sense it in kind? Do sharks recognize other predators? I had no idea. He didn't touch me, and that was enough of a victory for me.

Besides, my fingers were really starting to hurt. They weren't supposed to splay in the directions they did, and until I reset those bones, the tendons would keep stretching. I curled a lip at him. "Let me know when you have something worthwhile."

"You think it's that easy?"

"We made a deal–"

And there it was. The moment I thought I'd won. He snapped out a hand so fast, I blinked and missed it. He had a hold of the front of my skinsuit in one large fist, dragged me to the tip of my toes until I was nose to nose and eye to enraged eye. "You," he growled, "are losing any credibility you gained here. Don't. Push. It."

Losing? Like *any* of this was my fault. My curled lip turned into full-on teeth, violence screaming my head down. "Fuck you," I snarled back. I grabbed the front of his stupid suit, shearing raw agony through my malformed fingers. Aggression to raw aggression. *"You're* the asshole who offered this gig, *you're* the guy who runs a bunch of chuckleheads for analysts. Your teams have dropped ball after ball, and I–"

"Have proven over and over that you're not trustworthy," he cut in, furious enough that my eyes widened. Hard enough that for a fleeting moment, I was glad he didn't run the streets. Relieved I wouldn't have to face him on sainted terms.

He'd given me pause.

And for that, I punched him in the perfect face.

With my metal fucking fist.

Kaboom goes the shitsuit.

He didn't even see it coming; why the fuck would he? I'd played by his rules. Now he played by mine. My arm vibrated with the impact, forced him into a spin. His grasp loosened enough that I tore free and landed in a crouch then immediately stepped up to a fighting stance he'd never mistake for play. Fists ready, I stared him down when he straightened. Blood dribbled from his mouth, upper lip split deep enough to turn his top right teeth into a gory peepshow.

Cracked one. Served him right.

Raising the back of his hand to his mouth, he blotted at it without looking away from my eyes. Turned his head just enough to spit half a tooth and blood to the once-white floor, adding his mess to mine.

Fuck him. He made his own mess, throwing me in here.

"That," he said in deep, rasping tones I'd never mistake for anything but blind fucking savagery, "was your freebie."

My back heel turned. Just enough to brace, to test that ultimatum. But before I could do anything, the door slammed open. Armed goons in tactical gear filed in at a pace that wouldn't leave room for maneuvering between steel batons.

Two came at me right off the bat.

I pivoted on that same foot, sinking down into a low stance.

"Stop."

Another deep-throated demand. The diamond steel in Malik Reed's voice defied natural ability, and he wielded it with surgical precision. The two sec-goons froze, immediately easing into readiness I hadn't expected from mere security.

Well. At least that was better than anything his analysis department could come up with.

I straightened slowly, keeping the guards in my sights as I bent to pick up my clothes. My smile was no less bloody than Malik's grimace. I gifted him with it. "See you around, Malik."

"Go home," he said flatly. If his lip hurt, if his teeth ached in the cold seeping through the tear, I couldn't tell. "Cool off. We'll try this again when you feel like acting like an adult."

Yeah. Right. I had nothing to say to that. It killed me to let him have the last word. An order, no less. But I was just angry enough – tired, scared, strung out – that I couldn't push it.

The guards shifted aside to let me pass. More waited in the hall, Manticores held loosely. Nobody else passed me as I made my way out. Every muscle taut, I forced nonchalance I didn't feel. Step by step. Exit sign by exit sign.

I ended up in the lobby of the Mantis offices, stumbling through a door I'd never used before. The light pierced my skull with shattering precision. I forced myself to step into it, barely avoiding Hope's inquiry. It softened into a worried, sympathetic stare. Like she wanted to help. She watched me take those steps, clothes clenched in my twisted fist, and said nothing.

Neither did I.

Nothing for nothing, huh?

I felt her gaze drilling into my back as I stepped into the elevator. It closed on that silence and gave no fucking relief.

I'd earned nothing here but the satisfaction of punching Malik Reed. Nothing but the risk of tying my name to Mantis Industries. No answers, no help, no quarter given.

And as it turns out, decking Reed in the face wasn't as satisfying as I'd expected it to be.

# 20

My secret hideout wasn't all that removed from the usual shitty places. Busy enough that nobody paid attention to anybody else, removed enough that I'd be unlikely to run into familiar faces. The area wasn't in my usual turf, and the city is too big to know everyone everywhere.

I wasn't the only saint to duck into the area, either, and I doubt I was the only one who avoided doing it during normal hours. Fortunately for me, there were multiple ways in and even more ways out. Meant I could get my face off the grid for as long as I wanted to. Runners have avoidance down to a science.

There are places scattered between zones, technically part of the districts they're in but also oddly distinct, that are little but rows and rows and rows of narrow tenements. Townhouses, I guess, but stacked up like a crooked puzzle game meant for a six year-old on the impatient end of the scale. Ads are slightly fewer, but litter is higher.

Aside from the extra security I'd tacked on – my usuals: toxic capsules launched when my hand didn't hit the imprint, wires set to blow – the single door had deadbolts and more from top to bottom. Wouldn't stop a rocket launcher, or even some battering ram heavies, but I banked on the *secret* part to help with that.

Dragging my sticky, gritty, sorry ass into the place took far, far more effort than I wanted to expend. I'd barely even made it into the district when I'd all but collapsed under my own weight. With adrenaline worn down and every nerve screaming for relief, I trudged my way through blistering heat and crackling fury in the slim hope of some shuteye.

For once, I wanted to rest. *Needed* to rest.

I couldn't risk tackling anything else without pushing my nanos beyond what I'd already demanded from them. I still had to straighten my fingers. Still needed a recharge.

And a shower.

And a real bed.

And...

And instead of all of that, I stepped into my narrow entry, let the door slam behind me, and landed face first on the scuffed floor. The impact barely even registered under everything else. It was all I could do to breathe, taking in the cool tiles against my sweaty, bloody skin and the freedom of being off my feet.

Regurgitating the past twenty-four hours was *not* on my to-do list.

The failed source on MetaCorp, Incorporated – a setup by the cunting Good Shepherds. Indigo's refusal to include me on any runs, unwilling to recommend me to anyone else. Muerte's news. Shit, Muerte even showing up.

This last stupid job with the crowning shits of all shitty teams.

And nothing. Nothing, nothing, *nothing*. Just a bunch of punching assholes and getting my ass shot at, my info put on the market and–

"Gritfucking ratsucking motherfucking…" I was running out of ways to express myself. Giving up, I finished with a snarled, *Fuckheads.*"

Didn't help. Nothing short of killing every single smeglicker on my case would. And maybe a drink.

I forced myself to my elbows. Or elbow, as the seam at my shoulder pushed too hard into reinforced cartilage set around it. It crunched in ways that resounded in my gray matter. Smegging technical meatbaggery.

Clenching my teeth, I dragged my knees up. Struggled to shove my weight upright, cradling my metal arm with the crook of my other. My busted fingers faced the wrong direction, grotesque in every way.

I grimaced.

Booze first. I had to have some buried somewhere. Bracing my good shoulder against the wall for support, I locked my thigh muscles and managed a semblance of upright. My boots thudded heavily, an uneven process as I made my way through the small space.

Didn't have much. A few bits of furniture Hope had insisted I get – not that she'd know if I did. A bed; my first in a long time. Some cabinets. A cheap replicator for the clothes I printed up on the regular. No kitchen. Not a lot of these places had one. Most eat out at one of any trillion foodbelts.

"Finally," I muttered, spotting a few bottles discarded haphazardly by the bed. I staggered to them, relieved to find two held enough booze to start the process, and the third was almost full.

Tequila. The shit that runs like sewage.

And causes shit to run like sewage.

It couldn't possibly get any worse than that. I downed the first two and half the third before I shoved the first joint of my index finger into a dresser drawer and closed it hard enough to catch bone. The dresser held my backup weaponry. Made it heavy enough to do this.

With a sharp jerk, and a ragged run of swear words I made up on the spot, the entire finger snapped into place.

I did it three more times.

Then again over all four at the same time, where the last joints met the palm.

Finished the third bottle of tequila so fast, I hit empty before my nanos had finished clusterfucking the first finger.

Cold sweat congealed amid dried blood and worse, sending tremors up my spine and down into my arm. My fucking stupid hammerhumping piece of shit nanofactoried diamond steel arm that still hadn't. Cunting realized. It. Was. *Gone.*

"Screw," I said on a hard inhale, *"all of you."*

And now, if nobody minded, I was going to take a godforsaken shower. Radiation set to sandblaster.

I didn't want to get blood all over this bed.

# 21

Maybe I'd stayed too long in the radiation blast. I was still vibrating in place, my skin seared nearly raw. The ends left of my bleached hair had melted, leaving gooey strings all over the standup cubicle.

With the razor in my hand droning loudly and a half-empty bottle in the other, I stared into the spotted mirror and carved off the last quarter of my hair. It piled to the spotted floor, faded white edged with a dark coffee brown.

Wasn't sorry. Didn't care one way or another. I had no real attachment to my hair. Long or short, white or brown or black or blue or any shade I wanted, it didn't matter. With my height, whipcord body, intense hazel eyes and the aggressive bone structure under my mexi-anglo complexion, I knew I strutted it in every way but *cute*. I was beyond fine with that.

The buzzed remains of my dark hair would be cooler, and most of all, wouldn't offer any more opportunistic cunts the temptation of a handhold. I'd had enough of that one.

I dropped the razor, took a swig of bad tequila. Bracing my right hand on the counter, I let my head sink down, chin to chest. The razor still thrummed, left rattling on the aluminum surface.

Tired. *So* tired. So very frustrated. No Indigo. No team. No useful intel from the Battery location and no information on Knacklock's Kern or his people. No clues who leaked the video, and unhappy with the part of me who believed what Malik had said.

I was waiting on Indigo to track Hevin Kern, waiting on Muerte to lock down the fuckhole who'd targeted me. Waiting on Malik to pull his little lace panties up and deal with his shit.

As for Lucky…

I wasn't ready to tackle that one yet. I didn't know how, if I should. Didn't know if I was overreacting, either. I'd spent ten friggin' years building my cred out of Lucky's shadow, grateful for his education and respectful of his part in it. I'd come into my own, and he'd treated me like a real merc – blooded and proven.

Now I couldn't tell what was mine and what was his push behind the scenes.

I felt like it shouldn't bother me. So why did my throat squeeze when I thought about it?

No, no, no and no. All no, all the time. I ran it through my head over and over.

Going on the aggressive was only getting me screwed. I raised the bottle to my mouth. The smell of the stuff seared my nose hair, helping to distract me.

"Goddamn, your ass only gets better." A husky compliment edged with gravel, familiar and *right fucking behind me.*

I dropped the bottle, whirled around. The glass hit the counter and miraculously stayed upright. The bathroom spun. I had to brace myself against the steel edge to get the room to un-tilt. "Pissing hell!"

Muerte grinned, a somewhat blurry crescent of white

over vivid purple. I squeezed my eyes into a narrowed attempt at clarity. "Keslake, bebe. Your door was unlocked." She eased in to lean against the door frame, thumbs in her front pockets.

"The hell it was."

She shrugged, cropped violet jacket glittering. "Figured I should check on you."

"Yeah, fuck y–" I froze. Way too late. "*Muerte*," I said dumbly. "How are you here?" Not even Hope knew where I'd shacked up; I'd ignored all her offers and demanded cred in hand to pay for it. Boarding was part of the deal, but that didn't mean it had to be Reed's business.

Off the grid meant *off the grid*.

Half the booze haze vanished in a wash of adrenaline so vicious, I flinched. Fear spiked a second behind. "Shit," I hissed. Then, at her, "I'm blown, aren't I?"

Her gaze trailed leisurely down my naked body, newly shorn hair to muscle to the dragon curving at my side, hip and along my right thigh. "Play your cards right?"

I took one step forward, right fist clenched.

She raised both hands, warding off my venom. And another punch that wouldn't get us anywhere. "Not yet, Riqa. But it's going to be real close."

I sank to the floor. My spine rattled against the counter edge. My head rebounded off the same lip when I landed. Didn't even feel it. Ass cold on the floor, feet planted, I rested my forearms on my knees, hands limp, senses dragging.

Closing my eyes, my head fell back. *Thump*. "How bad?" I asked wearily.

"Just bad enough that *I* figured out how to find you from the network," she replied. Her voice came from a lower position; she'd crouched. "But then, I've learned to recognize the pendejo's patterns. I doubt anybody else is savvy to it yet."

I cracked open an eye. Yup, she'd crouched, weight balanced easily. Her hands clasped loosely, gloveless. *D-E-T-H* in brilliant red highlighted her left hand, each finger lettered above the knuckle.

She'd had that forever. Punched me when I pointed out she should have gotten a sixth finger for the *A*, just to be a dick. Our first fight. Hardly our last, but every time I saw those letters, I fought the urge to comment again.

"Here." She pulled a recharge from her belt, handed it to me. "You look like shit streaked on shit street."

"I know," I muttered. But I took the squeezable plastic, surprised at her thoughtful gesture. Smart runners carry recharges often, and there was usually a slot in our custom harnesses, belts, and bags for them to hook in. The muted green sludge – sometimes blackish purple, depending on the origin – had enough kick to keep our nanos from overcompensating when pushed; a kind of technological energy drink. Only less like piss and more like the bathroom at the tequila bar.

I hadn't intended to go so long without. Then again, I wasn't always as smart as I should be.

Downing this meant I wouldn't have to worry about the stress I'd put my body through already. A kindness, sure, but also practical as hell. I cracked the seal and tucked the capped straw between my teeth. "Gracias," I said around it.

No acknowledgment. Queen of goddamn avoidance. "You need a plan," she said instead.

"Yeah, no kidding." I dug thumb and forefinger into my eye sockets as I sucked up the sludge, trying to push the fear away. I didn't like fear. Fear meant I was unprepared, and that only made me angry.

Lucky's rule number one was getting put to the test here. Survive no matter what? It'd be touch and go for a while if the syphilitic diarrhea hit the fan. Up and comers I could handle.

Someone with enough juice on the line to locate my place?

That pissed me off even more.

I sucked hard at the recharge, swallowed a mouthful of it and clambered to my bare feet. I passed Muerte as she rose.

She followed me out. "And that plan is…?"

"Kill everyone."

Her chuckle snorted through her nose. "Plan for that plan?"

This time, I pulled the plastic away from my mouth and smirked over my shoulder. Caught her staring at my back. "Take a picture and I murder you."

She laughed, grating and loud. As ever. "No need, nena, I've got you locked in my memory banks forever."

"Flirt."

"Whore."

"I'm not your girlfriend."

"Your loss."

My smirk widened before fading out entirely. "Plan for the plan," I mused out loud. I booted up the printer, propped a naked hip on the counter it occupied. Drank some more. I could practically feel the little fuckers' feeding frenzy. I'd pushed it today. Again. Always.

I only had a few items in the printer's database, but I didn't need much more. Printing them up wouldn't take long. "I need to find Indigo."

"Yeah?" Muerte tucked her hands behind her, leaning next to the door frame. One boot braced against the wall.

"I probably know more than he does."

I shook my head. The printer beeped loudly, and I turned my attention briefly to the screen. Black cargoes, a lot of pockets for a lot of toys. Gray tank, loose enough to compensate for the breeze without getting in my way – I dialed up a skull print on the material for fun. Purple underneath, shitkicker boots I'd managed not to completely trash today, and a replacement for the harness I'd left behind at Mantis. Nice and casual.

As the device kicked in, I gave my attention back to my unwelcome guest. "I'd wondered if Indigo had leaked that vid," I said, "but even he doesn't know where my shack is. Whoever found me, he didn't do it through any sources he'd have access to."

"Koupra couldn't have followed you?"

I shook my head, grimly amused. "I haven't been back here in weeks." I didn't come here enough to have risked that much.

She let out a relieved breath that puzzled me. I tilted my head, eyebrows raised. "I'm glad to hear that," she admitted. "I was hoping I'd be able to lean on you."

Ah ha. The favor. I closed my teeth around the straw. "Uh huh."

"Favor for a favor."

"I get that."

Muerte nodded. "You know what's going down. You're prepped." I nodded. "So now I want an introduction to Indigo Koupra."

That stunned me into wordless silence. Then, eyebrows wrinkling, I asked, "Why don't you already know him?"

"He's got standards."

"You don't meet them?"

"Let's just say he's got a grudge."

"For the Squad?"

She shrugged. Guilty as charged. I hadn't known that.

"I want a run with him," she added.

"That…" My face screwed up in dismay. "That's not as easy. Why do you want it?"

"Because his cred is muy bueno and I want his business. Like Citywide Bank of Koupra," she replied seriously. "He's remarkably good at what he does, or so word says."

"I'll see what I can do once we find him. But, Muerte, I'm not exactly on his good side right now."

"Yeah." She nodded back. "I know. I'm also prepped for the letdown if he won't meet with you."

"Ouch," I muttered. "Don't jinx me. I can use all the help I can get right now."

"You're right." She made a symbol with both hands I didn't understand. "You are unjinxed."

I eyed her, took the last, long pull from the recharge pack. It crumpled. Then, swallowing, I threw it over my shoulder and asked blandly, "Have I told you to fuck yourself yet?"

"You have something in your teeth."

I gave her the same two-fingered insult the little shortmunch enforcer had given me. She smirked.

I got dressed fast, pulling the boots on last and kicking them into place on my feet.

Once in place, I stomped all the way to the tiny bedroom; she kept on my heels. Easing my arm through the harness didn't hurt as much as I'd expected. Tequila. Miracle drug of choice.

"First thing," I said, crouching in front of my dresser. "We need to find him."

"Call him?"

"Can't. Haven't gotten my protocols fixed yet."

"Ai." Muerte leaned against the dresser, looking down at me with a hand on her hip. "What about the Mecca?"

"Too early."

"Koupra's place?"

I shot her a grim little smile as the drawer I yanked out rattled. Loudly. "You think he's stupid enough to let anyone know where that is?"

"Not like *you* did on purpose."

"Not like he's stupid enough to let it out by accident, either."

"You said it," she chuckled, "not me." She rose on tiptoe, peering over my shoulder. Whistled at my stash. "You don't play around."

"Sure I do." I grunted as I lifted the trophy in my collection. The Valiant 14, my pride and joy. I didn't take it out as much anymore, not since I'd lost my first one, but I'd fondle it anyway. Maybe let Jad fondle it one day.

I tossed it on the bed, added extra clips beside it. Three interceptors, a smaller butterfly, two medium pistols – both Phelps & Somers 4884 Cougars. Clean firearm, easy to holster, with 11mm caseless rounds and a shocking rate of fire for its size. I generally didn't like them as much as my skull-splitting ammo, but didn't have much choice.

The Adjudicator had been taken by Reed's people. I'd fix that later.

"Not to make a bad day worse," Muerte said as I strapped my gear on, "but where *will* you go to get fixed?"

A good question. Rolling back in to Mantis and the lab there wasn't an option.

I didn't have to trawl around to know that any reputable chopshop wouldn't touch me. Especially now that everybody else knew Lucky had tossed me.

That left any number of lowcred chopshops, butchers with less talent than raw luck. I'd never had to go there, never had to risk it.

Because I'd had Lucky.

It always came back to Lucky.

I rubbed at my scalp, newly buzzed hair spiky against my clean palm. "I've got one option," I said slowly. I slipped one of the interceptors into the base of my harness, one in a sheath tucked into my boot.

The third clipped into a pocket, all but invisible in my baggy black fatigues.

"And that is?"

I slotted the butterfly into my arm, thumbing open the space I'd had built in to the diamond steel and releasing its mechanical catch. The clips for my Valiant wouldn't fit, but extra ammo for the smaller weaponry would.

Muerte watched all this with bemused amusement. We were no stranger to street warfare. "Avanza, already. What's the fix?"

"Lucky."

Muerte grabbed hold of my shoulder, spinning me around with serious concern harshing her smile. "Riko, that's not how it works."

I disengaged, but without heat. "I know," I said. I gestured with my free hand, a flail at nothing. "I know! But I don't have anywhere else to go."

Muerte muttered something I didn't catch, then added, "I want to reassure you, bebe, but I can't."

"*I know*," I repeated. I bent to collect the Valiant, pulled the strap crosswise over my shoulder. "Don't think I'm not aware. But as hard as Lucky is, as shitkicking stubborn, I'm counting on years of investment to keep my skin where it is."

"It's a fucking big risk."

"It's a fucking big problem." I waved her back into the hall. "We're going to Kongtown."

# 22

Muerte waited as I set my security in place. The doors locked automatically behind me. Which meant she'd jimmied them.

Which then meant I glared at her hard enough to make my eye sockets burn.

She shrugged, her version of innocence. Swiping her bangs out of her eyes, she pointed at her ride – a three-wheeled Hiki Cobalt with, I'd bet, bullet and shatterproof glass and no shortage of reinforcing. It'd seat two. Lucky me, I got to ride in back.

I mulled the plan as we crossed the cement to the trike. I didn't know if Lucky would actually shoot me. He might. Whatever I told Muerte, he'd never bent on his views. He'd told me to come back when I pulled my cred out of the shitter.

Instead, I was going back with my cred gone worse and a favor to ask.

By the time I climbed inside the Cobalt, I couldn't decide if I was going to shit my pants or pray. I needed Lucky. I needed him to come through. And if he zenned it long enough, he'd see my problem as something other than my own.

Besides, he owed me. I hadn't figured out just how

yet, but it was long past time for a heart to heart. Or a growl to growl. Or something.

I fastened the seatbelt as Muerte adjusted the seat. Wasn't going to risk that, either. Intelligent saints buckle up. The estimated amount of brains that get splatted on the interior of closed vehicles is legendary – especially among saints. You just never know when somebody's going to try to kill you, vehicle to vehicle.

Or rocket launcher to vehicle.

Bomb to vehicle.

Heavy to vehicle.

Like I said, legendary.

"You like?" Muerte asked as she threw a leg over the front seat. It sat like a motorcycle, but tilted forward, giving her full frontal view and side systems to gauge the rest. Three-sixty coverage and, let's face it, an incredible view of her lush ass as she locked her feet into place.

The engine purred like a goddamn lover. Muerte babied this thing, and she'd spent a literal fortune on it. I didn't have to ask to know it.

My turn to whistle. "Somebody's rolling in it."

"Was," she replied wryly, and patted the dash. "But she's fast and she won't spin out."

"Then," I replied, tucking one foot up on the back ledge of her perch, "let her go."

"I was hoping you'd say that."

"Like you needed me to," I scoffed.

She laughed. The trike did the rest.

Now I had to hope, pray, wish and whatever else desperate fuckers do that Lucky would give me a chance.

Best case, he'd help me out. Minimal fix, for old time's sake.

Worst case, the only saint I'd have taken a bullet for would put that bullet in me himself.

Lucky roulette. Time to put all my chips in.

The zones are huge. Too big to navigate without speed on your side, and Kongtown is no exception. I like the place. It's a teeming city crisscrossed with streets large enough for traffic and alleyways barely large enough for brats to squeeze through – running errands for the older folk, the pushers, the cutters, the bosses. Delivery is popular, food places dot every street and some of those back alleys. Ratruns intersect everywhere, as they do in every zone, and buildings tower so high they lean against each other in the older parts.

Every possible Eastern Asian character for every possible Eastern style of long since fusioned food flashed, popped, sizzled, flickered, faded in and out. Between them, fuckingly bright advertisements for flesh on display and for rent – girls, boys, ladyboys, boyladies, and everything in between. Need a vag but none of the conversation? A wet little pucker for your fantasies? There's tech for that, instead. Rent by the hour.

Visitors unfamiliar with the zone thought the whole district was one giant mishmash. Either they never learned just how turfed out it was, or they died for fucking with it.

Fortunately for us, riding through wasn't that much of a danger. Tourists come and go, people looking for food, sake, a fight, a bet, whatever. Kongtown is alive in ways so many other districts aren't – save maybe Deli and the rack. And possibly the FriqaChiquita's run, where a lot of the mexi folk carved out turf ages ago and refused to move. Not even the Kill Squad wandered up that way without a full group and an assload of munitions.

They'd win, if the Squad was anything like it used to be, but it'd cost.

Once we detoured away from the populated blocks,

bypassing some of the more aggressive borders, the streets narrowed. Signs lessened, never fully vanished. Made everything look shadowy as night crept in. Streetlights ran sporadically; most people this far on the outskirts string up their own generated lights.

Muerte pulled up to the crumbled curb. "You want me to stay?"

My chuckle lacked all humor as I unfolded from the back of her trike. The heatwave rolling through the shields this side of Fourteenth Divide had only gotten worse over the past few weeks, and night just traded shine for swelter. I squinted at her. "You want your cred to take a hit that bad?"

She didn't smile. "I'm here, aren't I?"

I hesitated. For the first time, I paused to look at her. Really look at her, and not just at her gorgeous legs and round ass in those temptingly short shorts. Under that boxy fringe of her red-tipped hair, her brown eyes met mine with an intensity I hadn't expected. Sincerity, I think. Or something determined like that.

She *was* here.

I frowned. "Why?"

Her crack of laughter sounded like surprise. "You're late to ask."

"Fuck you," I said, turning as she locked her beast. She tucked her palm against a side plate indistinguishable from the rest; a blue sheen rippled over it. Saint vehicle sec. Nothing else like it. "Why *are* you here? Do you need Digo's cred that bad?"

"Bad? No." She fell into step with me, surveying the somewhat emptier streets as the shadows began to stretch marginally cooler fingers across the area.

Dinnertime in Kongtown, central to far edges, was serious business. Even the ethnic tourists took part –

paid to take part, that is. Part of the experience, they said, and the residents were all too happy to charge up the vag for it.

"My cred's fine," she continued, shrugging. "The Squad's got good reach. But I need access to people that trust him, and unless he trusts me, I'd have to start at the bottom of the barrel."

"Leapfrog, huh?"

She snorted. "Wow, haven't played that since I was a kid."

I never had. I shot her a sideways glance and caught her gaze on me, shrugged at her and murmured, "Your funeral, chica."

"Don't take my lines."

The finger I gave her gleamed in the sun, freshly cleaned and irradiated.

Muerte laughed too much. Too loud. Too long.

Not loud enough to cover the sound of approaching engines. Several of them. Grating. Powerful. We stopped mid-step, halfway between her ride and Lucky's shop, and looked at each other. She tilted her head. I frowned.

We both turned toward the sound in unison, just in time to see two motorcycles and a souped-up racer shimmering in the heat still rolling off the streets. Couldn't tell much about the bikes, but the racer's colors screamed Kill Squad.

Only one reason for them to be this far out.

I whipped half around, seizing the open-mouthed Muerte by her low-cut collar. "You gritshitting *motherfu*–"

"Tranquillo, Riko!" She threw her hands up on either side, chin up, eyes firmly on me in what I assumed was an effort at wide-eyed sincerity. "I had nothing to do with this."

I snarled in her face. "Bullshit!"

Muerte apparently remembered enough to tell my everyday asskicking urge from bloody red *rage*. I was not feeling *everyday* right now.

She didn't move. Didn't so much as blink. "Think about it," she said slowly, calmly. "I need you, remember? I need Koupra."

"So you say."

The engines roared, rolling up on us fast. I spared them a quick glance – less than sixty seconds. Fuck, they were fast.

"Believe me," she said urgently. "I knew nothing about this, which means you need to get to cover *now*."

I didn't have much choice. And there wasn't much by way of cover – a few dilapidated cars that wouldn't stand up to anything heavier than a 6mm and sharp corners leading to twisted back alleys and ratruns. I'd have to take what I could get, and figure out who to kill once I did.

The first whoops and whistles reached us just as we both launched into action. Muerte ran behind me, close on my tail. I ducked behind the nearest car, rusted sides dented and flaking. Snatching one of my Cougars from the harness, I braced my arms on the roof of the car and waited. Finger on the trigger.

One little twitch, and the 11mm would take a smeghead down; we filed off our trigger guards as a rule.

Muerte didn't cover. She stood by the back bumper, arms crossed, staring down the encroaching riders. Much to my surprise, they stopped at a reasonable distance – though they made damn sure to skid in circles, wheels screeching. Classic Squad. Showy in every way.

Weapons out, they waited on their idling bikes in silence. We waited, too.

When the sunroof opened wide, I braced. My first

shot would set the tone of this whole thing, and I did *not* want Dancer on my ass if I could help it. I could hold my own better than I ever could as a teenager, but the Squad boss had gotten deadly refined with age. And a fuck-ton nastier.

"Muerte." A drawl. Not one I recognized, either. An emaciated man with the complexion of a Kongtown native leaned out of the gap, forearms loosely crossed on the car roof. He wore the same colors of the paint job – neon blue and crackling yellow, cut with black tags. His features, practically gray in the hollows of his yellow-brown skin, leered at her. Instinct told me that was his version of a smile. Not much flesh to dimple, but an affable sort of rictus.

She wiggled one hand at him. "Rictor." Rictus. Rictor. Of fucking course. "You're about two blocks off turf, brodel. What's going down?"

"She is." A nod at me. The bikers laughed. Didn't know one, couldn't see the other under her helmet. Gangs like the Squad see a high turnover – bodies rather than exits. I numbered among the few Dancer'd let go. Rictor waved his hand, dismissive to the side. "You wanna step out of the way or we gonna have to fight for the kill?"

I bared my teeth. "What the shit are you talking about?"

His sunken gaze turned to me. I heard weapons primed, clips set. One biker gunned the engine for no reason except it made his dick feel bigger. Muscled build, like a greaser gone to steroids, and his blue hair spiked up in a mohawk. The leer on *his* face wasn't a smile. He eyed me like fresh meat and that pissed me off. More jackwagons who hadn't earned the right. More disrespect.

I'd get one shot to launch this thing.

He'd be the first.

Rictor raised his voice. "Ai ai, the infamous Riko. You know the older Squad still mention you?"

"Yay." I sneered at him, full twisted lips and a gun barrel. "If you want revenge, you're about ten years too late."

He snickered, which prompted the others to laugh again. Fucking meatpuppets. Muerte shook her head. The exasperated look she gave me told me to shut up.

I was getting *real* tired of that too.

"No," he said, still laughing. "No, no." Another wave from his bony hand. Thick black rings covered each finger, chained at the joints. "Not revenge, the old bitch cut you loose fair and square. They swear you earned it." He appraised me, or what little he could see of me over the car's hood. "High praise, coming from the ladyboss."

I shrugged. "Don't ever let her hear you call her that."

He grinned, all uneven teeth in skin and bones. "I'll make sure to send your regards after we put you down."

I stared at him. Hard. "You're trespassing. You want me that bad?"

"It's nothing personal," he replied, lifting hairless eyebrows. "Your ass is up for grabs, and we're going to take advantage of it."

Ah. Shit. I'd prefer it to be personal. "What's your cut?"

"The glory of throwing your corpse at the Mecca."

Muerte coughed. "Idiot," she muttered.

I ignored her. "Let's think about this. Best case, you win, and then Shiva's saints carve you and your pussy posse up into teeny, tiny little pieces."

He looked down at his thrumming vehicle. Two more people in there, I'd bet. Then at the bikers with Dakon Insurgents in open view. Nice assault rifles, just hybridized enough to cross over with submachine gun rankings. Chewed out rounds at well over a thousand per minute.

They'd come loaded.

Again, a careless shrug. "That faggot won't push the Squad."

I laughed. Loudly. Mocking. "Aww, did somebody get bounced?" His lips tightened down to nothing. I wanted to rub my forehead, couldn't take my eyes off them. "Fuckholes, *please*. You're kidding me."

As if he had all the time in the world, Rictor lazily beckoned Muerte away. Again. Like he topped her in the ranks. "Step aside, nene. We're going to seize major cred today."

The mohawk waved, front wheel popping up. Showy bastard. "C'mon, baby, let's have some fun with this cyberbitch!"

"We're doing this *now?*" Muerte demanded. "Are you kidding me?" She took two steps toward the Squad.

Rage swamped me. Jammed ugly fingers down my throat and squeezed my lungs until they burned. Rage and – I swallowed hard – blame. Hers. Mine. She'd turned on me. Right at Lucky's doorstep, no less, where he'd witness every credburn the Squad dished out.

Betrayal by an established runner, a hunt called down by a gang run by a longtime ally...

So it'd all come true. Only this time, I put it together. "You cuntstain," I growled. "*You're* the source, aren't you?"

She didn't look at me.

# 23

I kept her in my peripheral. One shot, right? But who? If she turned on me, I'd have to drop her first. If she didn't, if she waited too long, I'd drop Rectum over there.

*Then* her.

Mohawk would have to wait.

"Hurry that ass," Rictor said sharply. "We gotta make some tread!"

She stared at him.

I stared at Rictor of the Bad Teeth.

We all kept each other in our sights, periphery to periphery. My finger tightened. Legs braced. At least I'd gotten a recharge.

Muerte turned to me. "Sorry, Riqa," she rasped quietly. "We knew this was coming."

"Only because you tricked me," I snarled, just low enough to carry her way. Up on his vehicular throne, Rectal looked bored, thin smile fading. I shot him a grim little smile of my own.

"Come on, bebe. I *told* you there was shit on your ass."

"Didn't know it smelled like you," I said tightly. I flicked a hard look at her.

She winked at me, glittering red dimples sparkling. *Winked.*

The nanosteel balls on that bitch.

I had one decision to make and I had a nanosecond to make it. Leaps of faith weren't my thing. A merc doesn't eat on faith, and I had nothing else to go on. No gangland saint turns on her crowd for shits and funsies; whatever Indigo could give her, Muerte would be committing suicide by Kill Squad, which meant she'd obey. Couldn't possibly be worth keeping my ass in her black book.

My target snapped to her just as she grabbed a firearm from the small of her back. I lived, breathed, shit my role on this street; I was damn comfortable as a splatter specialist, but Muerte juggled her roles with fucking finesse. She whipped her weapon out so fast, I blinked and missed it.

We were suddenly barrel to barrel, eye to eye, as I glared down the sights at the asshole of a fixer I'd let snow me.

One problem, though. I packed a Cougar, and 11mm caseless rounds were nothing to sneeze at. But Muerte carried a TaberTek 42 Mini, one of the smallest submachine guns out there. Easily holstered, it boasted 12mm rounds and easily switched from selective fire to full auto. It was the weapon of blackops and wetworks everywhere.

Sweat dripped down my back. Rolled down my temple. My heart slammed so fast, I struggled to slow my breath down. I was not ready for this. Was not prepped to go toe to toe with Muerte *and* her backup shitgoons.

My own ex-Squad. Guess I should have been prepped for this much, too.

I braced, taking three steps back from the car – Muerte in my line of sight and her crew still in my radius. Rictor held up both hands like he'd taken the fall on a carnival ride, rictus stretching ear to ear. "Whoa, whoa, little dead girl, don't go taking my kill!"

Muerte ignored him. I snarled without taking my eyes off her. "Eat my dick."

"Gonna try," he drawled.

Mohawk over there made tasty smacking sounds with his lips. "Muerte, darlin', you come back here."

She smiled. Shitfucking *smiled*. Like that wink wasn't bad enough.

Muscles tensed in her arm, twitched at her gun hand. I couldn't wait to find out why; rule number one: *survive*.

I shot first. The moment she so much as blinked, I pulled that trigger and stomped on any goddamn shitshred of remorse that I had to do it. Fuck that. This was the way of the street.

We'd played.

We'd all lost.

I'd be damned if I lost more than them.

Except she cunting sidestepped. Like she *knew* I'd take the shot. My aim missed her heart and hit her left shoulder instead, just as that sleek Mini of hers whipped back around to Mohawk and fired. *Batabatbat!* The echoes raced along the deserted street, rebounded up into the dark.

Three neat holes appeared across his forehead.

He froze. Blood dribbled down the bridge of his nose. It mimicked the crimson flow seeping down the back of Muerte's shiny jacket, but slower. Thicker.

She swore. Loudly, fast. Less imaginative than me, but harsher as she leapt for cover behind the rinkydink car.

I was wrong. So wrong. Gritting my teeth, I abruptly reset my aim and fired two rounds at Rictor. He ducked behind his reinforced shielding as Mohawk fell backwards off his bike. The greaser's souped up machine fell over, engine ticking and one wheel spinning.

Muerte's back hit the car siding, rattled it. "Sangano," she growled at me, rust on ground glass. It wheezed. "You fucking *shot* me!"

"Warn a bitch," I yelled as assault rifles and heavy pistols peppered the air. "I could have killed you!"

Muerte laughed, pained and angry and high on whatever decision she'd just made. Selling out your crew wasn't a great one. Bullets rocked the car frame, shook it bumper to bumper. Heavy ammo carved grooves in the softened asphalt on either side of us. "You missed," she said with irritating cheer. She tapped the car over her shoulder, gun barrel clinking grating emphasis. "Guess I'll need Koupra now more than ever."

"Making like you'll shoot me is not the way to prove your sincerity!" I rocked up, forearms braced, and squeezed off a few more rounds. Engines roared – the remaining bike growled the loudest; too heavy. Practically rattled. I didn't know much about mechanics, but I knew an overclocked joyride when I heard one. That thing would tear itself to pieces.

Not before she tried to run me down though. Which was stupid, but made it easy to guess the plan.

"Watch the car ramp," I added tightly. "I got this."

"I'll sit here and lick my wounds." A lie. As the engine got closer, vibrating the road, she dropped to the ground and lay down a thick spread of cover fire between street and the chassis we hid behind.

I say *cover fire* because ultimately, Muerte's aim was better than mine and she knew up to date Kill Squad particulars. One bullet tore into dead Mohawk's idling motorcycle, bounced around like a ping pong ball on sulfline.

The word *fire* was too short for how pretty that thing went up.

Rictor's car brakes shrieked. The vehicle spun wildly, avoiding the ball of fire and smoke as the frenetic mass of death rolled across the road. Short-lived, but it left black tar in its wake.

I jogged back a few steps, saw the second rider rolling in a dead straight line. Fast and hard. Helmeted, so she wasn't entirely stupid. Just dumb enough to pop a wheelie, spikes in the hubcap glinting, and use the lower hood of the car like a jump ramp.

She meant to jump us, force us to the ground, land and flank us from the other side. Probably shoot at us either from above or below with the short barrel assault shotgun she yanked loose from the strap on her thigh. Ballsy.

Not smart, though. I'd called that one. I was already on the move before her front tire hit the chassis.

Dimly, I heard Muerte screaming bloody murder – probably at me. Or at the fact the car crumpled beneath the combined weight of motorcycle, rider, and me. No idea if it pinned her. Would deal with that later. As the heavy bike jumped, I pushed off the windshield. It shattered beneath my boot, exploded in a spray of glass as I extended all fifty pounds of a nanofactory diamond steel clothesline – and about a thousand pounds of added force because I am that fucking good and this bricklicker's flash was nothing but chumheaded ego.

Her neck broke on impact; my arm-to-optics registered it the moment the rider's body tore off the back of the bike. She flipped twice. The machine spiraled midair, I landed on the other side of the car in a mind-bendingly painful crouch and the rider's body hit what passed for a sidewalk farther up the way. The sound of it, meaty and thick, somehow cut through everything else. Followed by the ragged crunch of metal scraping along the asphalt and tearing up layers of the stuff.

All within seconds.

Bullets stopped. Or maybe the searing scream in my head drowned it all out. That. Pissing. *Hurt.*

I panted heavily, flesh hand braced on the sticky ground and metal arm fisted beside my knee. I didn't dare shake it out. Couldn't hug it to my stomach to keep the shitting metal from straining my shoulder any more than it was. Not with that car on the other side of the two Squad gangers staring me down, and the fate of my next few moments hanging in the balance.

I refused to let that bonefucker see any weakness. I was going to be in enough trouble with Dancer's Squad already.

Slowly, Muerte eased out from behind the car. I saw her shadow as she stood, dusting off her legs. "He'll run," she said matter-of-factly. Like it was just another day. "Ass Wrecker over there doesn't like any odds that aren't rigged in his favor."

I stood with effort. My knees didn't wobble; score one for me. But I was tired. So damn tired. Metal arm hanging loosely by my side, flesh hand clenched, I watched the tinted windows of the Kill Squad vehicle for what seemed like forever.

Muerte stepped into line beside me. "In three…"

The engine revved up.

"…two…"

I scowled as the streetlights rolled up the windshield, throwing back a mirrored shine.

Muerte raised both middle fingers over her head. "…One." Smartass.

The car jerked. Backed into reverse, then spun out and peeled away.

A little more of my weight sank back onto my heels. I

shot her a look that I meant to be disgusted but probably just came across as *what the tits*. "That," I forced out, "was the dumbest shitting thing I have ever–"

She slapped a filthy, tar-sticky hand over my mouth, hard enough that my cheeks stung. Her fingers dug into the hollows beneath my cheekbones. "You," she cut in, ragged steel, "*shot* me."

I bit her palm. Sank vicious teeth into flesh and tar.

"Shit!" Muerte snatched her hand back, minus a patch of hardened asphalt and the chunk of meat between my teeth. I spat it out as she clenched her hand. "You are a crazy, *crazy* bitch," she hissed.

"Like you aren't." I wiped my mouth with the back of my flesh hand, likely smearing her blood instead of wiping it off. Grimly, I turned my back on the crackling remains of Muerte's life.

Not my problem. She'd made the call. What she decided to do from here was up to her.

As for me, I could now count on the Kill Squad on my ass every step of the way. Dancer would show next. I was too fucking skilled a merc for her to risk any more peons, and now I'd all but challenged her to do it.

The real question here, I thought grimly, was if Lucky would take their side. Cred was cred. Turning me in, skinned or otherwise, could be good for business. Unless I took down the Kill Squad singlehandedly, I wouldn't come out of this smelling pretty.

Another hurt, deep underneath the rest. A whisper that told me all those years counted for nothing.

I clenched my teeth, bent to pick up my gun, reloaded it because obviously my day wasn't going to get any shinier, and refocused. All I could do was try. Projection protocols repair, and – I winced, every step jarring ridged flesh at my left shoulder – maybe a dose of something to keep that shit locked down.

If he let me.

If he even saw me.

My chest ached. I thumped it hard, forcing the black hole I carried inside my ribs to shut the fuck up.

No leads.

Shattered cred.

At this point, I didn't even know if I had the backup I needed to proceed.

Did Muerte count? I shot her a narrow-eyed glare. She fell in line beside me. Her nanos had already sealed the hole in her shoulder – a through-and-through like that wouldn't do much to her.

I expected her to go all deep-thinker on me. Her life had just gone up in serious flames.

She could join the cunting club.

Instead, she sounded almost cheerful as she caught up and nudged my shoulder with hers. "Hey, on the plus side, at least you know I'm not your pendejo stalker."

I shook my head, eyes on Lucky's bare entry. "Dirty trick. You just blew up years with Dancer, for what?"

"So did you." She kicked at a few rocks, sending them skittering down the street. The somewhat less empty street, I noted, as the afterparty began to creep out of quiet tenements and dark alleys. They'd scavenge what they could, exchange notes on what they saw, make up wild stories.

Street theater was as much a part of this city as pissing on walls.

"I was planning to move on, anyway," she added. "Want bigger fixes to fuck with."

I'd just bet. Shaking my head, I gestured her towards a large warehouse door. Like most flat surfaces around here, it was marred with so much Kongtown border war graffiti that the original metal had long since stained. Layers and layers of the stuff.

Behind that door was Lucky's operating shop – large space, cement floor I'd had to rinse blood off so many times that I knew every discoloration, a single operating table. Because he was a man who prided himself on his work, he took one client at a time. Most banked on quantity, but Lucky's ratio of success skyrocketed beyond the norm.

He charged up the dickhole; it'd always been worth it.

Beyond the chopshop, his cramped little space. I used to live here, back when I was still new. Occasionally swung by once he'd shoved me out of the nest on my own.

I wondered if that's how he kept tabs on me. How he always seemed to know what I was doing. If he used that to make sure everybody else knew I was still under his thumb.

The lump in my chest wasn't anything more than the pain in my arm. The unraveling edges of my anxiety was just the slow bleed of wasted adrenaline.

The way my hand shook as we approached the cement steps wasn't fear. Or anger.

Best case or worst case, how Lucky dealt with me here would be the barometer for how I proceeded. He'd been around longer, fought harder, carved a space for himself so deep that even the best of the best watched themselves around him.

Either I'd get answers, or I'd get a bullet.

Maybe I'd be able to use Muerte as a shield.

I pounded on the door. Didn't really have the balls to walk in, not when I wasn't sure of my welcome. Which was a lie, and I knew it. I knew exactly what Lucky'd do if I walked right into his pad. He'd made that clear.

So I tried to stow my dick. Like, *really* tried.

The door thudded in its frame – he didn't bother to reinforce that shit. Did I mention nobody fucked with him? I'd only heard whispers of why. Living with him cemented the rest.

Muerte jammed her hands into the pockets of her little red shorts. "You sure he's here?"

"I'm sure he's *usually* here," I replied. I rose on tiptoe, shading my eyes to peer into the grimy window slot a few inches above my eye level. Too dusty to see much. Shadows in the entryway. "He takes off every so often, vanishes for weeks."

"Maybe he's gone."

Maybe. Or maybe he'd just decided to let me rot in the street. Maybe he'd dicked out so hard, everybody figured I was finally fair game.

My jaw clenched. Both of my fists balled.

Muerte stepped off the uneven cement stoop and backed up enough to study both sides of the warehouse. Looking for another entry. Surveying the upper windows; just as gross. Just as gritty. The roof was slatted aluminum, metal girders built into the sloping surface. I'd spent a long time staring up at those welded slats. Above them, crumpling aluminum siding too unsteady to risk squatting in.

Nope. Wasn't playing this game. Couldn't. This was all I had; a shot in the pissing dark.

Taking two steps back, I inhaled, sharp and quick, and kicked in the fucking door.

# 24

There are times when I look back and think I'd do things differently. Not often – I preferred living day by day. Hell, hour by hour. Saints live risky enough lives without throwing cockswinging competitions into the daily mix, and worrying about shit done in the past just led to more shit done to top it in the future.

The definition of zen.

As Lucky's front door slammed against the wall, rebounded hard and splintered off the hinges, I experienced one of those moments. I worried about my shit. What I'd done in the past, and what the hell I'd do in the future.

Now I had more reason to.

"Ai," Muerte said, half a laugh. "That's one way to make an entrance."

My stomach clenched. Wrenched in on itself and hurt so badly, I forgot about everything else. I shook my head, said quietly, "Doesn't matter."

"Que?" She pushed up behind me, peering over my shoulder. "Why?"

I stared down the narrow hall that doubled as a bottleneck should some motherfuckers get uppity *and* stupid, took in the dull floor, the sparkling dust motes

whirling in the air – upset by my entry. Thick enough to
choke on.

I didn't answer her. Couldn't. I stepped inside the
familiar foyer into the attached kitchen. Spotty tile, once
kept near-pristine but for the stains that wouldn't come
out. I'd spent hours cleaning it. A giant steel sink at the
far end for cleaning tools and what few dishes Lucky
owned. Shelves beside it that once held lopsided clay
mugs Lucky had made himself.

If I closed my eyes, I could see it as it was. Quiet and
clean, with illegally filtered hot water steaming as it hit
the bottom of the deep sink. I could almost smell the
coffee he'd made often, left simmering on a hotplate
at all hours. Like oil and pepper spray in one delicious
brew.

None of that remained. Not even the sink. Just torn
up piping and jagged holes in the tile where it'd been.

Muerte's boots clicked as she poked her head into
the only other door – Lucky's custom chopshop. She
whistled. It echoed back. "I got news, nena."

I already knew. And with every step, the void in my
chest got bigger. Deeper.

Blacker.

"I'm not," I muttered as I pushed past her, "your
girlfriend."

"No." Muerte's hand curved over my shoulder. I barely
felt it, wrapped up in the numb ache seeping under my
skin. "But maybe you can use one right now."

Goddamn pity everyfuckingwhere I went.

I'd known he'd kicked me out. He'd made it clear.

But he'd also left room for me to come back; said
to fix what I'd broke. He'd always been patient, stern
as balls on a nanosteel cock, and his methods had left
more bruises and broken bones than squishy warmth

and fragile feelings.

He was the reason I'd survived – no, *thrived*.

I'd always had Lucky. First before Indigo, before anything else.

Now I had an empty chopshop, shuttered windows, dust layered thick on every surface. The operating table was gone, ripped up from the foundations. Shaking off her hand, I looked up.

Nothing remained of the circular seal above it, designed to separate the table from the rest of the place. Lucky hadn't had to use it often; my clearest memory was a merc who'd swaggered in demanding too much tech with too little smarts to back it up. I never knew if Lucky had agreed to it to teach me a lesson I'd never forget, but I've definitely never forgotten it.

The runner's screams had echoed long after his converting meat became ash. The incinerator left nothing to chance.

Now it was gone. Everything, gone.

I staggered into the warehouse. Looked up the steel stairs, saw nothing but more dust, more shadows – more haunting echoes.

"Riko. Bebe…"

My breath locked down. My knees folded. Fists clenched so hard my optics registered steel-threatening pressure. Both fists hit the cement floor so hard, bones broke in one all over again. Cement shattered beneath the other – a spiderweb of dusted rock.

He was gone. Well and truly gone.

And I was well and truly *fucked*.

Fury clawed at me. Bloodyfucking*rage*.

And a sense of loss so deep, it knifed way past bone.

Throwing back my head, I screamed. Screamed myself ragged, screamed until I ran out of breath and

voice and the ache in my chest swallowed any softness –
any affection, any respect, *any* cunting memories – I had
left. Screamed my throat raw and left nothing but fire
and ash behind.

Muerte left me alone. She'd call it grief.

I called it betrayal. Straight to the bone.

She was sitting on a cement block, a nearly finished
cigarette between her fingers, when I finally stepped
outside. Two lines of dark gray smoke streamed from her
nostrils. "Hola." She stubbed out the remains, filterless
end left to smolder. "What's next?"

I appreciated that she didn't ask me any other
questions. Hell if I knew how to answer them. I bent
my arm slowly, straightened it again. Repeated it until I
no longer winced when my shoulder muscles stretched.
"Only one place *to* go," I said, searching the darkened
street. It hadn't cleared, but looked like business as usual.
Kids sitting on stoops, playing with whatever they could
find. Older crowd gathering on stoops, passing around
whatever they drank.

Teenagers starting young on the corners, making like
they weren't dealing whatever it was they dealt.

Babies. They'd learn, or they'd choke.

I sighed. "To the Mecca."

"Indigo there by now?"

I nodded.

"You think he'll have ideas for you?"

"I'm shit out of luck if he doesn't."

Muerte chuckled her raspy, broken chuckle and slung
an arm around my neck. "Chica, you ran out of that a
long time ago."

"Cunt," I muttered, and let the rest go. She wasn't
wrong. My throat hurt, ruined enough to grate when
I swallowed. My arm hurt, ratcheted up by a brain put

through the wringer and fucked for extra fun. My hand knitted; I was beyond an idiot.

So much for my hard-won cred.

The space under my sternum roiled.

Muerte, thank fuck, drove like she was batshit out of her mind. The Mecca wasn't all that far away from Kongtown, but north instead of near westside where Lucky's shop – where it *had* been.

I stared out the shielded window the whole ride. Didn't even peek at Muerte's deliciously squeezable ass. I guess I'd hit my limit.

Not even a little snatch to snatch action would pull me out of this one.

Goddammit.

# 25

By the time we rolled into the rack, dark had set in and the zone was in full swing. The Mecca's line circled the block. This time, nobody catcalled me when I bypassed it. Maybe the smeared blood and naked rage on my face warned them off. I'd wiped what I could off – dried blood itches – but fuck it.

The bouncer this time wasn't Jad; too bad, I'd left the Valiant strapped in my harness. Shiva allowed weapons, long as you knew the rules. I wasn't planning on shooting anybody, but I wasn't taking chances, either.

Most shops hire muscle and size, Jad being a sterling example of both. Lien Ta – shorten her name and she'd have your ass on the floor before you saw her coming – was neither large nor lean. She was short, pudgy, with apple-round cheeks and eyes sweeping up at the corners. Her complexion hovered between pale with a yellow undertone and brilliant red at her nose and cheeks, down her neck, and across her sizeable cleavage.

I love 'em short and round. So much to squeeze.

Unfortunately for me, Lien Ta wouldn't touch me with a nanosteel baton. She eyed me head to toe, gave Muerte the same treatment, and smiled sunnily at us both. "Going in for blood?"

"Not if I can help it," I replied. "Valiant's for later."

"I'll tell Shiva."

Of course she would. I shrugged. She jerked a thumb at the beaded curtain muting the chaotic strobe – a talent all bouncers learned early. "Don't fuck it up." I didn't have it in me to flirt with her. As I approached the door, she sized me up. "You're more subdued than usual."

Muerte raised a warding hand. "Don't go there."

"Rough day?"

"Mm."

I shoved the beads aside, stepped in just as I heard Lien Ta chuckle. "Too bad, I might have jumped her skinny ass had she asked."

I glanced back at her. "Liar."

Her smile lifted her cheeks, nearly swallowed her eyes as she spread both arms. "We'll never know."

I scowled. "I hate you."

"No, you don't."

Muerte dragged me away from the exchange. "Avanza."

Yeah, fine. I turned, surveyed the interior of the Mecca for signs of… hell, I don't know. Indigo. Theme. *Trouble*.

I smelled at least one. May have just been paranoid, but I wouldn't take any bets; the odds didn't feel right.

Music tonight pounded, but not the same way as it did when the Mecca revved up its people. The floor hosted a scattered handful of clubbers – mostly slummers banded together – dancing to the beat under the sliding, pulsing lights. Chairs and tables saw more than a few mercs sprawled in lazy comfort. Drink glasses glittered. Some empty, some filled with all kinds of colorful stuff. Lots of shot glasses.

A glance at the bar had me squaring my shoulders. No sign of Lance, but I knew one of the saints behind it. Andalais, a long-term tender who'd just as easily break a glass over your head as serve it to you. Depended on your attitude.

They liked *my* attitude. Usually. Today, they gave me a serious nod, the high knot of their braided foil-silver hair shining in the lights. Tawny gold eyes – they'd always sworn all natural – flicked to Muerte. Back to me.

I hesitated. "Shit," I muttered.

Muerte leaned in, her mouth by my ear. "What's up?"

"Blood in the water."

"Fun?"

"Doubt it." I lengthened my stride, putting enough *fuck off* into my pace, the set of my mouth, to make even the regulars back off. I hoped. Circumstances, as it turned out, had changed. I wasn't some street virgin fresh off the SINburn – I knew pissing well how many eyes tracked my progress.

And how many noted the Valiant strapped to my back.

No more playing around. By the time I made it to the usual back room, my lips twisted into a soundless snarl and my fists clenched openly at my sides. Blood in the water all right, and these motherfuckers thought I was the one bleeding.

"There shouldn't be this much interest in you," Muerte murmured. "Not on your normal turf." She stayed close to my back, thumbs hooked loosely in her pockets. The way she surveyed the club wasn't as casual as it looked – I noticed her lock eyes with some of the nastier mercs, hold them in her usual brand of *stand the fuck down*.

"Possible it's *because* I'm known here," I said curtly, pulling the beaded curtain roughly to the side. Beads today. Classy. "Digo–"

Eerily pale eyes in rich, dark skin snapped to me. Geometric tattoos on her head weren't vid-ink; she'd gone traditional white, needle to scalp.

Tashi. *Fuck me.*

The least friendly of my ex-team. She didn't trust me; she'd said exactly that to my face. She sat perched on the back of the booth, feet where her tiny ass was supposed to be, braced elbows to knee. A violently red lotus engulfed her right elbow, also tattooed in the old-fashioned way. A half-empty chute of something equally red fizzed gently on the edge of the table.

Next to the end of the booth, Boone rested one arm on the back of it. He towered over Tashi, typical bandana tied around his head and concealing the mass of wires that lined his skull. His wide foundation-replacement feet, diamond steel from waist to sole and wider at the floor, earned an impressed whistle from my tail.

Boone was slow to act, slow to think and extra casual for it. Except when he'd made up his mind, in which case he became an unstoppable tank. The weathered lines at his eyes, bracketing his nose and mouth, spoke of years longer than me on the street. Age meant experience; an invaluable bonus for most runners.

His tattoo was black, carved into his chest over his heart. Oddly sentimental for such a big guy.

It just made me miss my arm all the more; miss, a tiny voice said in my head, the team I'd belonged to.

Boone grunted a greeting. Neither angry nor welcome, just acknowledgment of my presence.

For her part, Tashi stared me down. Lush lips set in a thin line, and the bar under her bottom lip moved as she tongued the back of it. A sign of serious irritation.

I had no time for this. "Where's Digo?"

Boone opened his mouth.

"What do you care?" Tashi said, cutting him off. He raised his eyebrows, half turned to tilt his blocky head at her. She curled that lip at me. "He's not here, go the fuck away and take your trouble with you."

Muerte snorted a laugh, circling around me to fold her arms over her chest. Her gaze held Tashi's longer than I expected the splatter specialist to tolerate.

Again, that lip curl. "Who the shit is she?"

"Muerte," she answered.

Tashi lifted her chin. "Heard of you." Nothing good, given the grudge I hadn't heard about. Again, that jewelry shifted. "Squad know you're slumming?"

"Squad's got nothing to do with this."

"Right."

Silent, Boone turned his gaze to each person who spoke – he'd make his move when he decided it was time. Of the two, he was the least of my worries.

My fists clenched. Unclenched. I took a deep breath, approached the table. I didn't take the step up. "I need Indigo's help. You know where he is?"

Tashi grabbed her drink, looked down at it like it was way more important. "Fuck me, you need Digo's help," she drawled, sarcasm and shattered glass. No mistaking that for calm. Menace laced every syllable, lethal as her knives and twice as sharp. "Who could have fucking guessed? It's like you can't do jack and piss without his help." Now she looked up, meeting my eyes with violence in hers. Calm as her outward appearance was, she had eyes like goddamn windows to her internal hellscape. When she started, somebody died to stop it. "Go away. Indigo won't like it when I slit your throat."

Now Boone sighed, massive shoulders moving like a mountain avalanche. "Tash, you're harsh."

The skin over her cheeks went so taut, I expected them to tear like paper. "Tell that to Nanji," she spat, holding my stare.

I flinched. And then I got angry. Angrier. *Furious.*

"Listen, you pintsized twat–"

Muerte grabbed my left bicep before I cleared the step. Tashi only watched me, but every muscle hummed. Ready for me. A blade in reach; I'd stake my life on it.

Was ready to do just that.

Boone didn't have to stretch to reach my face. His whole fucking hand covered it, buzzed scalp to set chin. His thumb pressed into my temple. "Chill, Ree," he said, his low voice much, much calmer than ours. "Take a breath."

I pushed his hand away. He let me – I'd have to use far more force if he'd been serious. I inhaled loudly through flared nostrils, just for him, and eased back off the step. Muerte let me go. Real slow.

My only win here was that he'd palmed Tashi's face, too. She pushed it away with the back of her arm, tightlipped.

"Look." I put my hands down my sides. See? No facepunching. "I'm not bringing him trouble. I just need a name. Someone trustworthy who can fix my projection protocols." A lie. Big and fat. Muerte knew it, and to her credit, she said nothing to counter me.

I didn't have to spill my shit all over the team who'd left me behind.

Tashi, freed of Boone's block, held my eyes. Long enough that my scraped-together patience began to bubble into every bad idea I could form in the space of seconds – every one of them leading to Shiva busting my ass for all the cred I'd ever earn again. If not outright killing me.

Boone nudged Tashi's hip with that elbow planted by it. "She's still Ree," he said. "Digo still talks to her."

*Not* a reminder she liked hearing.

For all our instincts, our back-assward protective

streaks and our bonds, soured or otherwise, we all knew the same thing – what the linker says, goes. Saints who don't listen to their linker get very dead, very fast.

Tashi lifted a hand, white ink pale as frost scrolled over each finger. She gouged thumb and forefinger into her eyes, rubbed hard. "Fine," she bit out. This time, when she raised her head again, she'd regained enough of her usual calm – at least on the outside – to look at me without snarling. "You get one shot. Fuck this up again–" *Get one of us killed,* she meant. "–and you'll wish you'd gone necro with Nanji."

Boone nodded. Once.

Muerte let out a breath. "Seems fair," she said, graveled voice amused. Tash flicked her a glance, gave her another once-over, nodded.

It took a titsload of effort to unclench my fists. "Fine."

"Fine." Tashi stood, tall only because of the seat she stood on. She set down her drink; didn't touch the rest. "Don't know where Digo is."

"You call him?"

"No pick up."

I blinked at her. "You never lose him."

Bracing one hand on the back of the booth, she leapt over it with spiderlike agility. All spindled limbs and perfect landing. "I know," she said as she came back around. Next to Boone, she was laughably small. "None of us know where he is."

We all stared at each other, Muerte more bemused than worried.

Tashi was something of a personal bodyguard – she'd made it her mission early in our formation to keep tabs on him wherever he'd let her. At the very least, she could project him up and make sure he hadn't fallen into a sewer somewhere.

Which was more my style.

She didn't usually talk so much, left most of that to us. This conversation tapped her quota, and it also meant she was worried. If she didn't know where he was, not even if he was OK somewhere, then something had gone very, *very* wrong.

"*Fuck.*" I whirled, pushed Muerte out of my way – she sidestepped it easily. "I'll go talk to Shiva."

"Mm." Tashi hesitated. Then, like it hurt to say, she muttered, "Watch your back."

How sweet. "Stay here, compare ink," I snapped to Muerte. I left them to get acquainted, rolled through the club with violence openly etched in every step, every line of my body. I met stares and drilled them down. Left a wake of ruffled ego behind me; more runners considering what kind of boost my corpse would give them than I liked to know about.

Didn't have to roll far before Shiva materialized behind the bar, farther in than Andalais. They remained at their post, doing that thing that bartenders always seem to do when not pulling drinks – wiping down glasses and polishing up the bar.

Shiva liked the touch of class it gave the place.

Three patrons and me all aimed for the seat in front of her. A cool stare from exotic violet eyes convinced two of the patrons to find something safer to do.

The third blocked my path with a muscled shoulder.

Kilo.

She looked down on me with enough scorn to burn. Assuming I cared what some brave little heavy thought about me. "Get," I said softly, "out of my way."

"Get," she echoed flatly, "the fuck out."

I didn't know what Shiva was doing behind the much larger shield of the heavy. Didn't hear anything; wouldn't have mattered if I did. My vision tunneled down to Kilo. And the very intense lack of mercenary chatter behind me.

Even the slummers had finally picked up on the vibe. The smart ones made a quick getaway to the door – walking, not running. Running slummers make excellent targets, especially in bar fights.

"This a warning or a threat?" I asked.

"What do you think?"

"I think," I said slowly, "that your panties are bunched over the wrong saint."

Kilo's smile barely shifted her square jaw. Didn't reach her eyes. "Either way, little girl, you're walking meat."

My nanosteel fist drove so hard into her gut, no warning for her to brace, that her whole body bent. Blood splattered down her chin, peppered the front of my shirt.

Normally, I don't punch people in front of Shiva. It's bad for quality of service, and I did like quality service. Special circumstances required a little flexibility.

Kilo fell to her knees, gasping. Perfect height for me to slam my knee into her temple. She spun out, crashed to the floor. I turned, bared my teeth at the mercs who hadn't moved. They weren't really looking at me, as it turned out. Something much scarier waited patiently behind me.

A cloud of spicy smoke drifted my way. "Enough, darling. I'm not in the mood for blood tonight."

Shiva's voice fascinated me on some fundamental level. Sultry enough to ride the libido, smoky enough to muddle all sense of gender identification; I'd never heard her shout. Her diction was damn near educated, and her delivery perfect.

We all had theories on her origin. Few dared to speak them aloud.

I turned my back on the rest. Used Kilo's ribs as a stepping stone; her curses croaked.

Shiva eyed me, resting her elbows on the bar. "That wasn't nice."

"Nice'll get me in trouble."

The curve of her sinfully luscious mouth had its own fan club. I wasn't one of them – because I liked my ass where it was, and even I had waters too deep to jump in. So when it curved, I had the sense to read it for what it was.

Tolerance.

I eased onto the stool in front of her. "Sorry for the mess. Put it on Digo's tab."

She shrugged one elegant shoulder. Her style changed nearly every day, and today's was elegant androgyny. Pristine white, high-collared button-down, shimmering like Kongtown silk and threaded with glittering filaments. The collar was left open to her fine collarbones, hinting at what may or may not be hidden just one button down.

With pointed, unbuttoned cuffs barely hiding complicated silver rings at four of her knuckles, and narrow cigarette clasped between middle and ring finger, Shiva looked almost like any other patron hitting her bar. Her long, long hair – black as midnight today – braided up at the sides, giving her a magnificent fauxhawk.

Silver rimmed her eyes, shiny as Andalais' hair. The grab bag of ethnicities too mixed to pick out, bundled with some bottom-shelf Thai, gave her that exoticism sinners would take out several mortgages to claim.

Her midnight blue lips stretched wider as she reached across the bar and ran a hand over my buzzed head. "Soft." I let her. "Run into a chainsaw, Riko?"

I shrugged. "Two of them. Only one," I added with a glance over my shoulder, "is still railing my ass."

"You're such a troublemaker," she said, amused. She tucked a small shot glass in front of me. The smoke from her lips carried a spicy mix that was *almost* like cloves, but sharper. Personal blend, maybe. Didn't often see her indulging. "Nova?"

I nodded. You don't say no when Shiva gives you a drink. "I'm worried," I said flatly.

One handed, she poured raw green liquor into the glass, topped it with ash from her cigarette. "You're safe here." Her lashes flicked up, violet eyes touching mine. "For the moment. Your price is higher than most."

"Does everyone else know that?"

Setting the bottle behind the bar, she resumed her casual lean – a classic vid star in every way, right down to her siren smile. "They will."

If I survived whoever wanted to be made a lesson of first.

Not like I could complain. I'd take every one of these smegheads and mop the floor with them on any given day, but only if they came at me one at a time. Maybe two.

Three was pushing it. I hadn't done quite as well against three enforcers at once, had gotten my ass thoroughly beaten down by four not all that long ago, and this crowd fought dirtier.

She nudged the shot glass toward me with a long finger. "On the house."

If there was a catch, I'd deal with it later. I downed it in one. Hissed back a wild burn and set the glass – gently – on the bar top. The stuff sizzled all the way down. Left a hint of acid and spice in its wake. "Thanks," I rasped.

She took the glass, tucked it away, and straightened. "You're worried for Indigo, I take it."

Nodding, I clasped metal hand to flesh and hunched

in, easing the strain. "You know anything?"

She tilted her head. "What's your budget?" When I flinched, her throaty laugh drifted on a seam of smoke. Tucking one hand under her other elbow, she studied me in thoughtful silence.

I sighed. "You know I'm boned."

"I know." A wave of her hand, smoke trailing. "I don't feel the need to remove you."

"Yet," I muttered. I knew something, for once, that Shiva did not. Not unless Muerte had been chatting Shiva up behind my back.

"Yet," she agreed. "But as for Indigo, darling, I haven't seen him since last night." Her very white teeth peeked out from between those vivid blue lips. "He went home empty-handed. Much on his plate, our Indigo."

No ass in hand, huh? He sniffed after the ladies as much as I did, though he'd never admit it and played far subtler about it. Must have lots on his mind. I dragged one hand down my face. "Tash can't find him either. Have you heard anything?"

"No." Simple, one syllable. Eye to eye and saint to saint; I trusted this side of Shiva. She had no reason to yank me around. Her paygrade was so far above mine, I doubted I'd bring her more than pocket change for her trouble.

I wanted to be Shiva when I grew up. Except maybe less playing nice and talky-talky and also more obvious vag. What I *really* wanted was her impossibly ironfisted control on her own cred.

Nothing like losing it to reflect on what you did to lose it.

I sighed. "Afraid you'd say that." I pushed up from the stool, gave her a faint smile. "Thanks."

She inclined her head, gracious to the last. She'd be

gracious even when she spit on your corpse. Had seen it. Fucking magnificent.

I turned, hesitated again. Turned half around and dropped my voice. "Have you heard from–"

That enigmatic smile again. "Your drink is done, darling."

She wasn't going to give away anything she didn't want to.

I left with a nod of thanks, chewing on my own questions. Better I didn't ask after Lucky anyway. I'd done more than enough there. And if I found him, I'd do so much more than punch him.

I ignored every motherfucker in the room, left them grumbling in my wake, and ducked through the beaded curtain. Lien Ta waved from her perch on the tall, Jad-sized stool. "Watch your back, kiddo."

"I *know*," I snapped.

The front door slammed shut behind me. Half the line had disappeared – a sign that Shiva wasn't inclined to tolerate chumheads tonight. Tashi, Boone and Muerte huddled to the left, expressions serious as Muerte and Boone spoke. I made it halfway there when a man strolled into my direct line of sight, waving me down.

Casual denim, sturdy boots made for all day support. Woven, heat-friendly shirt unbuttoned at his neck, sleeves shoved over suntanned forearms. Tousled, too-long sandy hair pushed off his forehead, green eyes, five o'clock shadow on permanent lockdown… I could piece the bits together all day, if I had that kind of time. Could even describe the shape of his cock – three fingers wide and crooked to one side, for the record, and he really liked a finger in his ass when he came.

But I didn't have that time.

Abruptly changing direction, I grabbed two fistfuls

of his street chic shirt and barreled him away from the Mecca's door, the remaining line – fuck, away from any merc that'd roll out that door and start making guesses. "What," I snarled, low and in his face, "the shit?"

Detective Gregory Keith didn't smile. He grabbed my metal arm in a sweaty hand. "Thank God you're here. You need to come with me," he added, looking quickly over my shoulder. "Indigo needs help."

# 26

Purists don't like tech. They don't want it, or so they claim. Don't appreciate it, don't welcome it in their vicinity. And they especially don't touch it. Detective Douchedick had never once touched my nanosteel replacement, and that was *exactly* why I gave him the credit his urgency deserved. "Follow me."

He did. The others looked up as I shoved him across the semicircle, pushed him into place so that Boone's bulk blocked the Mecca's view of the detective.

"Who's this?" Tashi, I had no doubt, had caught a whiff of his blue blood.

"He says Indigo's in trouble," I told her.

She jerked like she'd just been slapped. Her whole body went ice cold, like a statue made of knives. She took a step into Greg's space, seized him by the front of his shirt and dragged him down to her eye level. "What. Do. You. Know?" Razors honed to precision violence.

He paled, hands up by his waist, fingers nice and loose. No weapons, no problem. No badge, either, I noticed.

"Indigo projected me about an hour ago," he said, stuffing as many words as he could into a breath. "Said a corp raid was circling Catcurry and I needed to come here to find his team for extraction."

"Why didn't he call us direct?" Boone wondered.

Greg slanted him a quick look. "Don't know."

"*Shit.*" I dragged both hands over my hair, a rough back and forth. "Shit, shit, fucking cuntsanding—"

Tashi shook him hard enough to snap his teeth. "Where in Catcurry?"

Those hands went up just a little higher, but his dark blond lashes narrowed. "All traffic's locked in or out for seven blocks around Catcurry's Central Market – data, communications, foot and vehicular traffic." For being eye to eye with death in pixie form, he was remarkably calmer than I expected. "Blackout on all sides. Indigo got a signal out to me, but it dropped halfway."

Tashi's grip on his shirt tightened to the point of tearing.

Muerte whistled behind me, low and soft. "What would they want in Deli?"

"What if they want Indigo?"

Boone studied me, putting a large, ungentle hand on Tashi's shoulder. Dwarfed it. "One linker is not often the target of a corp raid."

With obvious effort, Tashi let Greg go.

Something in my gut turned to a lump. A knot wound so tight, it pinched that ugly, numbing void I tried so hard to shut the fuck down.

I'd been part of that kind of trust once. That team.

I would again. Somehow.

"Did he just get caught up in it?" Muerte asked.

Greg shook his head, another wordless *don't know*.

"Market's about two-fifths of the zone," I said. "Where did he say he'd meet us?"

"He didn't," Greg said, straightening his shirt. "I'm sorry. The signal dropped before he got farther than coming here for you." When he looked up, he met my eyes. Not flirty. Not wheedling. Somehow, he seemed surer than when I left him. "I contacted a buddy on the force. Deli patrol's been advised to cut loose for the night." That gaze shifted to Tashi. "They've gone out for drinks in Kongtown."

"Then we get in there," I said flatly.

Muerte nudged me in the side, her voice a harsh whisper. "Also, maybe we should get out of *here*."

Tashi leaned around Boone to scope the area. Her narrow nose flared, neon glancing off white ink in myriad pastels. "Kilo," she muttered, hatred in her voice.

I followed her line of sight. Grimaced when I noted three mercs – Kilo included, that twat – gathering next to the chained-off, very small line. I don't know what history those two had, but it partly explained Kilo's attitude towards me. She stared our way. Maybe just at Tash, maybe me, too. Maybe at whatever we were hiding with our huddle.

Fuck.

"He's a cop?" Muerte asked me directly. I nodded. There wasn't enough time to explain exactly who Greg was before he got fucked over completely. "He needs to be handled before he's murdered," she pointed out. The gritty voice of reason in a knot of nerves. "Any takers?"

"Whoa," Greg managed. Alarm widened his eyes. "I can walk out–"

"Sorry," I told the detective. "You did good. Boone," I added, "hold him."

Boone grabbed his upper arms, spun him to face me. "What–"

"You see those saints behind me?" I didn't point. Just rotated an arm, warming up the joint. "Trouble. You'll get paid soon as we extract Indigo, so look mean and tough so I can punch your pretty face and get you out of here alive."

Tash stepped back, tucking her hands into the pockets of her loose yellow canvas pants. "Make it fast." She was as antsy as I felt, and our eyes met in a moment of tense solidarity.

Whatever else was happening here, we both wanted Indigo alive.

To his credit, Greg didn't fight. Maybe all this time rusting that badge with saints like me was beginning to rub off. "Make sure you call me if you need help," he said quietly. I'd never seen him so... serious? Not the right word. There was more hiding under his usually too-casual features. Determination, maybe. Something stronger than the boy-next-door rut he leaned so heavy on. "I'll do whatever I can."

I gritted my teeth. "Thanks," I said between them.

He nodded, the faintest tip, and tensed.

I prepared to deck him hard enough to ring his bell.

Was not prepared for him to launch himself at me. Surprised the shit out of Boone, who lost hold of one arm. The heavy reacted fast, tightened his hold on the other arm as Greg howled, "You fucking bitch, I'll kill you!"

Surprised the shit out of me, too. I leapt back a step, instinct kicking in. My arm lashed wide, a right hook I forgot to soften. My fist connected so hard, his head snapped to the side.

I didn't use my metal hand, which he better thank me for later, but I felt the impact of his jaw all the way to my elbow. Greg collided with Boone, who stepped back and let the detective collapse bonelessly to the floor.

Muerte howled with laughter; gritty, harsh and loud. As if we'd just tanked a chummer for fun. Although I'd bet real cred on the fact she'd just found it fucking hilarious.

Boone eyed him. Greg didn't move. "He's out."

*Finally.* A little bit of trust thrown my way, and from Detective Douchedick, no less.

"Dump him," I told the heavy. Didn't add it should be somewhere relatively safe, Boone could extrapolate. Greg would wake up sore, but he *would* wake up.

Words pitched to carry drifted our way, a mocking octave to the sound. Pushing for a fight, maybe. I ignored Kilo and her psychos. Tashi's lip curled so high, I expected to see fangs.

The heavy bent down, hauled the limp detective into the crook of one arm. "Want me to come?" The question was aimed at Tashi.

She shook her head, tapped her ear. They'd comm up later.

He nodded, stomped slowly away. I wish I'd had time to admire the sway of Greg's limp legs and ass as they left. I'd throw it in his face. Hauled like trash out of the rack. Tough guy.

"We should–"

Tashi's pale eyes turned to me. Ignored Muerte. "He asked for his team."

I nodded. A terse gesture.

"You aren't."

I couldn't argue that. So I nodded again. It was all I could do to keep from reaching for her skinny throat. I didn't need the reminder, goddammit.

Muerte took a step forward. I put an arm out in front of her, halting her before she could open her mouth.

Tashi's glance flicked to her. Without a beat, a long, spider-like hand flipped the thin knife she'd pulled without me noticing, turned the blade inward along her forearm. No warning. Just readiness.

"Madre," Muerte muttered.

I dropped my arm. "Let me ride with you."

"Why?" Tashi asked. A flat question.

I had a flat answer ready. "Because I owe Indigo my life, and I'm not going to sit back when he's in trouble."

She stared at me. She stared a lot. Eerie, and right now, uncomfortable. "Why?" she asked again. Flatter. Harder.

I wasn't sure I could explain if I tried. A tight ball of fear packed in my chest, and I couldn't tell if it came from everything I couldn't take the time to deal with now or borderline panic. Indigo had gone to Greg for help. It meant something.

Digo knew I'd signed the detective over. Knew I'd be the first one he'd go to. It bypassed the rest of the team, which made me believe he wanted me there.

I wanted to be there.

My mouth tensed, flesh fingers opening and closing. Why?

Muerte studied us both. "I hate to break the mood, but shouldn't we vámanos pal carajo?"

Yeah. We needed to.

*Why?* It rattled in my head. "Because he's family," I said, jaw aching with it. It cramped all the way down my throat, squeezed the heart I played I didn't have. "And I'll be fucked if I let some shitknockers take him down."

Muerte's chuckle accompanied Tashi's slow nod. "Don't go back on that." A warning. A threat. Tashi's gaze held mine for an uncomfortable moment more, and then she ghosted by us both, slipped off the curb with every intent to dart between vehicles. "Meet at the Central Market."

"Do you know where he'll be?"

She glanced at me, the briefest flash of pale, pale ice over a thin-boned shoulder. Neon caught the red lotus splayed on her elbow and lit it on fire. "I know where he lives."

She vanished before I could ask anything else.

My feet kept going, but the words left a dent. A sharp little corner of something I refused to let be anything else but anger.

I'd never known where Indigo shacked up. Nobody ever had.

Except Tashi. And it made sense, but *sense* was the last fucking thing I was feeling.

My flesh fist clenched so hard, my ragged nails left half-moons in calluses. "Muerte."

She pulled open the shield doors. "Ai?"

I climbed in. Stiff. Shaking. With rage. Just rage. Right.

She studied my face as I buckled in. Climbed in after, throwing her nanosteel leg over the seat. Her lips tilted, a *kind* of smile. "We'll get there," she said.

We had to. He was, fragile as the connection was, all I had left. I hadn't lied. He was family. The only thing I had close to it. And the only one with any chance of helping me. I needed his contacts and his team, I needed his bird's eye view.

I needed him alive, and I needed him to fucking trust me again.

Maybe hauling his fine ass out of this would help.

# 27

Catcurry isn't a zone, it's more like a neighborhood. A large one, but still just a piece of the overwhelming complexity of Deli. Technically called 57th Center 4A, only satellite layouts still label the area with the official name. Somewhere along the way, Catcurry stuck – a mocking indication of one of their more infamous exports.

Curry, and all its many flavors, is one of my favorite things. And it's not *all* curry in there, but like most things in this cesshole of a city, accuracy isn't really the point. If it was, I knew districts that should've been named Dried Babytoes. Wholesome protein and a great afternoon snack.

I'd take catcurry any day. Green stuff, not red; gives the meat a wild tang.

The market is always busy, and the shifts and stalls swap out day to night. Edibles and lamp-grown produce fill the place top to bottom, meat sold and cooked right on the street, animals penned up in cages ear to ass. Come night, the families fuck off and the rest of us defects slip in to intermingle, sell the shit daylight won't tolerate – and that is some very, *very* unusual shit.

As Muerte ramped up the engine and sailed through

three traffic lights nobody paid attention to anyway, I frowned at the barren edges of the market. Food papers, greasy wraps and more tumbled over the empty road – narrow enough that cars didn't fit and two-wheeled vehicles killed people daily. Shit had been left out, dropped, scattered around stalls.

Rats had found the untended cages closest to the road. The animals inside shrieked, eaten alive in a swarm of fur and teeth.

"Fuck."

"No bueno." Muerte pulled back the brake, threw the thing in a spin and squealed into a near perfect parallel park. Front facing out, like a damned smart runner with an eye on the getaway. Nothing greeted us, no corpcunts, no residents. Nothing. Sweat immediately popped out of every pore, smothered by the intense, sweltering weight of mid-depth summer. The lingering thickness of spice and heat and roasted meat settled heavy in my nostrils. Mixed with the usual aroma of piss, grease, animal shit and engine fumes, it flat out made my mouth water.

I'd murder just about anything for a good curry.

Neon signs popped in every direction, a smattered mix of languages that, like Kongtown, all looked alike to my uneducated eye. Same kind of spaces, though – you don't escape the dives, the foodholes, the flesh trade and the sleep-ins just by hopping zones. Every place has them, if you know where to look.

And no district escapes the flash of a corp raid. Company helos are easy to spot, large and black, with backdrafts like a flamethrower drawn in blue. Spotlights rotate in every direction, peeling back the dark spaces.

Made the location a breeze to find.

I flung up my hand to shield my eyes. Muerte popped her shades on, index finger securing them to her nose.

Cool bitch.

"Guessing *there*."

"No shit." I started running. Right down the center of the market branch, unslinging my Valiant as I pounded towards the chaos. In the back of my brain, I noted figures hiding in shadows of doors and behind stalls. Saw movement in upper windows, lights turning off in a desperate attempt to escape notice.

Not *my* notice. The enforcers flooding the area, and the SINless fighting them off. No sinner would dare. Not when any activity around corporate interests is guaranteed to be monitored.

The noise was deafening. Gunfire and shouting, fire left unchecked and crackling as it ate up nearby tenements, stalls, whatever caught and burned. The maze of streets and lanes, overhead bridges and below byways made the origin of all the fighting hard to pinpoint by sound, but the rest was obvious: follow the flash.

Getting there was a straight shot.

Or would have been, if a rocket hadn't gone so far off course that it collided with the fleshtoy shop directly over our heads. Screams erupted, wild and shrill. Muerte cursed as she leapt forward, pushing all her weight off her augmented leg. Her landing, less graceful than she probably meant to achieve, forced her into a hard tuck and roll.

I wasn't as fast, and I lacked the boost her tech gave her. The corner of the rise turned inward, then crumbled. Sheets of disintegrating stone, wood, plaster and fire. Girders, steel plates melted and buckled. Debris rained down around me – chaos in vivid color, furniture flaming out, bodies of unlucky gawkers who hadn't gotten out of the windows fast enough. Mirror shards glittered. Bodies hit the ground, some still screaming.

Some bounced. Cracked. Twisted.

I threw my nanosteel arm over my head, barely averted a chunk of metal from crushing my skull. Splinters exploded outward from a barrage of broken debris, stung my leg from knee to hip. I'd be plucking those out later.

After we all got out of here alive.

Corpses charred and blackened, adding to the mouthwatering smell of street food already thick in the zone. Which was nauseating, but meat is meat. It all smells the same.

As we pushed inward, more bodies appeared. Some had spilled out of vehicles, splayed loose and mushy in the street where they'd landed. A girl in a bright orange wrap, her dark hair glimmering in the light of flames consuming the stall behind her, lay face-up on the bloody remains of somebody else. Both were missing a large chunk of their faces, and the rats were just hungry enough to brave the heat. The faintest gleam of light eyes stared at me as I ran by.

Other bodies sprawled in every direction, so much char and bullet-ridden flesh.

More vermin would come later, starving cats and dogs prowling for food.

If anything survived the carnage we ran through, I wouldn't call it lucky. The raid had come in hard and bloody; *why* wasn't an answer I had yet. Indigo couldn't possibly be worth all this. Was it a coincidence?

The battlefield opened smack in the center of the market, like the intel had pinpointed the area but not the location. Barricades had been hastily erected across expanses of roads and grates, vehicles and hunks of cement, even the dead all piled together like a puzzle gone very wrong. Bullets peppered the road from every direction, shattered rock and windows, tearing through the grease paper plastered across some.

Screaming. Gunfire. Deafening whine of helos surfing backdrafts overhead. Straight chaos, and without Tashi here to guide us to Digo's shack, we'd have to cover more ground.

"Split," I yelled, and launched myself right over the first barricade. Muerte peeled off, vanishing somewhere along the outer rim.

Should have given her a comm. Hell, should *carry* the pissing things.

Landing jarred my knees. Poor form. No weapons came up at me – I didn't look anything like an enforcer, wasn't even wearing armor. Few nods as I landed. Most paid attention to the barrage of fire stemming from the other side of the barricade.

I glanced at the setup. Five mercs, a handful of others looking to hold down the spot. Some Deli militia, I think. Maybe saints, but probably not runners. Maybe sinners, too, but I doubted there were vidgrid achievements for murdering corp officers.

I didn't recognize any of them, but an older woman with hair hidden under a pastel green hijab lifted a spotted hand. The fire reflected off her skin in warm shades of copper and tea. "Are you helping?" she demanded.

"Indigo Koupra," I shouted back. Bullets zinged by my head. I ducked, crouched down and finished, "Have you seen him?"

The woman's laugh croaked. "The only things I've seen are a trail of dead and a vanguard of soldiers."

"I saw him earlier," volunteered a teenager. He held a Phelps & Somers Manticore like he'd been born to it, for all he looked maybe fourteen. The weapon dwarfed his hands; he'd learned to compensate. Mud and soot smeared his face and hands, and wraparound glasses covered his eyes. Smart kid. The lenses, though clear, fucked with facial recognition software, and the dirt made it difficult to visually pick him out of a lineup. Even his clothes were filthy, hair covered in dried mud. A real city guerilla.

I flashed him a hard smile. Fighter to fighter. "Where?"

He pointed with a sticklike finger. "Back behind Preet's."

Preet's. "Who?"

He took pity on me; I let him have it. This wasn't my district. He'd more than earned his superiority in it. "Two shops past the burning stall on the left," he shouted, and waddled toward me. Kept his head down, too. Whoever taught this kid, they'd done a fuckingly good job. "Look for the mural of Ganesh. Preet's door is on the right hand."

I frowned at him. "Who the fuck is Ganesh?"

We both paused as two mercs popped up from behind the barricade, rattled off belts of ammo. All sound drowned in the flurry, only to come screaming back when they ducked behind cover again.

The kid rolled his dark eyes at me. "Elephant," he shouted. "Big ears, long nose!"

"Oh. *Ganesh*," I repeated, like I'd known what the fuck. Religion stuff. Elephant god. Saint of, I don't know, trampling sinners to death.

If he rolled his eyes any harder, they'd explode in his head.

"Thanks," I added. I ruffled his crusted hair then and prepped to go.

"Hey!" he called. I glanced back at him. He backed up to the barricade, cheeky grin and crooked teeth firmly bared. "Tell Indigo he owes me one."

I couldn't help it. I braced one hand on the ground, grinning. "What's your name?"

"Jalender."

"Right." I touched my temple with two fingers. "I'll deliver the word. Keep your head down or I'll come back and piss on your corpse."

He laughed, shrugged and turned to face the barricade. He didn't stand and fight, I noticed as I scrambled around the crowd. He popped in and out. First on the left, then the right, sometimes in the middle for the random element. He fired precisely three shots every time.

The older woman tossed him clips. He worked them like he'd always known how.

That's the city for you. Breed 'em hard or breed 'em to die. Even the beggars have a few tricks up their nonexistent sleeves. To run, if not to fight.

The square the fighters had locked each other down in was a killbox even I wasn't stupid enough to run through. I had to go around, and to do that, I was going up. The nice thing about districts built on top of each other is the three-dimensional direction. Left, right, forward, backward... add up or down and any way in between, and that's how we get around.

Even better, as I retreated into the nearest tenement, no corporate guns greeted me. Just a lot of worried faces peering from open doors, crying kids and vidfeeds left on and loud throughout the floor.

I shot one wide-eyed woman a glance. "You all good?"

She peered fearfully over my shoulder. Nobody had followed me in. "So far," she said, worry thick in her voice.

I nodded. "Armed?"

She returned my nod.

It was the best I could do. Not everybody is cut out to

be a fighter. "Quickest way to Preet's?" I asked.

"Three floors up," said another man from across the hall, old voice hoarse. By the look of his skin and his bloodshot eyes, emphysema. So far advanced even his nanos were suffocating. "Take Bali's door, yellow stripe."

"Her fire escape," a man added from behind the fearful woman. Husband maybe. His turban matched her shawl. "Just cross it to the other side, hop down on the next roof, stairs down."

"Thanks," I said, and shouldered the Valiant. "Run if the shooting gets closer."

The old man smiled, yellowed teeth and jaundiced eyes wide. "Bring them to hell."

I loved communities like this. They're few and far between, but some band tighter than others. Long as you don't go pissing in their cultural dish of choice, they didn't mind helping in a pinch.

Tossing off another salute, I sprinted down the hall in the direction they'd indicated, found the creaking, old stairs and pounded up them. The carpet under my boots was worn thin, bare in spots, and slick with decades of accumulated wear. Not much to soften my approach.

Or the sudden echo, louder and heavier than mine. A man shouted, muffled. Two other voices joined in, and then gunfire erupted just as I hit the third floor.

Literally. Hit. The third. Floor.

# 28

A faceless enforcer rolled smack into my ankles, flailing arms and limbs catching me up. Wholly unprepared, I jerked wildly between ducking and jumping – and I missed every opportunity to avoid either. Automatic fire sprayed us both. Pain slammed into my thigh, momentum swinging me sideways. Most of the line of fire caught the fucker who'd run into me – saving my life. What a nice toolbag he was.

The other two enforcers went back to back, locked between whoever pinned them on the landing and me. Which wasn't a bad tactic, except I had a body shield and neither I nor the shooter on the other side cared about running a bullet through them both at the same time. And probably each other. I mean, *I* didn't care.

Obvious they didn't either, given the blood welling out of the through-and-through in my leg. At least they'd missed the artery.

Wasting no time, I opened fire. So did the other shooter. The soldiers dropped under the collective spray of two assault rifles, my Valiant and – by the sound – a Bolshovekia. Beautiful assault rifle, kicked like a drunk and killed like a dream.

Mine was better, though. Bigger. Juicier.

If a line of firepower carved uneven holes too close to my head, I'd take it in exchange for the splintered mess I made of the doorframe beside the other runner. One hand raised at me, a merc in full gear. The type who rolls around prepared, I guess. "Truce," said the modulated voice. Couldn't tell who or what. "This floor clear?"

I got to my feet, absently rolled the corporate corpse down the stairs. Thudded and clattered all the way to the next landing. "Civs from this floor down," I replied. "Not sure about the rest." I looked past his shoulder. "You see Indigo?"

"Never heard of her." The merc paused, faceplate reflecting a distorted version of me in its yellow-mirrored surface. "Last I saw, a squad pinned a handful of saints south of here. Maybe she was one of them."

*She.* I snickered.

The merc exchanged the clip of his Bolshovekia, dropped the spent cartridge and gestured with the weapon back the way he'd come. "Fourteen meters that way, trapped in a dead end."

"Shit," I said by way of thanks, and tucked the Valiant back into my harness. The thing was designed for easy reach and easier grab. Nobody smart runs around with an assault rifle half-cocked, especially when prepping to run balls out through an obstacle course. I'd need both hands and, all things considered, none of my other parts shot off by my own swinging weapon.

The merc, gloved hand painted a neon yellow down the center back, smacked my arm with theirs as I passed. "Watch it," came that oddly computerized voice. "This is a shitbig raid. MetaCorp's after someone worth burning the place down for."

I froze mid-step. Whipped back around. "How do you know it's MetaCorp?"

"You check," came the dry reply. They bent over one of the bodies, yanked a helmet off and tossed it away. A bit of digging, and they fished a black tag on a chain out of the body armor. The chain snapped in their hand, then glinted as they held it up for me to see. "Dog tags. Branded with MetaCorp's logo."

Shit. Shit fuck ass shit shit fucking snot.

"Who are they after?"

The helmet turned side to side as the tag vanished into a side pouch. "Heard one calling in a mayday, mentioned something about no sign of target. All I have."

"Great." I smiled thinly. "Luck, mate."

A brief, distorted chuckle. "Have fun, killer."

I left the merc digging at the second of three bodies, searching for another tag. Trophy hunter, I figured. Not sure if they'd keep the tags or sell them, but not uncommon for a saint.

MetaCorp. Unfreakingbelievable. They were everywhere I wanted to be, and nowhere I looked for them. Like they knew my shit before I did. There was no way this was a coincidence.

I ducked out the way I'd been directed, out onto Bali's fire escape. Another corpse peered up at me from the slatted metal, her helmet missing and armor shredded. No sign of her weapon, probably lifted. Guns are a good thing to collect. More useful than dog tags.

I shouldn't have stopped to check her over. Shouldn't have paused to breathe.

A clunk registered somewhere overhead. I looked up; too late. Too sidetracked by my spinning thoughts. Gunfire erupted from somewhere above me. Somebody screamed. It echoed, loud and ragged – mine. Blood splattered the wall behind me, exploded outward into the hall. Don't know if the merc was still there; didn't expect any help, either. This was my problem.

My flesh all but shredded off the bone of my right arm, joined the blood spatter in wet chunks as I spun with the impact. Agony lanced through my brain, whitehot fire and a whole lot of rage.

If I lost *this* arm to MetaCorp, I was going to burn the fucking place to the ground. Assuming they didn't beat me to it.

Worthless thoughts while I writhed on the gridded fire escape, screaming through gritted teeth. It hurt, fuck me, it hurt so bad I could barely see. My fingers, slick with blood, twitched as I struggled to get to my knees. To get behind cover, back around the corner. I heard voices, felt the impact of boots thudding up the rusted steps leading from the street below.

Everything blinded me. The constant barrage of lights, flashes, grenades, and helos blazing above the streets. The sheer, shrieking agony in what was left of my arm. The blood that had splashed up onto my right cheek and into my eye. Fire everywhere, piercing spotlights, flares in every color.

It was all I could do to get my ass on the platform, back against the wall. My tech arm had pulled the Valiant out, instinct and habit, while my flesh arm bled out at a rapid pace. Whatever time my nanos had bought me mending my thigh went up in smoke.

I was in so much trouble. I really, *really* wish I'd gotten my protocols fixed.

*Dammit, Lucky.*

Dammit, me.

"Riko!"

My head fell back against the wall. I sucked in ragged breaths, teeth clenched, cradling my ruined arm to my chest. At least my rotator cuff was still in one piece. Meant

I still had an arm free to murder the next motherfucker who came up those steps without worrying about losing the right one to gravity.

"Riko, *move*."

My name barely cut through sheer, blinding torture. Barely made it through a thick fog of fury and panic and pain. I couldn't even feel my heart in my chest, couldn't hear it pounding in my ears. It was too busy spewing my blood all over the place.

A dark shape came at me from somewhere other than the steps. I'd been ready for an attack from there. But instead of coming at me, the figure blurred into place from above. Or over? I had no idea. Just that one second, I was hearing my name and the next, there was a Manticore barrel shoved into my cheek. "Don't move!"

I tried my best to do exactly the opposite of that, swing my Valiant around to put bullet after bullet into whatever part of him I could hit.

Fucking meatsack wouldn't listen.

"Operator," said the voice, "Unit D has a lockdown on targets one and two. Send reinfor– *argh!*"

The figure jerked, lights catching on MetaCorp armor and turning into halos in my tunneled vision. Spots floated in front of my eyes. Black spots, white. Nanoshock, maybe. Or just raw bleeding hurt. The enforcer went sideways, split and turned into two figures. Shit. *Shit.*

"Riko, get the fuck up!"

*Who* the shit.

One of the figures leapt onto the railing as the other fell over, long tail of a blue-black braid carving a gleaming arc as he lined up a shot with another shadow in the double windows across the alley.

Oh. Indigo the shit.

Relief drowned helpless fury. "My side," I panted.

Talking hurt. *Breathing* killed me.

Yet another figure followed the path of the first, dropping directly into my line of sight from the rusted metal platform above us. I blinked. My hand was numb now, slippery and useless. But my tech arm, that remained nice and useable.

The enforcer focused on Indigo's back. Which gave me a perfect shot at the seam where leg armor thinned at the groin. Mobility is important. It's also a design flaw. My aim, tunneled down to a narrow point, held up just enough that all I had to do was angle my functioning metal limb.

The sheer rate of fire left no room for error; to say the Valiant carved a path up shit creek wouldn't do the mess justice. The guy screamed, faceplate muffling most of it. They'd be wired in. No reason not to be; this was professional stuff.

Which meant this one had already passed on this location and more would show soon. Operators. Always on track.

I struggled to get to my feet, back pressed hard into the supporting wall and boots braced against the porous platform. My arm hung useless from my side, black claws drawing fresh agony with every move I made.

The guy I'd anally violated with 12mm caseless bullets abruptly stopped screaming, making me the only one left. Indigo yanked a nasty looking serrated knife from the back of the enforcer's neck, flesh caught on the edges. The thing was twice as big as my interceptors, left three times as much carnage in its wake.

"Walk," he snapped at me, teeth bloody.

I locked my teeth, held my breath. Couldn't stop twitching. Too much muscle exposed, too many nerves recoiling. This would kill my nanos, shove me screaming into nanoshock. My vision was already going black. I hadn't hurt this shitting bad in a long time. My bottled shriek whooshed out on a guttural, "Shitpissingsuicidalfucking*fuck*–!"

One of his hands wrapped around my left bicep, narrow shoulders twisting with the effort to haul me off the fire escape grate. "Where're the others?" he shouted. It was the only way I'd hear him over the chaos in the zone and my own screaming brain. Pinning me against the bloody wall kept me upright, but my legs wouldn't hold me. And goddamn, I tried to make them.

Sucking in air, I managed, "Scattered to find you."

"How many?"

"Three."

"*Shit.*" He looked up, eyes flashing frenetic blue lightning in the wake of helo burns and scattered billboards. "Can you walk?"

"It'll seal," I muttered, then hissed in a wildly harsh breath as he bent and tucked his shoulder under my left side. He peeled me from my lopsided prop. My destroyed right arm swung loose; my shoulder pulled, fingers of visceral agony tearing up my senses. "I lied," I managed, white-faced, "it's going to fall off." What little blood I had left wasn't sticking around in the brain. "Jesusfucking–"

"Hang on, we're moving."

"Move fast." I sucked in air. "These asswipes have a target."

"I noticed. Now shut up," he added, "conserve your strength." He yanked me down the stairs, carrying most of my weight when my feet couldn't manage to hit the steps. They dragged behind us, jostling every bone in my body and my right side lit up like a fireworks factory gone very wrong. I threw my head back, jaw clenched so tight it cracked, and couldn't see anything, hear anything, *say* anything as I fought not to black out.

"Stay with me," he snarled in my ear.

"Fuck," I wheezed through aching teeth, "you."

"That's the Ree I know." A grunted compliment. "Keep it up."

He paused. Couldn't see why. Suddenly, he dipped, shoved his free shoulder into a door I couldn't see through my streaming eyes. The cacophony around us dimmed, then vanished altogether as the door scraped shut behind us. A man darted out from shadows, either from the room or from my tunneled vision, black on black. "Neela?"

"Māpha karanā." Indigo tipped – the room tipped? – and I heard him talking over my head, the response given. Something that sounded like my name, followed by a whispered *nanoshock*.

Yeah. Yeah, that seemed right. Blood and mucus streamed from my nose and mouth, more blood from the grated meat hanging from my arm bones. But there was grit between my teeth. Floods of the mechanical fuckers trying to keep up with the damage, replicating faster than they died off. Oozing from every orifice, every wound.

Too much tech in my body. Nanoshock left unchecked would convert.

I tried to say something. Anything. Managed a garbled rasp.

A dark hand covered my eyes. "She'll need a doctor."

"I'll find one," Indigo said, voice mangled. Faded. I reached out, trying to push through the hollow corridor of my consciousness.

I don't think I managed it.

In the dark forced by the hand on my eyes, I watched

Indigo's back get smaller and smaller. Until he vanished entirely.

Whatever was done after that, I couldn't stay conscious long enough to know what.

# 29

A thin finger poked me in the cheek. Twice. "She alive?"

"Can we eat her?" asked another – this one as familiar as shattered glass.

I cracked open dry, crusted eyes. Color oozed, fuzzed like a bad signal in horizontal streaks. "*Muerte*," I snarled. "You can eat my–"

A cloth soaked with sanitizer slapped me full on the face, dripped there as I struggled to get out from under it. Burnt my goddamn nose hairs. My body didn't move so well, muscles aching and slow. A dull throb in my head almost drowned out the fiery waves radiating up and down my right side, and the base of my skull felt like hot needles had been jammed into my chipset.

That cloth vanished, whipped away. "Don't kill her," Indigo said flatly.

Muerte's face tipped into my bleary vision. "Keslake, Riqa. Nice to see your pretty smile."

"Go die," I growled. I blinked fast, tried to get a sense of my whereabouts. Gritty ceiling, dingy gray. A mesh of crisscrossed lights painted the walls in myriad shadows and blurred colors, shifting with every blink and flicker. Thin mattress under me. My head pillowed.

By, I realized as Muerte patted my cheek, her lap.

Oh, for fuck's sake.

I tried to sit up. She reached over and thumped my clenched abs, forcing the air out of my stomach and weakening my attempt. I groaned instead.

"Stay," Muerte said, graveled voice stern. "We got your arm mostly back together and your nanos are recharging, but we're talking hours of damage here."

I winced. "I pass out?"

"Like an itty bitty baby," she teased. "Nanoshock set in real quick back there. Surprised you didn't go necro right in the middle of it all."

I bared my teeth at her, hoping some blackened reams of burnt out nanos still lined my teeth. Just for her.

Grimy boots thumped to a halt by my shoulder. "You," Indigo said, bending over so I could see his furious face, "are reckless. You should be dead. You *would* be, if it wasn't for me." Blue flame all but crackled out of his eyes, a searing blast of fury I might have whistled at if I wasn't so cunting tired. His lips chiseled down into a line so hard and tight, I wondered if spraining them was a possibility.

Could one sprain one's lips?

I had no idea.

Why was I staring at his mouth?

"She's currently stupid," Muerte said, gaze turned up to him. "Ignore her."

"I'm familiar," he replied between clenched teeth.

"Hey." I managed to get my left elbow under me, relieved to find it still worked. My right? Pretty much a big flopping dick. Fucking A. I grimaced. "I'm right here."

"Thanks to Indigo," came a low, even voice. Tashi. "Doc says you were shitclose to an incineration."

"Doc?" I squinted up at Indigo. "What doc?"

"Local," he said tersely. "Not good enough for

anything but a diagnostic and a splint. Barely agreed to do that after seeing you."

I sighed. No repair for me. And I was too tired for this fuckery. Letting myself fall back into Muerte's lap, I closed my eyes and muttered, "Thank you for saving me, Indigo Koupra, you god among linkers and incredible specimen of manliness."

"Asshole."

But something in those two syllables, something just faintly there under the salt, made me wonder if he'd be fighting one of those smirks if I opened my eyes.

So I didn't. Better, I thought hazily, that I didn't know.

I probably drifted off again. I can't imagine I didn't. My whole body was focused on healing, every nano pushed to the breaking point. I'd meant to rescue Indigo, and he'd saved my ass instead. Absolute opposite of our last run, where *he'd* tried to save *me* and I'd turned the district upside down to drag him out.

I'd fought off waves of flesh-crawling necros. He only fought off a couple MetaCorp enforcers.

I'd take that win all the way to the grave.

At least I'd gotten some decent help here. The first thing I realized as my eyes opened was that I didn't hurt nearly as badly as before. Second was that I hadn't died. So, that was solid.

I pushed myself to a sitting position, pleased when my right arm obeyed without too much complaint. I still *had* a right arm; guess I didn't have to burn everything down. This time. The splint had been removed, laying bare the carnage left behind. The meat was still knitting, splicing itself back together as my recharged nanos wove everything into place. New skin carved up sections of my tattoos, creating canyons of tender, too-pink flesh.

That sucked so hard. Vid-ink, at least, could be

refinished; pixels just need coding. But some of the more original stuff had been destroyed. Bastards.

I looked up, prepared to crawl off this thin mat beneath me. One twitch of my feet convinced me otherwise. I bit back a yelp, scowled at the needle shoved into the top of my left foot. Hollow and huge, it pushed mystery juice into the vein, dragging it from a cylinder on the floor. Also, it hurt like a cunt on fire.

As Muerte would say, no bueno.

Holding my breath, I reached down with my furrowed hand and wrenched it out. Which also hurt like a cunt on fire. Only like a cunt on fire that'd been kicked into the pubic bone for extra funsies. Too much for my delicate meat to handle right now.

"Fuck!" I shouted, grabbing at my foot and squeezing hard. "Shithole quack of a motherfucking syphilitic – *who the gaping asshole put a needle there?*"

A door across the plain, dingy room opened. I expected Digo or Muerte.

What I got was pale eyes and a razor's scowl. "You're noisy."

I shot Tashi a twisted grimace.

She took in my placement, the needle and IV hose discarded on the floor, and the cold sweat on my forehead. That eerie gaze slid to my healing arm, then flicked back to meet my eyes. "That was feeding your nanos."

"Nanos fed." I gingerly let go of my foot. Tested it. It twinged. Would bruise before it completely mended, but better than walking around with that huge cunting needle shoved in there. "Where's Indigo?"

Tashi regarded me in silence for a while. I let her, struggling up to my bare feet, looking down at my T-shirt and boxers situation. Green and black.

I liked boxers. They look good on me. But these were definitely not mine.

When I didn't fall over, Tashi finally beckoned. "I'll take you to them."

"Them? Muerte there?"

"Her, too," Tashi said without looking back. Enigmatic little pixiefuck.

"Do I need clothes?"

She shrugged silently.

I grabbed my boots by the door and stomped into them for extra foot protection. She waited. How nice.

I followed her into a narrow, dusty corridor, cradling my arm so it wouldn't jostle. The hall was dingier than the room I'd woken up in, with sad little lights guttering on and off and space made cramped by discarded furniture and abandoned junk.

At least, I thought as I picked my way gingerly around the sharper objects, I didn't fall over. I really didn't want Tashi to carry me.

Although knowing her, she'd just leave me with the trash.

She stopped five doors down and across the hall, rapped once with her sharp knuckles and pushed inside. "She's alive," she announced.

Another dingy room, dingy walls, dingy carpet stained to near black. Dingy windows with shades drawn, dingy lighting, just all-around dinge.

And two joes in bloody clothes torn wide, black skinsuits beneath. They'd been tied to a couple of very dingy chairs.

I pointed at them. "What?"

Indigo stirred from his perch on one stool, turning to look at me. "Not for you."

"No shit," I sighed. "Why are they here?"

From her corner vantage point, Muerte flashed me a thumbs up. "Scouts."

"Scouts?" I repeated dumbly. Then gave them a harder stare. "MetaCorp scouts?"

"Yup."

"Well, shit."

I was obviously late to the party. Under street clothes I wouldn't have glanced twice at, their skinsuits showed signs of wear, their faces the brunt of some heavy questioning. Unlike any joe off the street, both displayed that steely jawline of resolve you don't find by accident.

Given Indigo's irritated scowl and Muerte's folded arms as she stared at them, the men had obviously stuck to their invisible guns.

"And I thought I'd had a bad day." I grimaced, pulled at the too-big front of my borrowed boxers and slanted Indigo an eyebrow. "Thanks for the thought, man."

He glanced at the spacious area where a dick was supposed to be. Muffled a tired laugh. "You'll grow into them."

It was almost enough to make me forget the giant hole that lived inside my chest. For some reason, that only made it hurt more.

Made no fucking sense.

"So," I said cheerfully, studying the prisoners, "you're the MetaCunts stupid enough to get caught. Who bagged you?"

One stared straight ahead.

The other, an older grunt with pepper in his brown hair, flicked a glance at Muerte.

I raised both eyebrows at her. She shrugged. "Tashi did most of the work."

Behind me, Tashi replied, "They were easy to take down once their cover cracked."

"Tch." I braced both hands on my hips, managing to bite down a wince as my flesh spasmed over the bone, and bent to meet the gaze of the first one. Black hair twisted back into rows of braids, kept tight and severe. Dark rust skin and nearly black eyes, all locked down to sheer iron will. Impressive.

The older guy? He didn't look so confident through the fading bruises. Not that he'd spilled his guts, either.

Indigo shrugged when I tilted my head at him. "They're stonecold."

"You try a screwdriver?" I asked wryly.

Muerte coughed.

"Primitive," Digo sighed. And then, thoughtfully, "But not yet."

The older guy paled, red splotches standing out on his skin. He set his jaw.

I nodded. "Oh-kay." Straightening again, I stepped back. "What are we doing with scouts?"

"They'd be instrumental in data flow," Indigo said. He jerked a thumb at the sterner one. "I've seen this one around."

"So why not just crack their chipsets wide?"

Muerte's hands clapped once. "Ooh, good idea!"

Both went pale.

Digo shook his head. "I want to ask questions you can't ask data." Ugh. Such a linker. I'd rather kick people's teeth in than ask questions, so this wasn't my beat.

I shrugged, patted the scout's braids. "Let me know when you need me."

Was that relief ticking under the stony one's taut cheek?

"Yeah," Indigo said. "We've got this."

Ah, hell. Couldn't pass this one up.

Using the momentum of my turn, I lifted my front

foot and roundhoused it all the way back to the side of the younger one's head. The impact of my heel and his jaw cracked so loudly, the other guy jumped, yelping. His chair creaked.

My target's chair rocked all the way to the side, then fell over. He screamed in a deep, manly way. Very stern. Very soldier.

Very broken jaw.

"Riko!" Indigo leapt up, grabbed my metal shoulder. "We need them *alive*, remember?"

"He's alive." I shrugged off his hand, smirking.

Then shot Muerte a smeared metal finger when she added, "Can't talk, though."

"Get out," Indigo said to me, pushing me back to the door. Gently, I noticed. Shit. "Go back to sleep or something. Go fuck somebody. Hell, go rub off on the doorknob, I don't care. You are not helpful here."

It didn't hurt because he was right – of course he was right. It hurt because even though he'd have said the same thing back in the day, now it was just one more slap in a surprising amount of them. They added up. Even the harmless ones.

So I left. Not because he told me to, but because I was afraid that if I continued to stand up to his refusal to let me in, I'd crack something. His face.

My... Well. Something. Maybe something emotional. I didn't *do* emotions. They exhausted me. I was tired of feeling them.

I felt like a sack of meat at the end of a bungee cord.

Tashi watched me go. As I approached, she said quietly, "I'd rather just kill them."

I met her eyes. For once, they didn't spit daggers at me. Nodding faintly, I murmured, "I have a feeling there's more to this than a bunch of dicks being dicks."

"Once we knew where to find them, they were too easy to catch."

"Any idea why?" I pressed open the door with the one arm that hurt less than the other. For once, my left wasn't the bitchiest.

Tashi shrugged bony shoulders. "It's like they just gave up when they realized we weren't going to."

"You're scary when you run an assclown down."

She glanced at me. Back at the room – specifically, the linker righting the spilled chair. Then, quietly, "Thanks." Not for the compliment.

I flinched. "Don't," I replied, shaking my head. "It gives me ideas."

"Something has to."

"Pixietwat."

She didn't hit me. Didn't even acknowledge the insult with her recent barrage of violence. Tashi just huffed out a sharp breath I chose to take as a note of humor and let me go.

Look at that. A moment of solidarity. A breath instead of bitterness, like maybe it'd be OK. Maybe Tashi would forgive me, lead the way for the rest to give me a shot.

Snapped right back up on the bungee cord.

Exhausted to the point of resignation, I stumbled back to my empty room.

A man screamed behind me.

# 30

I went back to bed, but I didn't sleep. I lay flat on my back and stared at the ceiling, replaying what I could remember of the whole event.

Indigo had contacted the detective, not Tashi. The thought played and replayed in my head. He knew the detective would try to hit me up first. Greg didn't know the others. They only vaguely knew Digo worked a blue for info.

He'd all but hand-delivered an invitation. To help him. To watch his back.

I didn't know what it meant. Another thing to be angry about.

Now, MetaCorp was something else. *Something* had pulled them out of the gutter they'd been hiding in. If it was the same department chasing my ass, they'd managed to dodge me at every turn, avoiding every effort at pinning them down.

So what the tits brought them to Deli?

The only link was Indigo Koupra.

But how did they know?

I crossed one ankle on my upraised knee, metal arm tucked under the back of my head. I had to leave my right on the mattress. It still hurt when I tried to put pressure on it. Close at hand, I'd laid the Valiant 14. Just in case.

Far as I'd been able to piece together, we squatted in a place on the fringes of Deli – close to where its borders began to blend with Kongtown. Dunno if anybody lived on this side of the floor, but I suspected most squatted, too.

Either way, it was quiet enough that I was getting nervous. My raised foot twitched, fidgeted in tandem with nothing.

I had too much to think about and nothing but paranoia for my troubles.

When a rap came from the open door, I bolted upright, swore and grabbed my arm before it tore clean off. Not that it would. It just felt like it.

"Stop freaking." Indigo raised cartons of Kongtown takeout from the hall. "You've got to be starving."

I was. Whooshing out a pained breath, I scooted back, crossed my legs. The empty front of my boxers bagged. I resented that.

Digo sat across from me on the bed, lean legs folded in near perfect whatsitcalled. Like mine, but bendier. Lotus position, I think. Ironic.

He offered a closed carton in each hand. "Choose."

The smell wafting from each filled my lungs and nose with heavenly reward. I pointed.

"Dim sum," he said approvingly, "Good choice. I'll take that. You get gyoza yakisoba."

"Fuck, you're a jerk."

"True." We both fell silent as we cracked upon the cartons; Digo passed me chopsticks. I used them easy. Everybody south of the Fourteenth Divide knows how to use these. Kongtown food is a matter of life or death most days, and shops cropped up just about everywhere.

The takeout had cooled but it didn't matter. Cold Kongtown was just as good, if not better. I inhaled the noodles, looking down at my food instead of at the linker with me. I *was* starving. Tapped out of energy and tired of thinking. For a while, chewing and slurping was the only sound between us.

Eventually, as I slowed, Indigo's chopsticks clicked in my direction.

I eyed them, then searched his features. Nothing. No exasperation, no anger. Just his face. Doing nothing.

That silent thing, it irritated me. I frowned at him. "What." Not a question.

"The detective found you." Another not a question.

I nodded. "Traveled to the Mecca to do it." I searched every crevice of his expression, eyes to mouth and set of his shoulders. "Did you try to call me first?"

"Maybe."

"Why?"

A shadow of a smile. "Why'd you go get Tashi?"

"I was with her already," I replied. I looked back at my food, carefully tore a gyoza in half with my chopsticks. "Boone smuggled the detective out of the rack while the rest of us rolled in to Deli together."

His head tipped to one side, his own sticks clicking. A fidget. "I'm surprised Tashi let you come."

I didn't know if it hurt or just pissed me off. The carton dented between my fingers. "You're the one who projected Greg instead of Tashi," I snapped.

"Yeah, I did." *Click, click.* "You should fix your protocols." *Click.* "What about the rest of my team?"

Ouch. Extra fucking ouch. *His* team, huh? *Fine.* "Tashi's wherever you put her last."

"Lookout."

I shrugged, jammed my chopsticks into the carton.

Only a quarter left. "Boone had escort duty for your insider. Haven't seen Valentine or Fidelity in weeks."

"So, you came with two runners to tear the place apart."

No lilting question mark in that one, but it was definitely a question. I met his searching inquiry with a flat stare of my own. "You called for help." A beat. "I helped." Another, longer. "Also, some kid, Lavender or something, said you owe him one."

He smiled. For a moment, he *really* smiled, with that engaging way of his that turned his blue eyes up and edged endearing lines at each side of his mouth. It might have loosened that panic in my chest a little, if it'd stuck around.

Maybe he saw something in my face that said I'd taken that smile more personally than it was meant. It faded. "Serves me right, I suppose." He toyed with the dim sum in his carton. Dropped his gaze to the front of my... *his* boxers. "Good thing I carry spares."

"That's weird."

"You're wearing them."

"Also weird," I muttered, and set the carton on the floor by my primed Valiant. "So, you want to talk about the giant bloody Ganesh in the room?"

"Depends on the Ganesh."

"What?"

"Are we adding or removing a wall?"

I blinked, fingers tapping unevenly against my thigh. "I don't know?"

Indigo gave up the metaphor for me. "I mean," he clarified, "talk."

"By myself?"

"Humor me."

Another moment of silence. I was suddenly keenly

aware of the sharpness of his study – like his sister had, he saw more between the lines than was comfortable. I looked at my fidgeting fingers instead. Then, jaw squaring, forced myself to meet his gaze anyway. "I have a question."

He waited.

I took a deep breath. "Did you know that somebody's been convincing up and coming saints to take me on?"

"More than rumor?"

I nodded. "Targeted. No identity yet, but that same spunkdumpster got ahold of that vid you tried to crack."

The thick black fringe of his eyelashes widened. "Copied? Impossible."

I spread the fingers of my left hand, curved over my thigh. "The vid's going to be available to the highest bidder if I can't track it."

Those lashes narrowed. "For a fact?"

"Muerte dug it up."

"You trust her?"

"In this? Yeah." The skin on my healing hand twitched. Felt weird enough that I frowned at the fissures in it. "She was in the Kill Squad same time I was, but she'd stayed when I dicked out. I guess they decided to come after me without telling her." Outside Lucky's. I swallowed that knot hard enough to scrape all the way down. "Muerte gave them an enormously cheerful *fuck you*."

"She dumped them for you?"

"Apparently, she's ready to move on," I replied, dry as the dust coating every surface around us.

"Splatter?"

I shook my head. "She could have gone splatter specialist, she's good enough for it, but she's a better fixer."

"Good to know." Indigo sat back, bracing his weight

on a hand splayed behind him. The Kongtown carton in his other hand tipped back and forth. "About that vid. I'm positive nobody's gotten into my personal system. Not even a projector," he added.

"How would you know?"

His grimace carved deep. "I'd know." Then, "You sure Reed didn't do it?"

"Same song and dance." My back hunched, bones suddenly too tired to hold my own weight up. "No reason for him to do it. No reason for you to do it. There's nothing to gain by ruining me."

He didn't argue. Didn't gloat, either. "Glad you realize that."

My front teeth set together, jaw thrusting. I leaned forward again, a spike of anger flaring my nostrils. "Whose fault is that?"

"Whose fault tanked your cred to begin with?"

"Goddammit, Indigo–!"

"Sorry." Low. Hard to say, like he swallowed most of it back. "I know it's not all your fault." His empty fist clenched, both lowering back to his lap. The black cargoes he'd changed into did not, I noticed, have the too-large crotch problem. Apparently, I was the only one with a penis issue.

And fuck, didn't I know it.

Indigo exhaled. "It's been a rough few weeks."

"No shit," I muttered.

"Not just for you," he added flatly. A cutting reminder. "As far as anybody else cares, I should've taken you out the moment you came back without Nanji. We're feeling it, too, Riko. You aren't the only flag getting shot at."

I looked down at my knees. To hear him admit it felt like a slap. "Yeah," I said on a tight exhale. "I know."

"Do you?"

I deserved that one, too. I hated this feeling in my lungs. Hated the tight cramp in my guts, the oxygen turning to acid with every breath. Everything about this felt wrong, felt *hard*. It shouldn't have been this hard.

My fingers dug into my thighs. Tight enough to bruise. "I'm sorry." It tasted like bile and gasoline. The skin dented around my fingers faded to bone white. "I'm not great at looking at anything but the job in front of me. I'm used to having a linker to keep me on track, so I–"

"Again!" Indigo gestured heatedly with his food carton. "Why don't you get it? This *isn't* about you–"

"*I know.*" I closed my eyes, too tired to meet his intensity. Reframing my interest around something else, somebody else, took effort. I sucked at it. I had *never* claimed otherwise. What I could do, though, was nut up and meet him on his terms. Face to face. Eye to eye. Anger to whatever the fuck I could manage.

I'd called him family. I don't even know what that meant, but now seemed as good a time as any to give it a shot.

# 31

I raised my head. "Listen. I know exactly why I was cut from the team," I said, firming everything I had. Straightened my back, my neck, shoulders. My voice. "However pissed I was... no, I *am*," I corrected abruptly, "there's a reason I didn't wreck anybody's shit over it."

"Because we outnumber you?"

"Stop helping," I snapped back.

He shrugged. Waited. One foot uncrossed, planting on the floor beside the mattress like he had all the time in the world. He knew how uncomfortable I felt. *Knew* I had razor blades in my throat. I didn't do sorries. Or humility.

I'd never been backed into a corner like this before.

I looked down again before he noticed the twisted shape of my scowl. In my thighs, white welts flushed red. They'd go purple in minutes. Then yellow and green as they faded even faster. A minor hurt. A quick recovery.

Easier in the flesh than the head. Or the ego.

"I'm trying to say," I said to my legs, "that I get why I was tossed, and I'd've done the same thing if it was one of you. *But*," I added, too fast for him to interrupt. I raised my head, once more eye to eye. A goddamn yoyo. "I'll say it again. I would *never* willingly fuck you over."

Somehow, the single word I'd meant to frame with emphasis turned into a rising octave.

The carton crumpled in his hands.

"Not you," I spat out, anger slowly rolling up my insides. "Not the team." It ate at the rest of the shit I didn't want to feel, fueled itself into a wall between me and the ugly parts of me I didn't want Indigo's guilt-ridden fingers in. Or mine. "And not Nanji."

For a long, long time, Indigo said nothing. He only stared at me, searched my face. It went on so long that I began to doubt he'd heard me.

When he set the crushed carton on the floor by my empty, he did so with slow, deliberate care. "I want to know who killed her, Ree." His anger didn't go wild like mine. His had always been calmer. Blue heart instead of red flame. "I want to know if you lied to me."

So did I. About Nanji, about the mercs sold off and probably butchered like she'd been. I needed to know so much more, and that's why I needed Indigo again. I needed a place to start.

"Whoever set it up, whatever is behind it all, I *will* find out." His smile framed gritted teeth. "And if nothing else, this MetaCorp raid convinced me of one thing."

"Yeah?"

"I'm going to glue myself to your ass until I figure everything out."

*Shit and a half.*

I wanted so badly to smile. To take a relieved breath and punch him lightly in the chest and welcome him back. I couldn't. It wasn't that kind of promise. Scarred skin strained over my fisted knuckles. "Keep your enemies closer, right?"

He looked up at the stained ceiling. Shook his head and dropped his chin to look me in the face. "Keep your friends close," he corrected. Then, with a faint, tight smile, added, "You sit somewhere between the two, Ree. I'm not going to lie to you. But our goals align."

My mouth dried. Hunger and longing filled the space between my ribs. Anger and bitterness framed it. "What about the others?"

"I've talked with Tashi."

I blinked. "She agreed?"

A nod.

"Fidelity and Valentine?"

"Not yet," he told me, and pushed himself back to his feet. The empty carton by his foot tipped over, chopsticks clicking as they rolled out onto the floor. "They've been picking up side work for a couple weeks, I expect them to check in soon. I haven't spoken to Boone yet," he added before I could ask, "but he's more likely to go with the flow."

"He trusts you."

"Yeah. Get up," he added, offering a hand.

I didn't take it. One, all I had to take it with was my nanosteel arm, and I didn't like wrapping my fingers around flesh and bone unless I didn't care if I broke it. Two, my right hand hurt every time I tried to squeeze something. Fucking tissues would need stretching.

Three, the hell I'd take the help.

I unfolded my bare legs, grabbed one of my boots and wiggled it on firmly. "You think the rest will sign on?"

"If Tashi and Boone are game, they'll come around."

Back to a team. A real one, with real goals.

Goals that included fucking some corporate bullshit up.

I rubbed at my arm, bent to pick up the Valiant. If I looked ridiculous in a T-shirt and pair of package-empty boxers, I looked even more stupid with the assault rifle slung over my shoulder and street boots flopping around my bare ankles. "What if they don't?" I finally asked.

"Don't get my boxers in a wad," he replied mildly. He ran one hand over his head, pushing back his hair. Tendrils of blue tucked behind his ears as he gestured for the door. "One thing at a time."

A version of zen. Indigo had always looked farther ahead than now, it's what linkers do. But unlike me, he wasn't the type to get overwhelmed by choices.

He watched me as I passed him. "You've changed, I think."

He'd said that to me before. At the time, it wasn't nearly so thoughtful. I also thought that maybe, just maybe, he was right.

Too close. Wasn't going to touch that yet. I snorted, waving that away as he followed me out. "I'm tired of getting jerked around. At this point," I said, crass as I knew how, "I'll suck your pretty brown asshole to get what I need."

"Which is?"

"Knacklock's role in this clusterfuck."

"Oh yeah?" Smug. Maybe smiling? "Prepare to get on your knees."

I glanced back at him, single file as we forged through trash and debris. Yeah. A definite smile there, and arrogant as balls. "What'd you find?" I demanded.

"A link." He spun a finger in a circle; a suggestion I turn back around before I biffed it. "Just before the raid, a source came back with something I asked him to find. Turns out Kern's been dealing blackjack behind the scenes. With," he added behind me, "MetaCorp scouts."

"What, these jackmaggots?"

"Same ones."

"Well." Glee filled me. "Christ on an elephant wall.

Aren't I lucky?"

"Not yet. These chummers are well trained, endurance at insane levels." His sound of disgust carried more than a trace of impatience. "They even gave Tashi a go. Short of cracking their chipsets in hope of some data, I'm drawing up blanks. Might need an interrogation specialist," he added grimly.

Oh, damn. Serious work, then. Interrogation specialists fall into several street role categories, but they all have one thing in common – a wake of blood and a rep filled with broken souls.

"Valentine?" I asked. "I know he's not on board yet, but he's got the experience." Although he ran as our regular munitions specialist, he easily could have gone interrogation. Probably had for a while. He'd chosen the fight out on the streets instead; extra bonus points for corporation hits. Scary motherfucker, a real history of hard slaughterwork. We avoided any opportunity for a fight, neither of us willing to test each other under Indigo's watch.

Sexy, though. For an artificially sculpted fantasy.

"I'd prefer to avoid it," Digo replied. "Not until he hears me out and agrees to bring you back on." We approached the room, one of his callused hands pausing on the doorframe. "It's possible they don't know anything more than what they've immediately dealt with."

I shook my head, nudged his arm aside. "I've got a gut feeling."

His narrow shoulders rose with a deep breath. Squared with a sigh out. "I want to try and get them talking without cracking the chipsets. I have questions I want answered directly."

"You want to give them another shot?"

"As many as it takes," he replied.

"You realize that time is very much a problem for me, right?"

"I know."

I raised my tech arm, like a kid in class. "Idea. What about Jax?"

"We don't need him."

"But–"

"Riko." He tapped me on the forehead. Hard. "We can't use him anyway. Remember?"

Oh. I scowled. "Life was so much easier when going necro was just a scare tactic."

"Never was *just* a scare tactic," he replied, saying out loud what we both knew. "But yeah. We're not going near that fucker."

With that, he shoved his way into the room.

The door creaked as it opened – of course it did. Muerte straightened from her crouch in front of both men, who'd obviously seen some assault and battery. Stoneface's nose had reknitted, but crookedly. Blood coated both, dried to a rigid crust on their clothes.

The other guy's head lolled on his neck, chin to chest.

"Marital spat?" Muerte asked us, bland as raw balls. "Is it time for makeup sex?"

"Oh, shut up," I replied. "Anything from them yet?"

"Nope. The thing about nanos," Muerte added cheerfully, "is that it makes biting off your tongue a less than reliable suicide attempt."

My eyebrows skyrocketed. "They tried that?"

She pointed at the fleshy, stringy gob of pink and red on the floor by my foot. "They both did."

That explained the blood coating their chins, and the splattered puddle of it by each chair. The upright one stared at me when I approached, eyes empty. Dead men sitting. I bent to study the sheen on his face, the ashy pallor at the edges.

One eye flickered. A twitch of an eyelid.

I patted him on the head. "I'm not exactly a fan," I said to them, "but I'm fuckingly impressed with MetaCunt scouts right now."

Neither seemed to care what I thought.

"Hey, Indigo?"

He heard it in my voice. "Don't you dare," he warned. "We talked about this–"

"I know, I know." I really didn't have any more time. Touchy feely feelings aside, Indigo had said it himself. All he needed was data from their chipsets. "You'll have to ask your questions from Kern."

The Valiant slid off my shoulder. I caught it easily in my mending hand. Part SMG and part assault rifle, the baby could crunch out caseless rounds at an ungodly rate. Without the heat-baffled silencer attached, the number of rounds it could handle dropped some, but it wouldn't matter here.

There wasn't much left of the first enforcer's chest when I laid off the trigger. Blood and lung matter splattered everywhere, clung in thick gobbets to his buddy – who was visibly shaking. Face gone waxy pale, he stared pleadingly at Muerte's corner, lips trembling around a clenched jaw. "Please," he rasped.

My finger did love that trigger. He jerked back, chest splattering. Maybe a little *too* much. I let go, lowered the nozzle. Silence finally descended. Everyone stared at me. Including the dead guys, eyes wide open and mouths slack.

When Muerte's quivering lips turned into a laugh she couldn't suppress, Indigo lost it. "For fuck's sake, Riko, what the hell?" He strode past, shoving me out of the way.

"What?" I lowered the Valiant, tucked its warm metal behind my legs. "You said give them a shot."

Muerte's laugh went so high pitched, it cracked in and out through her broken voicebox. She laughed like her neck would snap, sagging back into the corner and pounding the wall with both fists as she howled.

The back of Indigo's neck went bloodred with anger. I'd never noticed before. Skin drawn tight at jaw and cheekbones, he rounded on me, finger dead to rights to my chest. That stung a little.

I deserved it. But not sorry; it was so incredibly cathartic.

"You better hope," he seethed, "I can extract something – *anything* – from their chipsets!"

Smiling, I spread my arms wide. "That's why I shot them in the chest."

I didn't think I could drive him any further into rage. It was all he could do to clench his fists and press them to either side of his head in pure wordless frustration.

Somehow, for some unfuckingknown reason I couldn't place, that ugly thing under my chest eased. A little. Just a little.

When he finally threw his hands up in the air, it was to growl, "Out. Go do something else. I'll be in touch with anything I find." His eyes narrowed to electric slits. "Assuming I find anything left." Then he growled something I suspected I'd be better off not hearing.

Better to leave before I pushed him any further than I already had. He knew me. Knew what it meant to bring me back on.

I just made the obvious choice a lot easier to make when it was the only one left.

Questions are good and all. The human angle often catches things raw data can miss, puts things together with instinct where even the most advanced tech still uses logic-based processors.

But humans lie, too. Or misremember.

If there was anything in their chipsets to find, Indigo'd find it. Better I gave him the time to do it alone. I left without further words. Not much to say after that kind of exit, anyway.

Muerte caught me one floor down. "Hey, chica, rocking the boxers."

"Go suck a necro," I said without stopping.

"Ease up, I'm on your side." She caught up fast, bent to consider my face. "That was funny as shit. Why so glum?"

I shook my head. I didn't know why. I'd gone from constant anxiety to cutting hysteria to warm and fuzzies and then walked out here feeling low as fuck. I didn't like the niggling little worm of an idea chewing on my brainmeat.

I'd stared into the faceplate of a MetaCunt op calling in for two targets, and it was *my* forehead in his sights. Locking me down while he called for backup? I was the most obvious threat, I guess. Maybe he'd tagged two more, and was just making sure I stayed off his back?

Didn't feel right. If I was just some saint in his way, he'd have blown me away right there. The obvious linkup between myself and Indigo, given our mutual run for Mantis a few weeks ago, made me wonder.

How had they found him?

How did they know I'd arrive to help?

Shit. "What time is it?"

"Almost six."

I sighed, knuckled at my aching eyes. Not nearly enough time for everything to stop hurting. "You think my shack's still safe?"

"Probably. At least for a little while."

"Great. I'm going," I lied, scanning the streets, "to go get some rest."

Muerte put a hand on my shoulder. "You still need to see a doc..." she began, but I shrugged it off. She frowned. Then resignedly shook her head. "Ai, Riqa. Your call. I'll go poke some fingers into some holes, see what crawls out."

Good. Information would help. Getting well away from me while I knelt to suck corporate dick was even better.

"Cheket," she said, backing away. "Don't get dead."

"Yeah, catch you," I muttered, and stomped away. Fast away. From Indigo's fragile trust and his habit of doubting my every move and his ability to see so deep under my skin that I felt like I needed a cigarette after it. Muerte's stare and her constant laughter. Tashi's uncomfortable solidarity.

I stomped away wearing boxers and a T-shirt and big, black boots and I still wasn't the weirdest motherfucker in the crowd.

I would be when I got where I was going, though. Malik's med-lab and Orchard's kindness were all I could get. All for the low, low price of hyperventilation and a nosy doc hellbent on my wellbeing.

Which was rapidly thinning out to *stressed as fuck*.

Having Indigo stuck to my ass gave me a sense of relief I felt like a tangible weapon at my side, but until we made some progress, I needed more than a calibration. I needed edges I didn't fucking have. It was long past time to roll the dice.

I flagged down an automated taxi, palmed the dash as a computerized voice welcomed me into the vehicle. My netware hooked up to the signal, ran a quick datascroll through my optics and hacked the console. Fed the meter enough to get me wherever I wanted to go. Hacked the map, too. Basic stuff. The software did all the real work.

Once the taxi lifted off, I leaned back in the scuffed plastic seat and closed my eyes.

Goddamn, I was tired. All I wanted to do now was get my cunting chipset fixed. Another fight. Another shitting showdown. Malik Reed would not like my presence in his offices. Not after last time. Hope would probably try to get in my way – would she be there this early? I had no idea. I figured all suits either slept at their desks or came in bright and early for that go get 'em day.

Either way, I'd find out. And if I was lucky, I wouldn't have to fight anyone to do it.

# 32

The way I figured, long as that automated elevator of theirs continued to let me up, Malik Reed could choke on my ladycock. Place like Mantis had all kinds of ways to keep out punks like me. So far, it hadn't locked me out yet.

I'd never actually been here this early. Kinda pretty, what with the enormous lobby windows open wide to violent pink and bruised purple streaks. Dawn hugged that low-hanging orange haze clogging the far wards and painted it in shades even more aggressive, and Reed's ever so tasteful color scheme picked up those contrasting colors. Tossed them around. No music played yet – maybe it was early for Hope, too.

She was already circling the desk as I stepped inside, features set in stern lines. A cup of something hot and red-purple steamed behind her. Smelled like organics in here. Fruity stuff.

She met me halfway across the lobby, arms splayed. "What are you wearing?" she demanded. Oh, sure. *That* was her first question.

"Latest street fashion," I replied blandly, sidestepped left.

She sidestepped with me, her lovely mouth a

secretarial line and eyes practically broadcasting Muerte's no bueno. "Mr Reed isn't in. You *really* need to start making appointments."

I stepped the other way, went sideways and skirted around her. "No, thanks."

"Riko!" Nude high heels covered good ground. She ducked around me, braced herself in front again. Red flushed her cheeks, her jaw set. In her light pink tweed skirt and silky cream blouse, belt matching her shoes, it was like she was the good girl in a dramavid and I was the villain of the moment.

Not even of the show, I thought moodily. Just the one scripted to rape the sweet girl so she could become the badass she was always meant to be.

Tired trope.

My smile must have turned a different way than I meant. Hope looked at me over her small framed glasses, and I would be fucked up the ass with whatever passed for Reed's personal pleasure rod if I'd stand here and be looked at like *I* needed the help.

I bent until my nose aligned with hers. "Get out of my way, Hope."

"No." Her eyebrows knotted – worry, not anger. Not fear. Worry and trust. "Please. Go get some sleep, Riko. You look exhausted."

Beaten, she meant. I looked *beaten*.

All the good things rolled out of the past twenty-four hours and it wasn't enough. Having Digo back in my corner, however cautiously, didn't outweigh the diarrhea of my cred. Of the chopshops. Of the fact I had to come back to godforsaken white tile just to get my tech fixed.

My patience snapped. She recoiled when I moved, took a defensive step back. My hands closed on her waist, dragged her up and pinned her to my side. With my flesh arm free, I caught her flailing arms by the wrists, pinned together.

"Put me down!"

I crossed the expanse of the chic lobby.

"Riko." Hope's voice wavered.

My jaw clenched. My chest kicked hard enough to turn my stomach, upend itself into the void spiraling wide between my ribs. "I'm not going to hurt you," I said flatly. Snapped it, rough and meaner than I'd meant.

Her teeth clicked together. She stopped fighting me, stared at my grasp on her wrists, tucked between us. Her cheeks had gone darker red, but much paler around the splotches. Didn't have to hit her to nail her where it hurt most.

I'd broken her trust.

And now I wanted to punch myself in the face. Wanted to sit down and apologize and explain to her that I'd had a rough fucking month, but I couldn't.

I wouldn't.

Everything about my world right now centered on one truth, the only answer that made any sense: MetaCorp wanted me. They'd linked up with Battery's chopshop. They worked with Kern's Knacklock shop.

They'd chased my ass into the Vid Zone, the thing that started it all.

I needed to be at peak performance. I needed more than that. I needed everything I could get my hands on, and I needed it now.

I needed Orchard to do it.

*Sorry*, I thought as I plunked Hope's ass on the top of the desk. It was higher than her legs could reach, one of those desks meant to provide a barrier elbow-high between her and clients.

Her cup rattled – real cunting porcelain.

Hope didn't move. Her fists clenched in her lap.

I didn't look at her face. Didn't want to see what expression she gave me as I left her there. I don't even know if she watched me go.

The back of my neck burned all the way to hell.

Cameras watched me, and I assumed security tagged me down every hall. Despite my entry – and yesterday's exit – nobody came tearing at me, no automated voices told me to stop.

Maybe Hope had alerted the lab. Maybe Orchard was just always there, always prepared for whatever came through the doors.

Maybe I was beyond caring what everybody else wanted to do.

This time, when I shoved through the doors into the already cold space of Orchard's... no, of *Malik's* lab, white tile was the last thing on my mind. Orchard, her hair twisted into a messy orange knot and her lab coat forgotten somewhere, met me with a metal cup of something steaming in hand.

I smelled coffee.

I smelled sanitizer.

And the smile that already curved her lips screamed *talk the crazy bitch down*. "Hey, you're here early–"

Fuck, no. I grabbed her by the upper arms, dragged her face to mine. The cup in her hand tilted, spilled the black brew over her skin, and then fell out of her grasp completely, soaking her denim and oversized blue sweater.

She flinched.

I tore the part of me that cared out and stomped it bloody into the spreading liquid on the floor. "Tech," I growled. "Fix my protocols. Pain dampeners, first tier." What else? "Skinweave, second generation processing."

Agility enhancements? No, I relied on myself for that. With pain dampeners, the risk of hyperextending my joints without noticing would put me on my face. "And tighten my fucking chipset before I tear it out."

Orchard shook in my grasp. Tiny vibrations that mirrored the strain in her neck, delicate cords taut all the way into the soft, folded collar of her high-neck sweater. Surprise and pain and something much, much deeper – something kinder than I expected or deserved – swam behind her eyes. One squinted, same side as the corner of her twisted mouth pulled up.

Fucking flowers from her hair. Her soap, maybe.

Orchard cupped my elbow in one hand – the only part of me she could reach. Gentle, too.

Goddammit.

"Riko." A very quiet way to say my name. Quieter than I was used to. "I'm willing to listen, but you need to let me go."

*No.* My fingers spasmed. "Can you do it or not?" I demanded, rasping every word. Something twisted inside me. Something ugly and raw; it fed the gaping wound inside my chest and tore it wider. Deeper.

We'd made progress, but Indigo hadn't filled it in. I didn't know if anything ever would.

Her flinch this time left lines bracketing her mouth. Her skin whitened around her freckles, darkening them. "Riko." Firmer. "You're hurting me."

Hurting?

This pampered little sinner didn't know the first thing about the concept.

And because that thought, violent and cruel, screamed through the front of my brain, I let her go. Shoved her away from me.

One of her feet slid in the coffee puddle and nearly

wiped her out entirely. She caught herself on the corner of a machine bristling with tubes while I skipped back three feet and jammed my hands behind my back. They fisted hard. Specs in my left optic scrolled from bone-threatening to steel-denting.

Fuck me. Fuck me with every goddamn thing possible, and skip the lubrication.

What was I *doing?*

Orchard righted herself, rubbed at her upper arm as she surveyed the mess on the floor. Ruefully, she shook her head. "I guess you don't want coffee?"

No. I wanted to scream. To throw a fist at her and make her run from me; *why* wasn't she calling for security? What the fuck did she stand there for, why did she look up from the stain and turn that rueful, gentle smile on me?

"Never mind," I snarled. "Forget everything." I turned around, fully intending to stride right the fuck out, but collided with the back of another stupid piece of tech in the way. Swore some more.

When a long, spindly hand cupped my flesh arm, thumb on an overly tender streak of shiny pink skin, I went still. Froze in place. Punching, I thought numbly, was my first impulse. So much so that my hand was already a fist, cocked at the elbow.

I squeezed my eyes shut.

*Blood on white tile.*

It didn't help.

*Guts dripping down cement.*

My teeth gritted hard enough, they creaked with the strain.

*Scattered hunks of black hair crusted in gore.*

Nothing made sense. Nothing fit; I couldn't keep it all straight. Memories that weren't memories, dreams that weren't dreams; what-ifs and almosts and fear and *wants*–

That hand tugged me around.

Copper in white. Light blue eyes ringed in burnt orange lashes.

These things were in front of me.

The smell of coffee.

The thick burn of sanitizer.

I hate it here.

Orchard's mouth moved, and as I stared at it, her words pushed through the buzzing, roaring cacophony pounding between my ears. "–panic, it's OK, take deep breaths. In." She inhaled deeply; a caricature of a breath. Let it out in just as overdone a fashion. "Out. You're not anywhere but here."

I *hate* it here.

Her nails, short and clipped to nearly nothing, left no dents as she tightened her grip. "Come on." Quiet voice. Firm. Level, like all she wanted to do was narrate the weather. "Step back into now, Riko. Focus." And then, stern like a teacher, "*Breathe*, Riko."

I breathed. Took in a gulp of air I didn't know I was missing until her voice crashed into my daze and oxygen tore my world back into pulsating, vibrant color.

Or what there was of it in this fucking white lab.

*I hate it here.*

I wobbled. For all her birdlike build, Orchard had a grip made for something other than fragile glass tubes and delicate equipment. She pulled me forward, turned me easily and sat me in the chair she must have evacuated when told I was coming.

My butt hit the soft padding.

Orchard crouched between my splayed legs, balanced between my knees, and looked up at me with those stupidly soulful crystal eyes. She could wait me out. She had the time. The inclination.

I didn't expect judgment from her. Wouldn't get it. She wasn't the type. Too godfuckinglydamn pure for my world.

I judged *myself*.

Her hands rested on my bare knees, which let her balance lightly on the balls of her feet. And gave her a perfect view of my face. Gone was the hurt. The wariness.

But the bright red patch on her nearly translucent skin, that still glowed.

I'd done that.

Orchard searched my face until she felt confident I'd come back. I guess I did. Suddenly, I found my skin impossible to wear, heavy and itchy and constricting.

Her mouth did that smile thing again. "Hey."

My lips peeled back from gritted teeth.

I wanted to say sorry.

I wouldn't. Still wouldn't. Not here. I wasn't; I needed what I needed.

My sorries had all tapped out.

She unfolded, using my knees as a brace, and stepped away. The stain on her sweater turned the bright blue fibers muddy brown. It dripped down her denim, tracing one skinny knee on the outside knob of her kneecap. "You stay put. I'm going to go change into scrubs."

I opened my mouth, managed, "I'll–"

"You," she cut in over me, and pointed at the usual place. Curtained room. White gowns all stocked up. "Will go put on a medical gown so I can keep the scan as clean as possible." Her gaze dropped to my healing arm. "And I'll pull up some rechargers for you."

Somehow, she wasn't yelling.

Crying.

Staring.

Whatever her responses could have been, she chose calm, matter-of-fact, kind. No matter how that burn on her hand might feel. I'd left bruises on her upper arm. Her nanos would heal it fast, but that wasn't the point, was it?

I was six sides of a thorny asshole, and for once, I didn't feel good about it.

# 33

When I came back from the land of the anaesthetized, Orchard was the first thing I saw. Or rather, her hair. Even I could tell my fascination with it was getting ridiculous.

She looked up from whatever work she did on her desk – no projections this time. She, like me, preferred tablets. Solid things to carry around, I suspected, rather than for security's sake. Her smile flashed, far too bright and open for the shit I'd laid on her.

I didn't get it. I didn't get *any* of it.

"Hey, you woke up quick. How're you feeling?"

No different, except more rested than usual. I frowned, sitting up easily from the usual table-bed thing. "What time is it?"

She checked the delicate watch on her wrist. It hung too loosely, she had to tilt her wrist to do it. Bright fuck-off green, not elegant at all. "Quarter past eight." Great. Still in too-early-for-thinking time. "Are you feeling better?"

I thought about it as I swung my feet to the side of the platform. She'd changed the crinkly paper shirt thing for comfortable recovery wear. This time, she'd given me white boardshorts and a white sports bra. Like she knew.

Bless her with whatever supreme power she liked.

I rubbed my scalp. "Head doesn't hurt anymore."

"Good start," she replied, scooting her heels off the chair seat and unbending from it. I couldn't fold up that small, too much muscle. "Your projection protocols are active again. I also checked out your arm. The replacement girdle has held up well. Aside from some minor cosmetic damage, you're in good shape."

I looked down at the matte metal. Poked at the extra ammo slot built in.

Still full.

When I looked back up, Orchard's smile was wry. "Yes, you are still armed." She pointed at a small pile of clothes, and the assault rifle hung over the back of a chair. "That's yours."

My bare feet hit the cold tile. I flinched, bit it back. Prepped for a spike of panic.

It didn't come.

I frowned at nothing. Thought about it all over again, checked in with my various body parts.

No sense of being watched.

No aching wound behind my ribs.

No deeply rooted need to murder every screwhead in the city.

Well. That was new.

Orchard watched me pad barefoot to the chair, pull the clothes up for inspection. Canvas pants – yellow, I noted in bemusement, like dark mustard – and a black, high-collar tank top. Nicer than I'd usually print up, but beggars and all that. Wasn't going anywhere I needed to impress anyone, anyway.

I needed some fucking peace and quiet while I waited for Indigo to crack those chipsets.

"Thanks," I said. I dropped shorts and top, pulled on

the underwear she'd printed for me, too. Slimfit white boxer-briefs – oh, yeah, she had my number – and another sports tank to keep everything in place. Also white.

Could've done without the white, but I figured her options were limited.

Orchard sat back down, stretched out her long legs. They crossed at thin ankles. "I did not," she continued, "implant any more cybernetics than what you already have."

I grimaced down at the button fly I struggled to snap together.

"You're already pushing yourself to the brink," she continued, "and the risk of hitting your threshold is too high. Even with our schematics and research, it's not a risk worth taking. This soon after nanoshock, recovery takes precedence."

Finishing the last button, I looked up. Not surprising she knew. Nanoshock takes its toll, and that shows up in scans. I nodded. "Fine."

I mean, what else was I supposed to do? In my state of zen, I recognized the logic. I preferred fighting necros, not joining them. I'd gotten impatient. Desperate.

Orchard's pale pink lips curved down, just a little. Her eyes settled on the ruined ink on my arm, though the scarring felt much less tender when I flexed it. "Be kinder to yourself, Riko. I can patch you up to a point, but I can't dose you up every time you come in here."

My brow furrowed. "Dose?"

"Anti-anxiety."

Well, that explained the lack of breath-shortening hysteria. I wasn't sure how to feel about that one, either. It was nice to breathe. It wasn't so nice to learn what it was I'd been missing in all the stress.

"Thanks," I said again, looking away.

"None needed. Just maybe go easy?"

Nope. Couldn't do that. I shrugged in answer. She, because she was too goddamn savvy to my shit, didn't push it.

The black tank was stretchy, but the collar took a bit of work to pull over my head. I missed the compressed hiss of doors from a farther exit, was too focused on tugging the fabric over the expanse of my cold abs and testing my internals for even a twitch of pain. Regardless of my eerily steady calm, the place was still too damn cold.

"Riko."

Ah, *shit*.

Orchard spoke up out of my line of sight. "Sir."

"Leave us, Dr Gearailteach." More snap than Orchard deserved. More authority than I would *ever* tolerate from him. But her? She had to suck it up and answer. Probably didn't think twice about it.

"Sir," she echoed. "Bye, Riko." The soft step of her footfalls faded, until they vanished behind another set of doors across the lab.

He barely waited for her to go.

"You," he told my back, "are not welcome here."

Shirt in place, boots in hand – at least my boots had lasted this far – I turned to meet Malik's icy stare. Man, I thought it was cold in here *before*. I smiled. Smirked, really. "Just leaving."

The ground he covered might have been intimidating for somebody else. I just watched him halt outside my reach. "Only *you* would cause chaos and think you can walk back into my offices like you belong."

I shrugged. And thank fuck, none of it hurt. "I don't *belong*," I said. "I'm just a contractor."

"Not anymore, you aren't."

I blame whatever Orchard gave me. The words didn't

make me angry. Didn't affect me me in the least bit. Another shrug. My smirk deepened.

His eyes narrowed. "You think this is funny?"

I shook my head, dropped my boots to the floor and kicked the one that fell sideways back upright. I focused on sliding my bare foot into it. Left Malik staring down at the top of my head. "I think it's a shitrolling riot," I replied. "What did you think would happen when you contracted a saint?"

Didn't have to translate the word. He knew. "I expected at least a modicum of effort."

I kicked the other one on, stomped hard to get them both in place. "Seriously, Malik. You're so smart, and then you're really very stupid."

That tic in his jaw. The tightening, subtle but there, in his shoulders. I'd learned to read him.

And he'd learned to read me. His mouth twisted in disgust. "You're out of it. What were you given?"

Whoops. "Nothing."

"What," he repeated evenly, "did my technician give you?"

Damn him. I did not want Orchard in trouble. This was not her fault; she was too shitting kind. "She fixed my chipset," I replied flatly, smile fading. "The anesthesia is wearing off." Boots in place, clothes on, I picked up the assault rifle and slung it over my shoulder. Paused, and added, "Your people walked off with my Dakon M422A. I want it back."

"You may trade it for the Valiant 14."

They say familiarity breeds contempt. Guess so. Right now, tearing off Malik's arm and beating him to death with it – in a very calm and collected way – sounded so much better than fucking him.

"The hell I will," I snapped. "It's mine."

"It was until you broke contract."

My eyes widened. Narrowed just as fast. "No deal."

"Then your Dakon remains with me."

"Fine." Whatever. The Adjudicator was a lot less rare than the Valiant, and a third of the price. I'd get another.

As I walked past him, a powerful hand wrapped around my metal arm, held tightly enough that I'd have to work to disengage. He'd done this before. Back then, it'd totally turned me on. Now, I scowled down at the shape of his fingers, the color warm against the cold matte metal. "You're about to expend *your* freebie," I warned quietly. "I've had enough."

"Everyone has." He dragged me half a step closer, biceps flexing impressively under his light gray suit jacket. So close that his mouth was only centimeters from mine. Not because he'd kiss me. Not because I'd kiss him.

I'd rather facefuck a piranha.

But this close, I couldn't miss the frozen fury in his eyes. Or misunderstand the ice coming from his mouth. "You may officially consider your contract severed, Risa Cole."

My flesh fingers twitched. "She died in that lab," I reminded him. So very, very softly. "You never had a contract with *her*."

"What I have," he replied evenly, "is you. Contracted or not. On my payroll..." His grip hardened, tugged me that much closer. "Or not."

His face. I'd go for his fucking beautifully arrogant face first and then I'd make him eat his own dick whole. Choke on it. Then I'd mail his cock-stuffed head to his wife for shits and giggles.

He let me go, a casual move, and calmly tucked his hands into his trouser pockets. Effortlessly posed, a goddamn model on a corpfuck feed with a less vapid stare and more deadly intensity in every line.

Screw him.

He knew my name. My gridded name, the one matched up with my DNA and my birth records and the SIN I'd carved out ages ago. He possessed my DNA – impossible to avoid. Orchard had been my only doc.

I'd had no other choice.

Now, I'd make one.

I stepped back out of his reach. "Is that a threat, *Malik*?" Venom in two syllables.

Even his shrug promised more trouble than I could handle right now. "Just a warning."

My jaw clenched. Every muscle locked so tight, I expected bones to break beneath. Not even Orchard's chemical helper put this one down. But what could I do? Short of a skilled 'jector willing to take this one on, I couldn't just murder him and expect that data to erase itself.

Or to vanish from the anglo records created when I was born.

Line in the white tile, drawn in blood. *Mine*.

Very slowly, with monumental effort, I turned. Continued to the exit, shaking.

He let me go. Only way I could describe it. Motherfucker *let* me go.

Not like I'd get far. He'd made sure of that.

# 34

If I could trust Muerte, she was the only one who'd found my flat so far. Meant I had somewhere to fester, and I very much wanted to fester. I had literally *nothing* else to do. Couldn't ream Malik dick to asshole. Couldn't make Indigo work any faster. Couldn't get Orchard to up my tech and couldn't find a streetdoc who'd do it without risk of fucking me up or over.

Couldn't hit the Mecca – even that place closed ass early in the morning for cleaning. And on the slim chance I'd meet any Kill Squad or other opportunistic meatheads, I didn't have it in me to fight.

All I had was a relatively unknown place to rack out, a lot of guns in it, and a stash of slank I hadn't burned through yet.

It was ultimately a start. Not a great one, but a start.

My door was still locked. Small favors. My place empty. Larger favors.

My stash untouched.

Awesome fucking world I lived in.

Banking on the fact that it'd take Digo more than a couple hours of effort to crack a company's chip sec, I snagged two envelopes of haphazardly measured orange powder. This stuff, it could be shot up, snorted, even eaten. Tasted like ass with a side of ratshit, but it worked.

In my case, I was too fucking worn to do anything else but dump it on the dresser in a messy pile and sit crosslegged on the bed, staring at it.

*Zen it*, right?

I counted out the problems in front of me.

One, somebody had stolen a security vid incriminating me in blacknet saint traffic. Two, that same pendejo had somehow figured out where I lived, and according to Muerte, they hadn't released any of it openly.

Three, it'd only be a matter of time before they did.

Four, the Vid Zone's chopshop lab showed signs of necro code in the databanks. Weaponizing it, according to Malik Reed. MetaCorp had wanted in there so bad, they'd taken on an insertion team *and* a metric spunk ton of murderous necros in the middle of a blight.

Five, Battery's location had been secretly owned by MetaCorp, and its databanks deleted only days ago. Given the timing, that was about the same time Greg and Indigo had been poking around there.

Six, the Knacklock shop and its doc had some sort of deal with MetaCorp, but if I wanted to hit that one, I'd have to wait for more information.

I stared at my fingers, five metal and one scarred.

MetaCorp was the common denominator here. But then...

So was I.

I squeezed my eyes shut. Six problems in front of me, and that wasn't including Dancer's Kill Squad, the up-and-comers sniffing around my ass, Lucky's disappearance and the protection he'd supposedly extended over my cred this whole time, the ruined art of my right side, my only access to med-tech cut off because Malik Reed's limpdick can't handle a punch...

I wondered if Orchard got in trouble.

I also wondered how long before Malik tried to fuck me with his records.

My forehead dropped to the surface of the dresser, a puff of slank dust exploding out in tiny grains. Stuff came in yellow and purple, too. Red, but that shit'd gone out of favor when the prime dealer got caught cutting the goods with raw chemicals. Killed a few unlucky suckers before they'd run him down.

I inhaled sharply, caught a nose full of the cloud. Swallowed it down.

"Problem number seven," I muttered to the dusty powder. "I am sober."

At least that one I could fix now.

I stayed on the bed, my legs hanging over the edge, my head on the dresser surface. My hands hung loosely between my knees. Which is how the projection caught me: slowly easing my brain into a slank haze while Orchard's medicated chill padded my calm.

I flicked out my tongue, licked up a patch of the orange dust in front of my face, and answered the call.

The box loaded up, Indigo's plain avatar popped in. Nothing fancy about it. He hadn't even updated it in years. "You racked out?" he said by way of greeting.

I nodded, not sure if my avatar had formed or not. I guess it had since Digo was looking at me.

"Muerte know where?" he asked shrewdly.

My nose wrinkled. He took that as a yes.

The first blast of advertising crawled across the walls. "News," he said, "stay put. We're coming to you."

Indigo was worse than Lucky sometimes. Worse than me. The connection dropped and I was left blinking, dusted orange slank trying to coat my eyelashes when I huffed out a tired laugh.

So much for festering alone.

And so much for my stash. Even I wasn't stupid enough to take more than a hit when possible opportunity came my way.

Swiping the stuff back into the packet it came from, I dropped it into the stashbox, licked the remains off my hand and set about prepping for company.

That meant sitting my ass down in the narrow hallway. Waiting.

Daydreaming in vicious color.

Slank isn't the kind of thing you want to take in a bad mood. It amplifies your state of mind, makes good times great and bad times ugly. I'd hoped it'd ride on the calm Orchard had chemically forced on me, but I guess I was just too wired for that.

Instead, I stared at my limp hands, one gray and one grayish complexioned under dusty brown, dangling between my knees. I thought about all the ways I wanted to tear out somebody's spine and whip it overhead like a stripper's LED G-string.

My day, I decided, was absolutely going to get worse. How could it not?

*Click.*

I looked up. "You're too fast," I shouted, "come back in ten minutes." Let the slank settle. I'd burn through this much too fast to enjoy.

Silence.

My eyes narrowed. I held my breath, straining my ears. Not like this place wasn't ass to mouth anyway. Flats in every direction, and sturdy walls or soundproofing couldn't mask every bit of noise.

Two fingers tapped on the tile beside my hip, flesh to floor.

*Clack.*

Street-honed instinct kicked in through fading burn. I kicked off the floor, went flying ass-first down the tiny hall as my door exploded. Splinters streaked in every direction, shrapnel torn apart by a wall of repeaters.

I was too winded to laugh.

Most of the time, nobody expects the occupants of a doorbuster to be floor-level at the start. Half the time, though, this kind of frontal assault is mostly about getting attention. Anything that draws blood is a bonus.

One hundred percent of the time, I stashed firepower everyfuckingwhere I could, ensuring I'd never be caught flat-footed. Should have known my place wouldn't stay hidden. Muerte had overestimated how much time I had to clear out.

The rapid rate of fire didn't slow down, suggesting more than a few shooters. Probably a crew. I kicked out the thin line of plaster disguising my first stash.

Not everything stayed in a drawer. Just the shit too big to hide.

The Cougars inside this one would do the job. I'd *rather* have my Adjudicator – I felt like I'd traded my favorite handgun for my assault rifle – but it'd do. Problem was figuring out which of my various exits hadn't been covered.

As the bullets ripped through plaster and supports, trashed the rest of my door from top to bottom, I picked up a third gun. A Phelps & Somers CounterTech II, always a decent backup against primitive fucks.

Only two knives – the rest had been lost to Mantis, too. Dammit.

And my Valiant. Left that hanging on the corner of the dresser because occasionally I'm smart *and* lucky.

But how lucky?

I chose an exit at random – the window in my bedroom

wall. It looked out over primo real estate: a shitty alley and the grimy facing of the place on the other side of it. Narrow space, too many levels down to risk jumping.

The problem had pushed their way into flats across the way. Form of mercenary fuckheads.

A shotgun cracked, thundered between the two structures and bounced back, louder and louder. The 7mm round hit the window frame over my head and shattered it.

I crouched, spared the direction it came from a glance. Two assholes, definitely saints, leaning out of a busted window. The bottom one had the shotgun, which he pumped for a second shot. Two-cartridge beast. Slow, but messy.

Couldn't see much of him, but his pal stood out. A lanky bastard with a shock of white hair on the top of his head and bright green bands around his elbows swaying his Viva Insurgent left to right – shit aim, decent coverage.

Awful line of sight.

I retreated a few steps. Voices shouted behind me. Unintelligible, except I recognized the tone of mercs on a mission. Didn't take long for one to run up on me. That one, I put a bullet in. As she sprawled, blood smearing my floor, two more flattened on the other side of the corner. Popped out just in time for me to shoot another. Side-hit – he'd been taller than I expected.

Two women, one brick house.

Way more firepower than I deserved.

Jamming both of my Cougars into the front of my pants – no more room in the back, and my harness had vanished – I turned and hauled ass. Braced one foot on the window frame and launched myself into the very narrow space outside.

Only two places to go, and one sucked worse than the other.

"She jumped," bellowed a woman, voice thick with a guttural accent. Russky, maybe. Unlike the anglo zoo, russkies integrated easily with everybody else. Only thing different is they kept tight bonds with each other, trusted each other over strangers, and so on. Their language hadn't rusted as badly as most.

I'd met a handful of russky runners along the way. Funny enough, most leaned to munitions specialists. And when it comes to russky-run companies, they run heavy weapons development. Crown of them was the Bolshovekia the merc pointed at me.

I clambered up the alley walls like a spider on steroids, oddly calm for the chaos unfolding around me. Thank you, Orchard. And slank.

And the brutal, icy rise of revenge brewing where adrenaline should be.

Didn't care about flight. As I leapt side to side, grabbing ledges and cracking wall and jamming my feet and toes wherever they fit, I pulled myself up with incredible ease. Searched for a place I could fight.

Would have kept going if a tanned hand hadn't snapped out of an open window I climbed past, grabbed my left foot and jerked me roughly inside. I had barely enough presence of mind to brace the sole of my boot on the wall before I ended up in a permanent splits, but my ass, back and side scraped hard into the ledge.

I landed on my back, gasping for the air punched out of me, and grabbed the pistol at my stomach.

A boot stepped on both, hand and weapon. "Don't shoot me, I'm here to help."

# 35

Detective cunting Greg Keith. I'd recognize that voice anywhere – it showed up on a frustratingly regular basis now that he considered himself one of us. I scowled at him through gritted teeth, struggling to my feet as more shouts, more gunfire, erupted below us. Thuds rocked the floor – boots, probably. A lot of them.

Probably a few heavies.

Definitely a lot of guns.

Place was too small for swords, so I had *that* going for me.

Greg, the moron, tried to help me up. I glared at him so fiercely, he backed up. "Whoa, don't bite, either."

I would, given half the chance. Savage him so bloody, he'd limp out of here and never hit the streets again. The detective was so far out of his league – and his fucking jurisdiction – that he'd shown up in the sinner's version of bare. No armor, one weapon – a Manticore. He'd moved up in the world.

I backed away from the window, sparks dotting the dark alley as the mercs aimed at nothing. Sound strategy – enough firepower, and somebody's bound to hit something. If they had any snipers lined up, though, I was dead bloody meat and a gray-pink splatter.

I held my side, bent over, gun loosely in my other hand and swinging by my knees. "Christ on a cunt," I managed, glaring at him. "What are you even *doing* here?"

He smiled faintly. "I figured you'd need extra help after the raid."

"Indigo send you?"

"Yeah."

"Why?"

"I was closer." His smile vanished, gaze searching the window and head cocked like he listened for oncoming fuckheads. "I have good news and bad news."

I straightened slowly, side aching. Orchard's dose of happy juice and the little bit of slank I'd swallowed weren't nearly enough to keep me mellow through this kind of shit. I pulled out my second pistol, easing a little farther into the room – a lot like mine, but no hall, I noted; clear space for shooting and no cover – and watched the window. "Cover the door." And then I added, "Tell me."

Greg, for all his stiff blue neck, stood at my back.

"Well." He held his pistol like a professional, at least. Double-cupped, barrel pointed up, elbows bent and steady. So cop, it hurt. "Good news is Koupra's on the way down, couple of people with him." Relief hit. "Bad news is that there's a bounty on your head pretty much guaranteed to set me up for life."

Relief fizzled. Boy, did he flinch when my metal hand pointed that second gun at him. Covering the window and the cop was easy. It was the rest I worried about.

Greg went wide-eyed, but fucking hell, he pointed his own Manticore right back at me. Straight-armed and stern.

I took a very brief second to approve of his reaction.

"Stand down," he said firmly. "I'm *not* here to kill you."

I met his eyes, death etched in mine. A promise of every nightmare the good detective ever had. That Manticore of his didn't waver. Guess he'd learned a thing or two on that job of his. A gun in his hands suited him. "Talk fast," I said flatly. "How much?"

"Koupra didn't give me specifics, but he said only one gang's been offered it."

"Shit." Muerte. She must have leaned on her contacts, kept tabs on the pendejo on my ass. "Which gang?"

The Manticore lowered, once more pointing to the floor. "Kill Squad."

"Fuck," I growled. "Fucking fuck fuckity cuntsniffing *mutants*."

I was boned. Boned, boned, fucked, boned. Whoever this guy was, he'd just reached out directly to the gang Muerte and I had pissed the hell off and offered them my head on a plate. There was no way they'd roll so far off-turf without a shitting good reason.

Both weapons returned to position, pointed at the window. Didn't see much happening. Heard a shit-ton of commotion Greg's way. "Swap," I said curtly. He did. I covered the door instead, prepped to blow it the fuck up. With limited weaponry and no extra ammo. Just fucking great. "Is your badge on you?"

"No."

I owed him more credit than I tossed him. I'd fix that later, if he survived this. "You ever face something like the Kill Squad before?"

"Don't know."

I gave it to him. Hard to know what the shit is until you've been in it before. "OK. Follow my lead and you may walk out with your ass intact."

His laugh rasped. "Got it."

I couldn't risk looking back. Boots and jeers followed by bursts of gunfire came at us from both sides. I had to trust he'd hold his own. And my back. "Shoot whatever the shit comes in."

"Christ," he said hoarsely, and then we had no time left.

The door busted open beneath the kind of boot that could only belong to a heavy. Didn't even stop to find out who. I had a bottleneck for as long as they tried to use the door, and I started firing before they considered blowing the walls.

Behind me, Greg hit my back, braced. I felt the recoil of his own discharging heavy pistol as more saints tried to swing into the window. Screams, blood, the whine of bullets too close for comfort – and under it, the faintest sound. A metallic clink.

I backed so hard into the detective, he stumbled. Turned into him, shoved him until he had no choice but to stagger towards the window. "Jump!"

"But–"

"*Jump, asshole.*" Firing back with my flesh hand, I grabbed the back of his T-shirt and practically threw him through the frame.

One.

A merc, midst of climbing up, shrieked as Greg's flailing limbs rolled her right off the ledge. He shouted. A runner with bright red eyeliner dropped, clutching their arm, while another leapt over and caught a 12mm in the face for his trouble.

They were practically killing each other. Kill Squad grunts, then. Cannon fodder.

Two.

Leaping backwards out of the window wasn't ideal,

but the alternative sucked bad enough to risk it. I had to drop my Cougars to do it, but I twined my tech fist tightly in the back of Greg's shirt and we fell together.

Three.

A deep, ear-rattling *boom* registered. The walls rocked as fire spewed out from the windows – probably tore through the floors. Casualties. Absolutely. Because saints, we're assholes. And we get the job done.

Eventually.

The blast shoved us together into the other wall, searing my back. I felt the fabric of my shirt singe and then burn away; the CounterTech shoved into the back of my pants went white hot, branding its shape into my waist.

Only thing that saved my Valiant was its fire-retardant strap.

We both shouted as we fell ass over knees over balls down the alley gap.

# 36

Reckless grenades are a thing of beauty: used the way some smeghead had used that one, and I suddenly had less to worry about. But real mercs? The ones with cred and experience? They don't run in like idiots. They wait for casualties. Either I'd wind up weakened, or competition would wind up dead – or both.

Somewhere in this mess, Dancer or one of her lieutenants would be looking for me. I needed to get Greg out of the line of fire before that happened. Preferably myself, too. I sure as necrotitties couldn't take on the entire Squad, and wasn't suicidal enough to try.

I hung from the ledge of an open window, fingers turning purple at the ends. Greg scrambled to get his feet on something – anything – to balance us out, my other hand wrapped around his wrist. I struggled to keep my tech fingers from overcompensating. A crushed hand would do neither of us any favors.

My meat fingers grated against the ledge. "Hurry!"

"I'm trying!"

"Get good," I gritted out.

I hurt. My back sizzled. I had to compensate for every shrieking nerve that pulled when I moved anything below my neck, and Greg's flailing made it worse. Pretty sure the back of my head had turned patchy, but at least I still had eyebrows.

No bullet holes yet. Small victories.

"Got it!"

My grimace might be mistaken for an encouraging smile; Greg took it that way. Ironic, given the smile he gave back looked a lot like panic.

Precariously balanced on the window ledge, he looked up, then down. His muscles strained, causing him to vibrate in my grasp. "Now what?"

I grunted. "See that narrow scaffolding?"

"No… Wait, yes." Hard to spot. It hugged a narrow section of the wall, rusted down to the bolts. A good tug would probably detach it from its crumbling moorings. What I planned would probably break it in pieces. "Don't tell me–"

"Grab it." With no more instruction than that, I dropped him.

"Riko–!" At least he didn't scream this time, though he turned *real* green around the edges. He flailed, smacked his hands and knees and feet and elbows and whatever else he didn't tuck in, scraped them bloody. Awful. *Really* bad. He needed to condition up.

Except no way would I encourage that, I thought grimly as I wrenched my arm back up onto the ledge, easing my meat fingers. They throbbed. I heard metal clang, a shrill sound, then bolts tearing loose. The whole scaffold creaked, probably bent, and Greg's shout cracked three octaves up. Another impact, and then silence. Nothing but the ever-present rush of a city that never fucking knows when to shut up and the murder spree up above.

As I braced my feet on the wall, I heard wearily, "You're a bitch, you know that?"

"Are you calling me that because of my vag?"

"No," he grunted. "I'm calling you that because I hope you go to hell."

"You're a bad Catholic." I held onto the ledge, turned, bent so the soles of my feet pressed flat.

"Christian," he muttered.

"Whatever."

He stared at me, hanging from both hands by the makeshift bridge. His feet swayed over nothing. His fingers were flat and abraded. The fact he'd managed to keep some of his cool impressed me.

I'd never tell him. Asshole needed to go home.

"You aren't–"

He obviously knew I was. As I pushed off from my wall, let go, I caught the other wall, skidded down that, and let go just in time to land on the collapsed scaffold. What used to be the top gouged into the brick, scored deep canyons. Greg shouted – most of which was prayer, I think, with some "Goddammit!" thrown in for extra bonus points – and swung wildly as the whole thing bent under my weight.

I crouched, held the bar under my feet for extra security, and peered between them at his panicked features. "Get a grip."

"You are not funny!"

"I'm a goddamned riot," I replied. I bent to grab one of his wrists with my free hand. He was too fucking heavy, and getting heavier by the second. My shoulder girdle twanged every time I had to carry him. Flinching, I jerked my chin over his shoulder. "You see that byway?"

"Holy Christ, Riko, n–!"

Yep. The amusing part of the whole thing was that he stretched out the *ooooooo* part of his protest all the way through the alley and into open air.

Gave it about a second before I stomped one foot on the nearest side bar and leapt after him.

He landed first, rolled over and over, a blur of filthy blue and abraded skin. The scaffolding snapped in half under the pressure I put on it, clattered and shrieked all the way down. I landed near enough to hear him cursing every way he knew how, balanced enough on my aching feet to turn my crouch into a guided roll, easing the shock.

Everything about this pissed me off. The rapid beat of my heart, echoed in chest and ears, the dull throb in shoulder and ankles. Burns were probably my least favorite – my back screaming with every move.

And I wasn't done. Not by a long shot.

I jumped to my feet, doing everything I could to shrug it all off. "Thanks," I snapped. "Run. I'll be in touch." If I survived.

"Wait," he wheezed.

I paused, crouched by his head, and set my CounterTech on the street beside his ear. Grimy, bloody, sweaty and half-dazed, he still managed to lift two fingers in a half wave. "You can't take on all of them."

I almost gagged. "How sweet," I said dryly, and patted his stubbled cheek. "You can't either, so go home and let it blow. And *don't*," I added as I rose painfully from my crouch, "stick your nose in this unless you want them shooting up your wife and kid."

He blanched.

I left him prone and bruised, dealing with the imagery I'd left him and struggling to regain his equilibrium.

He'd seen Indigo, he said, but where? I should have asked. Too late now.

At the end of the byway, where it turned into another layer of dirty street, the usual crowd hadn't dispersed.

Why should they? The shootout, whatever it was, was happening above them. Maybe, at worse, a body or two might splat in the middle of a crowd, or into the street. Maybe debris.

Shit happened on the regular. Doubt anyone would care, long as it didn't land on anybody. And had something worth pawning.

Crowds also meant cover.

"Riko!"

And cover would only work if I got there in time. Shit.

Valentine melted out of the crowd, a surprisingly effective move on his part. With broad, perfectly sculpted chest and shoulders, deeply bronzed skin, and white as ice short hair, he was not a man that looked like he could blend. The devilish goatee framing his mouth, like a fetishized desert fantasy, was black, contrasting in exotic flash. Every line of his beautiful body had been paid for – and perfection is expensive. He wore it well, *used* it well. Somehow, he didn't come off as pretty.

He came off as quietly dangerous.

I'd never been so glad to see him in my life. My shoulders relaxed, just enough to let me rub my face, clear sweat from my eyes. "Fucking hell, Valentine, I thought you were Kill Squad." I scanned the area behind him. "Is Indigo with you?"

Val shook his head, golden hoops at one ear glinting in faded daylight. Those were new.

Right. He hadn't spoken with Digo yet. After all, he'd been freelancing for a couple weeks. And now that I looked at him, it clicked: he'd have *no* reason to run into me here.

It took a long time for the sun to reach this far, which also helped keep the heat at bay for a while. Felt good on my grimy skin. Cooled off the excess jitters. My grin tipped crooked. Rueful. With my Valiant strapped behind my back and my pistols all gone, all I could do was shake my head at him. "Your timing really is the worst."

"Not really," he said. Then he shot me.

The first round hit me in the shoulder, where the metal shape of my arm turned into flesh. It glanced away from the diamond steel, which shoved it right under my collarbone. Bone splintered, a visceral crunch I heard as well as felt. Had no time to scream, swear; nothing but leap.

I moved forward instead of back, temporarily useless arm flapping behind me as I went for his throat. Or so he thought I would. Val learned fast; I'd done this move on him before, surprising the shit out of him at the time. Expecting it now, he skipped to the side, lining up a second shot that would have put a bullet into my head.

I knew better. He and I both knew better. We'd each built solid cred, and so much of it had been built on blood.

I dropped to the asphalt and spun on one hand and one foot, lashing the other leg out. It collided not with his ankle, but his knee. The front of my shin bent inwards, pushed in with so much force that at first, he braced. Then his knee snapped to the side.

Wasn't even close to fair.

He shot at me again. Went wild; hit my metal elbow as Val's teeth clenched around the pain I'd inflicted. He didn't do dampeners either.

I was so coming around on those.

The assault had already announced itself. People ran in every direction, some hitting the fringes to look up at the smoke. Brakes squealed and crumpled metal screeched as cars slammed into each other. A bicyclist went rolling ass over handlebars. Chaos as everybody got the fuck out of the way.

And there I was, bleeding from the shoulder, facing off against the one member of my old crew I'd never wanted to test in any way. I'd never even fucked him, much less fought him. Shit, we'd gone forever without arguing, either. Closest I ever got to a match was when he'd tried to block my access to Digo and I'd ridden his fine abs like a surfboard all the way in to Indigo's feet.

I thought we'd been cool.

"You're freelancing for Dancer?" My voice came out thick, hoarse. Pain, I told myself. Meatbaggery. I refused to be surprised anymore when somebody in Indigo's crew tried to kill me.

"Don't act so shocked," he replied, that mouth quirking to one side. Not quite a smile. Not a scowl. Lines of pain bracketed each side, framed beautifully by his thin black goatee. "Some of us are serious about our cred."

Ouch.

He braced most of his weight on his left leg, favoring that bent right. Unlike most of the mercs back there, he'd come prepped – tactical jacket, heavy pants with straps and buckles and pockets for his toys. No shirt under that jacket, which always amused me. It left that wide expanse of his chest and the narrowing definition of his abs and hip flexors bare. No tattoos. At least, not visible.

*His* lotus tattoo was white. Stamped on his ass, he'd said. I'd never asked to see.

One more reminder that mine had blown off. Figuratively and literally.

I eased down, hands low. The strain on my clavicle made my whole body tremble. It was already slowing, but it dragged me down.

And Val still had his gun.

My teeth bared. "You are making a mistake, Val."

"Knew you'd say that." He shook his head, hobbling back a step. Barrel pointed business end at me, he reached for something stowed behind his back. "I don't understand why you're so bitter. You know the laws of the street, maybe better than I do." A surprising admission coming from him. "Nanjali was one thing." He pulled out a short black tube. "Wasn't convinced you'd pull something like that. Boss still worked with you, so I figured I'd wait and see."

I watched him carefully. Gauged not his hands, but his eyes. Cold as stone, blank as ice. Not empty, not vapid, but precise and content. No regret there. Better yet, no pity.

"Heard some rumors," he continued. He didn't have to look to see what he was doing. Munitions specialists are experts with their tools. I heard a small clink.

A familiar one.

"Wasn't worth it until one of the Squad came around." One.

I fought to keep from flinching. "How much is Dancer paying you?" I demanded.

"Nothing. Dancer's not running this venture."

Two.

That made no sense. Dancer was a hands-on leader, not a wait behind the curtain type. I narrowed my eyes at him. "Who?"

With an obvious flick of his hand, he rolled the cylinder my way. Like I'd play fetch. Like it'd be as simple as this – be shot or blown to chunks.

I was disappointed.

With a shake of my head, I turned and kicked the cylinder away. It whistled past Val's perfect ear, hit something I didn't stop to see and clattered back and forth. I was already preparing to weave when I realized he hadn't moved.

And the cylinder hadn't exploded.

Worse, resigned amusement pulled at his features. Like *he* was disappointed.

*Thoop!* The awkward, vaguely uncomfortable sound of a monofilament net discharging. I twisted, swearing, and caught a face full of thin, tensile threads woven into a net too strong to cut. Way too fine to struggle free from.

A distraction.

I'd managed to dodge the bulk, but the thing had force. Hitting my face snapped my head back, forced my shoulders to follow. Torture ripped through me as my shoulder tore open all over again, and I hit that gutted cement like a sack of shit on a melting hot day. The burn scab ripped right the fuck off.

My voice strangled. The net spiraled as my face aborted its balanced momentum. It swung wildly, collided with the front bumper of a diagonally abandoned car and shattered out its windshield when the corner weights snapped into it. It left me staring up at city lights, roiling smoke and sparse patches of gray day.

No ads, at least.

Bright orange boots stomped into the muck by my face, splattering grime across my cheek. Fidelity bent over me. Orange cargoes and matching tactical vest was his thing. He even rocked orange hair. Because why the tits not?

"Rough day," he said.

I sucker punched him in the face; fast right jab to the nose from prone.

He yelped, stumbled back. Val laughed somewhere out of my field of vision – a genuine sound that, as my chest choked on the list of growing hurts, caused another pang of regret. Of loss.

Bitches. Both of them.

"She *punched* me," Fidelity yelled.

"You deserved it."

I struggled to my elbow – my flesh one. Goddamn, the other hurt. Again. Always. "Hey," I snarled, blowing dirt and slime away from my mouth. I fixed them with a glare I knew promised bloody fucking violence. "Quit yapping when you're trying to take me down, you cuntwagons."

Didn't realize until they both turned to look at me that their weapons were down. Monofilament discharger at Fidelity's feet, Val's Bolshovekia beside it.

I gawked.

White hair gleamed as Val tipped his head to his right.

I let my head fall back on my neck and saw an upside down version of Indigo, his lips all but vanished under the intensity of whatever he was feeling. Anger. Probably anger. Maybe into fury.

Couldn't tell.

In his hands, a Sauger Quad 78 – the 54's younger cousin; less spray, more impact. The quadruple barrel pointed directly at his own team.

Well. *Shit.*

"Back off," he said. Flat. Even. Serious as ballsweat, but meaner. "I'm not fucking doing this right now."

Hands raised, Val and Fidelity backed away.

I lay there, feeling like bukkake leftovers, and tried to decide whether I wanted to be emotionally angry, physically hurt, or mentally exhausted.

All three sounded like terrible ideas.

Debris drifted down on all of us, gently floating bits of singed insulation, probably people. I grimaced as a flaky clump of ash smeared under my eye.

"Freelancing, huh?" Digo's gaze remained on Val,

though he'd lowered the Quad enough to make it obvious he didn't expect resistance.

The merc shrugged. Then jerked, winged black eyebrows skyrocketing. He grunted in surprise, lifted up on his toes like an invisible hand had grabbed him by the head and pulled.

Muerte came around him, looking rather pleased with herself. "He's armed," she said, smacking her lips, "with the finest ass this side of the divide."

I snorted. Couldn't help myself. Indigo looked like he wasn't sure whether to laugh or swear.

Val just murmured, "Thank you," and accepted it like his due.

What a sweet fucking family reunion.

I growled under my breath, struggling to stand.

"Don't get comfy," Muerte said, surveying the surrounding area. "We need to clear out."

Indigo looked up. Then back. When he stashed his shotgun, the others relaxed. Just a hair. Enough to make me realize they'd taken him at his word. He would've shot them. Why? For *me?*

Piss.

His stare burned the motherfuckers to the ground. "You stupid sons of bitches should have talked to me first."

Fidelity opened his mouth.

Indigo's eyes narrowed.

Fidelity shut his mouth again.

Valentine glanced at me. "What changed?"

"You tell me," I retorted, grabbing my tech arm in my bloody hand. "You're so all shitting knowing." Setting my teeth together, I wrenched my arm back into my shoulder socket. My healing shoulder shrieked. I knocked it down to a strangled, *"Fuckingfuckholes."*

Muerte waved a hand at all of us. "Amigos? The Squad?"

Valentine ignored her.

Indigo did not. "Get out of my sight," he said grimly. "I'll deal with you fuckheads later."

I glared at them, every bone radiating menace. If my Valiant had slipped around to my side – easy reach – I wasn't going to point it out.

Didn't need to. Muerte's hand came down on my shoulder. The good one. Squeezed hard.

Valentine took a step towards Indigo, hands tossed up in exasperation. "Boss, you–"

"Not," Digo seethed, "now."

Linker done gave orders. Wasn't the first time, either. Indigo didn't snap often, but when he did, we left him alone. It was only partially personal. Valentine and Fidelity obeyed, leaving their weapons where they'd dropped them. When they passed me, they both shrugged, gave me a look I think I was supposed to read as *no offense*. "The creds were real good," Fidelity said lightly.

I shook Muerte's hand off my shoulder. "You tiny dicked–"

Fidelity smirked, but Valentine squared up. Muscle on muscle, murder in the buried glint of his eyes. He'd take me on. Without guns between us, I was more than ready to find out who'd scream first.

Giving up on comforting, Muerte snaked an arm around my neck. The Valiant at my side suddenly vanished, the strap burning a rough line as she pulled it around. Cold metal locked against my throat, jerked me back hard enough that I choked. If I moved, if I breathed hard, I'd crush my own esophagus. "Tranqillo," she said, slow and long and drawing it out. "Calm the tiny tits."

Like that'd help.

The unmistakable sound of a shotgun primed? That did the trick. Val and I froze in place.

Fidelity went still, too. Then smacked the larger man in the bronzed arm and strode away, back tense.

Cold eyes met mine. Then he turned and followed the orange wonder into the crowd. The panic had subsided when nothing else exploded in the tenements above, but too many shitheads still lingered. Waiting. Watching.

Sighing, Muerte released her hold on the barrel of my gun. "Seriously, Riqa. That would have been an ugly brawl."

I knew it.

I grabbed the Valiant, yanked it from her loosened grasp, and spun on my heel. "Valentine said Dancer didn't order the hit."

Muerte glanced at Indigo.

The linker let the Quad drop to his side, muzzle down, and matched my pace. "She didn't. One of her lieutenants did."

Well, didn't that just make sense. "Rictor," I snarled.

"If it's any consolation," Muerte volunteered, catching up to the both of us. "He's got a hit out on me, too."

"Oh, just fucking comforting."

Indigo let out a gusty sigh, the edges of his irritation torqueing it to gravel. "I'll deal with Fido and Valentine later. Let's go before any of them wise up to your escape."

I didn't like leaving behind a fight. But I still wasn't braindead enough to take on half the Kill Squad with only three of us.

Pissed and hungry, hurting and shitting tired of getting shot, I had no choice but to run.

# 37

Another day, another ride to Kongtown. This time, I closed my eyes in the back of Muerte's trike and let my bones reknit.

The ramen stall Indigo guided us to seated five, and the cook – a large man with long brown hair shaved at one side – spoke a bastard hybrid of Kongtown dialects too fast to follow all the way through. Based in Korean, maybe. Not sure. Ultimately, it didn't matter. We ordered. He delivered.

He left us the fuck alone.

Indigo propped an elbow on the bar, every line of his body broadcasting tired. I felt that. So did Muerte, if the chin she rested on her folded elbow was any indication. Her eyes closed by her large ramen bowl while steam wafted up from all three.

The half curtain hanging behind us kept too much of the humidity in, even with two small fans running on either side of the counter. *Tickticktick.* One wobbled.

Which also pissed me off. Really, very much pissed me off.

So much pissed me off that I had no more off to piss.

My teeth gritted, ground back and forth.

"That could have been worse," Muerte said without opening her eyes.

I snorted out a bitter laugh. "At what point does it get better?"

"Well, you could be dead?"

"Preferable," I muttered, rubbing at my shoulder. "I just got my nanos juiced, you know?"

She shrugged lightly. "I know, but hey, you're worth a fuck-ton of money. How's that for fame?"

"Wrong kind and to the wrong group."

"Picky."

I grimaced. She was yanking my dick and I didn't need it. Nobody wanted this kind of shit on them. I frowned at Indigo. "How did you know the Squad had taken the hit?"

"I know a guy," he said blandly.

Muerte grinned, shedding her cropped purple jacket. She stretched her tech leg out along the ground, propped on the bottom rung of another stool. "I'm the guy," she added.

"Another trail?"

Indigo nodded. "Muerte showed me the pattern. Once you know what to look for and who to ask, it's not hard to spot."

I picked up the wooden chopsticks by my bowl, tore them apart. They splintered at the connector. They always did.

Indigo's, I noted jealously, did not.

"And?" I pressed.

"And you're not going to like it."

Muerte jammed her chopsticks into her bowl, mixing the steaming contents without pulling them apart from each other.

"Dancer?" I asked. "Would explain the Squad's

massive run at me."

She shook her head.

Indigo was more careful with his ramen, wielding the utensils to pull ingredients over each other without ruining them. "I cracked the chipsets for the final piece. Guess who's got links in to the blacknet?"

Only one answer fit that question. I shifted on the stool, leaning back with a tired groan. "MetaCorp."

"Give her a medal," Muerte murmured. Then slurped noodles she'd somehow wrapped around her single, double-wide chopstick.

"What the fuck. What the actual shit." With each word, I got madder and madder. Guess I still had some piss left in me after all. "How? *How* do they keep finding me? Why do they want me? What the cunting *hell*," I continued, voice rising, "did I do to earn their dicks down my throat?"

He reached over with a lazy hand, flicked me in the forehead. "Shut up."

My teeth clicked. My chopsticks broke between my nanosteel fingers.

Muerte smothered a husky laugh.

"We're going to find out," he continued. "Kern's Knacklock location is the only shop still active, confirmed. If I can get there fast enough, I can get into his system before he shuts it down."

"We're going to hit it," Muerte translated helpfully.

I punched her in the shoulder. Regretted it instantly when my own burned. Not fully pulled together yet. The food would help. "I know what it means," I muttered. Then, "It's about time. I'm ready to tear this chummer's head right off his neck."

"Good." Indigo took a moment to eat, slurping sounds accompanying the effort. Wordlessly, the cook slid another set of chopsticks to me. Good man.

My slurping joined theirs, and as I soaked in the flavor, we said nothing for a while. Cars careened past us, too fast for the busy street. Joes yelled around us, laughed, spoke.

What I liked best about this place were the paper lanterns strung up in every direction, every color and pattern imaginable; surprisingly delicate for such an overly crowded zone.

There are neighborhoods in Kongtown that embrace that whole Chinese vibe and go all out, other places that roll with the muddled descendants of Japanese immigrants. They don't mix much, save for a few places that operate like the rack. Neutral as long as everybody treats it that way. Same with the Korean refugees who'd made it before all hell broke loose over there, intermixed and entrenched.

The busy districts don't initially look like it, but structure reigns in Kongtown. Even the overwhelming numbers of mixed-blood people choose lines, and there is a *lot* of that. Indigo, with his Deli heritage, would fit right in without a sideways glance – as long as he chose a side. It's not about purity, it's about adherence to the way it works.

The graffiti rolling corner to corner marks borders violently defended, and aggressively violated. Those who live in the middle work like messengers and diplomats between them – a kind of chosen side. One wrong move and somebody's head shows up on somebody else's doorstep. Whole families are slaughtered on the regular; peace is an ideal that mostly gets shafted by some up and coming gang looking to shake the establishment.

For some people, traditions are ingrained so deep

in cultural memory that even ignorant fuckers find themselves walking similar lines. For others, it's all about the fetishism of a violent, made-up era long since ground into dust. Honor is a goddamn joke, and swords are only as good as the asshole using them.

But then, that was true everywhere.

I finished my food first, droplets of ramen broth splattered on the counter around my empty bowl. "We need a team," I said.

"You, me," Muerte said, meat hanging from the end of her stick. It wobbled when she gestured, dripping. "Indigo, Tashi. What about Boone?"

Indigo winced. "I told him to kick Valentine and Fido's asses if they stepped out of line."

"Shit."

"Necessary evil."

Fuck those guys. I shook my head. "A linker, two splatter specialists and a fixer aren't going to be enough."

"Ideas?" she asked.

I glanced at Indigo.

He raised an eyebrow at me, sweaty forehead wrinkling as he polished off his food.

When I shrugged, he rolled his eyes. "If you can do it, do it. But you'd better make it fast."

"Who?" Muerte asked.

Nice to know that for all the shit, Indigo had been serious when he said he'd stick to my side. I guess I'd needed the boost of support.

My smile curved real slow. Real, *real* mean. "Pretty sure he's got tools to help."

I had a plan. Thank fuck and hallelujah to the magical elephant, I finally had a plan. And within twenty-four hours, I'd have answers to all seven of my biggest problems.

MetaCorp,        MetaCunts,        Meta-fucking-Cunts Incunterated. *Cunts.*

At this point, I'd give Malik Reed my ass if it netted me what I wanted from him.

Assuming *my ass* was code for *my fist*. I'd even give him the courtesy of a reach around for his trouble.

Now, if Hope would only pick up. I'd have to get through her to get to Malik, and I was prepared to fall all over myself in apology. There was no other way.

I took the opportunity to rest my meatsack, folding my elbows on the ramen stall's counter and my forehead on my crossed forearms. Over my head, Indigo and Muerte chatted. Good. We didn't have a regular fixer as part of our crew – *our crew*, I thought, tasting the words again – and if they'd hit it off, even better.

Favor more than discharged.

When the projected call connected, my attention switched fully to the box.

I blinked. Would have blinked, if my projected avatar had loaded.

This was not the Mantis lobby, like I expected. Nor was it Malik Reed's office.

Yellow sand, finely ground and spreading out far as the eye could see. Insanely blue sky, vividly saturated and bluer, clearer, than any sky I'd ever seen in my life. The occasional fluffy cloud. Turquoise ocean, white foam crests at the top of each wave, crashed into the sand, rolled up onto the shore and was sucked back into the surf.

It was hot. It smelled like salt and something so clean, I wondered if my protocols had glitched.

This was a *lot* of creds. And a shit-ton more bandwidth than I thought possible.

Fucking executive shits.

"You have nanosteel balls." Reed's voice, tenor lowered to cold anger behind me.

I turned. My boots only sort of crunched on the sand.

And then I choked back a laugh I figured wouldn't do me any favors.

"All this," I managed with a nearly straight face, "and you still can't lose the friggin' suit."

Dark eyes, sunlight caught in the black depths and glittering, narrowed. If he cared, I couldn't find so much as a twitch in the severe planes of his face. Not that I'd come to scope his fashion – or his taste in personal projections – but I couldn't help it. Sun, surf, sand, and a charcoal gray suit jacket over a white button-down, one of his eternal vests sleek around his trim waist. Matching trousers. Shiny black shoes.

Blue and gray striped tie tucked into the vee of the fitted vest. Perfect knot.

Should have looked stupid in the middle of all this pristine scenery.

Asshole looked good.

"When you are done ogling me," he said flatly, "you can get to the point."

I pulled my gaze back up to his face, tucked my hands in the pockets of my virtual cargoes and did my best to look like I'd reflected. "I've got an offer for you."

"No."

"Hear me out–"

No," he said again, and raised a dusky hand, a spiteful wave. "Goodbye, Riko."

"We're hitting MetaCorp."

*That* got his attention. Gaze sharpening, he folded his hands behind his back. "That gets my attention."

I knew it would.

I rocked back on my heels, but my feet didn't dig into

the virtual sand. His did. In fact, his blazer ruffled in the breeze.

*Ugh.* "Knacklock. There's a saint that runs it, and according to info picked up from a couple MetaCunt *scouts–*" I drew out the word. My turn for snide. "–he's dealing with the corp direct."

Malik's expression turned thoughtful. His mouth pursed faintly, posture unbending. So fucking cool. Asshole extraordinaire. "Your source?"

"My linker."

An eyebrow. "Mr Koupra has decided to risk your presence again?"

"Fuck you."

There. Hint of a smirk, cold glimmer turning sharply amused. "Your point."

"We need another hand to fill out the hit squad."

"You killed the last team sent in to one of your..." A pause. "...chopshops. You abandoned the most recent team I offered you. I am tired," he added, humor fading, "of training my people for your disposal."

My turn to smirk. I sauntered towards him, sand and metal firm under me. The sun was warm, at least. I knew what the sun's heat felt like, even if he'd programmed this one with less radiation burn.

He watched me approach. His shoulders shifted, a minute movement.

"Why, Malik," I drawled, coming to a stop so close, I risked my protocols again. "I thought you had a lot of tools to spare."

"Don't," he said, low and bordering on a growl, "push it. You have no right to ask me for anything more."

I almost bit back. My hands clenched in my pockets, heart slamming. Anger.

And a pulse in my snatch that couldn't help responding

to that thrumming voice of his. Authority pissed me off. From him, in moments like this, it made me want to crawl inside his skin and stroke myself off with it.

All that aside, I recognized the truth of it.

"Our last meeting sucked," I said bluntly. "To put it mildly. And I'm not asking you to hire me back on."

"Not in this lifetime."

"Not that I'd go," I snapped back. I straightened, backed off because punching him again sounded just as good as anything else, and I'd learned my lesson there. "But you want MetaCorp so bad, you were willing to risk those tools of yours, so I'm asking you for one more. One body with at least four guns."

Both eyebrows rose, came with a step forward. Like he'd clear the gap I'd made.

I felt pinned, stuck to the floor by nothing more tangible than his eyes. The waves crashed loudly behind us. His feet didn't crunch on the sand but pushed into it. The shiny gleam on his shoes collected a coating of dust.

Thorough. Expensive. So very meticulous.

He noted my stiffness, too. Took another step, removed that much more space. "Correction," he said, power and weight in quiet intensity. "You have asked for nothing."

My lip curled back in a silent snarl.

In the real space I'd pulled my attention from, Muerte laughed her harsh laugh. Guns, I thought in the back of my mind. They were comparing weapons.

My jaw set. I pulled my fists from my pockets, left them rigid at my sides.

Satisfaction touched his wickedly sharp features. Anticipation. "You are fortunate I found you useful, Riko." His head tipped. His hands unlocked from behind him, pulled aside his blazer to rest at his hips. So very powerful executive. So wow. "If you ask," he continued evenly, "I will consider it."

Asking would be the same as begging.

*MetaCorp*. I wanted them so bad, I could taste the blood in my mouth already.

My teeth gritted so fucking hard, I felt Indigo's hand palm my skull. "Seems to be going well," he said. Dimly. Wryly. A disembodied voice under the projection I faced down.

Malik Reed waited.

I stared.

He had no reason to look away.

Asshole. Screw his too-harsh-for-pretty model vibe. Red crept in to the fringes of what little patience I'd mustered. Shredded the only thing keeping me toe to toe and eye to eye; it wasn't even the shitting high ground.

There was nobody else who'd help me. Valentine and Fidelity had drawn their line in the sand, temporary or not. Boone was babysitting them, and I despised the fact he had to. They'd already tried to take me out once; one bad call was all it'd take for them to not just fuck me over, but Indigo, too.

No one else would be willing to help me on this crazy ride into shitville.

I lost.

I sucked in a shallow breath. "Will you," I said through clenched teeth, "give me *one fucking enforcer* so we can *burn* MetaCorp to the *cunting ground*?"

Silence. Cool appraisal. Jacket blowing in the wind, and sunlight adding a warm golden richness under his skin I wasn't used to seeing.

My jaw popped, eyelids straining with the effort I made to keep me from snarling outright and hunting his ass down in meatspace to rip out his intestines. I'd wear them like a dripping crown.

"*Please.*"

Jesus shitting syphilitic Christ, his smile wrenched a knife through my control and at least four fingers up my cunt. "So you *can* say it."

"I will," I hissed, clenching and unclenching my hands, "bring back a MetaCorp cock and fuck your lungs with it."

A small inclination of his head. "So you say."

"Are you going to help or not?"

Silence fell between us. Hell, even the sound of the ocean dimmed. Had I lagged him? I doubted it. The steadiness of this signal felt alien to me. Secure.

His mouth finally opened, assessing me toes to crown. Then, "Knacklock. Unless I am mistaken, 53rd and 716B West."

I nodded sharply. He'd done his homework.

"I will make arrangements with Mr Koupra."

I shut the pissing call down. Sweltering heat and cramped space came back to me with full force; I'd forgotten I was sweating through my clothes. "Ugh."

"Well?" Muerte demanded, leaning forward.

"Did you set it all on fire?" Indigo asked dryly.

"*You* talk to him." I thrust myself up from the counter, emptied of our ramen bowls. The stool scraped across the rough asphalt under us, clattered to the ground. "I'm out."

"Riqa–"

"Let her be," Digo sighed. "Those two are like gunfire and gasoline. One of them's gonna blow." A pause. "One way or another."

"Eat shit and die," I shouted back over my shoulder.

"Stay close," he shouted back.

Yeah, whatever. Not like I had a choice until Malik Reed sent his meatpuppet along.

Maybe I'd put a bullet in the unlucky bastard after the run. How's that for a message?

# 38

Two hours later, I stared as a sleek black van with blackened windows pulled into the lot we gathered in. It crunched over pitted asphalt and cement, slowing to a stop at a diagonal. I turned my incredulous stare on Indigo.

He shrugged. I guess Mantis didn't do subtle.

I rolled my eyes, followed them as Indigo led the way towards the windowless back doors.

"Spunkstupid," I sighed, one hand wrapped around the strap of my Valiant.

"It's not that bad," Muerte said, chuckling as she paced me.

I curled a lip at her without pausing. "Motherlovingpisslicking–"

Muerte's stiffened fingers popped me in the throat, fast and hard enough that I staggered.

My reflexes didn't save me from eating shit. I hit the lot on one knee, grinding a few layers of skin through my filthy canvas pants, and glared up at her. "The tits?"

"Enough already, yeah?" She offered me a hand back up. "It is what it is, nena, let it go."

Grabbing at my assaulted neck, I rasped hoarsely, "Not your girlfriend and blow me."

She clicked her tongue, laughter dancing in her wide brown eyes. "Make up your mind, you're giving me whiplash."

"Knock it off, you two." Indigo waved at us without turning around, a smirk in his voice. "Stop lagging."

"Go fuck a necro," I growled at her. Ignoring her offer, I pushed back up to my feet and jogged to catch up. Muerte, the whorebag, just kept grinning.

Some things never changed.

As we approached, the black doors flung wide. Black interior, too, except for various blue and green signal lights inside. Each indicated power fed to the racks it was attached to.

Racks, I couldn't help but notice as saliva pooled in my mouth, filled to the brim with weapons of death and rampant destruction.

The sucker Reed sent to play with me crouched in the back, digging through a crate of what I hoped contained armor and more weapons. Pistols, maybe some submachine guns for fun and profit. Knives or steels? Swords weren't my thing, but when Tashi showed up, she might enjoy a little something long and hard between her hands.

My grin spread ear to ear.

"Thanks for coming," Indigo was saying as I caught up. "You made good time."

The crate snapped closed. The enforcer stood. "Take what you need."

My grin froze.

I knew that voice.

Blood rushed to my ears. My fingertips tingled. Even the goddamn ones I didn't cunting have. "You didn't," I managed through teeth that felt like they'd grind glass. "Tell me he's only the escort."

Malik Reed levered himself out of the corporate van, sturdy combat boots squaring up on the asphalt. Skinsuit. Black, gray and white urban camos like his enforcers wear between runs, but with black plates overlapping his long, powerful legs.

To my disappointment, his chest armor had been scrubbed of all Mantis insignias. No aggressive letter, no gear labels. Nothing. I couldn't even get him tossed for being stupid. My fists clenched, weight locked down on my heels.

He didn't smile when he saw me. He didn't have to. Smug arrogance was just as bad. "Riko." A small nod. "Mr Koupra." Then, as his gaze landed on Muerte, he raised those defined eyebrows and added, "What shall I call you?"

She sized him up. Didn't offer a hand. "Muerte."

"Death." His lips twitched. My fists twitched too. Maybe they should meet. Again. "A pleasure."

"All yours," she said sweetly.

That's my girl.

Unruffled, he stepped back to clear the way. "As negotiated," he said, turning his full attention to Digo. "Armor and requisitions. Certain models are in testing stages and will require monitoring."

"Like hell," I snapped at his back.

Digo's hand came up behind Malik's back, universal sign of *Riko, shut up*. "No, thanks," he replied. "We're not on your dime." Then that hand turned into a middle finger aimed at me.

Muerte cracked a laugh, quieter than usual.

Yeah, I deserved that. Should have trusted his common sense. I was rusty.

Letting my linker figure out the run's needs, and getting the shit out of Malik's general sphere of existence,

I stepped to the edge of the lot and surveyed the glimpse of road beyond the crumbling wall. "Where's Tashi?"

At my shoulder, Muerte shrugged. She, like me, had managed to keep her favorite gun, though she had a rig to hook the Viva Insurgent on. Ugh, I'd need one of those too. One more thing to borrow.

Or steal, because fucked if I'd give it back.

"All right." Digo's voice, pitched towards us. "Hook up." His way of calling for a briefing. I liked it so much more than Reed's.

Who didn't move as we all pulled together.

I scowled at him. "Your job is done. Thanks for the gear."

"Riko—"

I ignored Indigo's sigh. "Go on," I insisted, making shoo-ing motions with both hands.

Malik, the asshole, didn't move. Hadn't, either. He simply looked down at a transparent tablet scrolling what I figured was equipment and did whatever he was doing. Ignored me, too.

My jaw set. Maybe he'd helped, fine. Maybe he'd pulled together more than I thought he would. Hooray. But he was still *him* and I didn't trust *above and beyond* as a concept.

Muerte jabbed me in the shoulder. The flesh one. "I hate to say it—"

My left hand darted out. Slammed up into the tablet. "Go swap out for your monkey," I snarled.

He'd never displayed much tech, not the obvious kind. No replacement limbs, no optics, nothing I'd ever seen openly. But sometimes, when I expected otherwise, Malik moved in a way that even his defined muscle and sleek grace shouldn't have been able to. As Indigo snapped out my name and the tablet tore up into the air

– destination, corporate facehole – Malik's grip shifted. His arm moved in a way I couldn't trace, like a snake made of liquid, and the device flipped over.

Once. Twice.

When it settled again, it was face up, settled firmly and flat on his palm, and his motor oil eyes drilled mine. "Riko." He tapped the tablet with his other hand, calm as I wasn't. "I *am* the monkey."

My mouth dropped open.

Muerte laughed, clapping me on the back. "Let's be amigos, yeah?"

I hated all of them. But especially Malik cunting Reed.

"If you're done," Indigo said loudly, "Riko, I'm going to need your cock out of your hands."

Sure. I'd shove it between Malik's girly lips instead.

I shut my trap because we weren't on Reed's dime, no, but we *were* on mine. My cred, to be precise. And Indigo's, now, too.

A map bloomed in the center of our circle, still in the shade afforded by the van. Indigo's chip projector was strong enough to compensate for ambient light, and he used it often when we planned. Handy tech. "Knacklock spans seven city blocks, about forty-five kilometers end to end." Indigo poked a finger into the thick red X dominating the northern end. "Hevin Kern's chopshop sits here." A block and a half.

"That's only about ten kilometers in," I noted, glancing at the lot around us as if it'd offer a clear picture. "And it's going to be under sec."

"It will," Muerte confirmed. "But when I called in a few favors, I found something interesting." She traced a line on the projection that spanned a longer path, roundabout through streets poorly designed, east to north. In its wake, a green line lit. "Because of all the traffic, there's less security coverage here."

"How does that make sense?"

"It's too convoluted," Malik said thoughtfully. This time, when he dragged a finger through the projected map, it left a stronger blue line, right down the center of the road. "This is more efficient and offers a near-perfect line of entry, but any attack will be seen coming."

Muerte nodded.

Indigo and I exchanged glances. "Where's Tashi?" I asked again.

His lips curved. His turn to be smug. "She's on her way."

Reed folded his arms across his armored chest. In a suit, he was damned impressive. In Mantis armor, thicker than it was even three weeks ago and altered for mobility, I knew offhand a dozen saints who'd try to tap that into next week. Not that he'd so much as give them the time of day.

I'd tap him with a bullet before I'd let him anywhere near my – admittedly aroused – orifices. Not unless I went out and picked up a designer version of syphilis first.

"You've evolved a plan," he said to Digo. Not a question.

I'd already expected as much. Indigo was my linker for so, so many reasons.

As if on cue, the roar of an engine bigger than anything I'd drive rumbled through the lot. We all turned. We all stared. Except Indigo, whose chuckle mirrored my sudden wash of glee. "You are the best," I gasped.

"You are dangerous," Malik said instead, watching the express truck tear up the ground it thundered across.

The battered cab came to a stop, wafts of black smoke belching from every pipe. The door swung open, and

Tashi – looking so much tinier against the enormous vehicle – poked her head up over it. "Somebody call for a battering ram?" No smile. Just near-white eyes in the sunlight and blazing white tattoos.

I was beginning to love those tattoos again. I liked it so much better when she wasn't trying to kill me.

Malik, the stonefaced bastard, surveyed the tableau without any sign of surprise or fear.

Muerte's laugh gave the idling, sputtering engine a run for its efforts.

"Yeah, I've already decided," Indigo finally answered. "Let's suit up."

# 39

Stop me if you've heard this one: a linker, a fixer, two splatter specialists, and a corporate dickhead walk into a chopshop...

Only *walk* isn't the word. Walking would have taken too long, exposed us to security. Not that we didn't get exposed. The shooting started about a kilometer away. Bullets rattled the cab, bounced off the trailer dragged behind.

Muerte hissed. "We've passed the first wave."

Indigo, lines carving yellowed tracks of *holy fucking hell we are doing this* in his face, jerked a nod.

We'd all comm'd up, helmets on. Same shit I'd worn the other day, with a HUD that outlined the team in green and bogeys in red. I hoped it worked better than the last batch. So far, it hadn't glitched.

All three of us had wrapped ourselves in the cargo netting, armaments secured and safety on just in case.

Cute that Mantis's supplied weapons still *had* safeties.

"Brace." In the comm, Malik's voice sounded so much more commanding. Asshole should've played operator. "First obstacle. Two more in quick succession. Then three between entry and structure."

"Speed?" Indigo asked, tone crimped tight. We

all firmed holds in the netting, pulled out as much as possible so we didn't break our limbs on collision.

"You don't want to know," he replied. Goddamn dry.

Muerte's snort ended on a, "Madre Dios," that I felt, for once, I could echo.

And then we ran out of time to think at all.

The cab plowed through three plain walls and two reinforced before jackknifing and rolling over three more. We didn't scream; we were professionals. Instead, we swore in all the languages we knew – I was the only one whose brain didn't process other lingual curses when pressed.

Rocked side to side and up and down, my helmet slammed against unyielding metal, my legs strained. One arm slipped out, and I jerked it back as hard as I could while the truck rolled again and again. My left arm held, shoulder girdle strong.

Outside the truck, thundering through the bowed trailer walls, echoes of our collision boomed over and over.

Indigo's plan put us smack in the middle of sec forces sent in by the whooping alarms.

As the cab came to a screeching, sudden halt, we untangled ourselves from the side netting, relying on knives and raw strength to do it. Mine being raw strength, just so I could get to the knife in my thigh-sheath. I had three more lined up, two at each leg, to say nothing of the amount of weaponry I'd helped myself to.

"Sound off," Malik ordered.

"One," our linker said, groaning.

"Two," Tashi added. Bitch didn't even sound winded.

"Three." Muerte.

I hit the ground – or the side of the trailer, I couldn't tell yet – and said, "Fuck off."

"Button it." That was our linker. I'd listen to him. Mostly.

Taking the lead, I kicked the back doors so hard they sprang open, thudded into three security guards getting ready to open them, and sent all three sprawling. Smoke and steam poured into the hauler from busted valves, cement cracked and crumbled overhead.

I opened fire before my feet hit the cement ground – looked like a large internal warehouse of some kind. Reams of plastic rolls lined one far wall, shipping crates piled beside them. Bare rectangles in layers of grime gleamed in the lights.

"They're moving out," I shouted behind me. "We too late?"

Muerte hit the floor next, kneeling to take out a sweep of secsmegs rolling in from the right. "Hope not," she replied. "I was looking forward to this."

Tashi and Malik met us on the other side, and as much as I fucking hated his guts, I admired his form. I'd never seen him get his hands dirty before. Right now, with his Manticore hitting every sec goon he aimed at and his defensive pace smooth as conservatory silk, I never would have guessed he wasn't one of us.

Maybe corporate executives went through training. Most were just too pussy to put it to the test.

We fanned out, one by one as we hauled ass, cover fire laying the groundwork for Indigo to get his data in the game. We closed ranks around our linker, even Malik. As the eye in the sky man, we needed him aware and focused, not bleeding out and useless.

"About thirty feet northwest," Digo yelled. Hard not to yell in this chaos, even though we were connected by helmeted comms.

Gunfire rattled the hollow garage, made everything

hammer and crack and echo and rumble. A few stray bullets pinged my chest armor, and one hit my helmet. I glanced down, whistled. Not one left a dent. "You finally made armor that works!" Even the heads-up hadn't faltered.

Reed said nothing. A definite professional. Boring, though.

Although Tashi didn't wear much armor as a rule, she'd made an exception this time. Given our lack of intel, it was the smart move. Underneath it, she rocked a level of dermaplating that acted as light armor, and she preferred mobility to extra impact resistance. Here, we had to shoot it out before we could get in close enough to splatter everything that moved.

I couldn't help but grin fiercely as I riddled three security mooks in black with half a clip of 12mm. It was even more gratifying than shredding the scouts.

Finally. This was my team. At least, enough of them to make me feel like no time had lapsed at all.

"Behind us," Indigo shouted.

"Noted," Reed replied, calm as ice. I focused front, swept the path ahead of us while Muerte covered my right. I trusted them to do their jobs, like I trusted nobody else.

Yeah, Malik Reed was a cunt. Okay, so Tashi had tried to kill me, still didn't trust me.

Indigo still cut me out of too much of the loop.

I had somehow killed his sister. We still needed to figure out how and why.

But goddammit, I *knew* these runners. And they knew me.

Enough of me to count.

"Brace," Reed added, seconds before the hauler behind us went tits up on the back of a magnificent explosion.

Fire and smoke and jacked-up metal went flying, hit the ceiling with enough force to spiderweb it, and skittered, shrieking. The impact of the blast rolled over us twice – once for the bomb, and second for the cab and trailer that came down like a ton of diesel-fueled bricks.

We all stumbled. Only Malik, who was ready, made no sound.

The rest of us varied curse to surprise to irritation. That was me. "Ballsy, asshole. How'd you know it wouldn't floor *us*?"

"Basic math."

I growled. "Eat me."

"Shut it, focus in," Indigo cut in. He crouched in the center of all of us, fidgeting with the personal comp unit attached to his forearm. No matter how slick and shiny his units started, no matter how fancy and high tech, Indigo always christened them with black. Even the inputs. Only he knew what he was typing and pushing and whatever.

Rather than project to everyone, his data rolled through optic projectors only he could see. The fact his processing ability beat that scroll at some ungodly rate, *and* that he was smart enough to work it on the fly, is what made him the best linker I'd ever teamed with.

We huddled around him, squinting through smoke, cement dust and debris and popping off shots at anything that moved. Some hit the floor, stayed there. Others ducked behind the stray containers, took potshots at us.

Some of those hit too damn close to home, while the unwavering inferno behind us turned it to sweltering hell.

"Hurry up," I snarled. "I'm tired of getting shot today."

"Hold your dick already," Indigo shot back. Behind his eyewear, his mouth worked – like he was crunching numbers. Formulating something.

I let him. This wasn't some balls new enforcer team, this was a group who knew how to cover a job.

Even Reed, who calmly took aim at everything that moved on his side.

I whistled in comm. "Why, Malik Reed, you shoot like a cop."

"Top of my class," he replied shortly.

Muerte tipped her head in his direction, dust smearing one side of her helmet in white and gray ripples. "You were a cop?"

He said nothing.

I covered Muerte. Swinging over her head, I tweaked the trigger just hard enough that a three-round burst chewed up the air in front of her face. A brave and stupid security specialist dropped, skidded. "Keep your eye on your side," I shouted.

She whipped back around. "Lo siento!"

"Sorries are for funerals," I growled, and shot the guy again for luck. I whirled back to cover my ground. "Digo... *shit*!" My turn to misjudge. Muerte cursed, slid in front of me fast enough to create eddies in the cloud of dust.

A security force in heavy armor froze. Had her – had us both – dead to rights with a Sauger 877 that would have chewed identical holes in the both of us. Anything we'd done would be too late, and everybody else covered their own sights.

I braced, swinging my Valiant up. Too late. All too fucking late.

The shots didn't come. No bullets. Not from that gun, anyway. From the other direction, Malik popped the trigger. The guy – girl? whatever – dropped like a bricksucking meatpuppet.

"Asshole," Muerte muttered, and then elbowed me. Hard. "Take your own advice, Riqa!"

"Fuck you," I snarled, shaking it off. Goddamn, I was tired of being shot. It never gets easier. Just another wave of pain to ride until you relearn how to breathe around it. She'd saved me one. Or, anyway, Malik had.

Why that enforcer hadn't killed us both made me wonder if he'd been a rookie. I'd seen it happen before.

Reed returned to his sweep. He didn't even gloat. On a run like this, you fucking well *gloat*. It's part of the fun.

"I got it," Indigo called, standing. "They've got heavy shielding up, all signal is blocked. We need to blow it."

"S'what she said," I muttered.

"Not to you," Tashi said quietly. Ha ha. "Where to?"

"Tash, three meters north-northwest," he replied, too professional to be amused. "Riko, cover her. Muerte, by me. Reed, take the rear, keep our asses clean."

Normally, that would have been *me* by Indigo's side.

I swallowed down the knife – I was too fucking awesome to be jealous – and hurried after the thin, ghostly splatter specialist. Made more sense to send us out ahead, anyway. We wrecked more shit.

Forging through layers of black smoke and heavy dust made me rethink my process. If some asshole got the jump on me because Reed's worthless helmets gave up the ghost now, I was going to haunt every last jerkoff in the building.

Indigo included.

That the rate of gunfire slowed, and then stopped altogether, wasn't what I'd expected.

"Last one down," Muerte reported. "Can't see shit in front of us, but looks quiet."

"Forward pair?"

"Quiet here too," I said. "What are we looking for?"

"This," Tashi said, coming to a halt at the far end of a recessed wall. She waved away a swirl of thinner smoke, popped a light on – attached to one of her steels, that was handy – and passed it over a tall cylinder set into the corner. Half had been set into the cement, the rest protruding outward. Tubes of metal ran over its surface, and as Tashi's light traced them up, they vanished into the ceiling.

"Well, fuck a truck," I said, surprised. "Think we've found it."

"Great. We're moving toward the southern edge of the interior, you need to dismantle that thing."

"Indigo."

"What?"

"I am not a mechanic."

"Engineer," he corrected, and Tashi chuckled faintly beside me. "I didn't send two splatter specialists for finesse. Take it down, or we're going in blind and scrambled."

Oh. Well, that made more sense. "This cover that shielding?"

"No doubt."

"Will this trigger a self-destruct in there?"

"Probably not."

I paused. "*Probably* not?" I repeated. "You don't know?"

"Riko." A thin edge of pride. "It's *shielded*. The only thing coming in and out of there are meatsacks intent on blowing holes in us, so if you don't mind?"

"Right, right." Tashi and I looked at each other, nodded in tandem. Putting her steel back into its thigh sheath, she withdrew her Sauger. She'd modded it. Better at closer range, which upped its rate of fire to serious crunch. Also heated the barrel at an ungodly rate, so not meant to be used for prolonged contact.

We stepped back far enough that if it blew, we'd admire the pretty colors without catching ourselves on fire.

"On three," she said.

"Come back when it's lit," Muerte added in the comm. "We're going to need you two."

Well, now I just felt all warm and mushy inside. "One," I said.

"Two," she followed.

In tandem, we said, "Three," and opened fucking fire on a tube of metal that hadn't done anything to us. Except exist.

Didn't take much. The whole thing lit up like a blue nova, sparks flying and metal crumpling, clanking. The lights overhead dimmed, a deep resonance rolling through the warehouse. I flinched.

The shield generator erupted in a series of electrical currents and went black.

So did the lights.

My head twitched violently to one side. I blinked hard. It twitched again, neck muscles spasming. It rolled down my left shoulder, jerking my tech arm. Everything around me vanished beneath a crashing hum; a wave of so much crushing pressure that I slammed my real hand into the side of my helmet.

It didn't help.

I crouched in darkness, hand pressed violently to my head, as my chipset went haywire. In my ears, nestled deep in my skull, the angry buzz of a million wasps threatened to sting.

# 40

*Abort.* I think that's what I heard outside my shrieking eardrums.

*Abort!*

I staggered up. "We are not aborting!"

Everybody went still. I mean, I think they did. Tashi's torch only cut so far into the settling dust. After an awkward moment, she put a small hand on my back, below the shoulder. "You're acting weird."

"Who said otherwise?" Muerte asked, dry as bone chuckle crackling the comm. "What do you think this is, easy mode?"

Shit. *Shit.* I shook my head, beckoned Tash as I stepped out of reach. "I misheard something," I muttered.

"Get over here," Digo added, "we'll need everything we can get for this."

Tashi and I forged back the way we'd come, tracing the smudges we'd made in the settling dust on the way to the generator. They were filling in fast. I could feel her glancing at me every few steps, gauging me.

This was becoming a problem in a big way. I'd already had my chipset recalibrated. It still happened. This one, though. This one hurt. I remembered the pressure last time my frequency had shifted, but I didn't recall the noise feeling so... thick before. Like a literal swarm of pissed off wasps bouncing around. It made my eardrums ache. Made my jaw hurt.

So bad that I almost didn't recognize it when tremors rippled under my feet. Almost. I jerked my gaze to the ceiling; more cement crumbled, fell all around us.

"Shit," Indigo hissed, and again. "Shit, shit, *shit!*"

"Failsafe?" Muerte asked, voice suddenly very, very serious.

"Shit," I echoed, and launched into a full sprint. "We need in there!"

"I know." Digo came into view, already running for the entry he'd found. A simple double door, built to slide sideways. It was already open, but nobody was running out. No gunfire, no bodies. No security. Not even bullets.

No necros, either, thank fucking Ganesh or whatever the hell a cosmic elephant was supposed to be.

Instead, as we approached, sparks lit in every direction. Electrical failures. Mechanical failures – shit, *engineering* failures, I don't know! We slammed into the large, single-room structure just in time to watch whole walls lined with banks of machinery pop, spark, and catch fire.

*Abort.*

A failsafe. Somebody had triggered it. But from where?

I clenched my teeth. "Are you shitting me?"

Digo slammed past me, flung a hand out to Muerte. "Go hit the upper bank," he said hurriedly, turning his back on us all. He worked fast, efficiently, pulling meatspace wires out of his comp unit and inserting its plugs into a system not yet burning.

I stared in rising fury as machine after machine went

up in smoke.

Muerte ran fast hands across the inputs arrayed in front of two monitors. One had shattered. The other scrolled through so much data, I couldn't parse it.

Tash and I stood watching them at work. I was impressed. Indigo often impressed me. Me, I felt like we'd hit a dead end – *crackle, pop, whoosh!*

Reed walked through the chaos, back straight, Manticore in hand. His helmet turned side to side.

Our tech gods pushed harder. Worked faster. The air inside turned acrid and sharp, plastic melted and aluminum warped. We watched the exit we'd come from. One exit, which seemed like a bad choice. Made covering it easier.

In my head, the fire fed the wild buzz until I could barely hear what the others said around me.

There had to be something here. *Had* to be. I hadn't busted my ass in a three-sixty just to find nothing after all.

"*Yes!*"

Followed abruptly by a rasped, "No, fuck!"

I blinked. "Which?"

Muerte skipped away as the last system in front of her shattered. "Lost it," she seethed.

"*Almost* lost it," Indigo countered. He backed away from his efforts, raised his arm unit. Fiery shadows painted his faceplate in demonic orange and red. "Let's boost before the place comes down on us."

Relief swamped me, so heavy that I almost sagged. He'd gotten something. *Finally*. Something good, too. No way this place held junk. MetaCorp wouldn't go to all this trouble, rig the place to burn, if there wasn't something important in here.

"Perhaps we should refrain from leaping to

assumptions." A longwinded counter to my relief. Malik's voice suggested curiosity.

"What?" I demanded.

"Reed, let's–"

"A door," he cut in. "A hidden one. There's more to this center than it seems."

Something beneath. I stared down the corridors as strings of melted plastic dripped around me. A fan of hot air spat flames and smoke behind Muerte, and she leapt ahead. "Somebody decide something," she yelled.

Digo and I, we looked at each other.

Neither of us had to speak. Not about this. We wanted so much more than just surface data. We needed in.

"Let's go," he ordered crisply.

Linker's orders. We all knew what we'd come for. Two of us just wanted more.

"Move," Tashi said sharply, the last of our line in the back. "Now!"

As we booked towards Malik's position, the damn place came down around us.

Malik got the doors open just in time. We all slammed through it. Muerte and Reed slid to either side, backs flat against the wall as a fireball rolled in on our heels. "Stairs!" I shouted, two octaves up.

I jerked suddenly, shoulders and waist armor cracking hard against the harness hooked around me. My head snapped forward, actually slammed chin to chest, and then the floor fell out from under me as I was hauled back. This time, when my shoulders slammed into the wall, all the breath whooshed out of me and the back of my head cracked against the anchor.

Malik's arm pinned me in place, faceplate turned my way – away from the roaring fire sucked into the open air. I couldn't see his expression with the backlighting.

Didn't keep me from snorting out what air I'd managed to take in and gasping, "Basic math, huh?"

"Hang on!" Digo's order.

We all did, until the fire faded and we could see again.

I was right. Past the larger platform we stood on, stairs vanished. Going ass over asshole on that one would've sucked.

Malik's arm dropped, leaving me to pull away and check the other side of the door. Indigo and Muerte, in roughly a similar position as I'd been, peeled away from their fire shield.

Tashi remained missing.

Indigo looked around. "Tashi?"

Nothing.

I ran to the top of the stairs, peered down it. No green signal. A platform led to the next set, curved left. "Tashi!"

The comm crackled. Then, "Here. Down. It's empty," she added. "And dark." Faintly, a blue glow bloomed. Her glows, always handy. "I don't see anything."

Indigo tapped across his comp unit. Rapid, without looking.

*Abort.*

My chin snapped to one side. Another spasm.

Nobody saw in the dark. I gritted my teeth. Another break in the worst of the buzz. I could still hear it, feel it, droning somewhere in the back of my brain, but not as viscerally.

I blew out a breath. "Hang on, Tash, we're coming."

Digo didn't argue. Reed filed in behind me. Too fucking close. I rocked an elbow back, digging in some space I didn't have to ask for. He faded back a step. Probably smirking.

My heart thudded. I was sweating in the armor, even through my skinsuit. These weren't temperature regulated – the only temp control suits Malik had brought required constant vitals reports. I wondered if anybody else was sweating, too.

Tash waited for us at the bottom of the stairs, two lines of glow sticks tossed out at ninety degrees. The initial area was too large to light up entirely. It felt...

It felt like the Vid Zone lab I'd crawled out of.

Heavy. Even as our footsteps echoed, even as the lights revealed nothing but open space, I felt confined. *Abort.*

My arm spasmed. Muerte tilted her head at me; inquisitive silence.

I shook mine.

"They must have started emptying this area first." Tashi pointed down one line of glow rods. "There's a faint line of something that way. Discarded, I think."

Great. "Another dead end," I muttered. I rigged up my Valiant, withdrew the Manticore I'd stashed from Reed's van. No Adjudicator still. "Asshole."

"Riko, Muerte, go check it out."

"I'll go," Reed countered, voice as cool as ever. He and Tashi should get together. Make beautiful icy babies.

I rolled my eyes. "I'll go too." Hell if I'd let him tread on my shit.

"Do it."

We both pulled flashlights from our gear, turned them on and held them crosswise under our guns. We paced each other. His light swept the area side to side, mine lit the way ahead. We both walked softly; he surprised me every moment in this shithole. I spared him a sidelong glance from beneath my helmet. Full circle coverage had its benefits. "Why the shit *are* you here?"

Reed's faceplate turned my way, but like I'd done earlier to Muerte, he said nothing. Not until we were closer to the outline Tashi had pointed out. My light slid over it, deepening shadows in the twisted shape and elongating one along the corridor behind it. "A body," he reported.

It splayed out like it *had* been discarded, flopped awkwardly within six meters of the corridor's entry. His face was turned down, chest crooked on one shoulder, legs scissored. Missing an arm.

No blood spattered around the corpse. No signs of a fight.

"Seems clear," I said as Malik's light flowed side to side. The others followed our trail across the cavernous interior. I tucked a foot under the body's armpit and rolled him over.

Bone, stained brown with dried blood. Skin flapped around one eye as he rolled, stuck to the floor it had been pressed against and tore off. Muscle peeled back with it, but clung to the shattered remains of one cheekbone and jaw.

One eye started blankly at the ceiling, orb exposed in its socket. The other had punctured, exploded in a putrid gelatinous circle. A spike of metal protruded through it, dotted with joints and with fine lights gone dark inset along it.

"Madre," Muerte gasped.

Reed bent, used the barrel of his heavy pistol to pull the corpse's jaw open. Wires, tangled and charred black, spilled from the body's throat. Along with it, strings of black ichor.

For the first time, Reed startled. He jerked his hand back, grunting.

Tashi made a sound caught between surprise and disgust.

Me and Indigo, we did neither. We looked down at

the twisted, alien face of a body gone necro and said in unison, "Not again."

I added, "Fuck my life," to mine.

# 41

"This is not where we want to be," Tashi said flatly. She stood as far away as she could and still be in cover distance, watching the body with what I assumed was suspicion. And horror. "Nobody said *anything* about necros."

We hadn't. On purpose. A stupid hope gone real wrong.

I stared deeper into the corridor, trying to see through the pressure squeezing my eyeballs. The dark and the tension surrounding us did me no favors.

"We've come this far," Muerte said, surprising me. Nobody had told her about necros either. "If they went to so much trouble to hide this, there's a reason."

"The reason," Tashi retorted, "got that fucker converted. No way am I next."

Malik finished studying the corpse, rose to his feet and turned. "I intend to push on." A simple statement. Matter of fact. Fuck what the linker intended.

Not a team player.

Then again, I struggled with that too. "I want to know what the tits," I announced.

"Fuck you," Tashi snapped back. Her voice rose an octave; the closest thing to scared I'd ever heard her.

Guilt tapped on my brain.

I shut it down hard. "Tashi–"

"We have no choice," Indigo cut in, his faceplate tipped up to the ceiling. Blue light danced along the tempered surface, catching the occasional sharp feature and angling it into deeper shadow. "The way back exploded. The only way out is in."

I heard teeth click audibly. Then, a less pitched, "Fine. But we kill anything that moves."

"Finally," I said, smiling grimly. "You're on my side."

"Shut up, Riko."

"You love me."

"Get fucked by a railgun."

Muerte laughed her graveled laugh and Indigo sighed.

I'd heard Tashi say worse. And this time, I trusted her at my back. Knives and all.

"Riko and Reed, point. Muerte with me, Tash covers our backs." A clip snicked as he slotted it into place. He carried a Sauger 877, like Tashi. They seemed to be one of Mantis's favorites – excellent security work, and even better necro-chewers. "We're going to keep this nice and steady."

Because last time, we'd all but walked right into a necro nest and gotten our flesh peeled off for it.

My hands shook. Rigging up my Manticore took more effort, and repeated efforts, than it should have. Indigo pushed my fumbling hand away from my back, slotted the heavy pistol in place for me. Of the five of us, only Reed noticed.

He bemused me. Saying nothing, he turned away again, prepped his own Manticore.

Digo bumped my shoulder with a light fist.

Silent reassurance. I squared both shoulders, shaking out my flesh arm. The tech replacement, so far, behaved.

Muerte stepped into line. "You really should grab something heavier," she said on the comm. "A pistol will only piss these things off."

"Aim better," he replied, and left it at that.

Humor cracked through my fear. Split enough of a canyon through it that I could take a deep breath. Snorting, I claimed space front and center and primed the Valiant for *fuck shit up*. The light I carried fastened to the barrel, providing easier light at the cost of weighing it down a little more. Nothing I couldn't compensate for.

And I'd be damned if I remained in the dark.

"Stay on guard," Digo said flatly. "And aim for their chipsets. Only way to stop these things is taking out their processors."

"Great," Tash muttered, and I couldn't blame her.

"Go."

Malik and I set the pace. We both held our weapons at the ready, though I felt laughably on top with my Valiant 14 next to the pistol his large hands made look smaller. Silence reigned around our parade of nerves and determination. Only our footfalls disturbed the eerie quiet, creating faint ripples that vanished in each direction.

No doors on either side this time. An entry corridor?

No. There'd been others leading away from that large vault.

*Clink.* I flinched. The edges of my light jerked.

"Stay calm." Malik's voice. Quieter. He'd switched to closed comms.

I openly growled at him.

When he chuckled, I seriously contemplated turning the Valiant on him and adding another corpse to the scene. "Don't fuck with me right now," I said quietly. "You have no idea my hair trigger."

"Believe me when I say that I do."

My teeth ground.

We closed in on the end of the hall, and another door sealing it. It didn't open as we approached, though its sensors for approach had been installed at the top of the door instead of at the panel beside it. Like it'd needed the top down view to scan.

"Locked," I said without checking.

Bypassing Reed on the right, Digo checked the panel and nodded. "Hold it."

As he worked his magic, pressing his gloved hand against the panel and tapping out commands with the other, Muerte and Tashi sidled up closer. "You really think there'll be necros?" Tashi's voice. Low and, fuck me, scared.

Smart merc's worst nightmare, right?

What was even worse than that was that I knew something they didn't. And as Digo's helmet turned to me for the briefest of moments, I knew I had to share. "I don't know," I said, "but there's one thing–"

"Don't get injured by them," Malik cut in. Smooth as hot oil, sharp as Tash's knives. "Especially the ones that leak."

"Leak?" Muerte asked, just as Tashi made a gagging sound.

Tough cunt any day of the week, but necros cracked that shell, apparently. Smart.

"After the Vid Zone's blight," he continued like neither had made a sound, "preliminary exams suggest they're learning to infect via nanos."

"No shitting way."

Muerte shifted, returning her attention – and the direction of her Insurgent – behind us.

"That's why we take them down fast and at distance,"

Indigo said, withdrawing from the panel. At the top of the doors, the scanner came to life. Green lines projected out, turned into a grid that took us all in.

It winked out. The doors audibly unlocked, then slid open with a hiss of compressed air. *Kssh.*

Ice rolled down my spine. My tech hand clenched on the barrel of the Valiant; numbers spiked in my left eye, threatening the structural integrity of my favorite gun. I struggled to unclamp each finger. Stared into the open space as dread speared sharpened talons through my eyeballs.

"Ai," Muerte breathed, little more than a croak.

Tashi's boots thumped as she jumped back. "What the fucking shit!"

Digo, Malik and I remained silent. Me because I couldn't speak – those cunting hornets had crawled out of my brain and into my throat. Swallowing stung all the way down. Shaking my head rattled my brains so hard, I *saw* thunder.

Indigo, maybe he'd been prepped.

As for Malik? Pride. Or maybe he really was as cold inside as he was out. Suddenly looking at a floor covered by the dead should have invoked something.

The smell hit us first. My nostrils flared, then my throat closed around the choking pressure surging up from my chest. I expected rot. I expected to smell the puke-inducing stench of fermented intestines and putrid flesh.

Instead, something metallic and substantial filled my nose. Freshly butchered meat. Recently shredded muscle.

A grotesque field of tangled arms and legs, shattered tech, and coagulating rivulets of blood. And bile. And probably worse. Acid underneath the meat; urine a faint burn under the copper odor of blood.

I closed my eyes.

*Get it off!*

Screaming. So much screaming, raw and terrified as nails and teeth and bare fingers peeled off armor like it was nothing and tore flesh from muscle and bone. Blood and gore, smears of rot, pus leaking from every wound and chipsets sparking as they hit the bloodied, gory ground.

"–ko?"

*Eradicate.* The word screamed in my brain.

*Abort.* More depth to it, like multiple voices screamed louder.

*Shut up.*

I sucked in a staggering breath.

"Riko!"

*Shut up.*

*Abort.*

"Get your shit together!"

*Eradicate.*

"Shut up," I croaked.

Hands grabbed my shoulders. Shook so hard, my neck popped as my helmet wobbled back and forth. *"Riko."*

*Eradicate!*

"Shut up!"

Cold air slapped my sweaty cheeks.

*I'm sorry.*

And then a fist.

*Hurry.*

I spun with the impact, stumbled to the side. My helmet clattered to the ground, one foot sliding in gummy fluid. I barely caught myself before landing face first into something that'd squish when I hit it.

My stomach sloshed. Twisted. Throat expanded as it

prepared to puke up whatever was left of the ramen I'd consumed earlier.

It was Tashi that jumped my shit, literally leaping onto my back so she could reach my neck. She wrapped an arm around my throat and jerked back so hard my face tipped towards the high ceiling. "If I can't," she growled in my throbbing ear, "you can't!"

"Come on, Riko." Digo, risking the soles of his boots to catch my left elbow. "Back it up."

"Oh, it's backing up all right." Muerte, the bitch.

Malik passed us all, picking his way around the corpses and squashing anything soggy on the way. "We're wasting time," he said, flat on the comms. In my ear, it sounded as if his voice hit a padded wall and stuck.

I swallowed hard against Tashi's arm. "Got it," I rasped. "Got it."

"Yeah?"

"Yeah," I managed.

She let me go, sliding back down to land with her usual grace. *Squish.*

My head hurt. My eardrums felt like somebody had played tug of war with both sides, and I'd lost my shit. Again. A subtle click on the comm. "Hey." Indigo's voice. Too quiet for anyone else to hear through his helmet. He still had hold of my arm. "You OK?"

Without my helmet, I couldn't answer without being heard. So I shrugged. Then nodded. Then withdrew my arm and took the Valiant he held out for me.

I couldn't explain it.

All I could do was forge on, searching for answers I didn't know the questions to. This time, when we closed ranks, I was very much aware of the others at my back.

One more burst like that, and I was afraid I would do to them what I'd done to a surge of necros in the Vid

Zone. I couldn't remember what that was specifically, but everything had been splattered when I came to.

*Eradicate*, huh?

I set my jaw. Tightened my grip on the Valiant and forged through the swamp of flesh and guts. This time, none of us had anything clever to say. Even Malik seemed stiff, shoulders rigid and footfalls hard.

As we all swept our lights, left and right in unified cover, doors inset on each side came into view.

Indigo swallowed. Audibly.

*Get it off!*

I shook my bare head. Hard.

"Do we check them?" Muerte asked, voice hushed.

"Do they lead out?" Tashi replied in the same tone.

"I don't—"

"They don't," I said, and then bit my tongue when all of them paused to stare at me. I grimaced. The shadowed space gathered up every sound, bounced it back and forth in eerie whispers. Felt like they jammed cold hands down my armor and grabbed my spine.

"Riko." Indigo's voice. Worried as hell.

"Placement," I snapped. "Use your fucking heads."

Made as good a sense as any. I could practically feel their combined relief as they accepted it.

Fuck me. I lied. Part of me knew that.

The rest of me had no answers.

*Hurry.*

When we reached the end of the vault, we all let out an audible breath. Even Malik. "I half expected them to start getting up," Indigo said, relief thick as the blood gelling behind us. "I never want to do that again."

"Has anyone asked why we had to do this in the first place?" Tashi, sounding spooked again but calm. She pushed up beside me as a large door blocked our way.

She hooked her modified Sauger on her rig – with less trouble than I'd had – and reached up to brace both palms on either side of her helmet.

It came off with an audible click, and lights around the rim of her collar flickered out. Her cheeks had gone burgundy, face dripping with sweat. She glared up at me, the irises and whites of her eyes eerily blue from our lights.

I frowned back at her. "Because MetaCorp is involved with Nanji's death in the Vid Zone and–"

"Yeah," she cut in, "I got all that. But what the hell is *this?*" She gestured back at the wall-to-wall dead. "Were they necrotech?"

*Yes.* "I don't know."

"What would you have done if they were?"

*Eradicate.* Heh. My mouth twisted into a grim smile. "Shoot them to pieces."

She thought about it. Turned to look at Indigo, who reached up and removed his own helmet. Sweat plastered strands of his dark hair to his forehead and cheeks. "We knew the Vid Zone was crawling," he said, "so this was a risk. But it was a working chopshop until recently." He shook his head, dropping his own helmet to the floor. It, unlike Tashi's, landed in something that squished. "Whatever happened here, it either happened fast or just happened to be contained when it went tits up."

Muerte coughed. "About that…"

Malik followed our examples and removed his, too. His face was neither sweaty nor reddened. He'd worn his own temperature-modulated gear. Asshooooole.

"We should move if we intend to get out," he said calmly. "If the authorities suspect an infection, we'll be burned down with the rest of the area."

Muerte pointed at him, her helmet still on. "What tall, dark and delicious said."

"Thank you," he replied, baritone mild.

I took a moment to press in on both temples with the thumb and forefinger of my right hand. Everything throbbed, but none of it in the kind of pain earned in a fight. My nanos had taken care of those. The hum in between both had settled somewhere around *hammer to the forehead* levels of noise. But it *had* faded.

Sucking in a breath that didn't help, I nodded. "*Oh-kay. Digo, break this bitch open.*"

Tashi backed up again, re-engaging her Sauger. We all did the same, sans helmets. Too hot. Too constricting.

Malik had no such excuse. He put his back on, and whatever the fuck he meant to imply, I read it as self-righteous. Because he didn't care if his vitals were recorded. Orchard already had scans of my brain going supernova in the middle of a necro blight. I did not need any more data in her – or Malik's – hands.

Digo's digital magic didn't seem to have any issues with the system down here. This time, he had it within seconds. Another hiss of air. Another click. The doors slid wide and every one of us braced ourselves.

# 42

*CHECKPOINT 4*

Bold letters in bright red painted the side of the wall. Beside it, the same kind of door we'd been cracking since we got here. The hall continued past, towards a larger entry with its doors wide open. Air steamed from the compressors, shooting a stream that hissed faintly from the sides.

I glanced back at Indigo. Deep blue eyes met mine, flicked to the checkpoint entry.

I nodded.

We had to get in there.

Tashi muttered. Then, "The exit?"

"The exit sign suggests so," Malik replied. Deadpan.

Muerte bent to peer around him. "What's in the other room?"

"Exactly what I'd like to know," I interjected. *Thank you, Muerte.*

Tashi's relief turned to a foot stomp – fucking cute – and a snarled, "Indigo, you infojunkie motherfucker."

"Don't leave me out of that!" Muerte waved at Tashi behind them, and then nudged Malik in the back. "Go play bait."

I snorted a laugh. But because this was a run and I

didn't want to risk getting caught with my linker down again, I paced Malik as he approached the checkpoint.

This time, the doors opened without help.

"Odd for a checkpoint," Malik noted. He swept the interior on the right. I covered on the left, back to back.

Our lights painted pale swaths through the dark. End to end. Top to bottom.

Broken tech. Smashed monitors. Charred plastic and blackened wires. Even the frames had been twisted. Monitors that had been set into the walls – for security purposes, most likely – left behind little more than gaping rectangles and dangling, still sparking wires. The sparks lit up small areas as they flashed. Only to leave the room feeling darker than before.

My lip curled. "I see why it was open."

"Unfortunate."

Behind us, Muerte and Indigo stepped in. Tashi walked in backwards, watching our asses.

Slowly, we all panned.

*Hssss.*

A buzz in my ear. Or was it in the room? I tipped my head to one side and shook it hard. As if I'd gotten grit in it. "You hear that?"

Indigo jumped. His light jerked. "Fucking fuck, Riko, don't do that."

I guess they hadn't heard it.

"Clear it," Malik ordered, and strode out farther.

Indigo rolled his eyes, then gestured silently at the rest of us.

"You can take the motherfucker out of the suit," I muttered.

"I told you–"

"Oh, sorry," I said sweetly as I covered my own radius. "I meant motherlover."

"Who isn't?" asked Muerte, laughing.

Her hoarse humor earned Tashi's hard, "Fuck off."

"Shut it," Indigo cut in. "Focus."

We did. The security checkpoint was big enough that we could all split it into fifths, surveying the carnage side to side. Frames still in one piece blocked the way in places, overturned counters and hanging grates blocking others. In the background, just above the hum, I heard them forging through the mess. Glass crackled and crunched. A sharp clang followed by a hissed, "Shitting ow!" earned Muerte a combined, "*Muerte!*" from three sources.

Reed's voice was not among them.

"My bad," she whispered raggedly.

After two minutes of excruciating silence, I reached the far wall. "Clear," I said.

"Clear," Reed echoed.

"Clear," Tashi said thirty seconds later, followed by Indigos, "Cl... *shit!*"

It happened so fast, Muerte and Reed didn't have time to respond. Tashi and I flanked Indigo's grid, and we were in motion the moment his *clear* faltered.

As the other two wrenched their lights around, Tashi and I were already shouting in unison.

"Get down!"

"Drop!"

Too late.

A body tore over a mangled counter, feet and hands scraping like an animal up its sides and off the surface. It was in the air before we'd finished verbalizing our reaction, and Indigo shouted as the thing tackled him head-on.

Nails grated across armor.

Blood rushed to my head.

Reed barked something I couldn't hear as my whole left side twitched so violently that I dropped my Valiant.

"Get it off me!" Digo screamed, fists full of the necro's filthy shirt and barely holding its gnashing teeth away from his face. He twisted, strained to move the bulky body, but the thing flailed and clung and threw all its weight without caring about hurting itself.

Tashi ducked low, arms streaming behind her as she streaked towards the clusterfuck. Her steels slid out from the sheaths at her forearms so smoothly that she had hands, and then she had sharp fucking metal throwing back blinding reams of light.

The cramp in my tech let go so fast I staggered.

Righted myself.

Juices dribbling down its chin, the necro suddenly jerked his head upright, impossibly red eyes fixing on Tashi. Optics. Total replacements, the kind that mercs who don't care about blending in pack around.

Tashi leapt for the thing's back, shouting, "Shove!"

Indigo braced every muscle he had and shoved. *Hard.*

No. Too slow. A nanosecond after Digo pushed, the thing grabbed two handfuls of floor and half-leapt, half-dragged himself forward, leaving Tashi to either land on Digo or compensate. She chose the latter, splaying her legs to frame Indigo, blades at the ready over him.

Linker first. Always.

I don't know how I knew it'd happen, but I was already in the air, tackling the necro in the chest with my left arm and shoulder shoved into its gut. The necro lurched, arms and legs splaying in the direction its momentum had been carrying him.

Something wet and loud ground in its body, right by my ear.

My eyes widened. "Sh–"

Too late. Again.

The thing opened its mouth in surprise, in sheer inability not to, and red and yellow bile gushed from its chest and throat. Chunks of meat splashed my cheek, my shoulder and chest. It hit the floor with an ungodly wet splatter.

I sealed my teeth under the strain of its weight, even as my skin tried to rip itself from the rest of me and crawl away.

Feet dug in to the floor, back muscles straining and heaving with every iota of strength I'd ever pounded into my body, I reversed the thing's momentum and bodyslammed it to the ground. Its back bowed.

Crunched.

"Don't shoot Riko," Muerte rasped. Red laser cut through, twitched as it tried to find a mark that wouldn't cost me another limb.

Reed didn't answer. The laser sighted at the thing's head, which lifted. It bubbled and frothed, scrabbling at the floor. I'd seen necros drag themselves along with wet and ruined intestine hanging from their legless bodies. I didn't expect a snapped spine to stop this one.

Malik's Manticore ripped a 12mm hole in the necro's skull. The report screamed through the checkpoint, cracked so loudly I flinched away. Wasn't aware I'd done it until the mirrored shriek in my brain abruptly went silent.

Made the leftover hum so much easier to deal with in comparison.

"That ain't gonna do it," Muerte said in the lingering quiet.

Tashi approached the squirming, dripping necro. Wordlessly, she grabbed her steels in both hands, angled them as if they were one blade side by side, and sliced through flesh, cartilage and bone like it was nothing.

I panted, resting both hands on my knees, the remains of the thing's bile turning sticky on the side of my face.

Muerte clapped me on the back as she passed by. "Don't puke again."

I didn't have it in me to reply.

The thing finally stopped moving. Blood and worse pooled and splattered in every direction around it.

"Anybody wounded?" Malik asked. Not like he cared, but like he cared about necro fluids in open wounds.

"Anybody feeling techish?" Muerte added.

I hadn't, thank fucking luck, ingested any of the shit on me. "No," I managed between gasps. I tapped one ear, wincing some. No sound. No pressure. "Didn't swallow anything either." But it smelled awful. I coughed as the pungent burn of necro vomit seared all the way into my brain.

Tashi swiped both of her blades in the air. Ichor and clinging flesh splashed to the floor on either side of her. "We done?"

Indigo and Muerte looked at each other – or I assume they did. She still had her helmet on. Something must have passed between them, because they both looked at me. When I only shrugged, Indigo moved around Tashi to study the body. Then he crouched and peered sideways at the head.

"It's Kern," he said after a moment.

"You sure?" I asked, frowning.

"Definitely."

"Well, shit."

Reed waited all of us out, studying the corpse of the necro. Without being able to see his face, I couldn't tell what he was thinking.

Muerte shook her head, removed her pistol from her rig and aimed at the twisted, shredded face. "Move," she said, and gave Tashi all of a second to do it.

Tashi did.

With better aim than I'd manage, Muerte fired. The head skittered away with the impact. She fired again. And again. Until the thing rolled and bounced like a ball and there was nothing left in the grisly mass to shoot. Just one big bloody lump.

When the last shot faded away, I eyed the remains and flipped Muerte a thumbs up. "Nice."

She holstered her weapon, grabbing her Insurgent with a shrug. "Seemed smart."

"Well, guess we go," I said with a sigh of relief. "Before something else goes wrong."

Tashi, for the first time in ages, smiled at me.

Muerte pointed at me. "Riko has to go first, she stinks."

"C'mere," I countered, "let me hug you."

Tashi and Indigo looked at each other. Looked at me. Then both pointed to the door. "Everyone else first," Indigo said flatly. His face, though. His face made me want to die with laughter. I never knew he could make that face.

"Oh, come on," I purred, and sauntered his way. "Want a celebratory snog?"

"Fuck no," he groaned, and hurried for the door.

Tashi stared at Muerte until she shrugged, laughing, and followed. Reed gave me a hard look. I spread my hands and gestured to him first.

As they picked their way through the scattered remains of the security checkpoint, I bent and palmed the lump of bloodied chipset buried in lumpy pink-gray mucus. It'd have answers. No doubt about it.

Pocketing the gory thing, I eased into a jog. "Hey, wait up!" I called. "I want to rub my love juices on yooooou...!"

# 43

Reed called for an extraction team the moment we surfaced. Then, wasting no time, he called for a burn team. A helo picked us up before the second team arrived. Reed's crew had come prepared with quarantine containers and radiation bunks – though they also disarmed us of all Mantis gear in the process. I'd gotten to keep the basic clothes, at least.

And the chipset I'd smuggled by.

Once cleaned and disinfected, we split and agreed to meet at the Mecca. For celebratory drinks and – Indigo didn't have to say it aloud – visual proof that I'd more than earned my place back with the crew. About fucking time. With any luck, the word would spread: mess with Riko, mess with the rest of the gang.

Fidelity and Valentine still needed to be convinced. Digo believed it'd be easy.

I wasn't so sure, but at least I'd learned when to stow my dick. At least a little. Indigo had finally come around – even if he'd done so with half a mind I was still responsible. I could work with that. Hell, if everyone else chose that route, that'd be just great.

We fight together. We win together. And we fall together. That's what makes finding family among mercs so dangerous.

•••

I was glad to be back. And this time, as I sauntered my way into the Mecca in skin-tight electric yellow vinyl shorts and black boots up to my barely covered vag, I brought the Valiant with me. So Jad could stroke it.

Tits on wheels, did he. Like a lover, but with none of the tongue action.

The smile he shot me over its nicely polished barrel screamed love at first sight. "You just made my life, baby girl."

"Aren't I awesome?" I asked, grinning. I held out my arms, showed off the lack of weaponry in long tight white sleeves and a low, low back. The front of the bodysuit sported an anthropomorphized version of a koala snorting a line of cocaine, and the words *Take it easy, mate!*

It wore an army hat. Because why the fuck not.

And so did I. One of those diagonal ones I'd found on a pack of street thugs rolling shops for creds. They'd gotten in my way, so I'd smeared them. And stole the hat.

Because why. The fuck. Not.

I tipped it to him as he gave me back the Valiant. "Shiva says you go in as you are," he told me, deep voice rich and serious. "The cut she'd take from anybody claiming your fine ass isn't worth the hassle, so you're probably all right for now." He paused. "It true you took out a MetaCorp station?"

Word traveled fast. At least half of it. Thank you, Indigo.

My grin stretched ear to shit-eating ear. "Fuck yeah."

He pushed out a large fist. "Fuck yeah," he echoed, and I bumped his knuckles. "Go see Shiva first thing. She at the bar."

Behind the beaded curtain, the place rocked, top to

bottom and side to side. Jam-packed with mercs and slummers, saints and chromers; the usual crowd plus the strays that always find their way in. The energy wasn't as rabidly violent tonight, but wild and, dare I say it, happy.

At the very least, the kind of happy that means you forget your bullshit for a while.

I tucked the Valiant into the rack I'd settled around my waist, so it hung diagonal over my ass. As I passed, I gave Shar a laughing wave. "Stop taking all the cute ones," I said. "And stop hogging the door."

He laughed, gasped mid-humor as a chromer I didn't know pinned him harder to the wall, balls deep and definitely gone on whatever Shar was dealing tonight. The guy had the look of a rich kid slumming it, with a chrome piece wrapped over his arm and a curved bar at his right ear.

But the way he fucked said he was no stranger to the vibe.

I grinned as both groaned in tandem, left the linker to his pleasures. He sure knew how to pick 'em. And if he was getting fucked so casually, the tension in the place had definitely slacked. Shar didn't sit on a cock if there was blood in the air. Too distracting.

The fact a horny linker with good taste had become my barometric warning system made me laugh.

As promised, Shiva poured drinks at the bar. She'd gone full Kongtown tonight, in one of those small floral dresses with a slit up the thigh, cap sleeves and straight collar. It was black on black, its sheen occasionally gleaming under the lights. When she moved, slick purple leggings cupped every fine definition of her legs. Her long hair had been twined into some ornate knot that miraculously didn't fall, and her makeup was black on black on black. Smoky eyes, pitch dark lips. Aggressive sweep of dark metallic gray at each temple.

The crowd was slavering over it. So very goth chic.

I claimed a meter of the bar, waited with my elbows planted on the surface. Didn't acknowledge it when a space opened up around me.

I was never unarmed. But now I wore it in the open. A sign of weakness?

Maybe.

But a sign of favor, too. Right now, I'd ride it all the way to winsville.

Shiva wandered my way, mimicked my pose. Black nails dotted with silver bits of paint winked at me as she folded her fingers under her chin. "Did Jad speak to you?"

"He did." I smiled, cupped my chin in my open palm. "Turned on that you care, Shiva."

Her lips curved. "Mind yourself anyway," she warned. "My fees are still in effect." And she wouldn't say no if they offered enough. Yeah, I knew how it went. "And please, darling," she added as she straightened. "Don't irritate me by flirting."

I swallowed a laugh, tried my best for straight face. Barely managed it as I saluted sharply. "Yessir."

"Go away."

But the fact her endless violet eyes gleamed in humor eased some of my own tension as I left. I'd gotten that radiation shower, now it was time for a drink. Everything had fallen in place. Digo had data to decrypt, which meant we'd learn what had been so important to hide in the sewage of the city.

Muerte had proven herself, so she'd probably made a good impact on Digo.

Tashi had sort of come around. At least I'd see her coming next time she pulled an interceptor on me.

Valentine and Fidelity didn't seem inclined to finish the job they'd picked up, or at least I hoped not. Boone hadn't commed in to say they'd slipped him.

The detective, in thanks for his stupidity near my shack, had earned the creds I was going to make Indigo pay him.

And for the moment, nobody else was jumping my shit.

Felt like victory all the way around.

So why, I wondered as I made my way through the usual Mecca crowd, did I still feel so uneasy?

Much to my surprise, Fidelity flagged me down before I hit the usual booth, waving me over to an array of padded furniture spaced out for casual hanging. The stuff was all curved and exotic, with graffiti art splashed all over. Someone had told me it was representative of the Buddha – another one of those eastern religions lapped up here in fantasyland.

It worked for Shiva. Which meant it worked for us.

I halted just outside the ring, arms folded and legs braced. I may as well have stamped *I will take no shit* on my chest.

Tashi perched on the back of one of the armchairs, feet on the arm rest and Fidelity sprawled in the seat under her. She'd gone torn-up denim, loose black tanktop and no bra under, which had more than a few looks scattered her way.

She ignored them. She always did. I appreciated that about her – we rocked what we wanted and broke who we didn't.

Fido and his orange surprised nobody – though he'd added some purple and yellow to the mix. Yellow shades reflected back the Mecca's whirling lights, shoved up into the wavy sweep of his black-brown hair. He raised a glass of blue – he'd ordered an Indigo. "Don't panic," he said, "all I'm armed with is booze."

"Who's panicking?"

He grinned. Neon orange capped his teeth, a dayglo grill. "I hear you ran a solid." I waited. "Listen, if Indigo's goin' to trust you, I'm giving him the benefit of the doubt."

My eyes narrowed. "Gee, thanks."

He shrugged, looked up at Tashi. "She's for you, too. So." He pointed at the couch. "Sit down. I ordered you an Indigo."

I paused. "Catch?"

He shook his head. "Don't fuck it up." But then he smiled. Really smiled. I hadn't realized how much I'd missed his stupid grill until I couldn't see it anymore. "Sit down, Ree. Join the club."

Not a full hand, but a big one. I'd take it. With more gratitude than I knew how to handle.

I glanced around, saw Val on the floor with a hot brunette, but no linker. "And where's Digo?"

"Said he'd be late," Tashi replied.

Fidelity kicked his feet lazily, two-inch flat heels winking. Orange sequins. I snorted a laugh. Tash looked down at her seatmeat, poking at the top of his head with a pointed silver nail cap. He looked up, swatting it away. "What?"

"Where's Boone?"

The fascinating thing about Fidelity, I noted as a waitress in a sweet little dress that mimicked Shiva's delivered my booze, was that for all his rich, warm brown skin, a flush of red bloomed *so* easily. "Why you asking me?"

"Because you want to jump his metal bones."

Fidelity waved so hard, I was afraid he'd slap himself

in hysterical dismissal. "No way, we're just partners!"

"You wish," I offered, earning a wide-eyed glower that way missed its mark.

I smothered my laugh into the rim of my glass, tipping the long, blue chute into my mouth. Not all that sweet, but richer than most would expect from anything blue, with a subtle way of sneaking up on you before clocking your brain into sheer stupid. A fine sheen of pale black floated on the upper layer – almost invisible against the rich booze underneath.

A kind of coffee. Stupid *and* wired. The Indigo wasn't a cheap drink.

Like the guy, I guess. Though he *was* a cheap lay.

And he was so late. I grumbled as Tashi and Fidelity argued back and forth; Boone had stepped out for personal business, I gathered. Once he'd been certain neither Fido nor Val would chase my ass down.

Funny Fidelity knew that and the others didn't.

Because *obviously*.

I surveyed the crowd as I nursed what felt like my first real break in too long. The Mecca thumped tonight, rolled a bump and grind beat that turned into sweat and rhythm. Not a thrash yet. May not go that way tonight.

I could probably push that, if I wanted. Dance floors easily turned to blood with the right steering.

Not that I planned on it. For all the fun I have thrashing my cares away, I'd done a hellish number on my meatsack recently. I'd rather hook up with somebody gentle this time around. Long, slow leisurely sex sounded like a day at a spa.

Not that I didn't know where to find *those* too.

Swarthy hands braced on either side of my head, dark against the paler paint smeared on the couch. Indigo bent over me, his braid swinging down to bat me in the face. I grabbed it, held it away from my face, and grinned up at the linker I thought I'd lost for good.

He smiled back. Like, a for real smile.

My heart thumped so hard, I thought my ribs'd crack.

I'd *earned* this. I'd worked my ass for this.

The pit in my stomach wasn't so sure.

"You look relaxed," he said.

"You're late."

"I'm right on time."

I scoffed, let him go so he could join me. Like Tash, he stepped over the back, but unlike her, sank to the seat. The other two looked up, waved, and continued arguing. About... I blinked. "Are they arguing about Valentine's tattoo placement?"

Digo shrugged. "Just got here."

"It's right at the center," Fidelity said, louder to include us. He turned in the seat, feet on the floor to paint the picture for us. "Right at the top of his asscrack."

"No, it's not," Tashi said, rolling her eyes. She braced a heavy foot on Fidelity's back, forcing him to bend forward on an *oof* of compressed air. "It's right on the glute. Left side," she added, jerking a thumb at him grinding between two very hot brunettes.

They multiplied around Val. Barbunnies. That deep-down promise of violence sculpted into his nature appealed to a certain set.

Only thing I could do was laugh.

"Where's your friend?" Indigo cut in. "Muerte?"

"Dunno." I scanned the crowd by the bar; Muerte wasn't a dancer. The leg, I think. She preferred kicking ass to grabbing it. "Said she'd meet us here."

"Maybe she's running intel on Val's tattoo," Fidelity said, snickering.

Goddammit, I couldn't stop laughing. It slid right up

my throat, poured out of my mouth with so much relief. That hole under my sternum, that aching void, I swear I felt it closing. Millimeter by millimeter. Edge by ragged edge.

Mostly.

I don't cry. Most I knew to do with this thick feeling was throw back the rest of my drink and slam it on the metal table. The noise of the club swallowed the sound.

It did not hide the sharp *clank* of boot to metal, or the screech of the riveted table legs as they left pale scratches in the cement floor. I blinked at it. Red, spiky. Attached to a leg bent at the knee, which led to a saint I recognized, hands in his pockets, leering down at me like he'd scored some kind of point.

"Rictor."

# 44

I lifted an eyebrow. "Your foot is on my table."

His sneer widened. "I found you."

"I'm sorry."

He bent, until I got an eyeful of platinum teeth in a skeletal skull. "You're worth a lot."

Uh huh. I inserted a hand between us. My flesh one. "Shiva know you're causing trouble?"

"Bitch better back down," said somebody else. A woman, black hair high and tight, bare, muscled arms folded across an equally muscled chest.

"You know this guy?" Indigo asked me.

I shrugged, gaze on Rictor's. He was built like a goddamn corpse, all bones and skin. I'd seen him in the comfort of his own vehicle. Hell if I knew what he'd do outside one. "Kill Squad," I said.

Tashi's eyes narrowed.

"Oooh." Fidelity's feet propped up on the edge of the same table, eyes alight. Teeth also alight. He'd taken the platinum as a challenge. "You piss off Dancer?"

"A few times," I said, smirking when Rictor's features got tighter and tighter. Meaner and meaner. "The first was when I shot her to get out of her gang. The recent one was—"

"Listen, you traitorous cunt," the ganger hissed, bending down until we were rictus to smirk. "Your bitchass just got paid for, so why don't you come nice and quiet?"

My smile faded. So did Fido's.

"You just paid the fee in the last ten minutes?" I scowled. "My timing is still shit."

Not *just* my timing, either. News traveled too fast to keep it quiet now. And second by second, more of the Mecca's regulars were clueing in. A hush fell over those nearest us. Even more so when another merc on the wrong side of the rails stepped out of the crowd. Then another.

I stopped counting. Bouncers started peeling the fringes back. Making room. We'd all get bounced next to work this out in the street.

Rictor didn't intend to wait that long. He straightened. "You gonna fight back?"

"Don't be a moron." I stood, dusted off the back of my shorts with my left arm. "Of *course* I'm not going to fight back."

At my elbow, Indigo stood slowly.

Tashi slid off the back of the chair, came around it, hands at her sides.

Fidelity whistled low and long.

"*We*," I corrected, relishing the word, "are going to fight back."

Fidelity moved. His leg flicked out, slammed the opposite table edge against Rictor's knee. Both clanged – knee replacement under those baggy pants? Fuck me. Still did the work. He wobbled sideways just as another one of his crew leapt over the back of the other couch – a three-seater, which left lots of room for Tashi to intercept.

My left hook righted Rictor's balance and then sent

him flying across the table yet again; more screeching, more clanging. Blood gleamed in the streaming lights, splattered wet and dark on cement.

A roar went up from the crowd.

Easy to rile them. Hard to figure out which one of them wanted to kill me when riled.

Bouncers moved in, but the crowd – eager for blood on any given day, when presented – pushed them back.

The best way to handle who was Squad and who wasn't was to drop them all, every single one that came at me. Fidelity and Tashi knew the drill, and Indigo was no slouch. I didn't go for my assault rifle, either – didn't need it. Not for this.

This was one more shot at patching my cred. Taking on the Kill Squad outside their turf could go either way – it depended on the outcome of this fight entirely.

Rictor whirled, came at me promising murder. He tackled me low at the waist, sent us both colliding into the two-seater. It tilted backwards, dumped us both in a roll I tried to top. Knocked my hat off; pisslicker. My head hit the floor and immediately jarred my senses. Pressure in my skull.

Disconcerting noise between my ears.

*Goddammit.* I'd just shaken it!

Fists blocked, arms locked, I struggled to get my knee under him, twisted my shoulders and jerked an elbow into his armpit. Just enough to get his ass off me and thrown to the side. He moved like a spider and tackled like a bruiser. Every contact hurt.

Bouncers pushed through, all wearing the usual black. Most carrying batons. Some fists.

Jad bent and plucked a struggling merc up by the back of the neck, shook her like a rag doll when she went for him. Didn't see what happened next, but I'd guess she wouldn't care – corpses don't.

You don't fuck with Shiva's bouncers.

Fighting back had always been allowed, if the hunters were too stupid to go for outright assassination, but I wasn't going to swing my dick in her direction. We knew to lay off the bouncers.

But this crew? They hadn't gotten the memo.

# 45

One of Rictor's elbows turned outward, swapped what I'd mistaken as meat for the tech buried in it. Barrels appeared where an arm used to be. I dodged too late – a sudden crack of a short-range shotgun blast rocked through the noise, the music, the shouting. It caught me square in the right side of my chest, shredding through the koala's admonition.

Never, *never* got easier, and shotgun shells only made it worse. The round tore through flesh and bone, spread a hole in my shoulder and under my collarbone that I *felt* rip wide. A lung popped. I staggered, fell to hands and knees as all the blood left my head. Made the ringing sound worse, overwhelmingly noisy. Aggressive. My blood, I saw as I struggled to stand, gushed to the floor. I slipped in it, boot heels drawing thin lines of red.

"Riko, fuck!"

"Now?" I rasped, going for funny and failing miserably.

The Kill Squad lieutenant's triumphant laugh cut short as Indigo tackled him, rolling him over and over in a flurry of blue glints of light and the domino effect that followed them into the crowd. Taken out at ankles and knees, bouncers and fighters and bystanders all collapsed, making a hot mess even worse.

An arm slipped under my metal one – orange and yellow. "Holy tits," Fidelity gasped. "Come on!"

"Not…" I gritted my teeth, shivering as the blood cooled down my side. Fuck, it was dribbling into my crotch. Not the kind of lube I'd've chosen for a night at the Mecca. I cursed, hissed what I had of any breath.

"Come *on*."

He dragged me away from the central ring. I looked back, saw Tashi standing her ground – which always covered a larger radius than anyone expected. With her knives in her hands, and her skills honed twice as sharp, she dropped motherfuckers in gouts of blood that didn't stop. Even when it mixed with booze on the floor.

Fido didn't see her stumble.

Didn't see her drop to her knees. Nobody had touched her; a gun? Rictor's one-shot surprise was toast, but others may have brought in slimmer weapons. Shiva didn't expressly disallow it.

Too much blood to tell what was hers. Her face hit the cement. Her back arched up, like she was cradling her stomach.

My head screamed. Crackled.

"Tashi!" I struggled, and Fidelity wrapped one hand around my metal shoulder like his grappling control would work on diamond steel. "She's hurt–"

"So are you!"

"*Fuck this.*" I flexed my arm, rotors grinding and whirring as the tech broke his fleshy hold. He snatched his arm back before I broke it – accidentally – and I turned back as he tried to recover his balance.

"Riko!"

I elbowed, pushed, shoved my way through the ring of fighters and not fighters.

A face got in my way. I left jabbed it. It sprayed blood.

A broad chest. I suckerpunched it with my right – screamed bloody murder and went blind with pain. Not that it mattered. I elbowed and pushed, chanted Tashi's name.

Pixietwat had once turned on me; she'd thought I'd murdered Nanjali.

She'd tried to kill me; she was protecting Indigo.

I knew these feelings. Knew that drive more than anything else. Indigo needed her more than he ever needed me.

But she'd given me a chance; run with me into a different kind of hell.

We'd protected Indigo together.

When I finally broke free of the tangled ring, Tashi was screaming in the center. They'd opened up around her, the closest gone wide-eyed as she threw her head back, eyes and mouth wide.

Black lines dribbled from her eyes. Like running mascara, but thicker. Finer. They gathered at the corners of her mouth. Spilled over.

Bubbled from the knife wound in her arm.

*Fuckgod.* Nanoshock. Hard. Fast. How?

One leg collapsed out from under me – too much blood loss. Didn't care. I'd drag my ass over to Tashi if I had to, get her the shit out of–

A shot cracked, with the unmistakable subsonic *thoom* of a sniper rifle heavily modded for close range. So, so much power. Less accuracy, but that didn't matter in close quarters. Tashi's jaw exploded. So did the base of her skull. Chunks of brain and bone flew, and the gore-streaked glint of her chipset skittered across the ground, smoking. Two patrons on the other side of the target went down screaming.

I yelled Tashi's name, struggled through blurred,

streaming vision to place the shooter.

Shiva stood on the bar, a goddess of death with a sniper rifle cocked against her shoulder. Her black lips were set so rigid, only the thinnest black line showed. Her features, for the first time, had gone hard as stone – similar to Indigo's in a lot of ways, especially when he got mad. Her eyes met mine. I think they did.

Nanoshock that advanced could just as easily turn to conversion. Maybe was.

She couldn't take the risk.

I couldn't believe it.

"Was she converting?" I heard.

I spun on my knees, metal hand braced. Barely held me up. "Fidelity!"

A streak of orange beside me, and then I was on my feet again. Stumbling, I leaned on the lighter man under my shoulder, tried to wrap my head around words that only came out garbled. "I know," he said in my ear. Thick voice. Like he was fighting tears. "I know, keep moving. What the fuck happened, I don't know... keep moving... I know..."

He wasn't talking to me. Maybe we both fought shock together.

Somehow, we made it through the crowd. Staggered to a back exit wired to scream the kind of alarm that sheared through music. He kicked it open. Everything shrieked. My head, my chest, my body.

Mercs and saints, sinners looking for a good time – they all streamed out around us. Some still fought, bursting through the open doors, tripping on anybody unlucky enough to be in the way.

Guns drew.

Knives glinted.

Fidelity stumbled as an ankle caught between his.

Mine? Fuck, mine. I went down with him. He wrenched free. "Go," he rasped.

I struggled to push my head up. Managed to straighten my arms; agony shredded through my side, my shoulder. My head. "Come on," I panted. "Indigo! We need–"

Fidelity, who had never been the rough type, grabbed my face in savage hands and dragged me so close to his that I couldn't possibly mistake the ream of black seaming his eyes. The whites had gone gray. Rapidly turned black. Blood at his mouth, nanobots duplicating so fast they pushed out of every pore, like gray sweat.

"*Go*," he repeated, and with near inhuman strength, threw me as far away from him – from the doors – as he could.

I collided with a trio of runners. We all went down together.

Elbowed in the head, stomped into the broken and pitted asphalt. Yelling, swearing. And louder than the others, shriller than I'd ever heard, Fidelity screamed as his body twisted, jerked.

My spine turned to ice.

I'd heard those screams. First in Lucky's chopshop all those years ago. Again, spilling from Tashi's mouth as she choked on blood and nanos.

I'd seen the way they twisted in Nanji's tech-broken body.

*Conversion.*

I didn't understand. Didn't get it. How? *Why?*

"It's her," yelled somebody – a woman's voice. High and scared. "Her gang is going necro!"

"Get away!" shrieked a guy too young to be in here, kicking hard to wriggle out of reach. I caught a boot to the face. Growled as I tried to roll away.

"People around her are converting!"

No. It wasn't me. I'd done nothing. So how?

MetaCorp?

What the hell? When?

Members of the Squad leapt into the fray, swinging modified bats and spiked boots.

I covered my head with my arms, drew my knees up to protect my stomach and the seeping hole in my shoulder as saints and sinners stampeded around me, over me. I had one shot. One smegging shot, and pride be fucked in the eye socket. Struggling to concentrate, I flipped my crackling chipset wide and projected the one shitting person I was so fucking tired of projecting.

Malik Reed's office bloomed into view. In it, the shape of Reed's avatar – shoulders, something suit-like. Before my connection even firmed, I braced my virtual legs and screamed, *"Extraction near the Mecca!"*

It was all I had. The connection shattered, falling to pieces as a foot slammed into the back of my head, grinding my jaw into the ground.

I didn't notice when a hand wrapped around my metal arm and heaved me out of the deadly flow.

Indigo. Indigo dragged me to my feet, bloody mask grim. "We have to go!" he shouted.

"Height," I rasped. The least I could do was run. And as my nanos overclocked to heal the gory hole in my chest, I realized whatever else, I'd be next on the nanoshock wagon. I needed a boost. A recharge. I needed something to shove in my face and convert to energy for the little fuckers before they ate me alive.

And all I had was white noise searing my eardrums and Indigo's hand in mine, dragging me bodily when all I wanted to do was collapse.

*What happened.*

What went wrong.

*Something* had.

But what.

*Where.*

These thoughts whirled over and over in my head, collided as lightning forks of torture ripped up my body. As I gasped through thick phlegm coating my throat, I slipped in blood, mud and grime. Indigo led the way, blood and mud soaking the back of his tight-fitting T-shirt. He'd gone casual, a dim part of my mind noted. But sexy. Black material. Words scrawled across it in digipaint. *Nice tech, wanna fuck?*

Classy. And so... *so Indigo.*

My jaw locked. Screw this noise.

When I braced both legs, Indigo snapped back in reflex, shot me an incredulous scowl. "What are you–"

"I pinged Reed," I cut in, thin. Tight. I hurt, shitfuck, I hurt so much. My vision crackled – gray snow, black snow. "We need to get somewhere high."

His jaw shifted, eyes filling with resigned fury. Determination. Fear.

Yeah. I felt that, too.

"This game again, huh?" he asked quietly. All around us, people yelled, guns went off. There'd be a lot of killing tonight. Two mercs hit nanoshock that hard in the open, and the necro hysteria follows. Anyone so much as twitches, they'd get one to the head.

I couldn't shrug. It hurt so much. Instead, I released his hand, pointed a metal finger up. My smile hurt too. "Helo, right? Up is better."

"There they are!" somebody howled. "Shoot them, kill them!"

And there it was. Indigo grabbed my arm again, shoved me ahead. "Got your back. Go!" That wasn't right. That was my job. I needed to protect him.

But he shoved a fist so far into my spine that I had no choice but to run. That, or French kiss the bullet with my name on it when I fell. These shittards were *not* fucking around.

Biting back a thousand variations on the word *fuck*, I ran. Indigo burned tracks on my heels. I ran like I didn't care that I was losing more blood than my nanos could patch together. Didn't care that Indigo's breath panted and broke behind me at regular intervals. We had *one fucking shot*, and there was no guarantee Malik Reed even heard me. I hadn't even stabilized before screaming it.

What the tits was a projection feed *for?*

Gunfire peppered the road at our feet. Pinged off metal sidings and whizzed by our heads. A grunt behind me, staggered footsteps, told me Digo'd been shot. I slowed.

He shoved me. "Don't stop, I'm fine," he gasped, teeth clenched. "Turn right up here."

"Right?" I didn't–

"Riko, *turn right!*" When I was too slow, he hooked my arm – flesh arm, only one he could grab – and practically ripped what passed for a soul from my open wound. I didn't dare scream; locked my jaw around it until I *felt* my back teeth crack in too many places.

He'd been on point.

The level dropped off abruptly, leaving a gap between this building and the next. We had no time to slow. No chance. "Shiva help us," Indigo muttered. Didn't have time to say or do anything else, but clench every muscle and sprint right up to the edge.

And jump.

Arms and legs flailed. My cheeks stung, sheer windforce as I slammed into the roof of the building, rolled and rolled. Graceless as balls. Bloody and covered in grit. Gouged to shit.

"Riko!" Indigo, hoarse.

Missing.

I panted for breath, struggled to get to my feet. Stumbling, tripping over myself, I staggered to the edge. Grabbed Indigo's clinging hand with my metal fingers. Tried so hard to be careful.

He flinched anyway. "Pull!"

That I could do. Bracing my knees firmly on the edge, toes planted into the graveled lot, I heaved him up. The muscles woven into my shoulder girdle clenched, pinged, but Indigo wasn't all that heavy. Not compared to the usual shit I did with this arm. He came up, swinging from one arm, grabbing the small pistol he'd put in his boot.

As I dragged him to the surface, he swung midair, sighted and put two bullets in two mercs rolling up fast. I threw myself back from it, carried Indigo with my momentum. We both hit the ground, far enough from the edge to provide cover. Too close to keep us safe for long.

I gasped for air, every breath torture, as I looked up. Nothing but neon and bright lights, advertisements and promises and *buy, buy, buy*.

No helo.

No help.

Indigo's hand clenched around my ankle. "Riko." A gritty rasp. "C'mere."

I didn't want to. Couldn't summon the energy, the will. Wasn't even sure my battered meat would allow it. I choked on gasps of air, flinched as it burbled at my shoulder. My ribs.

Tashi. Fidelity.

Why?

"*Riko.*"

Groaning, shattered in so many ways, I rolled over.

Dragged myself, fingers biting into the ground. Indigo's hand grabbed mine and pulled until I made it to his side. He sucked in air. Spat out blood.

Blackened.

Thick.

It spattered on his chest, already filthy. Gleamed in oily rivulets.

My world went cold. Empty. *Numb.* "No," I whispered raggedly.

He couldn't grab my hair, there was nothing left. He settled for seizing my chin, holding me still. I stared into his eyes – so blue, darker than Nanji's, but ohfuckinggod, exactly the same. Right down to the irises going black. Bit by bit. Too fast.

Too far.

My head screamed – fuzzed, grayed. I refused. I would not lose them all.

I smacked his hand away, grabbed his hair, jerked hard enough to pin his head down. Face to face. "Don't you dare," I snarled, on the ragged edge of collapse. "Don't you fucking dare turn on me, you smug son of a bitch."

His smile, a caricature of his usual, rimmed black. Black in his teeth. On his tongue, flecking his lips. Something I recognized all too well swam under those deep blue eyes. Something dark and alien.

"Too late," he said thickly. He choked, grating and bloody. Straining every nano I had left, every stretched ligament and the last of my blood flow, I dragged him onto my lap. Cradled his head up so the nanos flooding his blood found a way out. He kept trying to talk. Kept trying to burble something.

I flinched. "Come on," I whispered. "Don't do this to me. I just…" *I just got you back.*

He grabbed the front of my shirt, bloodstained koala

crumpling in his fist. "Riko, listen to me." Guttural and low. He dragged me close. "The data… I found something wrong." I shook my head; didn't care. His fist tightened, teeth bared. *"Listen to me.* It's big. Bigger th- than we thought."

I laughed, bitter and too much like a sob. "Obviously!"

"Muerte," he interrupted. "Need to…" He choked. Gagged. Managed, "Ask her."

"Ask her what?"

A shout. I raised my head, caught sight of a head ducking behind cover. They'd wised up to the killbox we'd made of the area. But also to the trap we'd set up for ourselves. There was no way out.

"Riko, listen," Indigo said quietly, wet and ragged. "I'm not making it out of here."

"The tits you–"

"Don't." He tugged on my shirt. I closed my eyes and let my head hang forward. Exhaustion. Anger. Terror.

So much loss.

"Find out," he ordered. "It's up to you. Find out before th- this goes v- viral." He struggled to say the words. "She knows. Muerte. She kn…" It died on a gurgle. He heaved out a breath that bubbled, from lips and the hole in his meat. "I'm s- sorry."

Sad eyes and a sadder smile. *I'm sorry*, Nanji had mouthed, silent behind a thick pane of tempered, impenetrable glass.

Brother and sister. Backbone of the team I'd made; the family I'd thought I'd found again.

Indigo's blood-smeared forehead bumped mine. "Never fucking look back."

"I hate you." My voice shook. Hard.

"Yeah." And he smiled.

The cunting bastard *smiled*.

Manticore rounds weren't made to be neat. Up close, they only got messier. The sound thundered in the narrow space between us, drowned out everything else but the screaming in my head. His eyes, a fierce ring of blue drowning in black, widened. Exploded outward, a wake of ruin. Warm, wet globules of flesh and brain splattered across my face. Thudded like rubber against my armor. His jaw shattered outward with the force of the bullet and I held his sagging, convulsing body up in my arms as the light faded from the eyes so much like his sister's.

I'd been here before.

I'd seen it just like this.

This time, I pulled the trigger myself.

# 46

As the shredded meat that had once been my linker – my best friend, the core of my whole fucking world – sank through my fingers, something inside me broke. This time, I felt it. My spine turned to ice. My body to stone. My heart stopped beating right the fuck there. I picked up his Manticore with raw, bloodied fingers and staggered, tottering, to my feet.

A gun knocked against the back of my head. Right over my chipset.

"You stupid cunting necrobitch," Muerte rasped behind me. Her voice, always hoarse, cut the noise across the rooftops with jagged contempt. "All you had to do was leave the chipset there and this would never have happened."

My fist locked around the Manticore's handle. "Muerte," I spat. It bubbled. I couldn't get a good breath. *Ask her.*

Oh, Indigo. I didn't have to. It came together in my head with a click I would have been ashamed of if I weren't so. Shitting. Angry.

Every muscle in my body locked. "*You*. I was right, wasn't I? *You're* the pendejo."

"I almost shit my pants when you said that," she

admitted. Her humor, always rough, darkened. "Figured you were too stupid. My bad."

My breath shook. "You set me up with the Shepherds. Why?"

"Ugh. Carmichael," she spat. "He was supposed to capture you alive." *Heathen cunt.* Of course.

I closed my eyes. My jaw ached from clenching it. My ribs were on fire. Every part of me wanted to collapse inward.

I refused.

"You," I said thickly. "Did you set the Squad on me?"

"Of course."

"And you turned on them?"

She shook her head faintly, sounding pleased. "Rictor and I cut a deal behind Dancer's back."

I wanted to call her a tool, but couldn't scrape it together. Dancer, I knew full well, would get her own back. So I swallowed the blood in my throat, spat what wouldn't go down.

The gun barrel dragged across my scalp, scoring a line of pain from chipset to ear. Then temple. Muerte wasn't stupid enough to get in front of me. Or to choose my left side. "I'm glad we had this talk." Aggravation littered her words. "It was getting embarrassing watching you, Riqa. I mean, I even *slipped.* That little twatwaffle wasn't supposed to get my scouts."

Her scouts. Hers. They'd kept looking at Muerte.

Because they worked for her.

MetaCorp scouts and Muerte?

Everything hurt too much to think through. Everything froze. Time had stopped for me. Even as blood leaked down my chin, as it pooled down my legs and joined Indigo's spreading crimson stain, I stared straight ahead. Focused every iota of my attention on every tiny twitch she made in my peripheral.

"Who?" I croaked.

"Who what?"

"Who paid you?"

"Ai." Slowly, she moved out a foot. Nudged Indigo's body with her toes. Checking for necro, maybe.

I'd solved that. There was nothing left of his chipset. Nothing left of *him*.

Blind bloody rage filled me. More than I'd ever known, deeper than anything I had ever tasted. Like blood and raw meat and gristle torn to shreds. Like a black hole burning red at the center.

And Muerte's face in my sights.

She smiled crookedly. "MetaCorp."

Right. My lips twisted. Bared bloody teeth. Pink foam spat from my mouth as I hissed, "Corporate *tool.*"

"That's funny, coming from you." The CounterTech's barrel dug so hard into my temple, skin broke beneath it. I clenched my eyes shut. Saw red and forced them open again. "A girl's got to make creds." A brittle smile. "It's no different than bending over for Mantis. Except in this particular case, you were encroaching on my employer's turf. Although I can't blame you," she added, chuckling with humor sharper than the moment deserved. "MetaCorp did try to fuck over your boss, too."

I tilted my head just enough to search her face. "If Knacklock was MetaCorp's," I managed through my teeth, "why the shit did you infiltrate it?"

"Two reasons. One, we lost contact twenty-four hours ago." She shrugged, glanced over when mercs across the way shouted. Four had popped up. Calmly, Muerte lifted the Insurgent held in her other hand and held the trigger down. She'd modified the clip.

The mercs went down, but I couldn't tell if they'd

dropped or were bleeding out. The others stayed covered.

"Protocols," she added calmly, "sealed the vault. My job was to get in there and get the data before it fell into Mantis' hands."

My breath shorted. My lungs wouldn't fill. The whole right side of my body was beginning to sag. Even anger, violent and desperate, couldn't keep me upright for much longer.

"Two," she continued, "you went and invited Malik fucking Reed as if he weren't part of the problem. I had to protect the investment. Collect or destroy. Turns out the fucking thing destroyed itself, and only this asshole walked away with anything at all."

At my feet, Indigo's blood mixed with mine.

I stared at it. Racked my brain. "I don't get it."

"Surprise."

Trails of dark black hair seeped into the crimson pool.

"Why go through all this trouble?"

"Because the job had always been to track you down." Muerte reached around me. Tugged the Manticore from my grip. "I'd hoped isolating you would make it easier." Her CounterTech II remained rock solid. She wasn't a borderline splatter specialist for nothing.

But then, I was so much more than borderline.

"You're worth more alive, but I'm under the same orders and I can't risk taking you in now. All this bullshit has gone too fucking far." Sighing, her voice softened just enough to piss me off even more. "If it's any consolation, I'm not happy about it. You were a damn good runner until they fucked with you."

Fucked with me?

I wanted to ask. My lungs wouldn't give me enough air to try.

"At least," she continued, her dark eyes empty of

laughter, "you got a second chance. I'm jealous, nena. I wish..."

Whatever it was she wanted to wish, she let it out in a short, choppy exhale. It sounded too much like regret. Her wide mouth turned down. "I know," she added without my saying anything. Like it all weighed on her. She didn't have the right. "You are not my girlfriend. So just be quiet and let me have the chipsets." Muerte cocked the CounterTech.

A worthless power move.

In the split second she took to swing her dick, I bent my skull into the barrel, turned and drove my frayed, bleeding elbow into her chest.

Agony ripped through my flesh. My lung gave up entirely, filling my throat with blood. Muerte staggered, surprise clearly etched on her features. Replaced by determined anger.

I watched it shift to fucking dread as my tech fist came around.

She pulled the trigger.

Fire dug talons into my pounding skull.

With the same turn's momentum, every joint cracking at me and every nerve screaming and screaming and screaming...

No. That was me screaming. Burbling. Choking.

And that was Muerte screaming, too, as my fist drove through her ribs. Bone cracked. Shifted. The numbers in my optics hit steel-bending digits and Muerte lost her footing. My meat flagged, but the arm Orchard had fixed up and the shoulder girdle she'd strengthened didn't.

Blood spewed from her mouth. Her eyes rolled back in her head.

She hit the roof's ground, rolled over and over and over until her boneless body collided with the walled ledge. Dust and grit floated in her wake, disturbed by her impact. The signs all around us flashed and flickered, meatspace neon that turned that trail of dust to a rainbow.

Muerte didn't move.

*Second chance.*

Slowly, as shouting spattered the makeshift cover, I turned around. Looked down at Indigo's body. Something purple and rubbery had hit the ground. Bounced. A lung. Part of one. Heh.

Spots floated in my eyes. Black. Heavy. I looked down at my arm.

More black.

My chest.

Black, black. And a fucking big hole.

Nanos dribbled from my wounds, thick and darker than blood. Thicker than Indigo's or Tashi's. Millions. Billions. It took so many to make rivulets like that.

Never fucking look back.

I don't remember turning away from Indigo's twisted corpse. But I must have. Because suddenly there was screaming coming from a skull I gripped in my metal hand and Indigo's brains made friends across my cheek.

Never fucking forgive.

A bullet pinged off my nanosteel arm. It ricocheted past my ear, scoring a thick line across my temple. Pain only drove me deeper into the angry wasps shrieking between my ears.

I don't remember what came next. Only that armor came apart like cardboard and meat tore like Kongtown lanterns.

No mercy.

Not for myself.

Not for them.

A trail of carnage before I die.

And black as night eyes burning into mine. *"Snap out of it."*

Why the fuck I did, how the fuck he did it, I don't know. At least I came to myself, one shoulder shrieking under Malik Reed's nanosteel grip, swaying in the center of a ring made of meat and bone and gore and brain and shit and...

Exhaustion swamped me. Even the .357 in my metal hand felt like too damn much to carry. Somehow, I was breathing. Not smoothly. Not deeply. But I hadn't died, and that was something.

Maybe, I thought numbly as my gaze slid slowly to Malik's, it was because *they*'d gotten to me. Maybe that was it.

Fucked with me.

"A second chance," I rasped.

Lights shredded my vision, spiraled and flashed. The backdraft of a settling helo raked across the roof. My skin, already scraped raw, felt like it peeled from every nerve. I shook in Malik's grip. Firmed myself.

"Riko." A low order. Fuck his authority. "Enough. You're done."

Heh. "Let me go."

He studied my face. Searched my gaze. When he let me go, I knew it was because the sedative had done its work. I felt it in my flesh. My veins. Working through all the damaged cells and brutalized muscles.

Across the roof, lit to a blinding shine, Indigo lay on his back. No more face. Just enough hair to flutter blue and black in the helo's wafting heat.

Muerte was gone.

My laugh twisted. "About time you showed," I croaked.

His jaw, carved in metal and stone, had ground so tight that I could reach out and trace the sharpened angles.

Wouldn't. Not unless I used the stolen .357 to do it, and I didn't want to. Wouldn't help. Wouldn't do anything at all.

I turned, wrapping my metal arm and the heavy pistol I carried over my ribs. How I wasn't dead...

My skin crawled.

Slowly, I picked my way through my grotesque handiwork. One foot dragged behind me. The knee split. I stumbled, righted myself.

Malik followed. He didn't offer to help.

He gave me that, at least.

Corporate drones swarmed the area, enforcers checking bodies, securing the perimeter. Everything they did best. Sealing, hiding, removing, erasing.

I wanted to laugh so badly.

"Riko." My name on Malik's lady lips again.

"What."

He stopped when I did. Gave me enough respect that I wasn't forced to stare at him as I knelt by Indigo's ruined husk.

*This would never have happened...*

"You took Kern's chipset."

My hands fell to my knees. Pistol pointed down at the rooftop. Indigo's lean, whipcord chest didn't move. Didn't rise. No breath. No pulse.

No chipset.

My smile cut like razors. Even for me. "I did."

Malik circled, shiny shoes dragging blood and gibbets with each step. He looked down at me. Implacable. Firm. "You need to give it to me."

I raised my gaze to his. "Why?"

"Because it obviously went viral."

I wanted to laugh to the point that my heart erupted with agony. Not on the outside. I'd never known anything like this.

*I'm sorry.*

Three times spoken. Nanji. Digo.

A whisper in that cunting chopshop.

"Did it," I croaked. Not a question. "Fine." Slowly, so slowly, I reached into the interior of my ruined, smeared boots. I'd tucked the thing there. Taped it in place, to give to Digo.

The tape tore in my bloodied, swollen fingers.

Malik's expression didn't change. He remained standing. The lights slid over his perfectly shaped head, picking out glints of brown in his close-cropped hair. Mine was longer. Even after buzzing it.

Longer, and dripping with the carnage I'd walked out of.

But I knew how to read him. I'd learned. His dark, short lashes narrowed. A fraction. The tension in his jaw; it shifted.

One hand came up. Palm to the sky. Ready.

"We'll get the data in the closed lab," he said. A promise. It rang like one.

I lifted the muck-seamed tech up to my face, balanced on two fingers and thumb. So small. A bitch to hit. But not impossible.

Muerte had missed on purpose. Shattered Kern's skull. I hadn't realized in time.

"I'd thought MetaCorp the common denominator." My smile pulled at both sides of my mouth.

Malik's gaze sharpened. Ice and oil, fire and steel. "Riko."

"Then," I said with effort, "I thought maybe Mantis was the common denominator."

*"Riko."* He took a step forward. "Get the chipsets!" His enforcers. Booted feet pounded. A helo whined. Harsh, shrieking.

Chipsets, huh? Plural.

He had too high hopes.

"Turns out," I said louder, hoarser, "I was right. But, Malik…"

For the first time, I watched Malik Reed lose his shit. Teeth bared in his perfect goatee, shiny shoes slick with guts and gore, he put all that training and muscle to use. Launched himself at me.

Too late.

Vicious rage, violent satisfaction, filled me as I spat around it, "You can't do anything without me." Rotating the .357 in my tech hand, I locked the barrel to the chipset. Pinned the chipset between metal and my gore-logged teeth.

*"Don't–!"*

I pulled the trigger. One finger, one click.

A blinding flash. Hands wrapped around my head, the gun. Shouting. Swearing.

Venomous. Savage.

The chipset carved a path through my brain the bullet only tore wider. The sound in my head cranked so high, so loud, so powerful that nothing else mattered.

The Maverick .357 isn't as big as my old Adjudicator, but it's more than enough to blow out the back of my skull.

No chipsets left.

*Go fuck yourself.*

I plunged into brutal consciousness.

# ACKNOWLEDGMENTS

*Nanoshock* has been a long time in the making. While Riko battled the demons she'd made along the way, I was battling mine – and they made this the hardest fucking book I'd ever written.

But I did it, and this kind of awesome shit doesn't happen in a vacuum.

Lisa Rodgers, you are and have always been the Indigo to my Riko. Without you, I'd have given up long ago.

Marc, Phil and the Angry Robot team: your patience, support, kindnesses and outright speed have been more than I ever dreamed could exist in the publishing dimensions. Thanks for being a back-asswards sort of reintroduction to a "people don't all suck" mode of play.

Stephen: I will always help you bury the bodies. Also murder them. Because I care.

Kevin: TO WORDHALLA!

And to everyone who supported me and continues to support me, to all my patrons, my amazing service dog donators, my very kind translators, my friends, and all my murderfriends: thank you.

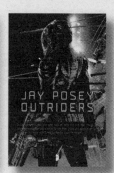
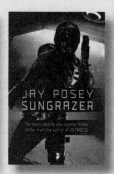

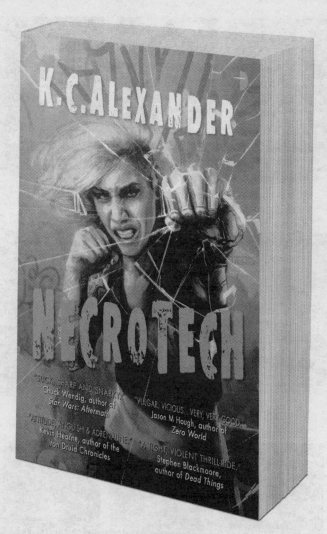

RIKO'S FIRST ... ESCAPADE.
READ IT, OR EXPECT CONSEQUENCES.